Call of the Mountains

A Catholic Novel

Annie Coffey

Bluebonnet Books, Inc—San Antonio, TX
ISBN: 979-8-9914045-0-1
eBook ISBN: 979-8-3305-2937-7
Library of Congress Control Number: 2024923465
Call of the Mountains: A Catholic Novel
Author: Annie Coffey
Digital distribution | 2024
Paperback | 2024

https://anniecoffey.com

Published in the United States by New Book Authors Publishing

Dedication

To my sweet daughter Mariah, who asked me to write her a book.

Acknowledgements

Thank you to Ascension Press for permission to use Father Mike Schmitz's homilies to write dialogue for the character of Father Joseph Machebeuf, the first Catholic pastor of St. Mary's in Denver City. You can find Father Mike Schmitz on Ascension Presents or on YouTube.

A special thank you to my dear friend and human thesaurus, Marie Immenhauser, who spent hours reading through this book and sending me insightful suggestions. I could not have done it without you, Marie.

Prologue

August 10, 1867

My dearest sister Betsy,

I was overjoyed to receive your letter today. I have already read it seven times from beginning to end. Your descriptions of even the most trivial of activities are always so entertaining, and many times I actually laughed aloud. Patrick twice asked me to share the reason for my mirth. He sends you his regards and wonders how Jared is faring. I encouraged him to devote more time to his own correspondence instead of always relying on morsels from my letters.

So many months have passed since you wrote your letter on December 26th, and I must wonder how much my sweet nieces and nephews have changed between the hour of your writing and the hour of my reading. How I long to see Fay, William, and Henry again, and to meet little Sophie for the first time! I hate the fact that the only way our children remember their cousins is through letters. They should be playing together every day, not separated by an ocean. I still feel so much regret about separating my children from their best friends. Time seems to race more swiftly each year. I cannot believe it has been almost eight years since we last embraced, dear sister. Of course, your children and mine are living reminders of how quickly the years have flown.

Charlotte is nineteen years old now and I was surprised last year to realize I've raised my best friend! She is funny and smart, and she cares so deeply for all those around her. She's grown into such a beautiful young woman. She has Patrick's deep blue eyes, and dark brown hair like you and me. She reminds me of you in so many ways, my sister. How I've always envied your inner fire and determination, sweetly masked by a calm and serene exterior! Charlotte is just like that; so sweet and delightful, unless someone is being treated unjustly. Then, she is a grizzly bear! She will make an amazing wife someday, but only the strongest of men will be able to handle her intensity.

Just as you and Jared are well-suited, she will need the right husband to complement her strength. So far, no young man has caught her eye.

Of course, there are so few of them around. I feel for today's young women. The war here devastated the male population. I know she longs for marriage and children, but I hope she will hold out for the right mate. You and I have both made such fortunate matches and I want the same for her. But where will she meet a potential husband? There are so few social gatherings here, outside of worship services. And since we are not in a city, the closest Mass is a three hour ride each way. It has been six long weeks since I've received the Eucharist. Patrick is hopeful that as more families settle around us, we will be able to build a parish in our small community and acquire a priest from our beloved Ireland. He even has a spot of land he'd like to donate for a church. It's a hilltop area with a gorgeous view of the mountains, and seems a fitting place for Our Lord to dwell in majesty. It would be lovely to attend Mass every week again. I am ashamed to admit that I took Mass for granted when we were growing up, Betsy. I remember feeling irksome if the homily was too long, or the priest too boring. Now I realize that none of that mattered. I was receiving Our Lord! How could anything else matter?

Our dear little Ruth (I can't help but say "little" although she is sixteen now) is still tiny and so delayed. I cannot complain about her health, as she is the picture of vivacity. It's just confusing that she remains so small in stature and has never advanced with conversation or understanding. Nevertheless, she is joyful and content- she fills our lives with love. I only wish I could know her better.

In contrast to Charlotte's loquaciousness, Ruth still possesses such a limited vocabulary. She is now able to communicate most of her daily needs and is finally able to visit the outhouse without prompting, which is such a wonderful blessing (as I'm sure you can imagine). But I do not know her heart as I know Charlotte's. What I would give to experience one day in Ruthie's mind! It must be a lovely place if her constant smiles and laughter are any indicator.

Brendan is only fifteen and has already surpassed his father in height! He is a brawny, healthy young man and it makes me laugh when I remember that at one time, he was no longer than my forearm. Oh, and those fat little feet of his! They looked just like building blocks! Do you remember? I honestly despaired of him ever walking! Now, he is on the move all day long and his little block feet have grown into the huge feet of a grown man! He brings so much sunshine into my life, and I thank God every day that he was too young to go fight alongside Patrick. I couldn't have borne it if he came back with that hollow, empty look Patrick had for a while. Sister, I know I've written you about how bad those first few months were. My formerly jovial, loving husband was a shell of his former self. I shudder remembering it. But, it was so beautiful to watch the children rally around their father. They brought him back a day at a time with their humor and unwavering love. We are so blessed!

Occasionally, when he thinks no one is around, Brendan will burst into song as he chops wood or works in the field. He has his father's deep, resonating voice and it thrills my heart. Do you remember that it was Patrick's voice which first attracted me to him all those years ago? It's fortunate that he sang so freely that day, else he would never have won the heart of so fair a wife! He said he was always too timid to sing at his own parish where everyone knew him but felt no fear to sing aloud while a stranger visiting Killarney. How foolish we humans are in worrying about what others think! If he had attended that Mass silently, I doubt we would have even met. I still laugh when I recall how I begged our father to go introduce himself. I remember you were so embarrassed by it! Oh, sister! I was rather impetuous, wasn't I?

Patrick and Brendan have been trying their hand with different crops and have found great success with potatoes, corn, cotton, and tobacco. I still have occasional bad dreams about the potato blight and ensuing famine, as I'm sure you do. It is doubtful any Irishman our age will ever take potatoes for granted again! I'm happy to have them in such abundance here. However, corn is definitely my favorite crop to watch grow. The green and yellow are so vivid, and the stalks grow so high. There's something almost majestic about a field of ripe corn. And it's much easier to harvest than the cotton. Brendan and Patrick tear up their hands every year bringing in the cotton. But I've developed a salve that seems to work very well in restoring their dexterity. Oh, Betsy! I look back over this last paragraph with embarrassment! When did I become such an old farmer's wife?

I miss you every single day, Betsy, and regret that our children are not growing up together. Despite my occasional homesickness for Ireland and you, I cannot regret our decision to move to America. This life Patrick and I have built together is more than I ever dreamed possible. I only wish the Gallaghers and Marshalls were on the same continent! Please tell Jared (yet again) that there is a growing community here with no general store as of yet. He could open the first one and become a very wealthy man! Imagine the legacy he would leave for your children and grandchildren. Remind him that he has a sister-in-law here in Colorado who would make his favorite pie every day in gratitude if he only moved his family to America!

With Greatest Affection,
Your Loving Older Sister, Annie

Chapter One

Tuesday, August 13, 1867

The sound of horses drawing up the long drive to their cabin was not uncommon. Now that the war was over, the Gallagher family encountered travelers at least a few times each week. It seemed everyone in America was either headed back east after failing to hit it big in the gold mines or headed further west in hopes of a better life. Some travelers were buoyant and happy, excited and eager to start a new chapter. Some were downcast and plodded slowly along as though every step brought them closer to despair. But all of them had one thing in common; when evening came and they saw a homestead in the distance, the lure of sleeping in a hayloft in a warm barn was always preferable to sleeping on the cold side of the road. They would knock on the door and ask for shelter, and Mother and Father were always happy to oblige. After all, it had not been that long since they were the travelers asking for warm shelter when they could find it.

Charlotte occasionally dreamed of traveling. She knew that once she married and started her own family she would like to live near her mother and father. But she wanted to see some of this great nation before then. It had been almost eight years since she and her family left Ireland to sail to America. The voyage across the Atlantic had taken close to ten weeks, and for ten-year-old Charlotte, that seemed like years. It had been extremely difficult, and something she hoped never to repeat. She remembered the horrible smells, the cramped conditions, and the lice. The lice were not even the worst part. So many people died during that voyage from malnutrition and dysentery. Charlotte felt that if people really knew what they were undertaking, most would never have done it.

No, she did not wish to sail again, but traveling from the east coast through so many different territories had thrilled her. It had taken over one hundred days to travel across the country from New York to Colorado in their covered wagon pulled by two strong oxen. At first, the days walking beside the wagon and the nights spent camping out under the stars had been

1

intoxicating after the stifling confinement on the ship. Then, weariness set in and the whole family longed to find a place to call home. If it hadn't been for the company of all the other families traveling in their group, the travel would have seemed interminable. But Charlotte, Ruthie, and Brendan had so many children to play with during the long days of walking. Every night seemed a party with campfires and banjo music and laughter. Looking back, it had been a magnificent experience, and one Charlotte would relish reliving.

When they began their journey in the east, there was talk of nothing besides the south's threat of succession and the possibility of war. Any time her father encountered another man, they began talking of the impending conflict. Charlotte was extremely glad they'd landed in the north where most people agreed with her family's views. No man should own another. She couldn't imagine how awful it would have been to travel through the southern states. It was a relief to discover that the further west they got, the less war talk there was.

Even at ten years old, Charlotte had been mesmerized by the ever-changing, always beautiful scenery. She'd often wished she could draw as well as her little brother, Brendan. Although only seven years old, he had a gift for recreating the sights of each day as they settled down to sleep. His drawing journal was completely filled by the time they reached Colorado! It would be a beautiful reminder of their journey here.

Charlotte remembered how difficult it had been each time another family stripped away from the group and went their separate way. She'd made some good friends all those years ago and still maintained regular correspondence with several of them. It would be nice to backtrack and visit some of her friends along the way. Or travel further west and see what else this grand country had to offer. Once they had arrived in Colorado, and her parents fell in love with this land, Father swore he'd never travel overnight again.

"Everyone and everything I love is right here," he always said. He usually followed that by giving Mother a wink.

Mother seemed to agree with him. She loved the life they were building. Charlotte remembered the first few weeks on this land. She remembered how exciting it had been to watch Father and Mother decide upon where the cabin would be built, and where the barn would be best located. They finally settled on an area where they were close enough to the stream to be able to haul water for all their necessities, but far enough that they would not be flooded out even in the heaviest of rains. In the years they had lived here, the stream had swollen over its banks twice, but never come close enough to feel threatening.

Those first years had been exciting, and Charlotte often felt they were in a race against time. Would their sod house be finished before cold weather hit? Would the well be complete before summer, or would they keep having to draw water from the stream? Would the crops be harvested before the first frost? Would the cabin be completed before Father left to join the Union army? It was always a race, but her family knew about hard work, and they generally got things done in time.

Now that the railroad was almost complete, travel would be so much quicker. That excited Charlotte. Yes, she would make plans to travel sometime soon. Perhaps Mother and Father would allow her to go if Brendan accompanied her. That would be so fun! Brendan was her very best friend. Oh, but she would miss Ruth! Ruth could never make the journey with them. There was something wrong with her little sister. Although sixteen years old, Ruth had not yet reached five feet tall. She was a tiny girl who barely spoke and carried a little doll with her every hour of the day. She could sit for hours, looking into the distance and laughing contentedly, or singing softly. There were no words to her songs, but she had perfect pitch and could often be heard singing Ave Maria or other beautiful masterpieces. She seemed so happy and content all the time. And never lonely. In fact, she often seemed to be conversing with someone the rest of them couldn't see. Charlotte sometimes felt like Ruth could see into another realm; that maybe she communed with God and the angels. Whatever it was that Ruth could see, it brought her great joy! She was always smiling, laughing, or singing happily. Just thinking of Ruth made Charlotte happy, and she began humming as she continued to prepare the garden beds for the upcoming fall crops, occasionally shooing the stupid, curious chickens who kept trying to supervise her work.

Suddenly, Mother's scream pierced the afternoon, and Charlotte looked up from the plot of dirt she was tending behind the cabin. Mere seconds later, she saw Father run out of the barn, carrying his rifle. His body seemed to fly for a beautiful instant before she heard a shot reverberate and realized he'd been hit; shot in the back. But where was the shooter? She quickly swiveled her head to investigate when Mother's renewed screams caught her attention and propelled Charlotte around the side of the house. There were no words for the horror awaiting her.

Two unfamiliar men were in the front of the cabin. Mother was being held around the waist by a tall, slender man in a faded blue uniform. She screamed and kicked and strained to reach Ruthie, who was in the arms of another, absolute giant of a man. Sweet little Ruth didn't even realize she was in danger. Her younger sister clasped her corncob doll, smiling and giggling as the huge man grabbed her dress by the collar and began to rip it from her body.

Charlotte stifled a gasp, then ran to where her father lay bleeding on the ground. She tripped over one of the chickens and practically fell over Father's body. She frantically attempted to pull the rifle out from underneath him. She could hear hoof beats growing close and knew she had to hurry. Suddenly, she was airborne as unknown hands lifted her up and pulled her against a hot, smelly body riding astride an impossibly tall horse.

"Look what I've got," the man behind her yelled as she wriggled to free herself. His breath reeked of alcohol and decay. He reigned his horse to the front yard and dismounted close to his associates, pulling her with him. She hit the ground hard, and he yanked her back to standing.

"We don't need old women or children when we've got this here!"

"Lordy, lordy, Fred," the man holding Mother said in admiration. "That there's a beauty!"

Without a pause, he pulled out his Starr revolver, pointed it at the back of Mother's head, and pulled the trigger. Mother slumped to the ground. Before Charlotte could even scream in horror, the man turned toward Ruthie. She was still smiling her beautiful, innocent smile as the bullet completely and utterly destroyed her face.

"Damnit, Archie! You almost hit me!" Ruthie's captor yelled as he jumped back in alarm. "I still wanted her, you fool."

He reached up with his huge hands and wiped blood and brain matter off his face. "Damnit," he said again, looking down at Ruth's unmoving body, "I've never seen such a tiny thing with such womanly curves."

Charlotte heard a primal scream and turned to see Brendan charging out of the woods towards them. Her strong, brave brother would rescue her, as he so often had these last few years. A rifle barrel whipped up on her left side. She heard the shot at the same time Brendan fell to the ground. Fred lowered his rifle as she whirled around to confront him.

"Why are you doing this," she screamed, and began pounding him with her fists. He easily caught her arms and began to laugh.

"I'm doing this because it's fun, little lady."

He turned to his horse, slid his rifle back into its scabbard, grabbed his canteen, and took a long drink. Then he spit on the grass and wiped his grimy face on his faded blue uniform sleeve. He wasn't as large as the giant, but there was no doubt he was the leader of this gangly crew.

"Bring him here," he growled to Archie. "I'm not done with him, yet."

Archie took off loping toward Brendan, his gait awkward and lumbering. When he reached Brendan, he kicked him in the side with his boot.

"Get up," he ordered, pointing his revolver at Brendan's head. Brendan held his injured shoulder as he slowly stood up and looked at Charlotte. She saw her own shock mirrored in his face.

"Move," Archie ordered.

Brendan began walking, with Archie following behind, his gun still pointed at the back of her brother's head.

"Tie him up there to the hitching post," the leader ordered in a sinister voice. "And make sure he's facing this way so he can watch the fun!"

With surprising speed, Brendan ducked and pivoted, shoving his elbow into Archie's neck. Archie's eyes bulged and he fell to the ground, grabbing his throat. Brendan lunged across Archie's body, reaching for the revolver, but the giant man was already upon him. He tackled Brendan to the ground and pointed his own pistol at Brendan.

"Dan! Stop," shouted the leader. "He can't see this if he's dead." Dan lowered his pistol and pulled Brendan over to the hitching post. Archie was still thrashing around on the ground, desperately attempting to breathe. Neither of his partners showed the slightest concern with the strange gargling noises. Dan was busy tying Brendan to the hitching post, and Fred was holding on to Charlotte with one hand while he tried to undo his breeches with the other.

Suddenly, Fred stopped what he was doing and stepped over to Archie. Pulling a huge knife from his belt, he quickly slit Archie's throat.

"Damn, Fred! What'd you have to do that for," shouted Dan in surprise.

"He was annoying me, and I want to enjoy this," Fred answered, turning back to Charlotte. Then, seeing the disapproval in Dan's eyes, he added, "Besides, his windpipe was crushed, and he was going to slowly suffocate. Good 'ol Fred just helped him along."

Charlotte stood like a statue. She simply could not process what was unfolding around her. Fred continued to loosen the ties on his breeches as she stood frozen, looking out over the bodies of her loved ones, past them to the beautiful mountain horizon, oblivious to what was about to happen. Suddenly, Fred threw her to the ground.

"Don't you dare," Brendan snarled, as realization dawned on him.

Fred laughed. "Oh, I dare! I'm going to have your pretty sister, and then my friend here is going to have a turn. And then I just might have a second go."

Brendan raged and cussed, but Fred just laughed all the more. With one knee on each side of Charlotte's waist, he kneeled over her, pinning her down to the ground. His grey eyes sparkled as he ripped open her bodice and put his hands all over her. She punched and scratched and screamed and bit, but it was no use. He was much too strong for her. Charlotte looked over at her brother. The pain on Brendan's face as Fred took her maidenhood pierced her heart. She was horrified that he was being forced to witness this. As Fred continued raping her, Brendan threw his head back and howled like a wounded animal. Charlotte turned her face away and tried to imagine herself anywhere but here.

Chapter Two

Tuesday, August 13, 1867

Thomas Linz closed his eyes and allowed every part of him to appreciate the cool breeze tousling his hair. He was hot and tired, and it had been one hell of a day. But he'd take the heat any time over the unrelenting cold he'd experienced the last few years; icy temperatures in the air around him and cold numbness in his own heart. The atrocities he'd witnessed and been forced to commit would haunt him forever.

Fighting for the Union had been a source of pride. Thomas loved his country and was willing to die to ensure freedom for all men. He was proud and motivated as he signed up to fight. But he had not been prepared for the reality of war. How could any human have been prepared for that? Fragmented memories knocked on the door of his consciousness, and he quickly pushed them away. Nothing good would come of allowing them inside.

The day had been a long one, and Thomas was ready to set camp. In addition to the physical exertion involved with a day on horseback, there was the mental toll. The world was a dangerous place these days, and he had to remain constantly vigilant as he traveled. His tattered navy-blue uniform afforded him a modicum of protection; after all, he had fought on the winning side. But America was a country divided. The Union had been preserved, yes. However, everyone had lost something in this godforsaken war.

He thought briefly of his parents and younger brother. Three-fifths of his family dead in a matter of months. And then there was Emily. What were her prospects? There were no eligible men left—at least none that possessed an untroubled soul. He tried to imagine his beautiful, caring sister married to the broken men with whom he'd served. Or worse yet, married to someone who'd been too cowardly to serve. No. He thought of how carefree and frivolous his early adulthood had been, so different from Emily's. The last four years of her life had been nothing but loneliness and heartache as she repeatedly lost friends and family alike. And yet, she remained so hopeful and resilient. He recalled his first glimpse of her upon returning from battle. She had rushed from the porch and run down the long tree-lined drive toward him in a most unladylike fashion! As he unmounted his horse, he'd nearly been tackled by her great hug.

Initially, Thomas relished being home in Ohio. The war had nearly destroyed him, physically and mentally, and the beautiful family home was a perfect place to recuperate. Emily had grown so much during his four-year absence, and he enjoyed getting to know the delightful young lady she'd become. When he'd ridden off to join the cause, he'd been twenty years old, and Emily had been only twelve. Although he'd loved her immensely, and she'd adored her older brother, their age difference left them with nothing in common; nothing with which to build a real conversation. Now, it seemed they were never at a loss for conversation. Emily had a brilliant intellect and an inquiring mind, and Thomas enjoyed his time with her more than he would have ever imagined.

But as the months passed, Thomas grew more and more unsettled. Life as he'd known it was no longer satisfying. He needed more than the frequent parties and nights at the social club. His comfortable, sedentary existence lacked substance. Cincinnati had grown and Thomas no longer felt at home there. He longed for adventure. He needed space.

Thomas tied Trigger to a nearby tree, grabbed his tin canteen from the saddle, and made his way down to the creek. He looked carefully in all directions before squatting down at the water's edge and using his hand to scoop up some of the crystal-clear water. It tasted heavenly. He removed the cork and filled his canteen. Once it was recapped, he set it on the ground and scooped several handfuls of water up to his face. It felt wondrous to wash away some of the grime. He thought about how nice a smooth-shaven face would feel but decided against it. He had to admit the thick, scraggly facial hair, while itchy and hot, seemed to be a protective factor of sorts. He was in no mood to chat with others on the road. The longer the facial hair grew, the less people approached him. These days, people saw him and sometimes moved to the opposite side of the road.

"I must look quite dastardly," he thought with a smile.

He stood and walked back to Trigger.

"Hey, Old Man," he said, affectionately rubbing the horse's neck. "Come have a taste of the best water in the world." He grabbed the reins and walked Trigger down to the water. This would be a fine place to camp tonight. The bank of the river was lined with thick oak trees and soft grass. He would be comfortable here.

As Trigger grazed, Thomas hunted for dinner. The area was obviously attractive to wildlife as it didn't take long for him to shoot a plump rabbit. He built a fire and then sat to prepare the rabbit for cooking. Until the aroma of the roasting meat began to assault his nostrils, he hadn't realized how hungry he was. He was grateful that he had some bread to go with the meat. Passing through Denver City earlier in the evening, he had purchased a few food items. What a luxury to have fresh bread!

After eating, he took a swim in the river and washed off all the grime from the last few days. The water was cool and refreshing and just what he needed after the heat of the day. Of all his prerequisites for potential homesteads, access to water was top of the list. It could be a river, stream, lake or pond. He wasn't picky, but a body of water was nonnegotiable! Of course he would add a well, but there was just something wonderful about swimming in the evening. It was as though you could wash away any troubles from the day and reset your outlook.

As the running water cleaned away the dust from the day, Thomas let his mind wander freely to his dreams for the future. There was so much work to be done, and he eagerly looked forward to all of it: finding the right property, building a home, marrying and starting a family of his own. Yes, the next few years would be busy and rewarding. Thomas felt so blessed to be starting this new chapter in his life.

Chapter Three

Tuesday, August 13, 1867

A fluttering against the skin of her forehead brought Charlotte back to consciousness. She hurt everywhere and her brain was completely out of focus. Her head was throbbing, and one eye was swollen shut. She slowly opened her other eye and looked around, but the tall grass surrounding her blocked her view of everything save the clear, starry sky above. The soft movements on her forehead resumed and Charlotte reached up and gingerly grabbed the culprit. As soon as she opened her hand, a tiny red beetle launched from her palm and flew away.

With much effort, she pushed herself into a sitting position. Her whole body screamed in pain, and the pain brought her crashing back to reality. A wave of nausea struck her insides like a hammer, and she leaned over and began dry heaving uncontrollably. There was nothing in her stomach, but her body continued to revolt.

Now she remembered it all, and the memories made her want to lie back down in the hope that she could will her own death. Her mind reeled. There was an incredible ache in her chest. She looked out over the grass and realized she was in a clearing less than two hundred yards from her home. She slowly stood up, noticing her torn blouse and blood-soaked skirt.

"Oh, my God. Oh, my dear God," she wailed. Tears streamed down her face as she began running blindly toward her home, toward her family, toward the end of her world as she knew it.

She halted her running and took a deep breath as she got closer to the homestead. The first body she encountered was her father's. She sunk to her knees, turned his solid, strong body over on its back, and instantly regretted it. His gentle green eyes were wide with shock and fear. Those eyes that always danced with amusement now showed only terror. Just twelve hours before, as Father and Brendan finished breakfast and walked out to start their daily chores, Mother had remarked that Brendan was catching up to Father in height. Charlotte remembered how their laughter had continued all the way out to the barn. What she wouldn't give for one more day with them both.

She thought of how her strong, brave brother resembled their father more each day. How could their lives be destroyed in just a moment? Charlotte looked toward the cabin. Her eyes had adjusted to the dark and she could make out Brendan's figure still tied to the hitching post in an upright seated position. Even from this distance she could tell that there was no life in him. She was filled with shame remembering that he'd been forced to watch as Fred violated her. Which of the evil men had killed him, she wondered. And at what point had he been killed? While she was glad that this was one death she hadn't witnessed, she fervently hoped it had been a quick death. They had already tortured her smart, courageous brother enough by making him watch.

The night air was cold, and Charlotte realized she needed to change out of her torn, bloody clothes. She stood up slowly and walked to the clothesline. She was about to grab her stockings and a faded cotton dress when she saw Brendan's clothes hanging a little further down the line. She left her dress swaying in the gentle breeze and instead pulled Brendan's shirt, breeches, and socks into her arms. Then she stepped into the barn.

The animals had settled for the night and the barn had a soft, peaceful feeling. Charlotte was comforted by the silent breathing of several horses. She slipped out of her clothing and quickly donned the boy's clothing. She'd never worn breeches and had assumed they would feel much like her pantaloons. She was wrong. Instead of a soft cotton texture, they were made of a heavier wool. The pants and shirt were much too big for her but felt protective in a way. As she tied a piece of rope around her waist for a belt, she began to feel safer already. She would be a boy now. She would be protected as a boy. Being a young woman had been too dangerous. Never again would she allow herself to be that vulnerable. Tomorrow, she would cut up one of her long petticoats to make a binding for her chest.

She went to the wall where her father's farm tools hung on pegs and grabbed his shears. It struck her that she would never see her father working with the animals again. As the tears began anew, she loosened her hair from its braids. It fell past her waist, wavy and soft from being braided all day. She grabbed big handfuls of hair and began chopping them off with the shears.

When her hair had all been shorn, she hung the shears back up on the peg. Turning around, she noticed the pile of dark brown hair on the ground. Its presence seemed to shout of some great deception. Using her feet, she shuffled the mass of hair so that it mixed with the hay covering the ground.

No one need know Charlotte had ever been here. She hid her women's boots and ruined clothes under some old grain sacks and exited the barn. Unable to bear the thought of walking past Mother's, Ruthie's, and Brendan's bodies to get to the cabin, she slowly made her way back to her father's body.

She knelt by Father's side, made the Sign of the Cross, and then gently closed his eyelids. He still didn't look peaceful, but at least she couldn't see his shock anymore. Charlotte remained at her father's side for a few minutes more, trying to gather her courage. She knew she needed to get to the cabin and try to find safety, but the thought of walking past her mother and Ruthie and Brendan...she didn't think she could bear it.

"I'll give myself a few more minutes," she thought as she lay down in the soft clover next to her father and wished with all her heart that she could join her family in the afterlife. "What am I supposed to do now," she whispered, as she put her arm across the broad chest of the empty shell lying next to her and began to cry.

Suddenly, she remembered the rifle. Her eyes flew open and she sat up, frantically searching the ground around her father's body. The rifle was gone. Those cowards had taken it. She had a fleeting moment of fear, worrying that the soldiers might come back and she would have no way to protect herself. But then she laughed. She didn't fear death, she welcomed it. She could join her family in the afterlife instead of being stuck here all alone. If those evil men returned, she would make them kill her, no matter what it took.

Chapter Four

Wednesday, August 14, 1867

Thomas woke in the morning, well-rested and well-fed. His eyes opened to see a canopy of tree branches above him, and he remembered the brilliant stars that had been twinkling through the leaves last night before he fell asleep. A man could get used to the splendor of this land.

He quickly saddled Trigger, then readied his bedroll and attached it to the saddle. He refilled his canteen and checked to see that he hadn't left anything behind. His travels had been interesting and beautiful, but he was weary of living out of a small saddlebag. He was ready to put down roots; to wake up in the morning and be able to start his day without packing up everything he owned. He smiled at the thought of a cabin and a real bed. It wouldn't be too long now.

As he rode west, he marveled at the scene surrounding him. He'd never "felt" beauty this way, as if the grass and trees and mountains were all too much for just one of his senses and demanded homage from his whole body. The colors were so vivid and the morning air so crisp and fresh. He felt an aching in his chest and realized his journey was over. He'd found his home. This was where he wanted to spend all his remaining years.

Now he just hoped he could find some land to make his own. From what he'd heard, the gold rush was winding down in this area, and there was land to be had. He hoped he could procure enough acreage to set up a modest homestead and farm. Maybe then he could send for Emily. He still wasn't sure that was a great idea. He knew her future would be easier if she stayed with Great Aunt Shirley in Cincinnati; better marriage prospects, a beautiful home on one of the finest streets in town. Emily was a very wealthy woman now and could live the rest of her life in a comfortable home with all the modern conveniences. If she stayed in Cincinnati, she would remain surrounded by friends and have access to all the social events the city had to offer. With him, she would live in a log cabin and have no social events to speak of. It didn't seem a good trade.

But Emily was determined to make her life with him. She had told him that several times and in no uncertain terms. Emily reminded him that Great Aunt Shirley was already an old woman, and when Shirley passed, Thomas would be the only family Emily had. In a span of only three years, Emily and Thomas had lost their mother, father, and nineteen-year-old brother, Michael. Emily insisted she needed her big brother in her life. If Thomas was honest with himself, he knew he needed her, too. He would just have to get a house built as soon as possible to welcome her. They could start with a log cabin and slowly procure the labor and materials to build something grand.

He rode on now with renewed purpose. Before this moment, it hadn't mattered which road he took, or where he ended up, as long as it wasn't Cincinnati. Now, everything had changed. He was looking for his forever home, the place where he would start a family and raise children and see his grandchildren play. This would be the Linz stronghold! His heart overflowed with peace, and the first sliver of joy he'd felt since before the war started. He was going to start over, far away from the death and destruction he'd experienced. He was going to build the life of which he'd always dreamed.

After another hour of riding, Thomas saw some buildings in the distance. As he grew closer, he could make out a cabin and a barn, and what looked like a person, maybe a child, digging. It was about time to give Trigger a break and a drink of water. Maybe the owner of this homestead could give him some good information about available land in the area. And, if he was lucky, they might offer a hot meal tonight and let him sleep in their barn after he toured the area. His stomach growled at the thought of sitting at a table and enjoying a home-cooked meal.

The buildings had an impressive backdrop of mountains, and Thomas wondered if those were the Rockies. When he stopped at Denver City yesterday evening, he'd seen them in the distance and been told he was getting close to the Rocky Mountains. He imagined what it would be like to wake up every morning and see that from his front porch. Those mountains made him feel so small, and yet gave him the feeling he could conquer the world, all at the same time.

He turned his gaze back to the property in front of him and realized that the child he'd seen earlier was now gone. They must have run inside to tell their Ma someone was coming. Thomas couldn't help wondering what the good lady would be making for dinner tonight. His hunting had been productive, and he hadn't exactly starved while traveling here, but a good home-cooked meal would be mighty fine.

Thomas looked up at the wooden arch over the entrance to the property. "Kerry Haven" was roughly burned into the wood. He rode slowly through the tree-lined path and up to the cabin. The property appeared well-cared-for, and the cabin looked well-built and sturdy. Contrary to his antisocial feelings of the last few months, Thomas realized he was truly looking forward to meeting the inhabitants. He took another look up at the beautiful mountains and sighed in contentment as he dismounted the saddle. He leaned over to tie Trigger's reins to the hitching post and straightened up just in time to see a figure hurtling towards him. He jumped aside, barely missing a shovel to the head. His attacker turned and prepared to take another run at him.

"Whoa, son," Thomas said, putting both arms out in front of him in a defensive gesture as he looked over the young boy standing in front of him. "I mean you no harm." He slowly walked backwards as he continued speaking in a soft, gentle tone. "Listen, just hold your ground and I'll be on my way. I meant no harm."

Charlotte raised her chin and looked him over quickly. She saw a pistol on his hip and a rifle attached to his saddle. She deduced that if he hadn't pulled one of them yet, he probably didn't plan to use them. Her mind appreciated the fact that the man had called her "son." It relieved her to know her altered appearance was believable.

"Did they send you back to finish me off," Charlotte growled, taking in the man's appearance. He was tall and broad-shouldered, and looked a bit older than her father. He wore a faded Union uniform, and his long facial hair was as unkempt as the scraggly black hair hanging below his dingy cap. She glared at him and attempted to look intimidating.

Thomas didn't know what to say, so he merely stared at the angry monster in front of him. The young man was a sight to behold. His short brown hair was covered with blood and sticking up in all directions. Oversized, blood-stained pants were tied to his waist by a length of rope and hung on his tiny frame. His face was filthy, and something, maybe tears, had left mud streaks down his cheeks. His right eye was swollen shut, with a gash running through the eyebrow. Thomas wondered if the boy's vision had been damaged, as well.

"Who did this to you," Thomas softly asked.

The boy continued to glare at him, then shook his head defiantly and walked back towards the barn. Thomas took this chance to quickly look around for additional attackers. As his eyes swept over the property, he noticed a body lying near the side of the cabin, and what looked like dried pools of blood in several areas of the yard and in the dirt near the cabin. He needed to get the hell out of here and fast!

Thomas mounted Trigger and turned to go. The scraping noises he heard to his left indicated the boy had resumed his digging near the barn. Thomas stole a glance in his direction. With a jolt, he took in the awful sight of four more bodies; these draped in blankets. Well, not fully draped. The heads and torsos of all four were covered, but the blankets were not large enough and left the lower bodies unprotected. Judging by the shoes, Thomas presumed there were two men and two women. Was this the boy's family? If so, he was digging their graves! Thomas's eyes flooded with tears, and he took a moment to clear his throat. Then he prompted Trigger to take just a few steps in the direction of the barn. He didn't want to startle the boy by getting too close.

"May I help you dig," he asked, when the knot in his throat allowed him to speak.

The boy did not answer. After a brief pause, Thomas hesitantly dismounted. He couldn't leave such a young boy to face this monumental burden alone. Without turning his back to the boy, Thomas led Trigger to the trough for a drink of water. As he did so, he couldn't help noticing bloody trails through the dirt and grass where someone had dragged the bodies. This poor little boy. He couldn't be more than ten or eleven years old, and it appeared he was now all alone in the world.

Thomas didn't have a shovel, and briefly thought about entering the barn to look for something with which to dig. Then he decided he couldn't risk turning his back on this ball of fury to search for tools. Loss and anger were a deadly combination, and this boy seemed to have plenty of both. Very slowly, he moved closer to the boy.

"Will you take a break? I'll dig for a spell."

The boy silently scooped two more shovelfuls of dirt out of the hole. Thomas realized he wasn't going to get an answer and was about to leave when the boy suddenly shuddered and gasped for breath. It appeared the young man was trying his best not to cry in front of a stranger.

"Listen, son. I would sure appreciate a drink of water, and you look like you could use a break," he said, tentatively reaching his hand out for the shovel.

After a few moments, the boy reluctantly handed it to him, whispering, "Thank you, sir."

His eyes never left the ground.

"Call me Thomas, or Tommy. And what shall I call you?"

The boy finally lifted his face and locked eyes with Thomas. Thomas was taken aback by the pain and distrust in those tired eyes.

"I promise you; I am not here for harm. I'll help you dig for a while and then be on my way. You have my word."

Thomas maintained eye contact and hoped the boy could read empathy and concern in his look.

Charlotte's mind was racing. What name could she use?

"My name is Charlie. Charlie Gallagher."

Then, she turned and walked toward the cabin.

Chapter Five

Wednesday, August 14, 1867

Thomas let out a long breath as he watched Charlie walk away. He needed to think this through. The body lying over by the house and the blood everywhere indicated these deaths had not been from natural causes. Hell, Charlie's physical appearance alone indicated something horrific had happened here! Thomas felt fury rising in his chest. What sort of person attacked women and children like this?

"Damn," he grunted aloud, realizing that the authorities needed to be notified right away. The party responsible for this massacre could be preying on another family at this very moment. He would discuss this with Charlie when the boy returned from the cabin.

He looked down at the hole at his feet. Charlie had certainly not made much progress, and Thomas wondered how long he'd been digging. The ground here near the barn was compacted and hard. He wondered why the boy had chosen such an odd place to bury his family. Normally, people wanted their loved ones laid to rest in a beautiful, serene spot. Then he felt stupid for even wondering. Obviously, Charlie was too small to carry the bodies to a more appropriate resting place.

Charlotte walked slowly toward the cabin. She felt weary, so weary she could have slept for days. There had been no sleep last night, only grief and dread and throbbing pain in her head. She looked ahead to the cabin and froze. The memories came flooding back and she thought she would be sick. To her left was where Fred had raped her. Ten yards further was where Brendan had been killed. Ruth and mother murdered right there. She couldn't walk through it. She wanted to run far, far away and never return to this horrid place. But she needed a moment away from Thomas to think this through. She took a deep breath and placed one foot in front of the other until she reached the cabin, then kept going, up the three steps to the porch and through the door.

It was shocking to walk into her home and find everything just as it had been yesterday before her world was shattered. How could everything look so normal? Her life was in complete shambles and yet, there were still flowers in a cup on the table. Mother's apron still hung near the fireplace and her Bible still lie in her rocking chair, as though Mother could walk in any moment and fold her in a warm hug. She could still sense her family's love filling the room.

Charlotte's resolve broke, and she slumped to the floor, sobbing. She didn't even care if Thomas came in and saw her crying like a girl. He obviously wasn't here to attack her, and she knew he'd eventually realize she wasn't a boy. She was a woman. She was a woman who had been grievously violated. She would never be the same person she was before. Rage and shame and devastating loss overwhelmed her. She threw her back her head to howl in pain as Brendan had done while she was being raped, but no sound came. Tears streamed down her face, and her body was wracked with sobs, but there was no sound.

"What an injustice," she thought. "Pain this deep should roar."

Her emotion spent, exhaustion washed over her, and she longed for nothing more than to climb into her parents' bed and sleep for days. But there were graves to be dug and bodies to be buried. And Thomas was out there waiting for a drink of water. She was pretty sure he'd only asked in order to convince her to let him help, but it had worked. She pushed herself up from the floor. There would be time to sleep once her family was laid to rest and she was alone.

She grabbed a soft linen cloth from the table to wipe her eyes. The excruciating pain shocked her. She'd totally forgotten about her face in the last few busy hours. Carefully, she blotted her face and eyes with the soft cloth. When she finished, she saw it was covered with dirt and blood. This wound needed to be cleaned before an infection set in. Hopefully, she could figure out how to bandage it.

Charlotte stepped out onto the porch and looked over to see Thomas was no longer by the barn. She experienced a brief moment of panic, and then saw the man's large horse still standing there. Relief flooded her when she realized Thomas hadn't left her, and she was greatly confused by this reaction. The last thing she wanted or needed right now was a strange man around. She doubted she would ever again feel anything but fear in the presence of a man. So, why had she been upset when she thought he was gone?

Charlotte walked the brief distance to the well and pumped the handle until water filled her bucket. Then she wet the cloth and attempted to clean her face. The swelling was astonishing. Carefully prying her eyelids open, she realized she could still see out of her right eye. She guessed she was lucky, although there was nothing lucky about the day she'd just lived. Horrible memories returned to haunt her.

After Fred finished with her, he climbed off and told Dan it was his turn. Charlotte took that opportunity to jump up and run. Her torn clothes kept tripping her, making it impossible to gain speed.

"Wait, Dan! Give her a fighting chance," Fred yelled, choking with laughter.

This was all a game to him. Charlotte ran as fast as she could, but she wasn't fast enough. Dan caught up with her before she even made it to the woods. He grabbed her braid and threw her down in a grassy field where she and Ruth had often played. She fought back with all her strength and managed to bite him hard on his arm, drawing blood. He recoiled in pain and then pistol-whipped her across the forehead. He must have knocked her unconscious because when she awoke, she was all alone. At least she'd not been aware as he took his turn with her.

"Excuse me, Charlie," she heard, and jumped in alarm. Charlotte raised her head and saw Thomas standing about eight yards away.

"I didn't mean to startle you, but I need to ask you a question before I dig any deeper," he said.

"Yes," she prompted.

"I…well, first…" Thomas paused to formulate his thoughts. "Do you know who did this to your family?"

Charlotte shook her head, and Thomas continued. "We need to notify the sheriff and try to stop them from attacking anyone else. How many were there?"

"There were three. One is dead, over on the side of the house. The other two must have left. I was unconscious, I think."

It was horrible to realize she wouldn't be able to just lock all of this away in her mind and move on from it. She was going to have to report it to law enforcement. She was going to have to put it into words and describe the despicable things that had happened. Thomas was right. Others were at risk. But she could change the story, just as she'd changed her identity. She could say it happened to mother, not to her. She could be Charlie. She could be the youngest brother. She could remain a boy. She felt safer as a boy. She never wanted to be a woman again.

"This is none of my concern, but I wanted to ask you about the location of the graves," Thomas began.

"I know it's the wrong place," Charlotte interrupted. "I just…" She looked down. "I just couldn't move them any further."

Thomas was relieved that Charlie didn't seem insulted by his critique. "Is there a certain place you think would be…better suited? I can carry them on my horse, one at a time. We can bury them wherever you like."

Charlotte immediately thought of the hilltop where Father always talked about building a church. That would be perfect. Mother, Father, Brendan and little Ruth, they'd be happy there.

"Yes, sir. I know a place," she answered. "Let me saddle a horse and we can take the first two bodies."

"Would you like to clean them up before we take them there," Thomas asked.

"I hadn't thought of that. But, I don't really want to see…."

"I understand, son. Just tell me if there are any personal items that you would like me to retrieve."

Charlotte was immensely glad he suggested this. She was still dazed and would not have thought of it.

"My mother has a locket around her neck and a rosary in her apron pocket. My father carries his father's pocket watch. I'd like those things, please. And my brother's boots," she added. "But only if you think that's appropriate."

Looking down, Thomas noticed that Charlie was barefoot. That seemed odd, as the cabin and barn didn't appear to be those of a poor family. "I think that would be fine."

Thomas was careful to place himself in a position to block Charlie's view before he squatted to remove the blanket from the woman's head. It took everything he had to not gag. The woman's face was…well, it was just gone. He could tell that she'd been shot in the back of the head. He gently removed the locket from around her neck and then replaced the makeshift shroud. He moved down to waist level and pulled the blanket aside. The apron had two large pockets, and he found a rosary in the first one he checked. He pushed the rosary and locket into his shirt pocket and stood. He took a moment of silence before moving to the next body.

This body was the largest, and Thomas assumed it was Charlie's father. When he pulled the blanket from his head, he was surprised to see a young man instead. It was apparent he'd been shot in the shoulder and then had his throat slashed. Thomas could not wrap his mind around the evil inflicted on this family. He quickly replaced the blanket over the face and moved down to remove the boots. These were fine leather boots and would serve Charlie well once he grew into them. Thomas was glad that Charlie would have something by which to remember his big brother.

"Are you able to remove his suspenders," Charlotte called. She was still standing close to the well and had no desire to move closer. She had already witnessed the utter destruction.

"I'll get them," he answered. Now the ill-fitting clothes made sense. Charlie was wearing the much larger clothing of his older brother. His thoughts turned to his own younger brother, Michael, who had always idolized him. Until Michael's death, they had been constant companions and best friends. His heart ached as he remembered he would never see his brother again. Young Charlie was experiencing the same horrid loss.

The next blanket covered the smallest body. Thomas turned and called out to Charlie, "Do you want anything from this one?"

"That was my sister. I think her doll is somewhere by the cabin. But I'd like a lock of her hair, please."

Charlotte chided herself. A boy would never have asked for a lock of his sister's hair! What would Thomas think? But the man didn't react at all. He just pulled out a pocketknife and knelt beside her sister's small body. Charlotte's throat burned with unshed tears for Ruthie, with her soft blonde curls and constant smile. How she would miss her!

Thomas approached the last blanket and was relieved to find that the man under it still had his face intact. He quickly located the pocket watch and covered Charlie's father again. Once he had retrieved all the items, Thomas took another silent moment to pay his respects. Then he turned and walked towards Charlotte.

"Here you are, son. I'm just so sorry that you're having to…" He shook his head, unable to finish his thought. Finally, he was able to speak again.

"What were their names?"

"My parents were Annie and Patrick. Brendan was my brother, and Ruth was my sister."

Thomas nodded his head solemnly. Charlotte accepted the precious items he handed to her and began walking to the barn. Once inside, she secured the locket around her neck, and put the rosary in her pocket. She tied the long blonde hair into a secure knot and added that to her pocket, as well. Then she quickly donned Brendan's suspenders and boots. They didn't fit at all. Looking around the barn, her gaze fell on the large bales of cotton on the far wall. She pulled several handfuls free and added some to each boot. That was much better.

By the time Charlotte came back out with her horse, Meg, and a second shovel, Thomas had wrapped each of the bodies securely in its blanket. Charlotte was so thankful that she wouldn't need to see the horror again. As she prepared to mount her horse, Charlotte reminded herself that she would need to ride astride Meg instead of side-saddle. She had put Brendan's saddle on her horse instead of her own but didn't want to forget and mistakenly climb up the wrong way. She'd occasionally ridden astride the horse when she and Brendan were out riding alone but would never have even considered doing so in front of Mother. Mother was a proper lady, and sometimes despaired of Charlotte's slack upbringing. Based on things Mother said about how proper ladies acted "back home," Charlotte was mighty glad to be growing up in the Colorado wilderness. It sounded near impossible to be and do all the things proper ladies were required to be and do!

"How old are you, Charlie," Thomas asked as they rode out to the hilltop.

Charlotte had Ruth's body draped over the saddle in front of her, and Thomas was carrying Brendan's body the same way. Her mind raced. How old would a boy be if he were her height?

"I'll be twelve next April."

She hoped that seemed accurate. She couldn't remember how Brendan had looked at twelve. Tears began streaming down her cheeks and she swiped at them with her sleeves. Brendan would never tease her or annoy her ever again. She would never hear him singing or see him swinging Ruthie around in the air.

"Oh, God," she silently prayed. "How am I going to survive this?"

Thomas must have sensed her mood because he remained silent for the rest of the ride.

The next few hours were grueling. It was decided that there was not enough time to dig four graves, so Charlotte suggested burying Mother and Father together in one grave, and Brendan and Ruthie together in another. She knew it was silly, but she didn't want Ruthie to be in the deep, dark earth all alone. Ruth had always adored Brendan, and Charlotte was glad her little sister would have their strong, protective brother with her for all time.

As she dug, Charlotte thought about the horrors of yesterday and the impossibility of the future. She couldn't stay here alone. She would need to make arrangements to move back to Ireland with her Aunt Betsy and Uncle Jared. But how did one even go about that? She didn't know anything about traveling. Tomorrow, she would ride over to the Crawford home and ask Mr. Crawford to assist her. The Crawfords and Gallaghers had only been neighbors for two years, but they had quickly become family. Yes, the Crawfords could take her in and help her through this tragedy. Maybe Mr. Crawford would even want to purchase the Gallagher land.

Oh, but she couldn't sell Kerry Haven! She had so many amazing memories here with her family, and now their graves would be forever here. How could she ever leave this place? Her heart belonged here with her loved ones.

She began to cry anew as memory after memory flashed through her mind; Mother and Father dancing on the cabin porch, Ruth spinning and laughing as Father played his fiddle; Brendan making them all laugh with his fast wit and brilliant humor. How on earth was she to survive without them? Who was she on her own?

Thomas, working on the other grave, thought about everything this young boy was facing. Even several years later, he still struggled with his grief every single day. Charlie was so much younger, and his family had died in such a horrific manner. He wondered anew how the boy would survive the tragedy. His heart broke at what lay ahead for Charlie.

The sun had begun to set as Charlotte and Thomas finished filling the graves and stood side by side looking down at the mounds of dirt. Charlotte had so much she wanted to say; there should be prayers and passages from the Bible and words of hope and encouragement. But all she could do was cry. Thomas just stood in silence and let her cry. Somehow, his quiet presence was a comfort to her.

As she stood there crying over the graves of everyone she loved, she made a bargain with herself. She could cry as much as she wanted tonight. Tomorrow, there would be no more tears. She would put today aside and never look back on it again. It was the only way she could survive this.

Finally, she wiped her nose on the sleeve of her shirt and turned to walk over to Meg. She was attaching the shovel to the saddle as Thomas cleared his throat. He stood several feet behind her, but she didn't turn around.

"Charlie, your bravery is astonishing, and I'd be honored to accompany you to the Sheriff tomorrow. However, I did promise to clear out once we'd buried your family, and I'm a man of my word. I'll not interfere if you don't want me to. What would you prefer?"

She stood in silence for a moment before speaking. "I don't want you to go," she finally said, choking on a sob. "Not yet please."

Thomas placed his hand on her right shoulder and gave a quick squeeze. "I'll stay, son. As long as you need me, I'll be here."

She felt guilty for deceiving this nice old man, but she knew she wouldn't be ready to give up her identity any time soon. Thomas would continue his travels tomorrow or the next day. There was no harm in keeping her identity secret for a few more days.

"I'm not harming anyone," she kept assuring herself on the ride back to the cabin. "I'm truly not doing anything wrong." Somehow, she still felt guilty.

The sky was deep purple now that the sun had dipped below the edge of the mountains. There was a beautiful dichotomy between the artistry of the night sky and the desolation in her heart. How could beauty still exist in the world, she wondered. Every lovely thing should have crumbled into black and white ash when her family was killed.

"First we need to sew up that gash," Thomas said, breaking the deep silence as they approached the cabin and barn. "Then I'll try to cook us something to eat."

Charlotte almost laughed at his suggestion. A man sewing up wounds and cooking meals!

"Yes, sir. I can show you where my mom kept everything, if you need."

"That would be good, Charlie."

They unsaddled Meg and Trigger and settled them into the barn with the other horses, then walked back to the cabin. Charlotte noticed Ruthie's little dolly lying in the grass and went to pick it up. She held it close to her chest and willed herself not to cry. It was no use. Ruth brought so much joy into every day of her life, and Charlotte didn't know how she would manage without her little sister.

When they entered the cabin, Charlotte gently placed the doll on the mantle above the fireplace and then pulled out her mother's sewing kit and her father's whiskey. She knew that the wound would need to be cleaned. She had seen her mother do this several times for Ruth, Brendan, and Father, but this would be the first time she had such a bad injury. She hoped she would be brave.

"Now this is going to hurt like hell. Are you ready?"

"As ready as I'll ever be," she answered with a tremulous smile.

Thomas smiled back with reassurance and then gently placed his hand on the top of her head and positioned her face at the correct angle. His touch was so gentle. Charlotte closed her eyes and imagined it was her sweet mother taking care of her. Then Thomas began dribbling the whiskey slowly over the wound and she took a sharp breath. She wanted to curse aloud, and then realized that she could. While it was never appropriate for a woman to curse, boys could do that without upsetting anyone.

"Tarnation," she hollered. Then, because it felt so good, she yelled it louder. "Tarnation!"

Thomas began to laugh. "I warned you, son. Hurts like the Dickens, doesn't it?" Now that he was able to get a closer look, he was glad to see that Charlie's nose wasn't broken. But the swelling was horrible. He wondered what the boy would look like in a week or two. Would he look like his father, or brother? Sadly, he had no idea how Charlie's mother or sister looked since their faces had been destroyed.

"Tell me about your family," Thomas said, as he worked. He knew the stitches would be as painful as hell, and he also knew the boy wouldn't want to cry in front of him. However, if Charlie cried while talking about his family, hopefully he would feel there was no shame in that. It made Thomas smile to himself- when had he become so protective of this boy?

"We came here from Ireland back in eighteen-sixty one. I was young, so I only remember a little about Ireland. My mother comes from a great big family and my father from a very small one. He always said one of the best things about marrying her was joining that boisterous family. They met in church one Sunday. My mother says it was his beautiful singing voice that first caught her attention. He did have a very strong voice, and I loved hearing him sing. Many nights, he would pull out his fiddle and play and sing for hours. My mother and Brendan and I would sing along, and Ruth would just laugh and smile. She loved music. We all did." Her voice trailed off.

Thomas wanted to keep Charlie distracted, so he prompted, "I noticed Brendan was already bigger than your father! How old was he?"

Charlotte laughed. "He was fifteen. And he was the best big brother any boy could ever want. He taught me to shoot from horseback and how to tell venomous and non-venomous snakes apart. And he was always up for a swim in the creek at the end of a hot day. He loved to swim." Her voice wavered, and she began to cry again. "I still can't believe I won't ever see him again."

"I lost a little brother myself, Charlie. It's been a few years, but I still sometimes feel like Michael will just come walking around the corner one day, and I'll realize this has all been a bad dream. Losing a sibling is just…I mean, you expect that your parents will die before you, but you never think about losing a brother."

"I guess we have that in common," Charlotte said through her tears. "How did Michael die?"

"He died on May 15, 1864. in the Battle of New Market. Have you heard of it?"

When Charlotte shook her head, he continued.

"Michael attended the Virginia Military Institute. Confederate General John C. Breckinridge was waiting for reinforcements, but they were greatly delayed. He decided to use the cadets from VMI, some as young as fifteen years old, to join the attack on the Union soldiers. Breckenridge must have been desperate to send such young boys into battle. I can't imagine his thought process. This was the first time in our country's history when a school's student body was used as an organized combat unit. I hope it will be the last. Michael was nineteen when he died. Knowing he wasn't due to graduate for another two years, I hadn't given a thought to his safety, so his death was truly a shock. And I didn't find out about it until much later. I still miss my brother every single day."

There was silence for a few long minutes as each of them thought about the beloved brothers they had lost too young.

"And what was Ruth like?"

Thomas was about halfway through stitching the gash and it was looking okay. He wished again that Charlie's face wasn't so swollen. It was difficult to pull the two sides of the gash together and he could already tell it was going to be an atrocious scar. He was thankful this injury hadn't happened to a girl. No young woman relished a scar across her face. But for a boy, it would just make him more desirable to the young ladies someday!

"There was something wrong with my sister. She was sixteen years old, but still acted like an infant. She couldn't talk very much. She laughed and smiled all the time, though. She was so joyful and innocent."

Thomas remembered the tiny body he had helped bury this afternoon. Sixteen years old? That was surprising.

When the wound was fully sewn up, Thomas cleaned it again with alcohol. He was impressed with the bravery of this boy and sent up a silent prayer that God would protect him from further loss.

"I'll make dinner since I know where everything is located," Charlotte said, standing up. "I hope oatmeal is okay. Nothing else is ready."

"That's fine, son. What can I do to help?"

"Will you start the fire while I draw water?"

"Absolutely."

Thomas stood and walked to the hearth. Charlotte grabbed an earthenware jug and left the cabin.

Thomas started the fire and Charlotte soon returned. She poured water into the cauldron hanging over the hearth and added oatmeal. Then she pulled a bag of brown sugar and a crock of butter and placed them on the table with two bowls and spoons. Soon they were sitting down to eat the meager meal.

"I just realized I've not eaten since yesterday morning," Charlotte said softly.

"I don't know how you were able to do everything you did the last two days."

For several minutes, they ate in silence. Suddenly, Thomas heard a thud and looked up from his plate. Charlie had fallen fast asleep, and his head now lay right in the middle of his empty bowl. Thomas pushed back his heavy wooden chair as quietly as possible and moved to pick up Charlie. The boy weighed next to nothing, and Thomas was again struck by the amount of courage present in this frail being. He hesitated a moment, looking around the cabin, and then carried him toward the only interior door. Balancing Charlie in one arm, he turned the knob and opened the door. As he'd expected, it was a bedroom. Thomas gently placed Charlie on what he assumed was his parents' bed and left the room.

Once out on the porch, Thomas breathed deeply. It was peaceful and cool outside, and he fancied some quiet time on the porch before lying down to sleep. He sat down in one of the rocking chairs and let his mind play out over the day. The beauty and excitement of his morning sharply contrasted with his horror and sorrow of the rest of the day. What had happened here was almost incomprehensible. He'd seen horrible things during the war, but those things had been done out of a sense of duty; a sense of fighting for one's beliefs. The senseless violence of these murders, well, it was just pure evil. There was no other explanation for it.

Exhaustion was setting in. Thomas dreaded sleep, but he knew it was going to be important to be well rested tomorrow. Should he sleep in the barn so he wouldn't wake Charlie if he screamed out during a nightmare? Or should he stay in the cabin in case Charlie awoke in the night and was afraid?

"Do eleven-year-old boys fear being alone," he wondered aloud. He certainly couldn't remember back that many years. It surprised him, though, that he already felt so protective of Charlie. Maybe he was just missing his own little brother. Thomas wasn't ready to let his mind go down that path, though. He stood up from the chair and stared out toward the mountains.

"Don't think about the bad stuff. Nothing good can come from looking back on that."

After one last glance at the stars and mountains in the distance, he walked into the cabin and quietly closed the door. To his surprise, there were now quilts laid out near the hearth. He was sure they hadn't been there when he stepped onto the porch an hour ago. He realized that Charlie must have woken and placed them there. Well, that answered his question about where to sleep. If Charlie wanted him in the house, he would gladly stay in the house.

In the bedroom, Charlotte lay awake in horrible pain. Her head was throbbing, but the pain in her heart was even worse. It felt like there was a huge, gaping hole in her chest that nothing would ever fill. There were no more tears left to cry and she just felt numb and alone. She heard the door open and then softly close. Relief surged through her as she realized Thomas was back in the cabin. Why she wanted him to sleep inside she couldn't comprehend, she just knew she did. Maybe his resemblance to her father made her feel safe. Maybe she just needed another human around. In a few days, Thomas would be gone, and she would have to adjust to the solitude. But for now, she was glad he was here.

Chapter Six

Thursday, August 15, 1867

Thomas awoke the next morning to the smell of coffee brewing and sausage frying. The cabin was pitch black, except for a candle which illuminated Charlie as he hurriedly worked to prepare breakfast. If Thomas didn't know better, he'd have thought he was looking at a gargoyle. Charlie's face looked even worse today than yesterday. The swelling had increased and his whole face was disfigured. His forehead stuck out inches past where it should be. Thomas again wondered what the boy would look like in a few weeks. Would he resemble his handsome father and brother? Even in death, it was remarkable how similar their features were.

For all his hideousness, Charlie certainly was a capable little lad. Until leaving for war, Thomas hadn't known a thing about cooking or making coffee. Men just didn't do those things! He guessed it was a different world now, and he was glad that Charlie would be able to care for himself without a mother or sister to do it for him.

His mind picked up the thoughts that had plagued him yesterday at the gravesite. What would become of this young orphan? Was there family nearby who could take him in? Or, if Charlie wanted to stay on at Kerry Haven, were there close neighbors who could support him? Life out here in the American west was difficult, and large families were needed in order to accomplish everything necessary to survive. A full-grown man would be hard-pressed to do it on his own. But a boy, alone? It just wasn't possible. The thought of Charlie leaving this property, and everything his family built here, well, it made Thomas sad. Charlie should grow up here, surrounded by the memories of his family and their love.

No, Thomas hadn't known them, but somehow, he knew they'd loved each other deeply. Charlie's love for them couldn't have come from a void. It took special parents to raise such a brave, capable son. His heart surged with a longing to have known them. He felt he would have loved this family. It was an odd feeling, missing people you'd never met.

"Good morning, Charlie," Thomas called, causing Charlotte to nearly jump out of her skin.

"Good morning, sir. That's the second time you've given me a start!"

Thomas laughed along with her, and she liked the sound of his laughter. Picking up the candle by which she'd been working, she walked over and lit a lantern that was on top of the mantle. She was shocked to see that Thomas was shirtless and quickly looked down at the floor. Hopefully, it was too dark for him to see her blush. It was probably perfectly normal for men to see other men without their shirts on. She just hoped he was still wearing his pants under the blanket.

"How long have you been awake? You looked so exhausted last night, I thought for sure I'd have to drag you from the bed this morning."

Charlotte hesitated, not sure how to answer.

"Did I wake you with my screaming?"

She slowly nodded her head.

"Damn, I'm so sorry." Thomas ran his hands through his tousled hair. "I—Ever since the war I have had these horrible nightmares. Sometimes, I wake up unable to breathe. Other times, it's just a lot of screaming." He threw back the blanket, stood up, and began folding the blanket as he continued. "I apologize again. You certainly needed your sleep after all you've been through."

Charlotte was relieved to see that he hadn't removed his pants before lying down to sleep. "My father sometimes had nightmares, too," she said, hoping to ease his guilt. "I felt so bad for him. He's the best … well, he was the best man I've ever met, and I hated how different he was when he first came back from the war."

There was silence for a moment.

"We certainly came home changed, didn't we," Thomas remarked.

"Yes. I imagine everyone did." Turning back to the small stove, she added, "I'll have this breakfast ready in just a moment."

"Thanks so much, Charlie. I'll head outside to check on the animals."

Thomas began walking towards the door. Then he stopped, and turned back to face her. "How far is the nearest town?"

"Denver City is the closest. It's a three-hour ride to the east. We'll find police there."

"Yes. I passed through Denver City on my way here. Give me five minutes," Thomas said, closing the door behind him.

He stepped out onto the porch and was awestruck by the brilliance of the stars in the night sky. If possible, they seemed even brighter and more magnificent than last night. He took a deep breath and stretched. His back was sore from all the digging yesterday. He thought of the four bodies lying in their freshly dug graves up on the small hill and turned in that direction.

"I'll take good care of him for you," he whispered impulsively. And then he wondered what had possessed him to say it. It seemed the most natural utterance, but it carried huge significance. He'd just made a very lengthy promise to people he'd never met. This boy would need to be looked after for at least four or five years. And yet, he didn't feel troubled by that thought. He smiled as he continued walking to the barn. With all his heart, he wanted to care for this boy. He wanted to continue the guidance and good training that Charlie's mother and father had begun. He wanted to see this boy grow into adulthood and witness what he would become. He wanted to provide all the brotherly love and wisdom he would have given to Michael and planned to give to Emily. He wanted to be a part of something bigger than himself.

Trigger seemed to have settled in easily with the Gallagher horses. There was a beautiful, strong gelding, along with three fine mares and a sturdy little pony. He had to admire Mr. Gallagher's ability to pick livestock. These were very fine creatures, and they were well cared for, as was everything he'd seen on the property. Thomas was happy to see that this place hadn't fallen into disrepair as so had many properties he'd seen on his travels out here. It was obvious Mr. Gallagher took pride in Kerry Haven and worked hard. Thomas wondered if Charlie would grow as big and brawny as his older brother. Brendan had no doubt been a huge help to his father.

Charlotte finished the sausage and scooped it onto two plates. She pulled the biscuits out of the oven, put the coffee pot on the table, and sat down to wait. The table seemed so large when set for only two people, and she fought back tears as she was flooded with so many happy memories made around this table. She abruptly stood up, needing something to do to get her mind off her loss. The flowers in the middle of the table were wilted and pathetic. She picked up the cup and walked toward the door. Just as she reached for the handle, the door opened. Thomas looked at the cup of flowers in her hand.

"I need to dump these," Charlotte said, trying to mask her emotion.

She walked past him and dumped the contents of the cup over the side of the porch as Thomas waited. Then, they walked back in together and sat down at the table. Charlotte felt Thomas was waiting on some sort of explanation.

"My mother loved wildflowers, and my father always made sure there were fresh flowers for her table."

"What a loving thing to do," Thomas said, as he began pouring his coffee. He placed two biscuits on his plate and took a deep sniff. "Everything smells great, Charlie. Your mother sure taught you well."

"I know it's odd for boys to cook, but Mother wanted us to be prepared for anything. Once Father left for war, it was just the four of us. Ruth was probably never going to be able to help around the house, and Mother knew that she couldn't do everything on her own and do it well. So, she taught me all she could." She was relieved that she hadn't needed to lie to Thomas, at least in this last exchange.

She bent her head and made the sign of the cross. Thomas stopped abruptly and lowered his head, as well.

"Bless us, O Lord," she began, and Thomas joined right in. "And these Thy gifts, which we are about to receive from Thy bounty, through Christ, Our Lord. Amen."

Their voices trailed off and Charlotte realized he must be Catholic, too. Although why that mattered, she couldn't say.

Thomas took a bite of his biscuit, and his green eyes grew wide. "Your mother did a damn fine job teaching you. This is the best biscuit I've ever tasted." He wiped some crumbs from his scraggly beard and continued. "I know grown women who would be jealous of your abilities, son!" Chuckling, he popped the last bite of the first biscuit into his mouth and buttered a second. "You may have to teach me this before I leave."

Charlotte felt herself blushing and focused intently on her plate. There was urgency to start their journey, and the pair quickly finished their breakfast without further conversation. "I'll get the horses saddled," Thomas informed her as he pushed back his chair and stood up from the table. "Yours is the black gelding, correct?"

"Yes. Her name is Meg."

When Thomas left the cabin, Charlotte moved to the water pot hanging over the fire and scooped out a basin of scalding water. Dishes were her least favorite chore, but soon she was done and ready to join Thomas in the barn. She doused the fire in the hearth and extinguished the candle and lantern. Then she opened the door and, as she left the cabin, instinctively grabbed her large straw hat off the rack by the door. Fortunately, Thomas had not yet exited the barn, and didn't see her mistake. Men didn't wear ladies' hats!

Charlotte grabbed Father's sombrero off the rack instead. She might one day decide to be a lady again, and it wouldn't do to have sunburned, freckled skin. She would protect her face the best she could while still pretending to be a boy. The sombrero hurt her wounded forehead, so she climbed the ladder to the loft and grabbed one of Brendan's soft bandanas. She folded it and placed it between the hat brim and her skin. It helped, but only minimally.

Charlotte stepped onto the porch and closed the door behind her. Thomas soon exited the barn leading Trigger and Meg. As she approached him, she glanced at the horses and saw that he had attached canteens and bedrolls to each of the saddles. Thomas followed her gaze.

"I wasn't sure how many days we would be traveling, so I prepared as best I could. Is there anything else you can think of?"

"I'll grab some food for us," Charlotte answered and ran back to the cabin.

Thomas checked the fit of the saddles one more time, and then began petting Trigger. The horse had been with him for close to two years now, and he was understandably attached to the strong, gentle creature. It was nearly impossible to find good horses following the war. More than a million horses had been killed in battle, and breeders were still trying to recover their supplies. That made Trigger all the more valuable.

As Charlotte quickly packed food from the kitchen and the cellar, she tried to calm her racing thoughts. She had not planned to travel closely with this man for more than a few hours. When he mentioned notifying the Sheriff yesterday, she envisioned a quick day trip to meet with the Sheriff and a quick return home. Now Thomas was preparing to be gone multiple days. She wondered what led him to believe they might spend more than one day on the road. How on earth would she hide her identity if they were forced to spend that much time together? Her mind was in a whirl, and she took a deep breath to calm herself.

"I can handle this. It's just a short journey. I've lost everyone I ever loved, and I'm still here. I can handle this."

Charlotte returned with the food supplies, and Thomas fastened them to his saddle. Upon leaving Kerry Haven, they rode in companionable silence for the first ten minutes. The night sky with its majestic stars surrounded them and held them close, almost commanding a reverential silence. Now the sun was beginning to rise over the horizon in front of them, and the sky was painted in brilliant colors. The world was fairly bursting with life, and it seemed permissible, almost necessary to speak.

"Tell me about your family," Charlotte said, turning to look at Thomas.

"My sister and I are the only ones left."

"I'm so sorry."

Charlotte felt sorrow for the kind old man and wondered if had been married or had children. How many had he lost?

"Thank you," Thomas said. "My mother was named Virginia, but everyone called her Ginny. She was beautiful and admired and I loved her dearly. I was the oldest of my siblings, and I think I was always a favorite of hers."

Charlotte almost remarked that she was also the oldest child, too. Relief washed over her as she thanked God she hadn't made that mistake. She would need to curb her loquaciousness and truly think before she spoke if she wanted to keep up her ruse. Mother and Father had constantly reminded her, "Charlotte, you've got to think before you speak."

"My father was named Matthew Linz. He was born in Cincinnati, Ohio and spent his whole life there. He practiced law and had a thriving practice. His parents were great friends with my mother's parents and had always hoped their children would marry each other. When my mother was sixteen and my father finished law school, they married. I was born soon after. My brother, Michael, was born three years after me. He was my very best friend. Emily was born almost six years later. She was the first girl in the Linz family for several generations and was adored by everyone. Despite being spoiled shamelessly, she has grown into a remarkable woman." There was pride in Thomas' voice.

"So, Emily is still alive?"

"Yes. She lives in Ohio. Emily was only fifteen when mother died. The family residence was closed up, and Emily went to live with our great-aunt Shirley Roberts. When the war ended and I returned to Cincinnati, we reopened our family home, and both lived there for several months. I enjoyed getting to know her again and spent some time getting my parents' affairs in order. My father's law partner, Mr. Gerald Stone, hoped that I would be interested in taking up my father's profession and continuing the partnership."

He stopped talking, and Charlotte sensed he was wrestling with his thoughts. She remained quiet. After several long minutes, Thomas began again.

"I just found that city life wasn't for me, anymore. I was born in Cincinnati and always assumed I'd live my whole life there. But, after the horror and filth and desperation of the war, I just couldn't do it. Everything seemed too crowded and loud. And there were memories of Michael and our pranks everywhere I looked. I had not a moment of peace. So, I turned down Mr. Stone and offered to sell him my father's portion of the partnership. He encouraged me to give it a few years. Apparently, he and my father made some very wise investments at the beginning of their professional endeavor, and Mr. Stone assured me he had no need for capital at present. He said he would prefer I leave things as they were and take some time to recover from the war before I decided to end the partnership. So, here I am searching for peace of mind and for my future."

He laughed wryly and looked over with a grin.

"Well, sir, I hope you find what you're looking for."

"Thank you, Charlie. I think I have."

Charlotte was curious, but unsure what she was curious about. What had Thomas found? Would he return to Ohio, or keep moving west? Her curiosity was soon satisfied as he began talking again.

"I spent the first few weeks of my westward journey feeling like I was running from something. It felt like I was trying to leave something awful behind; like I needed to hurry so I could outrun it. I wasn't sure if I would return to Cincinnati or start a new life in some isolated area where there was room to breathe. I just knew I needed to go. Then, a few days ago, I realized I was done. Yesterday was the first day I'd known absolute peace since going off to fight."

Thomas stopped abruptly and Charlotte looked over to find his eyes on her.

"I'm so sorry. That was callous. You lost your whole family that day, and I'm talking nonsense about finding peace. Forgive me, son."

Charlotte scanned the kind face and saw genuine remorse. "You didn't mean anything by it."

Thomas remained silent.

"Please keep going," she prompted. "I'm enjoying your story."

"Well, I woke up Wednesday morning feeling different than I'd felt in years. I felt whole and I felt peaceful. It didn't feel like I needed to run anymore. I think I've found my home."

Suddenly, his eyes narrowed, and Charlotte followed his gaze. Up ahead and slightly to the left, there was smoke billowing into the sky.

"That's too much smoke to come from a brush fire," Thomas said, as he spurred Trigger and took off down the road.

Charlotte nudged Meg into a run and followed him.

"I think that might be the Crawford's place," she yelled to him. She wasn't sure if he heard her over the pounding of the horse's hooves.

Five long minutes later, they reached the source of the fire. The Crawford's cabin and barn were engulfed in flame. Thomas jumped off his horse and ran toward the well, but Charlotte could tell it was too late to make a difference. The buildings were rapidly being consumed. Apparently, Thomas realized it, too, because he never even grabbed the bucket.

Charlotte slowly dismounted and walked closer to Thomas, who had pulled his pistol and stood scanning the property. She felt safer next to him. They looked around and saw the remnants of a massacre. Two bodies lay near the barn. She was almost certain they were Mr. Crawford and Daniel. Another three were in the yard near the burning cabin. MaryAnne Crawford and her baby girl, Margaret, lay together closest to the porch. Charlotte began to weep.

"Damn it," Thomas shouted loudly to the sky. Then he continued in a softer voice, full of regret, "It must be the same men who killed your family. If only we had come yesterday, we could have warned these neighbors."

Charlotte had nothing to say. She couldn't form words.

"Let's go! If we hurry, we can catch the bastards."

Charlotte felt sick to her stomach. Catch them? She didn't want to be anywhere near them. She wanted the officials to handle this, not her.

As if reading her thoughts, Thomas said, "I know you're scared, son. But you're the only one who can positively identify them. For some reason they left you alive, and you are the only one who can help stop them."

Charlotte mounted Meg and rode up alongside Thomas.

"If we pass through town on the way, we can notify the Sheriff and turn this mess over to him. All you will need to do is identify them once they're caught. I'll stay right by you the whole time."

Charlotte nodded her head but was still unable to speak.

"You're a brave boy, Charlie. I know your parents would be proud," Thomas said and then spurred Trigger into a gallop again. She followed along. She wished he wouldn't say things like that. His kindness made her cry even harder.

Chapter Seven

Thursday, August 15, 1867

Charlotte was enormously relieved when they arrived in Denver City. She had been praying for the last two hours that they would reach the town before they reached the outlaws. Her paralyzing fear began to subside as they followed a stranger's directions to the jail, located at the corner of Fifteenth and Market Streets. "Denver City Police Department" was painted on the front of the large, brick building.

They quickly dismounted and tied their horses to the hitching post before walking into the newly constructed building. There were four men in the front room. Three wore badges on their coats, and one just wore a suit and tie. There were audible gasps when the men saw Charlotte's misshapen face.

"We need to speak with someone right away," Thomas said urgently. "Time is of the greatest essence!"

One of the badged gentlemen came forward. He was tall and well-built, giving off a confident air. "I'm Sergeant Jason Albertson. How can I help you?"

He had a strong southern accent, and Charlotte was pleased that he was taking them seriously. She found him vaguely familiar but couldn't recall where she'd seen him.

"It must have been at church," she thought. "That's the only place I could have seen him."

Thomas reached out to shake the sergeant's hand.

"Thomas Linz," he said. "We're close behind two murderers and don't want to lose them. Can we fill you in as we ride?"

"Of course," Albertson agreed. "Do you know which direction they're headed?"

"No. Based on their direction between the attacks, I'm assuming they've come through here, but I couldn't guess which direction they will go now. This young man is Charlie Gallagher. His family was massacred. He can give you a description of the men."

"Wait just a moment," Albertson said, and turned to the other two men wearing badges. "We all need to hear this."

The men walked closer, and Albertson indicated Charlotte should begin.

"The leader is named Fred. He is about your height," she said, nodding her head to one of the officers. "He has stringy yellow-grey hair and a full beard. He's riding a huge, white gelding; very tall- the gelding." She shook her head in frustration.

Sergeant Albertson could tell the boy was nervous and rushing through his description. "You're doing fine, son. Just take your time."

"The other man is named Dan. He is the tallest, biggest man I've ever seen. He's bald and has a large, red moustache. His horse is grey. Both men were wearing faded Union Army uniforms. They have one extra horse with them now because there was a third man. He was the one who was killed at my place. Oh, and Dan has a bite mark on his right arm, about here," she said, indicating a spot on her right forearm.

"Let's go find them," Albertson said. "Grab some volunteers if you can and tell them to come armed. You go east, Phillips. Whiteley, you go north. You two will ride with me," he added, nodding to Thomas and Charlotte. "As we ride, you can fill me in on all the details, son." As soon as Albertson spoke the words, his officers jumped into motion. It was obvious that the sergeant was respected and obeyed.

Thomas and Charlotte left the jail, mounted their horses, and were soon joined by Sergeant Albertson. As they made their way through the bustling town, Charlotte scanned her head back and forth, looking closely at every man they passed. She wondered what she would do if she actually saw Fred or Dan. She didn't know how she might react.

As they came to the end of town, Albertson spurred his horse into a fast gallop. There was no time to talk as they sped along, hoping to catch up with the outlaws. After about twenty-five minutes of hard riding, they came upon a river. It was a good time to give the horses a short break and a drink of water. After dismounting and leading the horses to the riverbank, both men relieved themselves. Charlotte quickly walked off into the woods to urinate. Traveling with men was going to be difficult, she thought. This time, they would assume she was taking privacy for a bowel movement, but one could not do that too often. She would need to carefully monitor her water intake.

When she walked back to the riverbank, she crouched down and washed her hands in the running water. It felt so cold and fresh. Charlotte scooped some up in her hands and splashed her face. She could almost see out of her right eye again, but her face was more painful than it had been yesterday.

The skin felt tight where it had been stitched and her whole face burned with heat. She said a quick prayer that it wouldn't get infected.

The men had already mounted their horses, and Thomas was holding Meg's reins. Charlotte quickly climbed up on Meg's back and took the reins from Thomas with a "Thank you, sir."

He smiled at her and looked carefully at her face. She could tell he was worried about infection, as well.

"It feels a bit better," she lied.

"Well, I hope it feels better than it looks," Thomas said with a grimace. "It looks awful!"

"Can you see anything out of that eye," Sergeant Albertson asked.

"I can't open it very much sir, but it appears my vision was unaffected, thank God," she answered.

"Yes. Thank God for small miracles. We've made good time and I think we can slow our pace now," Albertson observed as they rode across a wooden bridge. "By the way, was your father Patrick Gallagher?"

"Yes, sir," Charlotte answered.

"I served with him under Colonel Slough in Company F of the First Colorado. Your father was an extraordinary soldier, Charlie. I'm sorry to hear he's passed. You know, we'd occasionally see each other in town and I always meant to ask him to come to lunch at the house the next time y'all were in town. I'm upset it never happened." He shook his head and continued to ride. "Maybe you could start telling me what happened to you and your family."

Charlotte felt she'd rather die than describe all that happened. But it needed to be done.

"It was Tuesday afternoon, and I was working in the garden behind the cabin when I heard horses coming up the drive. My brother was in the woods cutting some firewood, and my father was working in the barn. We all heard my mother scream. I saw my father run out of the barn with his rifle, and then he was shot in the back and fell. I ran around the side of the cabin and there were two men there holding my mother and sister. I tried to get my father's rifle out from under him, but a third man rode by and pulled me up onto his horse. He rode over to the other men and threw me on the ground. The large man, Dan, was tearing my sister's clothes off when my brother came running out of the woods. Fred, the same guy who shot my father, shot Brendan with his rifle."

The story was just pouring out of her. Thomas had been kind enough to not ask her any questions, so this was the first time she had to put the horrible ordeal into words. She was still in such shock that none of this even seemed real. She continued in a dispassionate voice; like she was just reciting her Latin or history lesson, and not telling of the moment her life was forever changed.

"It didn't kill Brendan, though. Fred sent Archie over to bring Brendan closer to the house. Archie was walking behind Brendan with a gun pointed at his head. Brendan crouched down and came up quickly, elbowing Archie in the throat. Archie fell to the ground and couldn't breathe, and Fred just walked over and slit his throat. Then Fred and Dan tied me and Brendan to the hitching post." Her voice dropped to a whisper. "They made us watch while they took turns raping my mother and sister."

Albertson and Thomas gasped, and Charlotte stopped talking, unable to go on for a moment. How glad she suddenly felt that this part was a lie. She realized that, as awful as her rape had been, it was infinitely better than it would have been to watch Mother or Ruthie hurt that way. Poor Brendan. He'd been forced to watch it happen to her, knowing that he couldn't protect her.

"What happened, then," Sergeant Albertson prompted after a respectful silence.

"After they finished, Dan pistol-whipped me, and I must have passed out. When I woke up, Brendan and Mother and Ruth were all dead."

Now that she was done with her story, silence hung heavy in the air. Charlotte snuck a brief glance over at the men riding next to her. Thomas and Albertson both looked furious and their righteous anger somehow made her feel safer.

"So, this all happened yesterday afternoon," Albertson asked in confirmation.

"No, sir. It happened Tuesday afternoon. By the time I awoke, it was dark. I worked to untie myself and then fell asleep next to my father's body. Yesterday morning, I dragged all the bodies over by the barn and covered them the best I could. Then Thomas showed up. He was wearing a Union uniform just like the others and I thought he'd been sent to finish me off. Once he convinced me he was safe, he helped me take the bodies to a more suitable place and bury them. It was late when we finished and then he sewed up my face. He's the one who said we needed to notify law enforcement so that they wouldn't hurt anyone else. But I guess we were too late."

Charlotte's eyes brimmed as she thought about the Crawfords. She looked to Thomas, hoping he would finish telling Albertson the details.

Thomas understood and picked up the story. "As we were heading towards Denver City this morning, we saw smoke. We followed it to a homestead and found more bodies. The brutal creatures didn't leave a soul alive. And this time, they burned down the buildings. You knew the family, Charlie?"

"Yes. They were the Crawfords. They arrived from Boston two years ago. They were our closest neighbors, so we saw them often. Mother and Mrs. Crawford were best friends and our families, well, we all grew to be very close."

"I'm truly sorry, son. You were lucky to survive," Albertson said.

After several minutes of deep silence, Albertson continued, "Do you happen to know why they left you alive? From what you say, it appears they've killed everyone else they encountered."

"The last thing I remember was biting the giant guy, Dan, on the arm. I bit him so hard it drew blood. He pistol-whipped me and I must have passed out. He probably thought I was dead."

"That bite mark will serve us well when we catch them. It helps with the identification. See, it's one thing to recognize someone upon seeing them again, or to pick them out of a line-up. But there's always room for error. The human mind can play tricks on you. However, you've given us identifying information before even seeing the suspects again. That makes it more reliable."

Charlotte felt a rush of pride. She wanted to catch the men who killed her family. The rush of pride was immediately followed by profound sadness. What did it really matter? Whether or not the killers were brought to justice, she'd live the rest of her life without her family. Nothing was going to bring them back.

"We're seeing more and more horrific crimes in the last few years," Albertson said to Thomas. "This war has decimated our fair country and turned men into monsters. There are so many shiftless wanderers who feel they have nothing left to lose. A man who has nothing left to lose can be a dangerous man indeed."

"Not three weeks before I left Cincinnati a neighbor killed his whole family and then himself. At first, the police thought it was a home invasion and homicide. But they soon realized it was not. Apparently, he left a crazy, rambling note about how he was saving his family from impending doom. I knew the man, but not well. He seemed a normal, successful businessman before the war. But friends said he came back delirious and troubled after fighting," Thomas finished. Then he asked, "Did you serve?"

"Yes," Albertson answered. "You?"

"I did."

Neither man said anything else for a very long time. Charlotte thought they were lucky not to have to put the horrors they'd experienced into words. She wondered how many times she would have to repeat her horror story if the killers were caught and taken to trial. Would she be able to remember her lies? She went through the story again in her head. Maybe if she mentally rehearsed it over and over, she'd not slip up and tell the truth about who was actually raped.

The horses kept up a steady clip-clop and Charlotte felt herself being lulled into sleep. Oh, how she wanted to wake up back in her own bed in the loft of the cabin and realize this had all been just a dream. Falling asleep while riding would not be good, though, so she tried to find something to distract her.

The countryside around them was green and thriving, despite the August heat. The road they were traveling followed the South Platte River and she could occasionally hear the comforting sound of running water. She thought of the stream back home and all the good times she and her family had enjoyed swimming in its depths. Some of her best memories with Brendan had been there. "Oh, Brendan. How will I make it without you," she thought for probably the hundredth time since his death. "I wish you had been the one to survive instead of me. You would know what to do on your own."

After several more hours of riding, Sergeant Albertson recommended that they set up camp for the night. Charlotte was dreading this prospect. How on earth was she going to keep her cover if forced to spend days on end with these men? They left the road and rode through the trees for several minutes until they came to a clearing that would be well covered and provide them with some concealment from passersby on the road. The river's running water could be heard much clearer now.

"Will you please take the horses down for a drink, Charlie," Sergeant Albertson asked, handing her his reins and then pulling the saddle off his beautiful horse.

"Of course." Charlotte reached out for Thomas' reins as well. He untied a long rope from his saddle and handed it to her.

"Will you also hobble them up somewhere with plenty of grass?" Thomas asked.

She nodded her head. He took the saddle from Trigger's back and set it on the ground. Then he undid Meg's saddle and set it down near his.

The river was just a short distance from the clearing and Charlotte marveled at the beauty surrounding her. Her heart swelled with grief, and she was afraid that she would be overcome. "No more crying," she said to Meg and patted the horse's neck. "It won't change anything, and I've done enough already." She looked all around her.

When the horses had drunk their fill, Charlotte led them to a grassy area and hobbled each of them. They would be able to move around and graze, but not run off.

"Goodnight, Meg," she whispered, throwing her arms around the horse and rubbing her left cheek against the smooth neck. "You're all I've got now." She stood that way for a few more moments, then slowly made her way back to the two men, picking up sticks and branches as she went.

Sergeant Albertson was working on a fire and Thomas was pulling a woolen blanket from his saddlebag. Charlotte set the kindling near the fire.

"Are you warm enough, Charlie,"Thomas asked as she approached.

"Yes, sir."

Just a few weeks ago, Brendan had used those same words when a cool breeze had begun blowing as they were out hunting together. Even in the summer months, the evenings got cold. Brendan had asked her that same question, and then removed his own jacket from his knapsack and placed it around her shoulders. Her heart was throbbing, and it felt like there was a huge, gaping hole in her chest. Would it always be this painful to think of her brother?

"Please, God, help me to survive this," she thought. "I know they're all in heaven with You now. Please just help me to be strong until I'm there, too."

Once the fire was flickering heartily, they sat down, and Charlotte began to pull food from her saddle bag. There were half a dozen biscuits from this morning's meal, along with some hard sausage. Charlotte could hardly force herself to eat. Every physical sensation seemed so dull now. Hunger. Thirst. The cold night air. She hardly felt any of it. The emotional pain was too strong to allow her to feel anything else.

After eating, the men sat by the fire smoking. Charlotte was about to lie down when Thomas asked, "Charlie, may I look at those stitches?"

She walked over to where he was seated on a log and knelt in front of him. The firelight danced on her face as he gently placed his hand on her chin and turned her head left and right. Thomas was immediately concerned by what he saw. The wound looked inflamed, and he feared infection. He pulled out a flask and warned her, "I'm going to apply whiskey again to try to stave off infection."

She took a deep breath. This time, instead of pouring it onto the wound, he pulled a handkerchief from his pocket and wet it from the flask. Then, he very softly blotted the wound.

"You okay," he asked as he worked.

She grunted in a sort of affirmation.

"That sounded just like something a boy would do," she thought, quite pleased with herself.

Once Thomas was finished with the wound, he patted her on the shoulder. "Again, I'm astounded by your bravery, son. That was a horrible story you shared today. I had no idea it had been so awful. Your family would be right proud of you."

Several tears escaped Charlotte's eyes and she inwardly cursed Thomas for his kindness. She wanted nothing more than to throw herself into his arms and cry until there were no more tears left. Something about this gentle, strong man made her feel safe, but too vulnerable. She needed to be tough and guarded, not vulnerable. She needed to be a boy.

Instead of giving in to her longing for comfort, she mumbled a gruff, "Goodnight," and walked to her bedroll, praying that sleep would soon take her from this pain. She pulled her mother's rosary from her pocket and began to recite the familiar, comforting words: "I believe in God, the Father Almighty, Creator of Heaven and Earth...."

"What do you think will happen to him," Albertson asked Thomas much later when the rhythmic rise and fall of Charlie's chest made it appear that he was sleeping. In truth, Charlotte lay awake in excruciating pain. Her forehead was throbbing, and try as she might, sleep would not come.

Thomas looked at Albertson across the fire and shook his head. "I don't know, and I find I can hardly think of anything else. It's consuming me."

"Do you know if he has family anywhere nearby?"

"I don't. He didn't seem to want to talk about himself much today, understandably. So, we talked mostly about me and my family." Thomas took a long draw from his cigar. "I'm hoping that there is family close by, or even some neighbors who can take him under their wing. I'd hate for him to have to leave his home, you know?"

"Yea. The boy's lost enough already. If he's able to stay in his own home, or at least stay close enough to keep up with it until he's grown, that would be for the best." He paused and looked over at the sleeping boy. "I'll say, he's a plucky young man."

"That he is," Thomas agreed. "Do you have children, Sergeant?"

"I do. My wife, Marnie, and I have three sons and two daughters. What about you?"

"No. I've not been married. But I hope to marry and start a family soon."

Charlotte thought Thomas seemed too old to be thinking of marriage and family. Wasn't he already her father's age? He would hardly be around to watch his children grow.

"What brings you to this area," Albertson prompted.

"I returned home after the war and realized I couldn't handle city life anymore. Everything was too loud and too crowded. I felt constantly irritated and on edge. I dreaded the constant socializing that was expected of me. It seemed to me that after the deprivation and isolation of the war years, people wanted nothing more than to attend balls and operas and dinner parties every night. I could see how much the interactions meant to my sister, Emily, and I attended for her sake, but it took its toll. I grew more and more irritable by the day until I became someone I didn't like at all. When I left Cincinnati, I had no real plans, I just needed to escape. Over the last few days, though, I think I've found my home. I really want to settle near here. There is something that calls to me and tells me I'm where God intends for me to be."

"That's a good feeling, indeed," Albertson agreed. "I feel that every time I look at my wife; that feeling of being right where God wants me, of being home."

Charlotte almost sobbed aloud at this. She would never feel this way again. Everyone she loved had been taken in a matter of minutes. God seemed very far away, and she felt so alone.

"Well, now I'm a jealous man," Thomas said with a laugh. "Where can I find one of those?"

"They're certainly not easy to find out here. You would have had much better luck back East."

"Oh, you can't imagine! There were so many women vying for my attention! It was absurd. I understand they have fewer men to choose from now, but good grief! It was overwhelming."

"Complaining about too much feminine attention! I've never heard the likes," Albertson exclaimed. Then he remembered the sleeping boy not far off and got very quiet again. "I met my wife when we were no more than children. I think I knew by the age of thirteen that I was going to marry her. She was the most beautiful creature, still is, but it was so much more than that. She seemed to glow with love. It's as though she holds a wondrous secret that makes her smile and look on the whole world with love."

Charlotte found tears coursing down her cheeks. How many times had she heard Father talk about Mother with this same sort of admiration and awe?

"Ah, I sound silly now." Albertson said, sounding embarrassed. He was glad it was too dark for Thomas to see his reddened face.

But Thomas didn't laugh at him. "I've not yet felt that way about anyone. But I'm determined to hold out for the real thing. I've seen marriages between poorly suited mates, and I've seen beautiful marriages. I want something very different from what my parents had. I want friendship, love, humor…I want it all."

Charlotte imagined that such a kind, thoughtful man would certainly find this sort of love. She hoped he would.

"Well, good luck to you, brother." Albertson chuckled again. "I still think you'd have better options back in Cincinnati. But I can ask Marnie to start looking. She's always eager to play matchmaker."

"Heaven protect me from matchmakers," Thomas said in mock horror and then stood up and stretched. "I'll take first watch, Sergeant."

"Sounds good. Wake me when it's my turn." Albertson walked over to his bedroll and lay down. He was snoring within minutes.

Thomas looked over to where Charlie lay sleeping. The boy was curled up in a tiny ball, shivering under the woolen blanket. Thomas grabbed his own blanket and knelt to arrange it over the boy.

"Father God," he whispered. "Protect this hurting boy and heal his sorrow. Please don't let his wound grow infected. Please help us find a way to keep him at Kerry Haven, God. And please help him to feel Your love and the love of his family every day. I ask all this in Your Son's precious name. Amen."

Charlotte felt so much love pouring through her at that moment. She silently added her prayer to Thomas'. "And God, please help Thomas find true love and the peace he desires. Amen."

As Thomas sat down by the fire again, he thought about everything Charlie had been through, and he was overwhelmed with fury. How could such evil be present in men's hearts? He recalled burying Charlie's tiny sister, Ruth. She was so fragile, so innocent. He couldn't imagine what Charlie felt as he watched his mother and sister be violated. Emily's face came to mind, and his heart burned in rage as he imagined himself in Charlie's position, having to watch someone harm Emily. He hoped that he and Albertson would be the ones to find the men and not one of the other officers. He wanted to kill those vile men with his own hands.

"Sorry, God," he whispered. "I'll let you take care of them."

Charlotte tossed and turned for another hour, before finally realizing that sleep was not possible while she was in so much pain. She stood up and wrapped the blankets around her shoulders before walking over to Thomas.

"May I come sit with you?"

"Of course." Thomas motioned to the spot next to him. He and Albertson had pulled over a large log while she was tending the horses earlier and positioned it as a bench. Charlotte carefully walked around the fire and sat next to him.

"You can't sleep?"

"No. My face is throbbing, and I just can't fall asleep. I thought maybe if you talked with me again, I might be able to."

"Am I that boring," Thomas asked with a laugh.

"No! I didn't mean that—"

"I was just teasing you," he interrupted. Then he looked over at her with a frown. "I wish I knew how to make it hurt less. All of it."

"Earlier today, before we saw the smoke, you were telling me about finding peace. I want to hear more about that."

"Let's move down here," Thomas said, sliding from the log to the soft grass and using the log for a backrest.

Charlotte did as he suggested. Thomas reached out and put his arm around the diminutive shoulders. Then he pulled the boy close so that his head rested in the crook of Thomas' arm.

"Now close your eyes and I'll talk as long as it takes, son."

Charlotte melted into him. She didn't care if this was what a boy would do, or not. She needed to be held. It was unfathomable how she could feel so comfortable with this man she barely knew, but she didn't care. She needed him.

"I finally feel like I'm where I belong. I want to build a life here in Colorado. When we get back to Denver City, I plan to visit the land office and see what parcels might still be available. I grew up in the city, but I spent enough time 'roughing it' during the war to at least pretend I know how to live off the land. I want to buy some cattle and raise beef. I want to breed horses. I want to farm enough to feed a wife and children. I want to live close to the land and rely on God for every aspect of my life. I think one of my problems in Cincinnati was just feeling too removed from God. Everything is right at your fingertips. You don't have to worry about survival day to day in the big city, and you forget your absolute dependence on Him."

He looked down to find Charlie looking up at him. The fire was dying down and it cast a soft glow on the boy's face. Thomas saw incredible trust in Charlie's eyes now. How could so much have changed in little more than a day? He kept talking about his future, all the while realizing that Charlie was now showing up in his plans. He wanted to see this boy grow up.

Eventually, Charlie's breathing slowed, and Thomas heard him softly snore. Relief flooded through him, and he hoped that the boy would get at least a few hours of deep sleep. He thought about moving Charlie back over to his bedroll but didn't want to risk waking him. He would sit this way all night if it meant Charlie wasn't hurting.

Several hours later, Albertson woke and stood up. He looked over to find Thomas sitting by the fire holding the sleeping boy next to him.

"Nightmare," he asked in a whisper.

"No, his head was hurting too bad to sleep. He asked me to talk with him until he fell asleep. I need to move, but I really don't want to wake him."

Albertson added a few logs to the dwindling fire.

"Your shift is over. Try to get some sleep."

He grabbed his rifle from near his bedroll and quietly walked away.

Chapter Eight
Friday, August 16, 1867

The next morning, Charlotte woke from a beautiful dream and was instantly battered by awful reality. "Oh, God," she prayed, "will every morning be like this? Will I have to remember anew every single morning?"

She opened her eyes and was shocked and embarrassed to find herself wrapped in Thomas' arms. The man's back was against the log with his long legs stretched out in front of him. She was seated next to him with her head on his chest and his arms around her. His warmth and protection were so comforting and she realized she had slept deeply for several hours. A wave of embarrassment overwhelmed her and she wondered how to remove herself from this compromising position. She carefully moved Thomas' arms and, when that didn't wake him, slowly stood up. Then she looked over to find Albertson sitting asleep with his rifle across his lap and relief flooded through her. Thank goodness he hadn't seen her sleeping like that on Thomas. She doubted eleven-year-old boys did that.

A strong wind whipped through the trees and the rustling sound pulled Charlotte's gaze upwards. It was that magical moment between night and day, when everything looks soft and other-worldly. She made a slow circle, taking in her surroundings, and then looked down at Thomas again. He was such a kind, gentle man; so much like her father. She was happy that he wanted to stay in Colorado, and hoped that he would settle nearby. Now that the Crawfords were gone, Charlotte really had no one left in her life, at least no one on this continent.

"Thank you, God," she whispered to the sky. "Thank you for Thomas." She took the blankets she'd been wrapped in and draped them over his shoulders to keep him warm.

As she quietly made her way down to the river, Charlotte noticed that she was able to see more from her wounded eye than she had yesterday. However, her face was throbbing and hot to the touch. The swelling seemed to have shifted and now her whole face was swollen. Pulling Brendan's bandana from her pocket, she wet it in the river and then pressed it softly to her wound. The pain was excruciating. She'd never had such a severe injury. Brendan was usually the one to have bumps, bruises, and cuts. Oh, how she missed him! He'd been her very best friend. He was so protective of her and Ruth, and he could make the family laugh like no one else.

Charlotte longed to strip down and bathe in the river. She felt violated and dirty, and wondered if she would ever feel clean again after what had been done to her. But there was not privacy enough for a full scrub. At least she could wash the caked blood from her hair. She submerged her head and rinsed her hair the best she could in the flowing water. When she flipped her head back up, she was shocked at how light it felt without the mass of hair she was accustomed to washing. Sometimes it took hours for the long hair to fully dry. This was so much easier! She ran her fingers through her hair several times and shook out the excess water. Already, she felt much better.

When done with her hair, she soaked the bandana again in the water and then tied it around her head as a sort of cold compress. She walked to the grazing horses and un-hobbled Meg to bring her down to the river for a drink. As Meg quenched her thirst, Charlotte smoothed the horse's mane and whispered to her. She found so much comfort in her sweet-tempered horse.

When both Thomas' and Albertson's horses had been tended to, she made her way back to the campfire. Sergeant Albertson was now awake and alert.

"Good morning," he called as she approached. He seemed embarrassed that he had fallen asleep on his watch. Then he noticed her makeshift bandage. "How's the wound today?"

"It's pretty bad."

Thomas was also awake. He stood up and rubbed his hand over his grizzled face. "I wonder if we should head back to Denver City and see a doctor."

"I was thinking the same," Albertson agreed. "If the outlaws were on this road, I think we would have overtaken them at some point yesterday. We kept a fast pace, and they were probably in no rush, not suspecting they were being followed. I can only hope that Phillips or Whiteley has found them and brought them in."

Charlotte was conflicted. She wanted to keep going, to do everything possible to find the men and prevent further slaughter. However, the longer she traveled with Albertson and Thomas, the greater the risk of discovery. And her wound screamed with pain. It would be good to see a doctor who could perhaps do something for her.

A few hours' ride brought them back to Denver City, where Albertson took them straight to a two-story brick house with a white picket fence and well-manicured lawn. It looked so different from the log cabins Charlotte was used to. A sign on the gate read: Joseph Groves, General Doctor.

"Dr. Groves and his wife, Clara, are great friends of ours. And you're going to love Big Viv," Sergeant Albertson said as he unlatched the gate. He led the way up the short walk to the wide front porch. Albertson knocked on the door and it was soon answered by a very large black woman.

"Well, hello, Sergeant Albertson," she said in a deep, resonant voice as a beautiful smile transformed her stern face into one of welcome. "To what do we owe this pleasure?"

"I wish it was a social call, Vivian. This here is Charlie Gallagher. He has a nasty gash on his head, and we're worried about infection. Is Dr. Groves in?"

"Oh, you poor dear," Vivian murmured as she looked at Charlotte's bruised and swollen face. "Yes, sir, he is. You all just come in and wait right here in the sitting room while I fetch him."

As Charlotte followed Vivian into the front hallway her eyes were drawn to the gleaming wood floors and graceful staircase. How her mother would have marveled over such elegance! Vivian led them into the sitting room; a beautiful, cheery room with tall bookshelves full of books. She longed to run her hands over the spines and take in every title. Instead, she took a seat and kept quiet.

"I'll be right back," Vivian said and hurried off.

Moments later, Charlotte heard boots on the wooden floors and Dr. Groves entered the room. He was a tall, thin man with a handsome, clean-shaven face.

"Why, he looks no older than me," Charlotte thought with surprise.

"Good morning, gentlemen," he said in a clear, strong voice. He was introduced to Thomas and then turned to her. "Let's see what we have here, young man. May I?"

"Yes, sir," Charlotte answered, although Dr. Groves had already removed the bandana and was peering intently at her wound.

"How did this happen," he asked, gently prodding here and there on her forehead and around her eye socket.

"I was pistol-whipped three days ago."

"And I stitched it up two days ago, but I'm afraid I may have done more harm than good," Thomas offered sheepishly.

"You did fine, sir, but it looks infected. I may need to open it up and apply salve to the interior of the wound. Come with me, son." He turned to Vivian. "Miss Viv, will you please bring these gentlemen some strong coffee and refreshments?"

"None for me, Viv. I'm going straight to the jail to see if either of my officers have found the bastar—sorry Viv, the critters who did this," Albertson informed them. "Then I'll come back for you both."

Dr. Groves place his hand on Charlotte's shoulder and they left the room.

"Thank you, Sergeant," Thomas said as he shook the man's hand. "I wonder if you could recommend a hotel. I have some things to tend to while here and don't want to ride back to Kerry Haven after dark."

"Hotel? There are a few. But I would be honored if you and Charlie would stay with my family. My wife hardly ever gets company, and she would be thrilled to have overnight guests. I know my children would love to meet Charlie. With your permission, I'll stop by my house on the way to the jail and inform them."

"That is too kind of you, sir. But a bed and a home-cooked meal sound wonderful. Thank you again."

"It's my pleasure."

Sergeant Albertson left the room. Thomas heard his footsteps in the hall and then the front door closed behind him. In a moment, Miss Vivian arrived with a tray.

"I'll bet you're famished," she said, as she set the tray down and began to pour a cup of coffee for him. "Now tell me sir, what on earth happened to your son?"

Thomas accepted the outstretched cup. "He's not actually my son. I only happened upon him by chance two days ago. His whole family had been murdered and he was all alone trying to dig their graves."

"Lord have mercy!" Vivian's hand flew to her heart. "That poor child. That poor little orphaned child."

She left the room muttering under her breath and walked straight to the kitchen. There, she began pulling out the ingredients for a cake. Big Viv, as her loved ones affectionately called her, showed her love through cooking. And she had yet to find someone who wasn't comforted at least a little by her pound cake. She and the Groves had only been in Denver City for three years, but Big Viv's pound cake was already well-known and coveted all over town.

In the exam room, Dr. Groves instructed Charlotte to sit on a tall stool near a bright hanging lamp. There was a slim, young black man scooping steaming water from a pot on a small stove into a wide basin.

"This is George Groves," Dr. Groves said, as he took a bar of soap and began lathering his hands with the hot water in the basin. "He's been working with me the last few years and is preparing to begin medical school early next year."

Charlotte could hear the pride and affection in Dr. Groves' voice.

"George, as you can see, there are stitches, which have been done moderately well. However, I am worried about these signs of an infection."

Dr. Groves gently touched several areas of her face. "We will soften the skin with this hot water and then drain the pus."

Charlotte found it comforting that he talked through everything as he worked. George dumped the hand washing water into a sink on the wall and scooped another ladle of steaming water into the basin. Then he handed Dr. Groves a folded piece of clean, white linen. Dr. Groves dipped the linen into the water and then wrung it out and waved it back and forth a few times to cool it.

"This may hurt a bit at the beginning," he warned Charlotte as he refolded the cloth and gingerly dabbed it on the wound. She braced herself for the pain.

"Is that too hot?"

"No. It actually feels quite soothing! I was afraid it was going to be awful, but the warmth…it feels good."

She looked up at him and smiled.

"Well, I'm glad," Dr. Groves said, smiling back at her. "The skin was drying out and pulling against the stitches. That, and the swelling, made for a lot of pain! The warmth from this clean water will soften the skin again and will allow us to drain the pus from the wound. Hopefully, we can clean it well and not have to open the stitches. Will you please rinse this and then continue to hold it steady on the wound while I get the salve," he asked, as he handed the linen to George.

George nodded his head in agreement. Taking the wet compress, he rinsed it in the steaming water and then wrung it and let it cool just as Dr. Groves had. He peered carefully at the wound before gently applying the compress again.

Charlotte was curious about the young man.

"Where are you from, George?"

"I'm from North Carolina. My mother belonged to Dr. Groves' father and I grew up alongside Dr. Joseph and Miss Clara, although I'm the oldest. When Joseph turned eighteen, Master gave me to him as a gift. I went along with him to medical school in Washington DC. As soon as we got there, Dr. Joseph immediately freed me. I stayed with him, but it sure felt good to be my own man and not someone else's property. When Dr. and Mrs. Groves got married, they asked me if I wanted to come to Colorado with them. I jumped at the chance. Dr. and Mrs. Groves are the best people I've ever known. I would follow them to the ends of the earth."

George's smile was genuine and filled with joy. Charlotte sensed he was a man who had big dreams for his future.

"How exciting to be starting medical school soon. Which will you attend?"

"Rush Medical School in Chicago is the closest school that accepts Negros, so that's where I'm going. I plan to study hard and earn top marks. Then I'll come right back here to my friends as soon as possible."

George continued gently swiping at the pus which was now oozing out from between the stitches. Again, he rinsed the cloth and then dumped the water in the sink. Pouring a new ladle of hot water into the basin, he soaked the cloth and applied it again. Charlotte felt such relief. Now that some of the pressure was being removed, the wound was no longer throbbing. She took a deep breath.

"Am I hurting you," George asked, quickly pulling the cloth away from her forehead.

"No, I'm sighing because it feels so much better. It's not throbbing anymore!"

"It certainly is a nasty wound. But I'm hoping Dr. Groves can get it cleaned adequately without removing your stitches. I imagine you've had enough pain for the time being."

Dr. Groves returned with a small glass container. George removed the cloth from Charlotte's forehead, and Dr. Groves' face lit up. "That already looks much better. Good job, George."

"Thank you, sir."

Charlotte could see the deep affection between the two men. What a prodigious friendship theirs had been. Playmates had grown into master and slave and then into best friends. It filled her heart to see that equality was not just a lofty dream. People with good hearts would make this into a reality. She imagined that by the time she was her parents' age, or Thomas' age, blacks and whites would live side by side in perfect equality.

"Would you like to apply the salve," Dr. Groves asked George, while holding out the small container.

George nodded. "Let me wash my hands again."

Charlotte couldn't believe how good the salve felt. For the first time since she'd regained consciousness on Tuesday night, she wasn't experiencing excruciating pain. She thought she might be able to sleep tonight without having to bother Thomas. Again, she felt embarrassed for her childish behavior last night.

After liberally applying the salve to her wound and gently wrapping her head in a clean bandage, George smiled.

"Well, young man, you're all done for now."

"I can't thank you both enough. I think I might be able to get some real sleep tonight. I've been in too much pain to fall asleep these last few days."

"You're a brave lad, and I know you'll be romping around soon," Dr. Groves said, as he clapped her on the back.

George began cleaning up the medical supplies and Charlotte turned to follow Dr. Groves back to the sitting room. Thomas jumped to his feet as they entered.

"Charlie did great, and we didn't have to reopen the wound. My assistant and I cleaned it and drained it. That relieved a lot of the pressure. Then we applied a salve that should help ward off infection while also keeping the skin from drying out and pulling against the stitches. I'm going to send this salve with you, and it needs to be applied morning and night until it is all used up. However, I would very much like to see Charlie again tomorrow to check on the wound. Would that be possible?"

"Yes, doctor. I actually have several things to accomplish before we leave town. Sergeant Albertson has graciously offered to let us stay at his home tonight."

Charlotte felt a surge of anxiety mixed with excitement upon hearing this news. She dearly wanted to be back in the cabin, surrounded by everything familiar. But she dreaded the long ride and facing the emptiness awaiting her at home. She dreaded the loss of daily contact with Thomas. Surely, she would only see him sporadically after he purchased his own property. And, truthfully, she longed for more time with all these wonderful people. Sergeant Albertson, Vivian, Dr. Groves and George had all been so caring. She knew that loneliness and grief were all that awaited her at home, and she was scared she wouldn't survive it.

"Wonderful! The sergeant is a great friend, and Clara and I usually end up over there several nights a week. I will come by tonight to check your wound. For now, I'd like you to settle in and get a good long rest. If you wake this evening for dinner, that's fine. But if you sleep through till tomorrow morning, that's even better."

"Yes sir. I think I'd like that second option!"

"Well, that's because you haven't tasted Nora's cooking yet. The Albertson's cook is the best I've come across." Then Dr. Grove's voice dropped, and he looked quickly behind him to make sure no one was listening at the door. "Although if you tell Big Viv I said that I'll never forgive you!"

Everyone chuckled at that comment.

"But seriously, I want you to get as much sleep as you can, Charlie. Your body needs it."

Dr. Groves thought Charlie's mind needed the rest even more than his little body. When he'd left the exam room earlier to get the salve, Big Viv had filled him in on the loss of Charlie's family. This poor boy was going to suffer emotionally long after his head wound healed.

"Thank you, Dr. Groves," Thomas said. "I look forward to visiting with you tonight."

"I'll see you tonight, then."

When Joseph Groves left the room, Thomas and Charlotte made their way out the front door and sat down in two of the rocking chairs on the wide, shaded porch.

"Charlie, I'm guessing these must be Brendan's clothes that you're wearing," Thomas said, as they waited for Albertson to return.

"Yes, sir."

"I understand that you want to keep everything that belonged to him, and you can certainly hold on to these until you grow into them, but do you have clothes that fit you at home?"

"Not really."

Charlotte was trying to figure out where Thomas was going with this conversation.

"I just had a big growth spurt and outgrew my breeches and shoes. Mother was going to sew me some new pants as soon as she had a chance. She just never got around to it."

"I brought very few things along on my trip from Cincinnati and need to buy quite a few items for myself before we leave town. Would you mind if I purchased some for you, as well? I won't make you wear them if you'd prefer to stay in Brendan's clothes, but...."

"That would be fine, sir. More than fine," she stammered. "I would really appreciate that. I can pay you back when we return to the cabin. I know where some money is put away."

"Don't you worry about that, son."

Thomas clapped Charlotte on the back as he stood and walked to the front door.

"Let's see if Vivian has a piece of paper and pencil handy. I'll trace your foot to take with me to the shop."

Vivian was happy to produce paper and pencil for such a worthy endeavor. She helped Thomas trace Charlie's feet and informed him that he could find premade clothes at the dry goods store down the street from the Albertson's house.

"Now Thomas, you set this young man up with some nice clothes, and I'll get him fattened up to fit them," she said, giving Charlotte a playful jab in the stomach. "You're much too skinny, Charlie, but give Big Viv some time. I'll soon take care of that."

Charlotte had to laugh at the wonderful, bossy woman. What a force of nature she was! It felt good to have someone fuss over her, but it made her sad to think that her own mother would never be cooking for her or teasing her again.

"Why, Vivian, are you giving Charlie a hard time," a booming voice asked, and the three porch occupants turned toward the front gate. "I might have to call law enforcement on you."

"I'd be careful about that, Jason Albertson. You know those officers of yours like me better than they like you!" The feisty lady returned his jest with a wink.

"Too true, Big Viv. Too true. I know they'd pick you over me any day of the week."

Albertson turned to look at Thomas. "I stopped by the jail and neither officer has yet returned. But, in better news, my wife is simply delighted to have you both stay over tonight."

"Please tell your beautiful wife that I'll be sending two of my pound cakes over with the good doctor when he comes to check on Charlie tonight. One is for Charlie, and one is for the rest of you to share."

Charlotte was already walking down the sidewalk towards the horses, but when she heard this, she impulsively ran back up the porch stairs and threw her arms around Big Viv for a hug.

"Thank you, Miss Vivian," she said, barely able to hold back her tears.

"Oh," Vivian exclaimed, speechless for the first time in her life. This poor, sweet boy was breaking her heart. "You call me Big Viv, Charlie. I can tell we're going to be good friends."

"Why don't you all come over tonight with Dr. Groves," invited Albertson. "You tell George and Clara I want to see all of you tonight for music and cards and Big Viv's famous pound cake."

Thomas and Charlotte mounted their horses and followed Jason Albertson the few blocks to his house. The Albertson house looked very similar to the Groves house, but it could not have been more different in energy or noise level. Before the visitors had fully dismounted their horses, several tall boys ran out the front door, jumped off the porch, and raced down the sidewalk towards them. Charlotte was caught off guard and stepped closer to Thomas without consciously thinking about it.

"Good grief," Sergeant Albertson said in mock rebuke. "You three will have our guests thinking I raised a bunch of wild hooligans!"

Thomas sensed Charlie's change in demeanor and assumed the boy was just exhausted and overwhelmed from the day. Protectively, he said, "I'm under orders to make this young man lie down and rest until Dr. Groves comes to make his rounds tonight."

"George and Vivian and the Groves will all be coming over tonight, so you'll have plenty of time for fun and games, my boys. For now, let's help Mr. Linz and Charlie get settled in."

"I'll take the horses and get them fed," offered the oldest boy, grabbing the reins to all three horses and turning towards the small stable behind the house.

"Let me do quick introductions first," said Albertson. The boy turned back to face them. "This is John David, our eldest. He's eighteen."

John David waved and then walked away with the horses.

"This is Damien and he's sixteen," Albertson said, pointing to the tallest of the boys. "And this little rascal is Fulton. He's fourteen and the baby of the family." The proud father grabbed the awkward, skinny boy and tousled his yellow hair playfully.

"Father!"

The boy protested gleefully as he tried to break free from his father's bear hug. Charlotte's heart was breaking at the familial love surrounding her. She desperately needed to be alone before she was overcome with tears. She wished bitterly that Thomas had never agreed to spend the night here. Each new person she met seemed a painful reminder of the loving family she would never see again.

Just when she thought it couldn't get worse, a diminutive woman with blonde curls and a delightful Southern drawl called from the porch, "Welcome! I'm so glad you're both here."

To her great embarrassment, Charlotte lost her composure and began shaking with sobs, right in front of everyone. A boy would never do this!

"Oh, sweetheart," the woman said, rushing down the sidewalk to Charlotte. "Come with me and we'll get you down for a rest. You must be utterly exhausted."

Charlotte allowed herself to be led up the walk and into the house. Mrs. Albertson led her upstairs and into a small, cozy room with two beds covered in beautiful, feminine quilts.

"Please excuse the feminine décor," Mrs. Albertson said, as she turned down one of the beds. "I've put you and Mr. Linz here in our girls' room. They'll sleep downstairs in our room tonight. Now, would you like to go right to sleep, or would you prefer a bath first?"

Charlotte thought of how luxurious a bath would feel right now. But would she have enough privacy? And, she didn't have any clean clothes to change into after a bath.

"I think I'd prefer to sleep first. Mr. Linz said he is going right now to get some new clothes for each of us and then I'll have something clean to put on after bathing. Is that okay? I don't want to get the bed dirty."

"Oh, fiddle-de-dee! Don't you worry a bit about that. Just lie down and relax. Would you like me to send Mr. Linz up to wake you for dinner?"

"Yes, please, ma'am. Thank you so much for your kindness."

"It's my pleasure."

Mrs. Albertson winked at the young boy as she walked out and gently closed the door behind her.

Charlotte unlaced the boots, removed her long socks, and pattered over to the dresser which held a pitcher and wash basin. Now that Mrs. Albertson was gone, she was rethinking her decision to sleep first and bathe later. She was filthy and would likely leave the bed linens a stinking mess if she lay down without washing. At least she'd thoroughly rinsed her hair in the river this morning. She wet the hand towel next to the basin and quickly washed her arms and feet the best she could. Then she dusted off her pants and shirt. This would have to do.

As she sank into the soft mattress and closed her eyes, she thought back to the promise she'd made to herself on Wednesday; the promise of no more crying. What a fool she'd been to think she could be stoic. She stopped struggling with her emotions and let the tears flow freely. There was so much to mourn. She would never see Ruthie grow up, or see Brendan marry and raise kids of his own. She would never again sit down to a meal with her family and hear them recount the trivial occurrences of their day or share their dreams and goals. She would never get another warm hug from her strong, wonderful father, or hear Ruth sing in her sweet, innocent, wordless way. She would never again hear Mother say "I'm so proud of you, Charlotte," or see Father look at Mother with such obvious love that it made Charlotte long for a husband of her own someday.

She thought, then, about her future. What should she do? She knew that she had two main options; she could stay in Colorado and attempt to make a life on her own, or she could return to Ireland where she would be surrounded by family who loved her and could share in her grief. She knew which choice made the most sense. Even had she been a man, it was impossible to survive out here alone. She loved Aunt Betsy and Uncle Jared and had fond memories of her cousins. Yes, she would return to Ireland, as soon as the criminals had been caught.

The salve removed her physical pain, and the crying slaked her emotional pain for the time being. Within moments, Charlotte was fast asleep.

Chapter Nine

Friday, August 16, 1867

After leaving the Albertson home, Thomas first visited the land office and made his inquiry about available lots. He also informed the clerk about the demise of the Gallagher and Crawford families and asked if the office had records for the Crawford's next of kin.

"They'll need to be notified of their loved ones' deaths,"Thomas said.

"Our office is required to reach out to them. I'll send a telegraph this afternoon with the notification. If no one in the extended family wants to take up residence there, this land parcel will revert to the government. The Crawfords had not yet completed their five years of residence to permanently own the land under the Homestead Act."

"May I put my name in for it if they don't want it? I don't mean to sound unfeeling, but it is in the precise location I'm favoring."

Thomas realized that if he were able to procure this property, it would allow him to stay near Charlie and be a support to him. And he would be near those glorious mountains.

"I can return in a few weeks to see if you've received word yet. In the meantime, I'll check out any available lots you may have. Now, what needs to be done in order for the Gallagher survivor to complete Homestead requirements?"

"Let me see," the clerk said, looking through his files. "Well, it appears this land was purchased back in 1861, before the Homestead Act was passed. The Gallagher family owns their land outright; seventy-five acres." He looked up from the paper. "I can make note of the change in ownership if you have the full name and date of birth of the survivor."

"I'm afraid I don't have that information." Thomas was embarrassed by how little he knew about Charlie. "Perhaps when I return in a few weeks, I can bring the young man with me."

"That would be just fine. Here are the coordinates for available lots in the area."

Thomas looked down at a printed list of coordinates. Some had been scratched out, but there were still plenty from which to choose.

"Perfect! I will return around the end of the month to claim a lot. Thank you for your assistance."

Thomas turned and walked out the door. He needed to get the clothes purchased before the Dry Goods store closed, and a glance at his pocket watch revealed he didn't have much time. Luckily, the dry goods store was just one block over. Thomas entered the large, brick building to find it bustling with customers. He looked around, overwhelmed with all the noise.

"May I help you," a cheerful voice asked, and he turned to find a young woman at his side. "I work here and can help you find something if you need."

"That would be great. I find myself a mite overwhelmed with all the activity in here."

"I thought you might be, sir. What is it you're looking for?"

Thomas handed the saleswoman the paper on which he'd traced Charlie's feet.

"I need a pair of men's boots, some pants and shirts, socks and underclothes for me and my...son." It was a small lie, and much easier than explaining the whole long story.

"He is about this tall," he said, indicating chest-high on his tall frame, "and very thin."

"I'll start gathering these things. Please feel free to look around or wait up at the front of the store."

Thomas walked around and was surprised by how much the store had to offer. Several bins of candy caught his attention, and he decided to purchase some hard candy for the children and a box of bonbons for the adults to enjoy this evening. In no time at all, the assistant was back at his side. She efficiently showed him several pieces of clothing in his size and several boys' items.

"Why, you've found everything I needed. I'll take it all."

"Wonderful," the young lady exclaimed, and led him to the counter to complete his purchase. Before leaving, Thomas handed her several dollars.

"I would never have been able to locate all of this on my own. Please keep the change for yourself," he said with a smile, and left the store.

When Thomas returned to the house, Mrs. Albertson led him up the stairs and to the bedroom he would share with Charlie that night. She softly knocked on the door and waited for a reply. When there was none, she slowly opened the door. Charlie was curled up fast asleep. Thomas was relieved to see how much better the wound already looked. Dark, ugly bruising still covered the young boy's face, but the swelling was much improved from that morning.

"This bed can be yours," Mrs. Albertson whispered to Thomas, pointing at the unoccupied bed. Thomas laid a wrapped parcel at the foot of Charlie's bed and set a small pair of men's boots down on the floor under it. The parcel contained two pairs of pants, drawers, two pairs of socks, and three shirts that he hoped were the right size for the boy. Then Thomas joined Mrs. Albertson back in the hallway. He softly closed the door, and followed his hostess down the stairs where his own parcel of clothing waited.

"Charlie opted to sleep first and bathe later, but if you'd like a bath now, I can have the boys bring the tub in."

"A bath would be amazing," Thomas said. "But please let me bring the water."

"Oh, those boys need to keep busy, and you're probably every bit as exhausted as Charlie. Just sit down for a moment and I'll bring you some lemonade. Dinner will be at half past six, and Charlie said he'd like you to wake him. I imagine he'll be mighty hungry."

"That sounds good. I'll wake him after I bathe, and he can go get cleaned up before dinner. I know he'll want to look his best around everyone."

He sat down and soon Mrs. Albertson returned with the lemonade.

"This is delicious," he exclaimed, after his first sip. "Thank you again for your hospitality, Mrs. Albertson. You and your husband have been a godsend."

The genteel woman smiled warmly at him.

"You're very welcome, Mr. Linz. I'll send the boys to get you when the bath is ready."

Thomas was happy to finally have a quiet moment to sit and relax. It had indeed been a long day and so much had happened even in the few hours since they returned to Denver City. He was pulled from his thoughts when a young man appeared at the doorway.

"Your bath is ready, Mr. Linz. Please, follow me."

"Now, remind me your name," Thomas said as he followed the young man to the back bedroom where a metal bathtub had been set and filled for him.

"I'm Damien, the middle boy."

The young man smiled shyly.

"Well, thank you, Damien," Thomas said.

Damien nodded his acknowledgement as he left the room and closed the door behind him. Thomas stripped out of his filthy clothes and sank into the hot water. It was the first true bath he'd had since visiting a bathhouse in Missouri. Of course, he washed every time he came to a river or pond, but there was nothing like a nice, hot bath. While he would have loved to soak until the water was too cool to enjoy, he hurriedly bathed and dressed himself in his new clothes. He wanted Charlie to be able to enjoy a bath, too. Dinner was less than thirty minutes from now.

Thomas made his way back up the stairs and knocked again on the door.

"Come in," he heard from inside.

"How did you sleep, Charlie," he asked, as he walked into the room.

"So good. Now that my head isn't hurting, I really slept well."

"I came to let you know that Mrs. Albertson prepared a bath if you're ready. I figured you would like to bathe before dinner. And here are your new clothes and boots."

"Oh, thank you!"

"You're very welcome."

Thomas turned toward the door. Charlotte picked up the boots and the clothes parcel and followed him downstairs. Mrs. Albertson met them at the bottom of the staircase.

"Well, good evening, Charlie," Marnie said with a sweet smile. "Wait a moment while I grab more hot water for your bath and then I'll show you to it."

Minutes later, Charlotte lowered herself into the steaming bathtub with a sigh. Baths were such a rare treat, and even better when you didn't have to draw and heat the water yourself! She closed her eyes and let the hot, soapy water soothe her sore body and battered soul. Although she was exceedingly embarrassed about crying in front of the Albertsons this morning, she looked forward to visiting with them all tonight. And it would be good to see Big Viv and Dr. Groves again, as well. When all the warmth was gone from the water, she finally stood up and looked through the new clothes. She was shocked to see how much had been purchased.

Thomas looked up from the book in his lap when he heard Charlotte talking in the hall.

"It's nice to meet you both. Have you met Mr. Linz?"

"Not yet," a female voice replied. "My mother said he's in the sitting room. It's right here."

Thomas rose to his feet as Charlotte followed two young ladies into the room.

"Thank you so much for the new clothes and the boots. They fit perfectly."

Thomas couldn't believe how different the boy looked in clothes that fit. He appeared taller now that he wasn't being swallowed in Brendan's large clothing.

"You're welcome, son."

Then he turned to introduce himself to the Albertson daughters. "I'm Thomas Linz," he said, with a slight bow.

The two girls giggled at his gallant gesture.

"I'm Miss Sarah Albertson, and this is Miss Julia Albertson," the taller of the two said. "Mother said dinner is ready and we should bring you both to the table."

Dr. Groves had not been exaggerating about the talents of the Albertson's cook. Nora was a remarkable cook and, even with very short notice, she had prepared a delicious dinner for the visitors. Thomas relaxed as exuberant conversation surrounded him and drew him out of his shell. Even Charlie seemed to be more at ease. He wasn't talking much, but he responded when spoken to, and occasionally laughed at the antics of the lively Albertson boys. Thomas looked around the table and realized he couldn't wait for Emily to meet all his new friends. In that moment, he felt sure that bringing Emily to Colorado was the right decision. He smiled to himself and then caught Sergeant Albertson looking at him with a humorous grin. There was an unspoken question on the sergeant's face.

"Is this what you're after," he seemed to be asking with his eyes. Thomas nodded his head and smiled back at his new friend.

He realized this was exactly what he wanted; a big, loving, joyful family. It was what he'd dreamed of for years. He looked at Charlie sitting across from the table. The boy would certainly be missing his family right now. Thomas imagined that this closely resembled mealtimes at the Gallagher table. Suddenly he remembered something.

"My mother comes from a great big family," Charlie had said, as Thomas was stitching his forehead.

Were they all still in Ireland, or had some of them immigrated to America? Thomas simultaneously felt relief that Charlie had family and would not be alone, and sadness that he might leave him. Leave him? How could Charlie leave him when he'd never been his to begin with? It wasn't like Charlie was his son, or even a distant family member. He felt growing frustration with himself. He needed to focus on his goals and quit trying to control a situation over which he had no influence.

"And what about you, Mr. Linz," Sarah asked with a smile.

"I beg your pardon. I'm afraid you caught me woolgathering."

The five children laughed, and Mr. Albertson rolled his eyes. "My silly children want to know when your birthday is. Birthdays are always a good excuse to have Big Viv's special desserts, so they like to keep track of everyone's birthdays and pester her for cakes!"

"My birthday is November 11, so they'll have to wait a while," Thomas answered.

"You and George Groves share a birthday," John David cried. "You're birthday twins!" Then, turning to his mother, he asked, "Does that mean we'll have two cakes on their birthday?"

"You'll have to discuss that with Big Viv tonight," Marnie answered. She turned to Thomas. "You would think we starve them."

"Did you accomplish everything you needed today," Sergeant Albertson asked Thomas a few minutes later.

"Yes, I had a very productive visit to the dry goods store, as you can tell by the fancy new clothes Charlie and I are wearing," he joked. "And I got a list of available land plots to check out over the next few weeks. The clerk at the land office is doing some research for me and I'm planning to meet with him again at the end of the month to make my choice."

Thomas noticed that Charlie seemed very interested in this last scrap of information.

"Oh, that's wonderful," the boy said. "I hope you'll end up close to me."

"Do you plan to stay here then, Charlie," Sergeant Albertson asked, and instantly regretted it. "I'm sorry. That was rude of me to ask."

"Well, I need to write to my aunt and uncle in Ireland. I don't yet know exactly what I should do. Mr. Linz has offered to stay with me for a while, and, well…" her voice trailed off and she looked down at her plate.

Everyone at the table was quiet for a few moments, and then Thomas quickly changed the subject.

"Sergeant Albertson, I noticed that you have a Catholic church down the street, and I'd love to make a visit before we leave in the morning. What can you tell me about it?"

Thomas talked daily with the Lord, but there was something special about praying in an actual church.

"Why, that's St. Mary's," Marnie cried excitedly. "The Groves attend Mass there, and I'd love it if Mrs. Groves would show us around the church tomorrow. Actually, with all the new construction, there's so much more to see in Denver City. Why don't you stay another day or two? There's no need to rush off. You could attend Sunday morning Mass and then we could all meet here for lunch afterwards. I'd love to send you off to Kerry Haven with a full stomach."

Thomas looked over at Charlie. The boy's tentative smile was all the answer he needed.

"We would love to. Thank you for making us feel so welcomed here in your home."

A knock on the door caused instant excitement among the Albertson boys. All three of them jumped up from the table and ran to the door. Sarah and Julia were more demure and polite, but they too stood up and asked to be excused. From the front hallway the boys' exultant shouts of, "Dr. Groves! Clara! Big Viv! George," could be heard.

"From our sons' noise, you might think we seldom saw these friends, but we just had them over this weekend," Jason said sardonically. "Good grief, but they get excited!"

Charlotte and Thomas followed Mr. and Mrs. Albertson to the front parlor where everyone was greeting and hugging as though they hadn't been together just the week before.

"Mr. Linz, Charlie, I'd like to present my lovely bride, Mrs. Clara Groves," Dr. Groves said, his face beaming with pride. "Clara is my childhood sweetheart and Denver City's most accomplished midwife."

"It's lovely to meet you," Thomas said, taking her hand and gently pressing his lips to it. Clara gave him a beautiful smile and then turned to Charlotte.

"I've heard so much about your bravery, young man," she said kindly. "How is your head feeling this evening?"

"So much better. I'm very thankful to your husband and to George."

Big Viv moved forward and handed Charlotte a cake. "Don't you share this with anyone else, young Charlie. They all have their own to share."

"Thank you, Vivian."

Charlotte's eyes welled with tears, and she turned to place the cake on a nearby table. Why did everyone's kindness threaten to undo her?

"Who's open to a card game," Dr. Groves asked.

"How about Euchre," Marnie suggested. "I'll get the cards if you gentlemen will set up the folding tables."

Soon, there were three separate games of Euchre being played, and the house buzzed with happy chatter. Sarah, John David, Charlotte, and George made up one table. Joseph and Clara Groves, Thomas, and Fulton made up the next. Big Viv, Marnie, Damien, and Julia sat at the last table. Jason

Albertson was the odd man out, but he laughingly insisted that it was important he remain mobile and alert to ensure fair play at all tables.

"We don't tolerate card cheats in this here establishment," he boomed.

Charlotte soon found herself laughing along with her companions and thoroughly enjoying the game. She felt a brief pang of guilt about her joy, and then realized this was what her family would want for her. They would want her to enjoy life's goodness and not be drowned in grief. She looked across the table at her partner, Sarah. The young lady was beautiful and appeared to be about the same age as Charlotte.

"We would definitely be friends if I was myself tonight," she thought.

Although they weren't allowed to talk to each other about their cards, Charlotte realized as the evening progressed that she and Sarah seemed to be communicating strategy to each other through different facial expressions.

"I know what you're doing," George accused good-naturedly after an especially egregious wink between Sarah and Charlie. "Don't think I can't see what you two are up to!"

Sarah laughed and then pulled her face into a pretty pout.

"Oh, Mr. Groves! How could you even think such a thing? I'm wounded."

Sarah's flirty tone of voice indicated George's suspicions of underhanded dealings were right on the money. Charlotte thought she detected romantic feelings between the two. She thought about what a beautiful couple Sarah and George would make, and then wondered if a black man and white woman would be allowed to court each other.

Thomas glanced over to the next table and was happy to see Charlie laughing with the other young people. He wondered again what the future held for the boy.

"Returning to his large family in Ireland is probably the very best option," he thought as he looked down at his cards.

Charlie would undoubtedly be better off with an aunt and uncle and plenty of cousins close to his age, than with a bachelor who had no experience with children. In Ireland, Charlie would have access to educational opportunities and social opportunities the likes of which would not be present back at Kerry Haven. Thomas had almost made peace with this proposed outcome when Charlie's laughter caught his attention again. He looked at the boy and instantly felt deep sadness at the thought of not being a part of Charlie's future.

"Sergeant Albertson, will you sit in for me for a couple hands," he asked, standing up. "I'd like to take some air."

"I'd enjoy nothing more than assisting Mrs. Groves in beating these young bucks!"

Albertson took his place across from Clara. Joseph and Fulton's laughter followed Thomas as he stepped out onto the front porch. The night was cool and clear as Thomas made his way down the sidewalk. When he reached the street, he looked to his left and right. Spotting the church in the distance, he turned and began walking. He was weary beyond belief and his mind was a jumbled mess. He suddenly wanted nothing more than to pour this all out before the Lord. Entering the side door of the church, he could see nothing save the red glow of the tabernacle lamp. He took a moment to let his vision adjust and then carefully made his way into a pew and knelt. Only after kneeling did he notice the quiet presence of another gentleman a few pews in front of him.

"Father God," Thomas silently prayed, "Thank You. Thank You for the gift of faith. Thank You for the blessings of these last few weeks. Thank You for being with me every step of the way. Thank You for my safe travels and for these new friends. Thank You for sending me clarity about bringing Emily out here to live. Thank you for all of it!"

He took a deep breath and continued his silent conversation. "I come to You tonight confused and disquieted, Lord. I know you brought me into Charlie's life for some purpose. I'm happy he won't have to face his grief all alone, and I'm honored that You are allowing me to be part of his life. But I long to know Your will for me right now. Am I simply called to help him get to Ireland, or do You want him to stay here? I already feel so attached to him, Father, and I don't understand that. I long to stay with him and guide him as he grows up. Is that just grief over Michael that I feel?"

Having poured out his heart, he quieted his mind and sat in silent contemplation. Suddenly, the other man stood up and turned to go. Thomas saw his white collar and realized it was a priest. The priest smiled at him and Thomas smiled back. He knelt for a few more minutes of gratitude and then stood and made his way out of the church and back to his friends.

Only thirty minutes had passed when Thomas returned to the Albertson home, but Clara, Joseph, George, and Big Viv were already saying their goodbyes. There were big plans for the next day. What had started out as a request to know more about the church had grown into a full tour of Denver City's reconstruction and it seemed most everyone wanted to attend.

"It was so nice meeting you both," Clara said, as she hugged Charlie and shook Thomas' hand. "If no little babies decide to be born tomorrow, I plan to join you all for your tour."

"Goodnight," Big Viv said. "I'll be skipping the tour, but I'll see you tomorrow night at dinner."

Thomas was exhausted, and thought he might fall asleep before he even made it up the stairs. However, Charlotte felt rested from her nap and wanted to talk.

"I'm so excited to walk around and see everything tomorrow," she said, lying on her back with her hands behind her head. "Everything is changing so much since the big fire. I can't wait to see what has been completed since the last time my family was here."

"Do you miss Ireland, Charlie," Thomas asked sleepily.

"Sometimes. But I think I like it better here. I know I'd have an easier life with my aunt and uncle, but I don't really want to leave the cabin and the land and all my memories. It will be a very hard decision to make."

She rolled to her side, facing the next bed. Seeing Thomas in such close proximity shocked her and she suddenly realized how improper this was. She was a young, unmarried woman sharing a room with a man. Her mother would die from the shame of it all. Then Charlotte remembered Mother was already dead, and began to softly cry.

Thomas heard the sniffles.

"You've made some wonderful friends here, Charlie. I know that you'll have people who love you, no matter where you decide to live."

The boy continued to cry, and Thomas was unsure how to proceed. Certainly, Charlie would prefer that he pretend to not notice the crying. It would be too embarrassing. Thomas silently prayed for wisdom. Thankfully, it wasn't long before sleep came and lulled him away from his thoughts about Charlie.

Chapter Ten

Saturday, August 17, 1867

The next afternoon, a happy, tired group returned to the Albertson home after an eventful tour of the city. Marnie immediately ordered Charlie upstairs for a nap.

"I don't want Dr. Groves saying you overdid it on my watch," she said cheerfully.

Charlie followed her orders, and Thomas decided he wanted to go for a shave. The scraggly hair had served its purpose during his travels, but he no longer felt the need to keep people at bay. Besides, he was damn tired of the itchy scruff.

"I'll be back in time for dinner," he informed Mrs. Albertson. "Is there anything you need while I'm out?"

"No. Between Big Viv and Nora, I think we're in store for a fine feast."

Thomas walked two blocks to the barber shop he'd seen earlier in the day.

"Good afternoon, sir," the barber greeted him as he entered.

"Good afternoon," Thomas replied. There was a young man in the barber's chair receiving a shave, and two older men who looked to be in their sixties were seated awaiting their turn. Thomas sat down in the next seat and closed his eyes as the shop's occupants resumed their conversations.

His mind played through the events of the day. He'd enjoyed every moment spent with the gregarious group. They'd walked through the finer areas of the town, stopped for tea and sweets at the City Bakery and Restaurant, and finally enjoyed a picnic at the park. Thomas was warmed as he witnessed Charlie's growing friendship with the Albertson children. Some of Charlie's shock had worn off and he seemed less dazed. Of course, the dark bruises and ghastly wound still caused strangers to stare as they walked past, but Charlie hardly seemed to notice.

Charlie's excitement increased with each new sight, and he especially enjoyed the Old London Hospital; a busy drug store selling all sorts of medicinal tinctures, bandages, and first aid supplies. They purchased a few items to take back to the Gallagher homestead. He realized that so many things he took for granted, or found mundane, Charlie was still excited about. Charlie notified them that when the Gallaghers traveled to Denver City for Mass, they always came and left on the same day. And, because all the stores and businesses were closed on Sundays, he'd never visited any of them. Thomas loved witnessing the boy's awestruck joy.

He dreamed of taking Charlie to Cincinnati where he and Emily could introduce the boy to all the beauty the city had to offer. There were museums and opera houses, ballets and symphonies to attend. All the things he'd dreaded only a few months ago seemed enticing when he imagined seeing them through Charlie's excited eyes. He was soon smiling like a gigglemug and hoped none of the men in the barbershop had noticed.

"Ah, I think this young buck is in love," the old man next to him cackled as he elbowed Thomas playfully.

Thomas opened his eyes to find all four occupants of the barber shop staring at him.

"Not love, just daydreaming," he said good-naturedly.

"That silly grin looked like a man in love," insisted the barber, as he accepted payment from the current customer and brushed off the chair.

"Don't I wish," Thomas joked, raising his hands in a deprecating gesture. "Where would a man find a quality young lady to court around here?"

"Oh, you've come to the right place, mister," one of the old men said with a grin. "Why, Jasper and I know all the good families in Denver City."

"Jeb here is worse than an old lady when it comes to knowing the town's goings-on," Jasper said, pointing at his companion.

"Now just a minute, Jasper," Jeb began, when the barber interrupted.

"Both of you are as gossipy as old hens. That's why I don't mind you congregating here in my shop for hours on end. You provide such entertainment for my other patrons."

The barber pointed his finger back and forth at Jeb and Jasper. Thomas burst into laughter as the two old men sputtered in mock indignation.

"Why don't you come have a seat and tell me what you need," the barber said to Thomas.

"I'm happy to wait my turn."

"Oh, we're not waiting in line," Jasper said. Then, as though realizing he had just proven the barber right, he shook his head and looked down at his lap.

"Didn't I tell you they just came in for the gossip," the barber asked, as Thomas and the old men howled in laughter.

Thomas sat in the chair and got comfortable.

"What would you like," the barber asked.

"I want to look presentable again. It's been a while since I needed to interact with others, and I'm afraid I've grown rather shabby."

"Well, alright. A haircut and shave. Clean face, or leave a mustache?"

"Which do the young ladies prefer," Thomas called to Jeb and Jasper.

"Oh, definitely leave a mustache," Jasper responded.

"Yes, you definitely want to keep a mustache. I've personally found it drives the young ladies wild," Jeb quipped.

That sent the two old men into renewed peals of laughter.

"Mustache, it is, then," Thomas said.

He relaxed into the chair, and listened as Jeb and Jasper presented the names and family histories of all the eligible young ladies of Denver City. Not only was their conversation enormously entertaining, but Thomas felt sure he would find a wife in no time if the two old men had their way.

Forty-five minutes later, he walked out of the barbershop feeling like a new man. He reached up and ran his fingers through his short, wavy black hair. It felt sensational and he was glad he'd had it trimmed. Best of all was his face. In the last few months, he'd forgotten how good a naked face felt. There was a skip in his step as he climbed the stairs of the Albertson's porch and knocked on the door.

"Well, my heavens," Marnie exclaimed when she opened the door. "I thought," she began, and then started laughing. "I thought you were much, much older, Mr. Linz. I thought you the same age as the Sergeant and I."

Thomas stepped into the house and Marnie closed the door. At the sound of their mother's laughter, several of the Albertson children came into the front hallway.

"Goodness gracious," Fulton cried. "Is that you, Mr. Linz?"

There was a quizzical look on Thomas' handsome face.

"Do I really look that different?"

"I honestly would not have recognized you if we passed on the street," Julia said in astonishment.

"Nor would I," agreed Sarah. "You look years and years younger!"

"Well, I guess my disguise worked. I always use a scraggly appearance to trick my way into unsuspecting households so I can steal the fine silverware."

The Albertson children burst into laughter again.

"Well, I just counted the silver and it's all there," Sergeant Albertson said. "You shaved too soon."

"I hope I haven't kept you waiting for dinner," Thomas offered when the laughter died down.

"No, you're right on time. We've already set the tables and we're just waiting for our other guests to arrive."

Just then, another knock sounded on the door.

"Fulton, will you please go upstairs and wake young Charlie," Mrs. Albertson asked.

Jason turned to open the door and Fulton bounded up the stairs. Thomas' appearance triggered a second round of incredulity as Clara, Big Viv, Joseph, and George entered the house. Thomas had begun to feel embarrassed over all the fuss and was relieved when everyone calmed down and began to claim their seats around the two tables set up for tonight's meal. Charlotte was the last to come into the room, her face flushed with sleep.

"How is my young patient faring today," Dr. Groves asked.

"Much bett— Oh good heavens," she cried aloud when she saw Thomas. She stood frozen in place, staring at him for a moment. Then she shook her head and turned to Dr. Groves.

"I'm feeling much better," she finished, and took the open seat between Fulton and John David.

"We all reacted that way, Charlie," John David said, and everyone at the table laughed.

"The difference is remarkable," Sarah commented in her sweet, feminine voice, and Charlotte felt a quick tinge of jealousy. Had Thomas decided to shave because there were pretty girls in the house? She knew he wanted marriage and a family. Maybe he fancied the pretty Sarah Albertson. Charlotte tried to assure herself that Sarah liked George. Yes, Sarah and George liked each other too much for Sarah to be interested in Thomas, she thought to herself.

Thomas noticed Charlie was silent and withdrawn for several long minutes as the conversation flowed around him. He wondered if the boy was upset about something. Was his head hurting again? Or maybe he was just not yet fully awake from his nap. Thomas sometimes felt disoriented when he first woke up. Perhaps that was why Charlie was acting so odd.

Jason Albertson stood up and cleared his throat. "I want to thank you all for joining us tonight. Friends are a rare gift, and something we should never take for granted. Let us thank God for this food and for new friendships."

All who were present bowed their head, as Jason led them in a blessing. The meal was delicious, and Charlotte attempted to savor every bite. She would not eat this well again anytime soon. Although she enjoyed cooking, she never had access to any variety when it came to ingredients. She stole another glance at Thomas. Heavens above, he was beautiful! He had a sharp jawline and a fine mouth, and for the briefest of moments, she imagined what it would be like if he kissed her. Her body burned as she remembered falling asleep with him by the fire on Thursday night. She would never have approached him for comfort if he'd looked like he looked now! She'd only seen him as a gentle old man. How foolish she felt.

Tonight, instead of cards, there was music. Joseph Groves and Jason Albertson were grand fiddlers, and everyone sang along boisterously. Thomas looked over several times to see that, while smiling and clapping to the beat, Charlie was not singing. This seemed odd since the boy had mentioned more than once how much his family loved music and singing. Perhaps he was just feeling timid around the older boys. There were some who thought it unmanly to sing. Thomas remembered feeling nervous about stuff like that during those years between ten and twenty. It was a tough time for a man.

The truth was, Thomas' appearance had shocked Charlotte to her core and she couldn't recover her equilibrium. He was at least twenty years younger than she'd believed. From the first sight of him, she assumed he was her father's age or older. Now, he was a handsome man in his twenties who set her heart aflutter. She looked across the room to find he was staring at her with concern in his eyes. Her face burned and she looked quickly away. This simply would not work. Everything had changed when he cut off that scruffy facial hair. He'd ruined everything!

Thomas was relieved when the music began to wind down and the Groves group said their goodbyes. He sensed that Charlie was not feeling well, and wanted to talk with the boy alone. Maybe he could figure out what was troubling him.

"Goodnight and thank you for a wonderful evening," he said to Marnie and Jason as he took a lantern and turned to Charlie. "Let's get to bed so we can wake early for Mass tomorrow morning."

Thomas put his arm around the boy's shoulders as they walked up the stairs. Marnie smiled as she watched them go.

"I'm so glad they have each other," she said, wrapping her arm around Jason's waist and looking up into his eyes. "They have both lost family, and no one should face this world alone."

Thomas had shared his story during the last two days, and Marnie understood the loss he'd faced. Everyone had lost so much during the bitter war between the Union and the Confederacy. She wondered how the nation would ever recover.

"And I'm so glad I have you," Jason answered, smiling down at his beloved wife. "God truly blessed me with you, Mrs. Albertson."

Charlotte's heart pounded as she walked up the stairs with Thomas' arm draped over her shoulders. What would have seemed like fatherly protectiveness only yesterday now made her feel as though she might faint. How was she going to get out of this sticky situation? Thomas was going to accompany her home tomorrow, where they would be totally unchaperoned for days, if not weeks. Should she just expose her betrayal now? She could send a telegram to her aunt and uncle tomorrow and ask Mrs. Albertson to house her until they replied. Betsy and Jared would certainly invite her to live with them and she could escape the mess she'd made here.

"Let's look at that wound," Thomas said, pulling her from her thoughts. They were in the bedroom now, and he brought his right hand to her forehead as his left hand held the lantern close to her face.

"Oh, God help me," she thought, quivering at Thomas' nearness. For a brief moment, she wondered what would happen if she closed her eyes and lifted her face to him. Would he kiss her? She'd never been kissed before.

"Charlie, I can't get over the difference. The swelling has gone down so much. Why, I hardly even recognize you now!"

"Well, that makes two of us," she said, sharply.

Thomas laughed aloud and then realized the young boy wasn't making a jest.

"Are you upset with me, Charlie?"

Thomas was still standing so very close to her. There was a confused, wounded expression on his face and Charlotte regretted her harsh tone.

"No, not upset," she said, looking down at the floor as she searched for an explanation. "It's just that you used to remind me so much of Father, and now you don't."

She turned away from him and walked over to her bed. She couldn't think or even breathe with him so close to her. Sinking down to the bed, she sat with her head in her hands. "I guess I just feel...I don't know, alone again."

Thomas stepped over and knelt down in front of her. "Charlie, look at me."

She lifted her head and let her hands fall to her lap. Tears were flowing freely down her face now.

"You're not alone. Charlie, I'm not going anywhere. I plan to settle in this area, and you're stuck with me until I find my own land and build a cabin on it. That's months away, at least. You'll probably grow sick of my company."

Charlotte didn't accept the handkerchief he offered or respond to his humor. She simply removed her boots and wordlessly lay down with her back to him.

Thomas had no idea how to respond to this slight. He stood up and looked down at the sad, hurt little boy. Taking a deep breath, he turned and sat on his own bed to remove his boots and shirt. Then he extinguished the lantern and lay down to sleep. Who knew a haircut and shave could cause so much damn trouble!

When he awoke the next morning, Thomas was surprised to see the bed across from his was empty. He glanced around the room, but Charlie was nowhere in sight. Thomas figured he must have risen early and gone downstairs to visit with the Albertson boys. He stood up and stretched. It felt so good to sleep in a real bed. He almost wanted to stay a few more days in Denver City just to avoid sleeping on the floor again.

His thoughts jumped to the Gallagher cabin, and he wondered where Charlie and his siblings normally slept. All he'd seen was the bedroom he presumed to belong to Mr. and Mrs. Gallagher. Realizing this was all in the past tense now made him sad. He'd been hurt by Charlie's behavior last night, but he would need to be patient with the boy. Grief was a powerful, confusing emotion and he would probably witness plenty of conflicting behavior from Charlie over the next few weeks or months. Thomas had been absent as Emily processed her grief at the loss of first their parents and then their brother. He wondered how his sister had handled the losses. Already traumatized by the war, Thomas had grown increasingly numb and withdrawn after each loss. Word of Michael's death had almost killed him. Only the unceasing activity of each day's fighting kept him going. He often wondered how he would have handled it if there hadn't been a war, and he had been a gentleman of leisure in Cincinnati.

The sound of voices downstairs brought Thomas back to the present moment. He needed to finish getting dressed for Mass. Sergeant Albertson had lent him a proper coat and Charlie was given one that Fulton had outgrown. They would look presentable. He wet his hands in the washbasin, then quickly washed his face and smoothed his hair before heading downstairs. To his dismay, everyone was waiting for him.

"Well, don't you look dashing," Mrs. Albertson greeted him as he descended the last few steps. "We'll have no trouble finding you a fine wife. In fact, Mrs. Groves can probably point out a few eligible ladies at church this morning."

"Between you and my friends from the barber shop, I may be married off before the end of the year," Thomas cried in amusement as they all started walking to the church amid laughter and good-natured teasing about his matrimonial prospects.

Each and every Albertson seemed to have an opinion about which of their neighbors would make the best wife for Thomas, and laughter consumed the whole, happy group. All except for Charlotte. She did not enjoy this conversation at all and instead found herself consumed with jealousy. She couldn't bear the thought of Thomas falling in love with another woman. Not when she wanted his love so badly. The crazy thing was, she had his love. He loved her and wanted nothing more than to comfort and protect her; only he thought she was a boy named Charlie. What a mess she'd made of things, and try as she might, she couldn't think of a good solution. She'd spent hours last night weighing this option and that. None of them ended well.

Either she kept her secret and ran off to Ireland, never to see him again; or she admitted her betrayal and Thomas hated her for deceiving him. He had trusted and protected Charlie immediately, no questions asked. How would he feel when he discovered "Charlie" was a lie? He would be so angry, and she couldn't blame him.

When the group reached the beautiful church, they found Dr. and Mrs. Groves, George, and Big Viv waiting outside for them. The Albertson family said their goodbyes and kept walking toward the First Baptist Church of Denver. Dr. Groves pulled open the heavy wooden door and ushered everyone in. Charlotte felt uncomfortable entering the sanctuary without a veil on her head. Mrs. Groves of Miss Vivian would surely have lent her one had they known she was a woman. That thought brought her even more guilt. Thomas wasn't the only one who would feel betrayed. All her kind, wonderful new friends would feel betrayed, as well. And Marnie might never recover after finding out she had put Thomas and Charlotte together in a bedroom. Oh, the horror!

Sitting in the quiet church, Charlotte remembered a verse from Sir Walter Scott's poem, Marmion: "Oh what a tangled web we weave, when first we practice to deceive!" Yes, she had certainly spun a tangled web. Her only option was to run. She could never admit she was a woman and destroy poor Mrs. Albertson's proper ladylike sensibilities. She would send a telegram to Betsy and Jared today before leaving Denver City. Then she would return to the cabin with Thomas and keep up her pretense through the next few weeks until he came back to Denver City to check on the land grant.

Suddenly, she was struck with a wonderful thought! Maybe Thomas could simply take over Kerry Haven. She no longer needed it, and she had heard him tell Mr. Albertson how much he loved the area. If Thomas settled there, he'd not need to dig a well or build a cabin and barn, or even buy his own livestock. He could have it all! And she could avoid the shame and humiliation of admitting her lie. She breathed a sigh of relief. Now that she had partially untangled her web of deceit, she could concentrate on the Mass.

Thomas glanced down the pew to find Charlie staring at the altar and smiling widely. The boy's face was practically radiating joy. Thomas was relieved that Charlie had recovered from last night's anger. It was going to be a rocky road, but he felt sure Charlie would survive his losses. He had such strength of character for someone so young, Thomas thought with pride. Then he turned his attention back to the Mass. Everyone was now standing for the Gospel reading.

"A reading from the Gospel according to St. John," Father Joseph proclaimed, in a deep, resonating voice. He traced his thumb in a cross over the page and then traced a cross on his forehead, lips, and chest.

"Glory to you, Lord," the congregation answered.

Thomas traced a cross on his forehead, lips, and chest. He loved the symbolism involved in sealing the words of the Lord in his mind, in his words, and in his heart.

"Jesus said to them, 'I am the bread of life; whoever comes to me will never hunger, and whoever believes in me will never thirst. But I told you that although you have seen me, you do not believe. Everything that the Father gives me will come to me, and I will not reject anyone who comes to me, because I came down from heaven not to do my own will but the will of the one who sent me. And this is the will of the one who sent me, that I should not lose anything of what he gave me, but that I should raise it on the last day. For this is the will of my Father, that everyone who sees the Son and believes in him may have eternal life, and I shall raise him on the last day.'

"The Jews murmured about him because he said, 'I am the bread that came down from heaven,' and they said, 'Is this not Jesus, the son of Joseph?

Do we not know his father and mother? Then how can he say, 'I have come down from heaven'?

"Jesus answered and said to them, 'Stop murmuring among yourselves. No one can come to me unless the Father who sent me draw him, and I will raise him on the last day. It is written in the prophets: "They shall all be taught by God." Everyone who listens to my Father and learns from him comes to me. Not that anyone has seen the Father except the one who is from God; he has seen the Father. Amen, amen, I say to you, whoever believes has eternal life. I am the bread of life. Your ancestors ate the manna in the desert, but they died; this is the bread that comes down from heaven so that one may eat it and not die. I am the living bread that came down from heaven; whoever eats this bread will live forever; and the bread that I will give is my flesh for the life of the world.'

"The Jews quarreled among themselves, saying, 'How can this man give us his flesh to eat?'

"Jesus said to them, 'Amen, amen, I say to you, unless you eat the flesh of the Son of Man and drink his blood, you do not have life within you. Whoever eats my flesh and drinks my blood has eternal life, and I will raise him on the last day. For my flesh is true food, and my blood is true drink. Whoever eats my flesh and drinks my blood remains in me and I in him. Just as the living Father sent me and I have life because of the Father, so also the one who feeds on me will have life because of me. This is the bread that came down from heaven. Unlike your ancestors who ate and still died, whoever eats this bread will live forever.'

"These things he said while teaching in the synagogue in Capernaum. Then many of his disciples who were listening said, 'This saying is hard; who can accept it?'

"Since Jesus knew that his disciples were murmuring about this, he said to them, 'Does this shock you? What if you were to see the Son of Man ascending to where he was before? It is the spirit that gives life, while the flesh is of no avail. The words I have spoken to you are spirit and life. But there are some of you who do not believe.'

"Jesus knew from the beginning the ones who would not believe and the one who would betray him. And he said, 'For this reason I have told you that no one can come to me unless it is granted him by my Father.'

"As a result of this, many of his disciples returned to their former way of life and no longer accompanied him. Jesus then said to the Twelve, 'Do you also want to leave?'

"Simon Peter answered him, 'Master to whom shall we go? You have the words of eternal life. We have come to believe and are convinced that you are the Holy One of God.'"

Father Joseph paused reverently for a moment. Then, he held the Book of the Gospels up in the air and said, "The Gospel of the Lord!"

The congregation responded, "Praise to You, Lord Jesus Christ!"

As soon as everyone was seated, Father Joseph began speaking. Thomas noticed he had no notes in front of him, only the Gospel.

"In last Sunday's Gospel, we heard about Jesus feeding a crowd of five thousand with five loaves and two fish. Then, that night, He walked on water. I think you'll admit this was a big day for Jesus."

Father Joseph smiled, and there were a few chuckles from the congregation.

"Today, we read about the crowds that He'd fed coming to look for Him. Jesus knew that they came not because they believed in Him, but because they longed to see further miracles. Jesus said to the crowd, 'I am the bread of life; whoever comes to me will never hunger, and whoever believes in me will never thirst. I am the Bread that came down from heaven.'"

"Now, there were three groups of people listening to Jesus. There were the crowds who simply wanted entertainment. They were not disciples; they just came to be entertained. They are referred to in the Gospel as 'the Jews.' The second group is 'Disciples.' These are the ones who left everything; their homes, their families, their friends, to follow Jesus. The third group is the Apostles. Hold onto those three distinctions because they will be important in a moment."

"So, first, the crowds murmured amongst themselves about Jesus saying, 'I am the Bread come down from heaven.' Then, we hear that the crowd questioned His words. They have moved from murmuring to questioning. But Jesus continued. 'I am the living bread. Whoever eats this bread will live forever. And the bread that I will give is my flesh for the life of the world.' Now the crowd moves from murmuring to quarreling. We read: they now quarreled amongst themselves saying, 'How can this man give us his flesh to eat?' Does this sound like they think Jesus is speaking symbolically?"

Father Joseph paused and looked from one side of the church to the other. "No. If they thought He was telling another parable, they would not be bothered. When He said He was the gate, or the vine, or the Good Shepherd, no one quarreled. But at this moment, they are taking Him literally. They say, 'How can this man give us his flesh to eat?' If Jesus were speaking symbolically, this would have been the perfect moment for Him to say, 'No, you misunderstand me.' But instead of clarifying, He emphasizes and magnifies His claim. Not once, or twice, but five times, Jesus renews His claim. He says, 'Amen. Amen, I say to you, unless you eat the flesh of the Son of Man and drink his blood, you do not have life within you.'"

"Secondly, Jesus says, 'Whoever eats my flesh and drinks my blood has eternal life and I will raise him on the last day.' Then He says, 'For my flesh is true food and my blood is true drink.' But Jesus is not done yet! He continues. 'Whoever eats my flesh and drinks my blood remains in me and I in him.' And lastly, 'Just as the living father sent me and I have life because of the father, so also the one who feeds on me will have life because of me.'"

"Jesus knows that the people are struggling. Yet, He doesn't back down, or cry out, 'I'm not speaking literally.' No, He ratifies absolutely that He meant what He said. He repeats it five times in five different ways."

"We continue reading: Then many of his disciples said 'This saying is hard. Who can accept it?' Let me ask you all," Father Joseph said, looking out at everyone in the pews. "Is a symbolic statement hard to accept? No. No, it's not. It's only symbolism."

"However, Jesus was not speaking symbolically. He asks them, 'Does this shock you? What if you were to see the Son of Man ascending to where He was before?'"

"Where was Jesus before," Father Joseph asked. "He was in heaven. He made the heavens and earth. He can make everything out of nothing. He can take bread and wine and turn it into His body and blood."

"If we continue reading, we see that 'as a result of this, many of his disciples returned to their former way of life and no longer accompanied him.' This is the only time in the entire Bible when someone left Christ. And what did He do? Did He run after them and explain that He was only speaking symbolically, and they should come back? No. He doubled down. When Jesus says, 'Amen, amen I say unto thee,' we know that what is coming after this is a solemn oath. It means 'I stake my life on this.' It is a very serious claim. If Jesus stakes His life on the fact that we must eat His body and drink His blood, who are we to say that the communion we receive is merely a symbol, or a remembrance of His passion? Who are we to deny His true presence in the most Blessed Sacrament? If Jesus was willing to lose His followers over this, we should understand that He meant what He said. As Catholics, we must believe in the true presence. We must believe that we are, in fact, consuming the real body and blood of Christ every time we receive communion. To not believe this is to cease being Catholic."

"Let us pray that we will grow each day in our belief in Christ, Our Lord, truly present in the Eucharist. Amen."

With that, the priest turned and walked back to his seat near the altar. The church sat in silence for several minutes before Father Joseph stood and began the profession of faith.

Chapter Eleven

Sunday, August 18, 1867

The homily was powerful, and Charlotte felt completely refreshed as she walked out of the church alongside her friends. They made their way over to the pastor, Father Joseph Machebeuf. Charlotte prayed he wouldn't recognize her. Then she realized she was worrying unnecessarily. Of course, he wouldn't recognize her dressed as a boy without any members of her family. The church had only been here for seven years, and her family attended sporadically at best. She thought again of her father's dream of building a local parish. Her heart ached with missing him.

The boisterous group made their way back to the Albertson home, still talking about wives for Thomas. Charlotte was determined not to let it bother her. She couldn't allow herself to care if Thomas ended up with Abigail Price, or with Mary Johnson, or any of the other eligible young ladies being proposed by the eager matchmakers. She would be in Ireland soon and could push Thomas Linz straight out of her mind.

After a filling lunch of cold cuts, bread, and cheese, Thomas and Charlotte began their goodbyes. It would have been so difficult to leave their wonderful friends if not for the fact that Charlotte would see them again in a few short weeks. Mrs. Albertson handed them each a packet with more food, and Jason gave Thomas directions to the telegraph office. Then they rode off amid cries of, "Goodbye!" "Be safe!" and "We'll miss you!"

"I'd say we made a good impression," Thomas said, turning to smile at Charlie. "Have you decided what you want to say in the telegram to your aunt and uncle? This will be difficult information for them to receive."

"I have thought and thought about it, but there is no good way to send such horrible news. Do you have any advice?"

"Not really. Maybe the telegraph operator will have some suggestions. After all, he does this every day and has probably sent many death notifications."

In just a few minutes, they arrived at the telegraph office. When they explained what they needed, the operator looked troubled.

"I can send your telegram to Ireland, but I have a few caveats. Transatlantic telegrams are very, very expensive. At a minimum, we're looking at approximately a hundred dollars."

Charlotte gasped. It was an obscene amount of money, and there was no possible way that she could afford that.

"I can pay for it, Charlie," Thomas said softly. "That's not a problem."

Charlotte looked at him with wide eyes. When he'd purchased all those premade clothes on Friday, she had begun to wonder if he might be wealthy. This offer to pay for the telegram confirmed her assumption.

"And you might not want those you're communicating with to feel pressured to spend a fortune responding to you. You might prefer to send a letter even though it takes longer."

"Oh, I hadn't thought of that," Charlotte said, dejectedly. "I can't ask that of Betsy and Jared."

They thanked the operator and left the office.

"Can we stop at the post office," Charlotte asked as they walked back to their horses.

"I'm sure it will be closed since today is Sunday. Perhaps we could go home and write our letters for posting next time we're here."

She nodded her head but didn't look at him.

"I know you're disappointed, Charlie, but this might be for the best. If you left soon, you'd be crossing the Atlantic at the coldest time of the year."

Still there was no response.

"Are you in a rush to leave? I understand if you feel it will be too difficult to return to your cabin. Would you like to ask Dr. and Mrs. Groves, or the Albertsons if you can stay here in Denver City? I'm sure they would be happy to host you until you are able to make arrangements with your family in Ireland. And I could bring anything you need from the cabin when I return."

"No, it's just…I don't know. Everything's fine. I promise."

Thomas waited for a few moments to see if Charlie would continue.

"Let's go," Charlie finally said.

They turned their horses to head for home. When they reached the edge of town, Thomas spoke.

"Selfishly, I'd be pretty happy if you stayed until the spring. I'd like to be able to introduce you to Emily."

"You've decided to send for her," Charlotte asked excitedly.

"Yes. Sitting around the table with the Albertsons the other night, I realized that Emily would love it here, and there are more opportunities than I'd realized. I worried that she might not have the same prospects here that she has in Cincinnati. But Denver City will continue to grow and will eventually provide anything we need. While I don't want to live in the city, and still plan to find land near your homestead, all the modern conveniences will be only a three-hour ride away. And I know she will absolutely love our new friends."

Charlotte was torn. Knowing that Emily was coming to live here made her want to stay all the more. How she wished that she hadn't disguised herself in the first place! She wanted so badly to stay in America, to stay here close to her family's graves, to stay in the cabin that held so many wonderful memories, and to stay close with all the wonderful people she'd grown to love over the last few days. Most of all, she wanted to stay close to Thomas. They rode in silence for a long time before she spoke again.

"Thomas, I've been thinking about something. If you want, you can just make your home at Kerry Haven. I'd like to know someone was living there who loved the land as much as my family did. And perhaps you could visit their graves sometimes. You wouldn't have to rush to dig a well or build..."

Thomas had pulled his horse to a stop. Once Charlotte realized he was no longer beside her, she stopped talking and turned back to face him.

"Charlie, I would be exceptionally honored to take over your family's homestead. You have no idea how much that would mean to me. I will pay you a fair price, and you can set it aside for your education, and to buy a home someday to start a family. It will be a substantial amount."

Charlotte looked at his earnest face and beautiful green eyes. She wished she felt the same joy she saw in that handsome face.

"I keep wishing you could have met my family," she admitted, prodding Meg to begin walking again.

"I know I would have loved them. The state of the property indicates they were hardworking and took pride in their work. And, if you are any indicator, Charlie, your parents were great role models. The way you talk about Brendan, I imagine a courageous, caring young man; and it sounds like Ruth brought joy to everyone she met. Yes, I would have loved them."

Charlotte simply nodded. Thomas was correct about each of them, and she felt her loss keenly.

"It's hardest in the morning when I first wake up," she said. "I forget that they're gone, and I wake so happy. Then I remember and it knocks the breath from my chest."

"I still feel that way, too. Especially about Michael. I sometimes think of something funny I need to share with him, and then it crashes into me anew that he's gone. He would have been twenty-three next month."

Charlotte laughed, and Thomas looked at her in confusion. This wasn't a laughing sort of conversation.

"I'm sorry. It's not funny," she giggled. "Only, I thought you were so much older, and I thought your siblings were older, too. I figured Emily was an old spinster. Then, when you got a haircut and shave…"

Charlotte paused and looked directly at Thomas.

"How old are you, actually?"

"I'm twenty-five. I knew the scruffy appearance kept me from unwanted attention, but I had no idea it made me appear geriatric!"

"Well, it did!"

"Nevertheless, Emily is hardly an old spinster. She's eighteen and the most beautiful girl ever! Of course, as her older brother, I am inclined to think thus. I hope she'll find good friendships with Sarah and Julia Albertson. I imagine I'll be riding this road often bringing her back and forth! And who knows, maybe John David will catch her eye."

"Oh, who's playing matchmaker now?"

Again, Thomas marveled at how easy and entertaining their conversations were. The horses' hooves kept a rhythmic beat on the dirt road, as Charlotte tried to make a mental list of all that she would need to do before leaving for Ireland. She thought about how long it generally took for Mother's and Aunt Betsy's letters to reach the other. It could be several months before her aunt and uncle even received word of her family's deaths. And then, several more months until she received their response to her request to live with them. Of course, she didn't really need to wait for a response. She knew the Marshalls would welcome her with open arms. She planned to leave as soon as arrangements could be made for her travel to New York. What a relief that she would have money from the sale of Kerry Haven to fund her trip.

Then, doubt crept into her mind. Would she be allowed to leave the country before the criminals were found? After all, she was the only one who could identify them. Oh, but that would uncover her deception! No, she couldn't have that. She had already decided that she would leave for Ireland as a boy. She wanted to leave with the love and admiration of all her new friends intact, and without wounding any of them with her betrayal. If the criminals were found and brought to Denver City, they would likely recognize her and call her out as a woman. That would ruin everything!

On the other hand, if they were not caught, other families all over the territory were in danger. She's seen firsthand that their violence was not an isolated event. She thought about what she'd seen at the Crawford homestead.

"Tomorrow I plan to go bury the Crawford family," Thomas said, as if reading her thoughts. "But I don't think you should come with me."

"Thank you, Thomas," Charlotte said, overwhelmed with relief and gratitude. "I don't know if I could bear the sight of my friends' dead bodies."

"I agree."

They rode on for a few minutes in silence. Thomas didn't deserve to carry out the horrible task alone, Charlotte thought. And besides, now that her time with him was limited, every moment seemed more precious. Once she left for Ireland, she would live the rest of her life without ever seeing him again. She decided to be brave and help with the graves.

"Actually, Thomas, I think I'll go with you. That's a huge task and it's not fair for you to do it alone. You didn't even know them."

Thomas looked over and smiled a weary smile. "Charlie, I've spent the last five years surrounded by death and decay. I've seen things on and off the battlefield that I'll never forget, no matter how long I live. I wish I could get the memories out of my head, but they'll never go away. You're only eleven years old and have already suffered more trauma than most people suffer in a lifetime. If I can protect you from one more set of bad memories, I want to do it."

His eyes were full of pain.

"You have the rest of your life ahead of you. Let me protect you from this."

She merely nodded her head and looked away. His words had pierced her heart. The rest of her life. The rest of her life in Ireland with her aunt and uncle and cousins. The rest of her life without wonderful, captivating, handsome Thomas.

She thought of herself five years from now. She'd be twenty-four and likely an old maid. After the pain of what those men had done to her, she knew she never, ever wanted to be married. How could women endure that night after night? Besides, no man would ever measure up to the one riding next to her. She would constantly compare any potential suitor to Thomas, and certainly find them lacking. She had always dreamed of a beautiful marriage like that of her parents. How could she now contemplate settling for someone she didn't truly love? For she knew in her heart that no one would ever come close to Thomas, and how could she live with someone who was only second best?

There would never be a day, probably not an hour in a day, when she wouldn't think of Thomas and wonder what he was doing back in America. Her mind pictured him happily married and settled in the cabin where she'd lived all these years. She imagined him sitting down to meals with his wife and children. She imagined him sleeping next to another woman every night. It was all she could do to stop herself from turning to him and telling him that she was a woman and that she loved him! From telling him that she wanted to be the one sitting beside him at meals. She wanted to be the one raising his children. She wanted to be the one lying beside him at night. But then, she remembered Fred's savage attack and her body recoiled from any thought of marriage, even to a man as wonderful as Thomas.

"So, Charlie, what did you think of Father Joseph's homily today," Thomas asked, out of the blue.

"He's always a good speaker, but today was especially powerful. Nancy Crawford and I often debated the True Presence in the Eucharist. Her family was Presbyterian, and they believed the communion they received was only a symbol of Christ's body and blood. I wish she could have heard Father Joseph's scriptural proofs today. I tried to explain it to her several times, but I know I never explained it as well as he did today!"

"I grew up Lutheran, myself. My parents baptized me Lutheran, and we attended Trinity Evangelical Church every Sunday. When I was seven years old, I began attending St. John the Baptist Catholic School, since our Lutheran church didn't have a school. My parents denounced Catholicism, but they wanted the best education for me. So, there I was. The young, energetic priests all followed the academic model of Father John Bosco — have you heard of him?"

When Charlotte shook her head, Thomas continued.

"He's a priest in Italy who has devoted his whole life to educating street children, and orphans, and young boys who always seem to find themselves in trouble. His teaching methods are based on love instead of punishment and he's had great success with the roughest boys around. Anyway, the priests who ran our school used his model. I can tell you that, although the academics were rigorous, every student in my class felt seen and understood by our teachers. I think their charisma was what initially drew me to Catholicism."

"Wow, I've never heard of him, but he sounds amazing!"

"He is. I always think that if I ever travel to Europe, I'd like to go meet him. His life's work has impacted so many! Anyway, after two years at the school, I decided that I wanted to become Catholic. I was only nine at the time, and the priests encouraged me to keep studying. I think they knew how my parents would react. Meanwhile, I was going home in the afternoons and teaching Michael and Emily everything I'd learned during the day."

Thomas chuckled softly.

"They both idolized me when we were kids. I sometimes grew annoyed with their admiration, but I hope I was never cruel to them. It's so difficult when I think of the 'what-ifs. Sometimes, I still can't believe Michael is gone."

He stopped talking and a profound sadness enveloped him. Charlotte searched her mind for something to say. She wanted this conversation to go on and on forever. Should she ask him about Michael, or would that just make him feel worse.

Suddenly, Thomas burst into song. At first, she was shocked and a bit confused. What was he doing, singing at the top of his lungs right in the middle of the road? What if someone heard? She looked at him questioningly, but he just winked and kept on singing. She couldn't help laughing at his reckless joy. Moments later, she found herself joining in the song. She easily picked out the melody, and for a brief period their voices danced together; his deep and strong, hers clear and high.

Then, abruptly she stopped in alarm and her hand flew to her mouth. Hers was a woman's voice. What would Thomas think? She turned, wide-eyed, to find him stifling a grin.

"Charlie, you'd better enjoy that true, clear voice while you can," he said, chuckling. "Once your voice starts to change, you'll never sing so beautifully again. Trust me son, you've got some awkward years ahead of you. I remember the voice cracking and embarrassment."

Thomas shook his head and chuckled. "Very awkward years. But you've the voice of an angel today- enjoy it!"

With that, he resumed his hearty singing. Charlotte laughed at his comments and then continued her melodic artistry. She marveled at how beautiful their voices sounded together. Damn it, she thought. One more yardstick she'd use when measuring up potential suitors in the future. Did they sing as well as Thomas?

The sun had set behind the mountains and twilight was quickly approaching as Kerry Haven and the Gallagher cabin came into view. Thomas was mesmerized by the colors streaking across the sky.

"Have you ever seen anything more beautiful," he asked, waving his arm to encompass their surroundings.

"This is my very favorite time of the day," Charlotte answered. "I've always loved how the colors get so bright, and the harsh lines seem to blur. It gives everything a dream-like appearance."

"Charlie, that was almost poetic! Speaking of poetry, I sure could use more of those delicious biscuits. Do you think you could whip some up while I tend to the horses and unpack our saddle bags?"

"I think I could do that," Charlotte answered, with a smile. "When you realize how easy it is, you'll have me doing the hard tasks while you whip up the biscuits!"

"You definitely need to teach me before you leave, Charlie. And that's an order!"

Again, the thought of Charlie being elsewhere made Thomas sad. He wished the boy would stay. Thomas knew he would need help managing the large property, and it would be years before any future Linz sons would be old enough to assist him. He hoped that if he had sons, they would be as courageous and full of character as the young man riding next to him. Perhaps in a few weeks, when Charlie had recovered somewhat from the shock of losing his family, Thomas would present the idea. There was no doubt that Ireland was a better option for Charlie, but he should at least have the choice to stay.

Once he unsaddled Meg and Trigger, Thomas grabbed a half-filled grain bag and walked towards the pasture. He shook the bag as he called out to the other horses in the pasture. They must have been accustomed to receiving grain in the evenings because it didn't take them long to answer his calls. As he tended to the horses and gave Meg and Trigger a good brushing, he looked around the barn. It was well-built and organized. There was a loft above him, and he wondered if that was where Charlie and Brendan had slept. Barns were such warm, comfortable places to fall asleep.

Thomas let his mind wander over what he needed to accomplish during the next few months. On Saturday, before his haircut and shave he had stopped at the post office and mailed a brief letter to Emily. The letter outlined his plans to settle here and informed her that he could now receive letters at the post office in Denver City. He liked to write a few thoughts each night before falling asleep and had mailed her a letter each time he passed through a town with a post office. Now, he finally had a place for her to send return correspondence. It would be so great to hear from her! He dearly missed his sister and hoped she had not changed her mind about joining him when he settled. He was sure she'd be happy here.

His trip from Cincinnati had taken ninety-two days on horseback. He needed to find out if train travel between Colorado and Ohio had improved since the last time he checked. No matter how they traveled, the trip would be arduous, but traveling by train would be infinitely better than by carriage or horseback. And, if Charlie traveled with him to Cincinnati to bring Emily, that would at least get the boy closer to New York and his transatlantic voyage.

After he finished unpacking the saddle bags and returning the bedrolls and other supplies to their proper places, he walked to the well and rolled up his sleeves. Then he pumped some water into his hands and washed his face and arms. He used his wet hands to smooth back his hair. It felt good after the dry, dusty ride today. Night had fallen, and he looked from the beautiful mountains to the sturdy cabin where soft light spilled from the windows. He could hardly believe that this picturesque setting was going to be his home.

He entered the cabin and left his boots by the door, next to Charlie's. The difference in their shoe sizes made him smile. He again wondered if Charlie would end up as tall and muscular as Brendan had been. The boy was currently so small-framed that it seemed improbable. However, he was only eleven. Surely, he had plenty more growing to do.

The wonderful smell of biscuits permeated the cabin and Thomas' mouth began to water. He didn't see Charlie anywhere and assumed he was in the bedroom. The closed door indicated this was likely. Thomas decided to set the table while waiting for Charlie. He quickly located the utensils and plates stacked on a shelf near the oven. Then he noticed the empty cup that Charlie said was for flowers. After another quick glance at the closed bedroom door, he grabbed the cup, stripped off his socks to leave by the door with his boots, and stepped back outside. He knew there were a few wildflowers near the well.

While Thomas was busy in the barn, Charlotte had quickly prepared the biscuits and put them in the oven to bake. Then she took a pitcher of hot water into the bedroom and poured some into the washbasin. Taking off her shirt, she carefully unwound the petticoat strips she had tied together to bind her chest. The bath and new clothes on Friday had been wonderful, but since she had not taken other material with which to conceal her breasts, the petticoat binding had been on her for nearly a week now. It was ripe! She quickly submerged a clean linen cloth into the hot water and washed her face and neck. There was no longer any drainage from her wound, but the cloth came away covered with dirt and grime. She would take dirt and grime over pus and blood any day! She rinsed the cloth and then bathed her chest and arms.

When she heard the door open, she hastily dried off, wound a fresh binding around her chest, and fastened it tightly. The petticoat had been voluminous enough for her to make several bindings from its pieces, and this would allow her to rotate them for washing. She pulled her shirt back on and tucked it into her pants, then lifted her suspenders back up over her shoulders.

Stepping out into the main area of the cabin, she was surprised to find herself alone. That was odd. She was sure she'd heard Thomas come in, but perhaps it had just been her nerves playing tricks on her.

It was time to remove the biscuits from the oven, and Charlotte grabbed the potholders she had made with her mother last year. Then she opened the oven door and carefully pulled out the pan. She turned around to see Thomas placing a cup of wildflowers on the table.

"You weren't supposed to catch me in the act," he said with a sheepish grin. "Since I no longer look like your father, I thought I'd try to act like him at least. You said he always put wildflowers on the table for your mother."

Charlotte's eyes filled with tears. "Thank you, Thomas."

Dinner was a simple affair, especially after the meals they had enjoyed with the Albertsons.

"I'm missing Nora right now," Charlotte said, looking across the table at Thomas.

"I was just thinking the same thing. I guess I'll need to make sure my dedicated matchmakers include culinary aptitude as one of the requirements for any young woman they want me to meet."

Thomas laughed and Charlotte wished she could join him in his mirth. Objectively, she knew this was funny. In any other circumstance, it would have been absolutely hilarious. But the thought of Thomas courting pretty young ladies didn't make her laugh; it strangled her. She began to cough, and took a sip of water to try and clear her throat.

"Are you alright," Thomas asked, standing up. He probably thought she was choking on a biscuit, when it was just pure jealousy causing her trouble. She held up her hands to signify that she was okay.

"Just need to clear my throat," she croaked. A few more coughs had her breathing normally again.

Charlotte stood up and moved to sit in her father's rocking chair. She was exceedingly curious about what type of woman attracted Thomas. As painful as it might be to hear about his ideal woman, maybe upon hearing his preferences, she could convince herself that Thomas was not for her.

When Thomas joined her in the living room, she prompted, "Let's return to your comment about womanly requirements. What exactly are you looking for in an ideal wife? I mean, I deserve to take part in the matchmaking competition with the Albertsons. I may know just the woman for you."

"Well, young Charlie, I guess you do deserve a chance to pick the future Mrs. Linz. Of course, I'd say the fact that we'll be living together for the time being gives you an unfair advantage."

Oh, heavens! She wanted an unfair advantage at winning his love, not at picking out someone for him to love.

Thomas was serious now.

"Honestly Charlie, that's a good question. My ideas about the ideal woman have changed so much in the last ten years. I used to believe a pretty face and nice figure were the most important things. When I think of all the beautiful young debutantes I escorted to this or that social event before the war, I sometimes can't fathom it."

He stopped and looked right at her.

"Charlie, you would not believe how pretty some of these young ladies were!"

Charlotte wasn't sure how to respond. Did eleven-year-old boys already notice women? She knew Brendan often praised the beauty or the poise of young women they knew. But at what age had that begun? She couldn't remember. She ended up just nodding her head to encourage Thomas to continue talking.

"There were a few that my parents thought especially suitable," he said, staring ahead as though lost in memories. "But they were just so boring! I would call on them once or twice and realize I enjoyed better conversations with their parents or siblings than I did with them. I couldn't imagine a marriage where I spent evening after evening in awkward silence. That would be pure torture."

He stopped talking, and Charlotte felt that she needed to contribute more than a head nod.

"I always loved being around my parents after dinner. They could talk about anything or nothing and still seemed perfectly content to just be near each other. Most nights, Father would read aloud while Mother sewed or knitted. Brendan once commented to me that it just felt safe. That was the word he used- 'safe.' I think I would agree."

"My life was very different from yours," Thomas said, staring into the empty fireplace. "It wasn't until I was fourteen or fifteen that I really spent any time around my parents. They were wealthy socialites and were seldom home. I spent my early years surrounded by housekeepers, nannies, tutors, and maids. I assume that my parents loved each other, but I can't remember ever witnessing it firsthand. I want to do things differently when I'm married."

Several quiet minutes passed with only the sound of crickets chirping outside. It was such a familiar, comfortable silence.

"I want a marriage like Jason and Marnie, or Clara and Joseph," Thomas finally said. "I want the joy and the laughter and the teasing. I want someone to look at me the way they look at each other. And I want a whole passel of children. What about you, Charlie?"

Charlotte didn't even try to formulate an eleven-year-old boy answer. She just nodded her head in agreement.

"Ah, you're too young for such lofty conversations! I'm probably boring you to tears."

She wanted to tell him that no conversation had ever bored her less. But she needed to react as if she were an eleven-year-old boy.

"A little bit," she said.

Thomas exploded with laughter, and she couldn't stop her smile. Apparently, she'd responded perfectly for an eleven-year-old boy.

"Are you ready for bed," Thomas asked thirty minutes later.

"Yes," she responded drowsily. It had been a lovely evening talking with him, but she was ready to be alone with her thoughts. "I'll sleep upstairs in my own bed tonight. You should take the bedroom."

She walked to the bedroom and removed her extra clothes. Then she climbed the ladder to the loft.

"Goodnight, Charlie," Thomas called up to her.

"Goodnight, Thomas," she answered.

Chapter Twelve

Monday, August 19, 1867

In the wee hours of the morning, Charlotte awoke cold and shivering in her bed. She rolled over to snuggle with her sister. Little Ruthie was always so warm and cozy, as if her internal temperature was set slightly higher than that of others. Charlotte's outstretched arms found only the cold, empty edge of the bed. She let out a mournful wail as reality enveloped her.

Charlotte heard her parents' bedroom door swing open.

"Charlie," Thomas called. "Charlie, are you okay?"

She wanted to answer him. She wanted to stop the awful ache in her chest. She wanted to just die and not have to deal with this pain anymore. The wailing continued as if coming from a dark place deep inside her chest over which she had no control.

Thomas ran carefully across the cabin in the pitch black and hurriedly climbed the ladder. He could hardly bear the pain in Charlie's voice. It pulled him back into the moment when he'd first learned of Michael's death. He lay down next to the wailing boy and pulled him close.

"It's all right, Charlie," he whispered. "I'm here. Just let it all out. I've got you."

Charlie's agonizing wails almost broke the dam in Thomas' heart. All the pain Thomas had so carefully kept bottled up since learning of his little brother's death burst forth. It took every ounce of his resolve not to fall apart. He had no concept of time or place; he only knew he hurt.

When the sun began to pull itself up over the horizon, a soft glow filtered through the small window in the loft. Charlotte awakened to find herself staring into Thomas' sleeping face. Lightning crackled through her body at his nearness, and she carefully pushed herself to the other side of the bed. The movement woke Thomas, who sat up, yawned, and stretched his arms toward the ceiling.

"Are you okay, Charlie?"

Thomas ran his hand through his hair. Although it was August, the loft was unseasonably cold this morning. Charlotte immediately missed the warmth of his strong body lying on the bed beside her.

"I'm better now. Thank you."

Charlotte noticed her voice was shaking. Now that Thomas was sitting up, she lay staring at his broad, muscled back. She quickly sat up and wrapped the blanket around her tightly.

"Was it a nightmare?"

Thomas had turned around and was looking intently at the small face. The swelling was almost gone, but the tiny, black stitches matched the ugly black bruising on Charlie's cheeks. Now that both lids opened all the way, Thomas didn't think he'd ever seen eyes so vibrantly blue.

"No, I don't remember dreaming anything last night. I was just really cold when I woke up, and I—"

She stopped talking just in time and turned her head away. It would not do to have Thomas think that Charlie made a habit of crawling into bed with his sixteen-year-old sister.

"I thought about how warm Ruth's hugs always felt on cold days. And then it was like every other morning has been. I remembered she's gone. I remembered they're all gone."

She looked up into Thomas' kind face.

"I'm so sorry I woke you."

"You have simply evened the score. I'm the one who woke you with my screaming that first night," Thomas said, attempting to lighten the mood. He stood and walked to the ladder. "I'm going to go start some coffee brewing and get dressed to ride to the Crawford place."

"Thomas, I don't want to be here alone. What if those men come back?"

Thomas could hear the shakiness in Charlie's voice.

"I doubt they will backtrack, but we can certainly go together. I'll prepare the bodies, and you can decide where we should dig the graves."

"Sadly, the Crawfords already have a cemetery of sorts. They lost their twin babies last year. It was horrible."

After a hasty breakfast, Thomas and Charlotte set out for the Crawford home. The air was brisk and smelled faintly of pine. Just as she had yesterday, Charlotte concentrated on the beauty of her surroundings. She wanted to soak in every image. She knew that she wanted to remember this breathtaking country for as long as she lived.

Stealing a glance at the man riding next to her, she let her mind wander. Did Thomas have any farming experience? Would he be able to work the land as well as Brendan and Father did? He might have to hire one of the Albertson boys to come help occasionally. Even with Mother, Father, Brendan, and Charlotte busy from morning to night, there was always more to do each day than could be accomplished in a day's time.

She wondered what her life in Ireland would be like. She only had very vague memories from her childhood there. But even those memories bore no resemblance to the life she would now lead with her aunt and uncle in Killarney. Killarney was a large town with hotels and a rail station and so many shops. Her Uncle Jared co-owned a thriving general store that his grandfather, Jon Marshall, had established in the 1820s. Together with his brother, Darren, Jared kept his grandfather's legacy alive. She would be living a very different life than she lived here in Colorado. Instead of mountains and plains surrounding her, she would be surrounded by busy streets and buildings. These mountains called to her and she wondered if she would still feel their pull even across the ocean? Instead of the deep quiet she'd grown used to, she would live in the noise and bustle of the big city. Granted, it would be a relief to start over in a place where memories of Brendan, Ruthie, and her parents did not assail her every moment. And she knew she would be very happy with Fay and Sophie. It would be so lovely to have sisters with whom she could gossip and attend community gatherings. She'd never had that with Ruthie. A wave of guilt passed through her. But it wasn't betraying her love for sweet, innocent Ruth to long for female company.

Thomas began singing again and she laughed to herself. The man had no fear of what others thought. There weren't any other travelers on the road right now, but there could be at any moment. Yesterday she had begged him to stop singing when they saw a carriage approaching in the far distance. He accommodated her, and they passed the carriage in silence. The moment the carriage passed, he immediately resumed his boisterous song. She had been mortified! Seeing no one in either direction, Charlotte decided to join him, and the rest of their ride to the Crawford property was spent in song.

When they arrived at the front gate, Thomas stopped his horse. The burned remains of the cabin and barn were about a hundred and fifty yards ahead.

"Alright, Charlie, which direction is the cemetery?"

"It's past the cabin and through those trees," she said, pointing to the west.

"I'd prefer to get things cleaned up a little before you come down there. Do you mind waiting here?"

"No, let me take Trigger and Meg down to the trough. I won't look in the direction of the cabin."

He handed her the reins and took off walking toward the homestead. Charlotte could see several big, black turkey vultures around the house and barn. The thought sickened her. It had now been four or five days since they were killed. Would there even be anything left to bury? With a heavy heart, she began leading the horses to the trough.

She heard Thomas yell, and looked over to see him flapping his arms in an attempt to disperse the vultures. Hus efforts were not producing much of an effect. The birds would fly away from one spot and then return almost immediately when Thomas moved to the next spot. Had her dear friends been torn apart by the nasty birds?

Thomas took out his pistol and fired several shots into the air. That finally caused the birds to fly away some distance. They landed about fifty feet away from him. She saw Thomas walking about and realized he was going from one body to another. He bent down a few times, and she guessed he was retrieving personal items. Finally, he began making his way back to where she stood with the horses, who were contentedly eating their fill of the lush green grass around the water trough.

"Charlie, I'm so glad you didn't see that. There's not much…there isn't a whole lot left to bury," Thomas said and rubbed his hand over his face. "I'm so sorry. We just didn't have time on…we didn't have time when we left on Thursday."

In his anguish, he was tripping over his words, and she felt bad for him.

"It's not your fault, Thomas."

Reaching for his hand would have been the most natural thing right now, except that she was a boy.

"What should we do?"

"I'm going to collect the remains into the grain bag I brought, and we'll bury them all together. We can eventually make separate grave markers with each name."

He turned to untie the empty bag from his saddle. Then he quickly pivoted back to face her.

"I almost forgot about these."

He reached into his pocket, pulling out a pocket watch and a locket.

"While at the land office, I got the address for their next of kin. We can mail these items to them when we're in Denver City."

Charlotte turned the locket over in her hand. She knew this locket well. Her friend Nancy was so proud of it and had worn it every day since her mother gave it to her last year for her sixteenth birthday. It was a family heirloom which had belonged to her mother and grandmother before her. Sweet, fun-loving Nancy had not a mean bone in her body, and yet she had died in such a horrible, violent way. It just wasn't right.

"The Crawfords were really good people," Charlotte said softly, and placed the pocket watch and locket in her saddlebag.

Thomas was holding the grain bag and a shovel in one hand. With the other he reached over and squeezed her shoulder.

"I know it's hard to remember this sometimes, Charlie. But the world truly is a good place filled with mostly good people. We can't let the evil ones ruin our outlook."

He turned and began walking back to collect the remains. She knew he spoke the truth. And yet, it was so difficult to understand how God allowed such horrible things to happen to good people.

Her mother's words rang in her ear: "Charlotte, if God stopped every bad thing from happening, it might be lovely, but it would cost us our free will. He is perfect love, and He wants nothing more than for us to live in perfect love. But He will not override our free will. Evil exists in the world not because God wills it; only because He loves us too much to control us."

Charlotte wondered how the three men who had carried out these atrocious acts had become so evil. She firmly believed that all babies were born with a blank slate and great potential. What people grew up to become was determined by their upbringing and experiences. So, what had these men experienced to turn them into such merciless killers? She decided she didn't want to follow that train of thought and shook her head as though to clear it.

She looked over to see Thomas shoveling. With a shudder, she realized there weren't even actual bodies to place in the grain bag. How horrific!

Soon, Thomas was waving her over. She pulled the reins gently and the two horses stopped eating and began to walk behind her. As she drew close, an overwhelming stench assailed her nostrils. A wave of nausea hit her, causing her to lean over and throw up on the grass. How had Thomas worked over here for so long? The smell was absolutely horrible.

"Sorry, I forgot to warn you," he said with a grimace. "It's been so hot these last few days, and they've been here for a while."

Charlotte used her free hand to pinch her nose. "The cemetery is over here," she said in a nasal voice. She began walking briskly away from Thomas and the large, very full bag he was carrying. What an undignified way to be buried, she thought. Her poor friends!

When they reached a beautiful grove of trees, Thomas saw two makeshift grave markers. There was a slight breeze rustling through the oak leaves and causing the wildflowers to dance. What a fitting place this was to honor the dead. Charlotte and Thomas took turns digging the grave and were done before the sun had reached the middle of the sky. Digging a grave for this bag was very different from digging a grave for a full-length body. As they stood over the mound of dirt covering the whole Crawford family, Charlotte wished she had remembered to bring her family's Bible. After her remorse over the lack of ceremony when they buried her family, she should have remembered it. Thomas led an Our Father, and they stood in silence for a few more moments.

As they walked back towards the road, Thomas stopped.

"Let's gather these poor, hungry pigs and we can come back tomorrow for the cattle."

The four pigs were released from their pen and seemed ready to follow their rescuers without argument. Thomas wiped his forehead with a bandana.

"Are you ready to go home?"

His question caused Charlotte's throat to close and her heart to swell. She nodded her assent.

Home. With Thomas. Home. It was a lovely thought. She climbed atop Meg and waited for Thomas to fasten the shovel to his saddle and mount up. His face was covered with stubble, and she wondered if he was going to return to the shaggy look.

"Are you going to let your facial hair grow out again?"

He hesitated before answering.

"I haven't decided yet. It caused one hell of an uproar when I had it shaved. I'm feeling like I should maybe have left it."

"Thomas, I'm sorry about that—"

"No, it wasn't just you," he interrupted. "Everyone made such a fuss that I really felt embarrassed. I prefer it shaved, but…I don't know. We'll see."

"Well, I think it looks better shaved."

"Thanks, Charlie," he said. Then he looked more closely at her face. "I guess you'll have to start shaving soon, yourself. How old was Brendan when he began shaving?"

"I don't really remember," Charlotte had to admit. Then she laughed and continued. "What I do remember is this ridiculous little mustache he grew last year. Mother hated it with a passion and begged him to shave it off. Father thought it was funny and encouraged Mother to just not worry about it. 'He'll shave it before we go to Mass next,' he'd told Mother, while giving Brendan a stern look. Father was always kind, and he had a wonderful sense of humor, but we knew not to disobey him. He was not one to accept disrespect or argument. We all knew that he meant what he said. Anyway, Brendan ended up shaving it not for Mass in Denver City, but because Nancy Crawford hadn't liked it. Brendan fancied Nancy, and her distaste was all it took for that mustache to disappear. My gosh! We certainly teased him about that!"

Charlotte ended with a sigh. How sad that Nancy and Brendan were both dead now. So much had changed in not even a week. A week ago, she was surrounded by a loving, happy family. A week ago, she saw herself traveling for a spell and then marrying and settling somewhere near her family and raising children of her own. She imagined being a farmer's wife and enjoying a life very much like she'd always known. A week ago, she'd never met Thomas. A week ago, she'd never been in love. Love? Was this love, she wondered. Yes, love. She was sure that this was love.

The slow pace of the pigs doubled the travel time back to Kerry Haven. They finally arrived, sweaty and hungry.

"This heat is just oppressive! I think I'll go for a swim after lunch," Thomas said. "How far away was that stream you mentioned? The one that Brendan loved."

Charlotte wiped her face with a bandana.

"You're right about the heat. This is miserable. The stream is only about three hundred yards past the house. It's so cold and refreshing. You're going to love it! It may be my favorite spot on the whole property."

"That sounds perfect," he said, dismounting from Trigger with a grunt. "Oh, I'm looking forward to a few days out of the saddle. Maybe tomorrow we can walk the property, and you can fill me in on your father's plans."

"I'd like that," she said, sobering at the thought of all the projects her father would never accomplish. She looked over at Thomas. At least he would be the one purchasing the land. She knew it would be well maintained, and cherished. She only felt sad that she wouldn't be around to see it all.

"Now that tomorrow is settled, would you prefer lunch preparation, or horse and pig duty," Thomas asked with a grin.

"Definitely lunch!"

Charlotte climbed down from Meg and handed Thomas the reins. "We can have cheese and sausage with the last of the biscuits for lunch, and then I want to cook a real meal tonight."

"A real meal? Anything that fills the belly is a real meal, Charlie."

"You know what I mean," she argued. "Something that you smell before you even enter the cabin; something that makes your mouth water and your stomach growl. Something delicious."

"Sounds like you're describing those biscuits of yours," Thomas countered, good-naturedly.

"Well, you sure are easy to please," she said, shaking her head. He turned to lead the horses into the barn, and she watched as he walked away. She thought about the bolt of lightning she'd experienced when they woke together this morning, and her face flushed. Oh, why did he have to be so good-looking?

Before entering the cabin, Charlotte visited the root cellar and grabbed everything she needed. She thought about all the hours the family had spent building the cellar and the pride they felt as each new crop they harvested added to their stores. Mother had been so skilled in her gardens. Charlotte wondered if she would ever garden again once she moved to Killarney with the Marshalls. She would miss gardening, but not the damn chickens! She hoped to never own chickens again.

Laden with vegetables, Charlotte walked through the door to find Thomas already in the cabin. He was eating one of the leftover biscuits.

"Sorry," he said sheepishly, wiping crumbs from his mustache. "I didn't know where you were and thought I could sneak one before we sat down to eat."

"Your excessive love for those biscuits truly amuses me."

Charlotte set down the vegetables on the chopping block. "We're going to have stew and cornbread tonight. I hope that will suffice."

"Ah, stew," Thomas replied, in mock rapture. "I can't wait!" He thought about how fortunate it was that Mrs. Gallagher had taught her sons to cook. This skill would serve Charlie well in the future.

"Tell me about your family in Ireland, Charlie. Do you know much about them?"

Charlotte grabbed the dried sausage and cheese, and placed them on the table. Then she reached up to the shelf and removed two plates and the bowl of biscuits that sat covered with a linen cloth. She sat down at the table across from Thomas and they bowed their heads to pray.

After the blessing, Charlotte answered his query.

"My mother was the oldest sibling of the Winchester family. Betsy is four years younger, and then there were two brothers, Robert and William. William died young, and Robert never married. He raises goats and sheep in

Killorglin, and regularly visits Betsy and her husband, Jared. He didn't think the name Robert suited him well, so instead he went by his surname, Winchester. I remember him being the most fun adult I knew. All of us children looked forward to Uncle Winchester's visits. Betsy and Jared had three children when we left Ireland; Fay, William, and Henry. Sophie was born six years ago, so we haven't met her. Betsy, Winchester, and Mother wrote to each other often, and it was always so exciting when we visited the post office in Denver City. Mother would read the letters aloud so we could all enjoy them. Letters are, of course, a poor substitute for visiting in person, but Betsy and Winchester wrote so well that I feel I know them all."

She stopped to take a bite of cheese.

"The Marshalls- Betsy and Jared and their children, live in Killarney, on the northeastern shore of Lough Leane. I remember the lake being very beautiful. Uncle Jared and his brother, Darren Marshall, run a general store. I remember Darren would always sneak us candy when we visited the store." She paused to eat a bite more.

"It's astonishing that you remember anything at all," Thomas commented. "You must have been so young when your family left."

Charlotte realized that, had she kept talking, she could have easily revealed her lie. She needed to remember that she was claiming to be eleven, and would have been only around three years old when her family emigrated.

"Yes, I have only a few vague memories. Most of the information I have is from Aunt Betsy's letters. I do remember that Killarney was a busy city. I'm curious to see it again. And I'm very much looking forward to getting reacquainted with my cousins."

Thomas smiled. "I'm happy you'll have family that loves you. There's nothing better than family." He thought about all that Charlie had lost. No one would ever replace the boy's siblings or parents, but at least he would be surrounded by love.

"Do you need some rabbit or squirrel for the stew," Thomas asked a few minutes later as they were both finishing their lunch.

"That would be wonderful! I was going to use some of the salted pork, but fresh meat would be so much better."

"Wish me luck, then!"

Thomas grabbed his rifle and left the cabin.

Charlotte began cleaning and chopping the vegetables. Dinner would be delicious! She had never minded cooking but hated the tedious, boring prep work. Aunt Betsy and Uncle Jared kept a cook, and Charlotte thought how nice it would be to have someone else doing prep work and cleaning up afterwards. Yes, she could grow accustomed to that. But life would be very different in Killarney. There were so many things she would have to change in order to be a "proper lady." In Killarney, so many of the freedoms afforded her in Colorado would be cause for scandal. No longer could she ride her horse where she pleased, or take long solitary walks. It would no longer be acceptable to go out without a suitable chaperone. And, if anyone in Ireland ever found out about her unchaperoned acquaintance with Thomas, she would be ruined! She would have to be so careful when she talked about her life here. She smiled to herself as she thought of how scandalous her current situation was. And yet, after their first meeting, she'd never felt a moment of alarm around Thomas. How she wished she didn't have to leave him or her life here.

She sighed. And then remembered one last thing, perhaps the worst thing, about life as a "proper lady." Once she embarked for Ireland, she would be expected to wear a corset and stays every waking hour and not just on Sundays for Mass. She hated wearing corsets and thought them ridiculous. All the things she used to find so detestable when Mother talked about "proper ladies" would become her daily reality.

Once she finished chopping, Charlotte scooped the onions, carrots, and potatoes into the cauldron. Picking up the empty earthenware pitcher, she quickly walked out to the well. The beauty of the mountains never failed to delight her. After living most of her life looking at the majestic Rockies morning, noon, and night, she wondered what it would be like without them. She hoped that Aunt Betsy still took frequent walks to the lake. Charlotte knew she would go crazy surrounded by buildings all day. Even during her family's brief visits to Denver City for Sunday Mass, she craved the solitude of home. How she would miss the silence!

As if on cue, a gunshot shattered the stillness. Charlotte chuckled to herself. Thomas couldn't have planned that better! She wondered what he'd found. Would they be eating squirrel stew, or rabbit stew tonight? She was not curious for long. By the time she had added the water to the cauldron and built a fire in the hearth, Thomas walked in carrying a large, skinned rabbit.

"Excellent," Charlotte said.

Thomas sat down at the table, placed the carcass on the cutting board, and began removing the meat from the bones.

"You won't believe how perfectly timed your shot was, Thomas. I was at the well pumping water and my mind drifted to the noisiness of Killarney and how much I will miss the still quietness of life here. Right then, your shot rang out and broke the silence. The irony of it gave me a laugh."

Thomas looked up with a playful smile. "It took a great amount of planning, I tell you! You'll not find another with my split-second accuracy and precision."

His laughter filled the cabin, and she longed to stay in this moment forever. What would happen, she wondered, if she just admitted her true identity? Could Thomas ever love her? He was already so protective and caring of her as Charlie. Could he love Charlotte? Could he forgive her for hiding her identity if he knew she had only done it out of fear?

She allowed herself to imagine marriage to Thomas and a life spent here, living with the freedom to which she was accustomed. A life filled with his smiles and laughter and kindness. A life filled with his love. Was she brave enough to tell him who she was?

"Now this can simmer while we go swim in the stream," Thomas said, interrupting her beautiful reverie.

She was shocked to see that he had already added the meat to the cauldron and was washing his hands over the washbasin. Her face grew hot, and she hoped he couldn't see her blush.

"I," she stammered. "I need to have some time alone to concentrate on the letter to my aunt and uncle."

"Aw, but you've earned a break," Thomas argued. "And I will solemnly promise to leave you in peace this evening so you can write." He could understand that Charlie didn't want him around when tasked with such an emotional letter. But there would be time for writing later. "Please come with me," he pleaded.

The heat was stifling, and Charlotte longed to cool off in the stream almost as much as she longed to spend time having fun with Thomas. But there was no way she could go swimming without revealing that she was a woman, and she wasn't prepared to tell him just yet. She needed time to think about the best way to talk with him. Obviously, he'd be upset, but hopefully she could present it in a way that didn't anger him more than was necessary. She needed to plan her approach.

"I'll walk you down to the stream, but then I need to come back and write," she said, trying to sound firm and decisive. "Besides, the cornbread isn't going to bake itself!"

"Too true! And if your mother's cornbread recipe is as good as her biscuit recipe, I certainly don't want to miss out!"

"My Mother would have loved you. She was always so pleased when we liked her cooking, but I don't think any of us ever got as excited over even her best meals as you do over simple biscuits."

"What can I say," he chuckled. "Simple biscuits have won my heart."

"How sad," Charlotte said, raising her eyebrows and shrugging her shoulders. "I guess our matchmaking contest is over before it even really began. There will be many heartbroken young ladies in Denver City tonight." And one right here, she thought, ruefully, as Thomas doubled over in laughter.

When Thomas stripped off his shirt and laid it over the chair, Charlotte had to look away. The sight of his bare chest did peculiar things to her insides. She suddenly regretted offering to walk him to the stream.

"Well, let's go," he said, turning toward the door. "How deep is this stream? I can't wait to cool off."

The stream was a five-minute walk from the house, and they chatted the whole time. Charlotte concentrated on looking ahead, constantly fighting the urge to turn and stare at his broad shoulders and strong arms. She was finding it difficult to breathe.

Thomas was pleasantly surprised to find the stream wider than he'd imagined. The thick trees along both banks provided cool shade and the crystal-clear water looked incredibly inviting. Before Charlotte realized his intention, he had stripped off his pants and drawers and walked naked into the water. She quickly turned around.

"I'll see you back at the cabin," she called, before rushing off. Good heavens!

Thomas was baffled by Charlie's behavior. He'd assumed that once they reached the stream, he would be able to convince the boy to stay and swim. But Charlie was halfway back to the cabin already. Oh, well. The water felt unbelievably refreshing, and was so deep in some spots that he couldn't touch the bottom. He looked around and was surprised that Brendan and Charlie hadn't put up a rope swing over this deep area. That would be one of his first projects this week! He remembered the hours of fun he and Michael always had on rope swings when visiting the Ohio River. There was nothing like that brief moment between releasing the rope, and being enveloped by the water. Sometimes he felt he might be able to fly. Thoughts of Michael were still painful, but he could now focus on the happy times. He smiled more often than not when he remembered his little brother. What a life they could have made out here together! Michael would have loved everything about this place. At least he could bring Emily to share in the adventure.

When Thomas grew chilled from the icy water, he made his way to the bank and pulled on his drawers. Then he lay down on the soft grass and let the August air warm him. He still couldn't believe his good fortune. Kerry Haven was beyond anything he could have ever hoped to find.

Charlotte returned to the cabin flustered and out of breath. She had never seen a naked man. Her family swam in the stream almost daily during the hot summers, but her father and Brendan always left their breeches on out of respect for the ladies of the family. Again, her face flushed at the thought of his broad shoulders and long, muscular legs. She was infinitely thankful he hadn't turned around. A bare backside was shocking enough! How would she ever be able to face him at dinner tonight? The embarrassment would be overwhelming.

After stirring the contents of the cauldron, she sat down at the small desk in the living area and pulled out a piece of paper. It was time to write to her aunt and uncles to notify them of her family's demise. She sat in distracted silence for several long minutes. Finally, she realized she was still far too flustered to form coherent thought. The sooner she left for Ireland, the better. Thomas' presence was becoming far too disturbing.

She stood up and began pulling out ingredients for the cornbread. It was much too early to begin baking it, for it would only take about thirty minutes to cook, but she desperately needed something to do. Otherwise, her disobedient mind would keep wandering back to things no proper lady should be pondering; like how sensational it felt to wake up with him this morning, and what it would feel like if he kissed her.

An hour had passed when Thomas returned to the cabin to find Charlie sitting at the table with a large stack of letters. There were tears streaming down the boy's face, and Thomas felt horrible for invading his privacy. Those must be the letters from his aunt and uncle.

Thomas was at a loss for what he should do. Would it be best to put his shirt on and leave the cabin again? Should he encourage Charlie to talk more about his family? Damn, he had no idea how to handle the situation.

"I was just reading through all these letters from Ireland," Charlotte offered, weakly. She couldn't bring herself to look up at Thomas. Then she cursed herself. Her stupid infatuation with this man was going to ruin their easy camaraderie.

"I tried to write to tell them about Mother and Father and Brendan and Ruth, but I...I just couldn't find the words." Her heart felt like it might shatter into a million pieces.

Thomas moved one of the chairs until it was right next to Charlie's. Then he sat down and pulled the boy into a hug.

"Charlie, I wish I knew how to take this pain from you."

He brushed the boy's hair back from his tear-streaked face. Charlie's blue eyes met his, and Thomas almost gasped at the pain he glimpsed in their depths. "I can only promise you that it will hurt a little less with time."

After several long minutes, Charlotte pulled herself from Thomas' embrace and sat up straight in her chair. How was it possible to feel so wonderful and so horrible at the same time? Her heart was simultaneously breaking at her horrific loss and rejoicing at Thomas' touch. Was now the right time to tell him? She wanted him to keep holding her forever, but she wanted him to hold *Charlotte* close, not Charlie.

Before she could decide whether to speak up, or stay silent, Thomas stood up and walked to the hearth.

"This stew smells delicious!" he exclaimed. "You continue to astonish me, Charlie."

No, she decided. Now was not the right time to tell him.

"Thank you. How was your swim?"

"Extraordinarily refreshing," he answered turning back to face her. "I can't believe you and Brendan don't have a rope swing in one of those trees!"

"We actually did, until it snapped a few weeks ago," she said, laughing at the memory of Brendan hurtling through the air holding the broken rope. It felt good to laugh. All the uneasiness she felt only moments ago dissolved. How easy Thomas made it to love him.

"Now that I would have loved to see! Who was on it when it snapped?"

"Brendan was, and boy did he fly! It was hilarious. I've never seen Ruth laugh so hard. She just kept saying, 'Again! Again!' Ruthie never went into the water with us, but she enjoyed coming down to the stream and watching us swim."

"I love hearing you talk about them," Thomas said softly, looking to make sure his words didn't hurt Charlie. "It makes me wish I'd known you all before the tragedy."

"Me, too," Charlotte answered. "They would have loved you." Then, she cleared her throat and stood up, asking, "Who's ready to learn how to bake cornbread?"

Thomas pulled his shirt back on and came to stand next to her. "This might be a dangerous skill for me you to teach me," he said with a grin. Charlotte shot him a quizzical look.

"Well, if I learn to make too many delicious things, I might never leave the cabin again."

"Good grief! I've honestly never seen someone so enthusiastic about baked goods!"

Chapter Thirteen

Monday, August 19, 1867

They sat down to dinner later that evening and Charlotte was pleased when she tasted the stew and cornbread. Both had turned out better than usual.

"Mmmmm…these are perfect," she said, with a satisfied sigh.

"I think this might be the best cornbread I've ever tasted. Of course, it probably just tastes so good because I made it myself."

Charlotte chuckled and shook her head. He had an effortless way of making her laugh and she couldn't get enough of it.

"Yes, you're terrifically gifted. I'm so glad you showed me how to make this. Maybe next time you can teach me how to make the stew."

Thomas' green eyes sparkled with amusement. She'd never seen such beautiful eyes and she loved the way they crinkled in the corners when he smiled.

When Thomas had finished his third serving, he stood and covered the cauldron with his plate. "I will sleep like a hibernating bear tonight."

He stretched his arms wide as he yawned. Charlotte stood to begin cleaning and putting away the food, but Thomas stopped her.

"You cooked. I'll clean up. But let's just visit now. I need to digest my dinner before I begin cleaning." He walked to the living area and sat in Mother's chair. "I'm really interested in knowing more about your family in Ireland, Charlie. Would you feel comfortable reading some of the letters aloud?"

"Of course. I would like that." She picked up the letters from the desk where she'd placed them before dinner.

"April 3, 1860

Dear Annie,

I can't believe it's only been three weeks since you and your family left. It feels so weird to not have you just a few doors down. A hundred times a day I think of something funny I want to tell you next I see you. Or something I need to ask you.

How I miss our daily chats! Coffee and tea aren't nearly as nice when I drink them alone. I continue to serve at the soup kitchen you and I started so many years ago. But it's so different without you by my side. The number of needy families continues to drop, thank the Lord! Yesterday, we only had thirty-five people come through the line. It's unbelievable to think that there were years where we averaged two hundred a day! How thankful I am that our country continues to recover from the famine.

I'm hoping and praying that you are having a safe, calm voyage. Every time I hear from anyone who has made the trip across the Atlantic, I wonder if I will ever have the courage to do it. Jared assures me we have a future in America once the time is right, but I confess I find the prospect daunting! Of course, the older the children get, the easier it will be, I suppose.

There's nothing really exciting here to write about. William and Fay have each lost several more teeth. They look so cute and funny with their snaggled smiles. I love this age! I will close this boring letter before I put you and me both to sleep. Please be assured of my constant thoughts and prayers. Your little sister, Betsy"

"September 1862
"Oh, Annie! Your last letter had me laughing uproariously! I cannot believe Charlo—

Charlotte quickly corrected herself,

"I cannot believe Charlie painted Ruth's pony! How funny that must have been. Did Ruthie love it? I can almost hear her sweet, infectious laughter."
"Henry is now attending St. Brendan's Seminary with William. As you can imagine, he is overjoyed and proud to be attending school with his big brother. Many students come from far away and take room and board at the school. I feel blessed that I have my boys at home with me each evening. Their constant noise and messes can feel overwhelming, but I know that they are mine for such a short time. Soon, they will be married and have families of their own, and I will miss these days."
"I allude to marriage, but lately William talks often of the priesthood. He's only twelve, and much could change in the next few years, however, I love the idea of having possibly raised a priest. What an honor that would be, dear sister! I always thought our dear brother Will would end up ordained. Can you believe he's been gone seven years now? I still miss him every hour of every day. What fun we all had growing up! Did any four siblings ever love each other as we did, Annie? You and Winchester and Will were the best friends a little sister could ask for."

Charlotte choked back tears. She and Brendan and Ruth had loved each other that way.

"I think we both experienced that sort of sibling bond," Thomas said, softly. "It sounds like you and Brendan and Ruthie sure did."

Charlotte nodded, and then kept reading.

"Fay is thirteen now and attends Loreto Convent, a secondary school for young women. She is intelligent and dedicated to her studies, resulting in the highest marks in her class. Jared and I are so proud of her accomplishments. Her future husband will have a wife that is not only well-versed in running a household, but also smart and educated. And she's so generous and helpful around the house. I simply don't know what I'd do without her sweet temperament and amusing conversation.

Sophie is a delight and is spoiled by the whole family. With her constant smiles and her abundance of hugs she brings sunshine into every day! Oh, sister, I wish you could meet her. Keep praying that we will soon be together in America. I know it will happen eventually.

Jared and Darren are doing so well with the general store that they've decided to open up a second location! As Ireland continues to recover from the great famine, Marshall and Sons can hardly keep their shelves stocked. Grandpa Jon pops by occasionally, but I think he knows his sons are great managers and he can relax. He and Donna are such wonderful people and I'm so thankful every day that I married into this loving family.

I close this letter and seal it with all my love and affection. Your little sister, Betsy"

"December 23, 1865
Dearest Annie,
It's so odd to be writing you Christmas greetings, knowing that you will most likely be reading this letter in June or July! I always get a bit sad around Christmas and Will's birthday. He would have been thirty-three tomorrow. The children and I will make a cake and we'll enjoy his favorite meal for supper. With relief, I find it's easier to think about him now than it was a few years ago. I no longer feel that sharp stab through the heart. It's more like a constant, dull ache. But I remind myself that Will has just won the race and crossed the finish line ahead of us. We will all be together someday in Heaven. I wonder if he will still have his odd sense of humor. How he could make me laugh! Do you remember when I burned my nose laughing at Will? I had just taken a very hot sip of tea when he described that mangy dog down the street. The scalding hot tea shot out of my nose and I was in pain for several days!"

"Who was the funniest of the three of you," Charlotte asked Thomas.

"Definitely Michael. He was funny and mischievous and always in some sort of quandary. My little brother could find trouble like no one else! I remember one time when he accidentally set the carriage house on fire. He must have been about six years old and had escaped from the nanny. Emily and I were still in the school room working on our lessons when we heard a commotion in the kitchen. We arrived in time to find Michael gesticulating to the cook. He was panting and out of breath. 'Fire! Fire,' he finally managed to yell as he pointed out the back door. By the time we ran outside, the kindly old coachman, Jacob, was frantically pumping water into a bucket. Michael and I grabbed more buckets and, within a few minutes, the three of us had the fire out. Michael begged Jacob not to tell our father. We promised that we would repair all the damage. We were so scared. Michael didn't want to get a beating, and I didn't want to see him hurt. Well, Jacob took pity on him and said he would not offer any information to my father. 'But, if he asks me, you know I won't lie,' he said."

"Did your father ever find out?"

Thomas chuckled. "No, he never did. My father always had his horse brought around to the front of the house for him. And, when he returned to the house, he always dismounted at the front steps and had the horse taken back to the stable for him. He never did see the damage, and we worked with Jacob to get it all repaired."

Thomas laughed again. "Jacob was a good, kind man."

There was a lull in the conversation, and Charlie yawned deeply.

"I'll clean up down here, son," Thomas said. "Why don't you get on to bed?"

"Yes, I probably should. After all, this wound has healed so well," she gingerly touched her stitched up forehead. "The last thing I want is to fall asleep while climbing the ladder and bust open the other side!"

Thomas snorted in laughter, which made Charlotte laugh, too. She stood up from her chair and turned toward the ladder. Then, she pivoted and walked to Thomas' chair. Leaning down, she gave him a big hug.

"Thank you so much for everything, Thomas. I don't know what I would be doing right now without you."

With that, she turned and swiftly climbed up the ladder and to bed.

Chapter Fourteen

Tuesday, August 20, 1867

Charlotte awoke to thoughts of Thomas. She needed to tell him today. The deception was gnawing away at her. She simply could not continue to lie to this wonderful man. They would spend today walking around the property, and she would have plenty of uninterrupted time to tell him. How would he react? She couldn't bear the thought of him leaving or asking her to leave. She wished that she could just remain here as a cook or housemaid. Thomas could build his life around her and she could stay here, close to her family's graves, her mountains, and all that was familiar.

She quickly dressed and went downstairs to start the coffee and begin preparing breakfast. Thomas must have heard her, for when she returned to the cabin with a jug of water from the well, he was seated at the table. He was tousled and barely awake, but his smile lit up the room.

"Good morning, Charlie," he said with a huge yawn. "What recipe will you be teaching me today?"

She laughed. "Today you will be learning tortillas."

"Tortillas? I've never heard of them."

"Oh, just wait until you try one. They're delicious! My mother learned to make them from a Mexican trail cook when a group of miners stopped here on the way to the mining camp. They'd come from South Texas, and we heard so many interesting stories from them."

"Excellent. I'm always ready to try new food items."

Thomas came to stand beside her at the stove. He yawned and scratched his chest.

"Is there coffee? I need coffee to awaken my culinary genius."

"Oh, Thomas," she said, shaking her head as she grabbed a mug from the shelf and handed it to him. How did his every comment make her so happy? "The coffee will be ready in a few minutes."

"Where do we begin," he asked.

"Well, the tortillas are more labor intensive than the eggs, so we start with them. I'm making a double batch so we can have them for a few meals. That is, if someone can control himself!"

She grabbed a small bag of salt and a larger bag of flour and turned to the table.

"First, we wipe off the table, which I've already done. Next, we begin setting up our ingredients. Will you grab those two bowls, please," she asked, pointing to a pair of large blue bowls on the highest shelf.

Thomas procured the bowls and set them on the table in front of him.

"We'll need one and a half cups of warm water," Charlotte instructed, pointing to the cauldron of boiling water hanging over the fire in the hearth. She handed him a ladle. "Five of these should be just about right."

Thomas scooped five full ladles into the large bowl and returned to the table.

"Next, you'll add two teaspoons of salt."

He grabbed the spoon and quickly added two scoops of salt to the steaming water in the bowl.

"Now, we'll wait a few minutes for the salt to dissolve into the water, and for the water to cool to room temperature. In this bowl, we'll mix the flour and lard." She indicated a large bag of flour and a crock of lard. "Measure out four cups of flour and one cup of lard."

Thomas added both to the bowl and then turned to Charlie for the next instructions. The boy looked exhausted. How had he not noticed that before?

"Did you sleep okay last night, Charlie?"

"Not great."

"Was I screaming again?" Thomas wondered if he would ever get past the night terrors and sleep peacefully through the night.

"No. It wasn't you. I keep having nightmares of the attack and I wake up in a panic. When I'm finally able to calm my racing heart, grief takes over and I lie awake for hours reliving old memories."

"Oh, Charlie," Thomas said, and moved to put his arm around Charlotte's shoulder. He pulled her close to his side. "I know from experience that it helps if you talk about it. The more you talk about your loved ones and remember the good times, the less it hurts. Please know I'm here to listen anytime."

"Thank you, Thomas," Charlotte said, turning to face him. "I truly don't know what I'd do without you."

There was so much more that she wanted to say to him. He was standing so close to her and again, she pondered what his lips would feel like on hers.

"I think the coffee is probably ready now," she stammered and pulled away from him. If Thomas noticed the high color in her cheeks, he didn't mention it.

He poured a cup of coffee and then returned to her side.

"Okay," she said in a matter-of-fact tone. "Use this fork to mix the lard and flour together."

After they mixed the salt water into the flour-lard mixture, Charlotte showed Thomas how to knead it. Then they let the dough sit for a few minutes before turning it out of the bowl onto the floured surface of the table. Rolling the dough out thin enough was more difficult than Thomas had imagined. The first few tortillas he cooked were way too thick and resulted in hard, ugly disks. He tasted one and grimaced. Once they both stopped laughing, Charlotte patiently showed him again how to roll the dough thinner. It was one of the best mornings Thomas had ever experienced. This boy was so witty and fun.

"What would you like to see first," Charlotte asked once they'd finished breakfast and cleaned up their mess.

"I'd like to start by walking the perimeter. I worked it out last night and, if this property is a square, each side would be about two thirds of a mile."

"It's more of a rectangle, with the north and south sides shorter than the east and west. But it's still something we could walk in a few hours. I can't wait for you to see it all!"

Thomas grabbed his hat and two canteens hanging on the hat rack. Charlotte grabbed her father's sombrero. Once the canteens were filled at the pump, they set off. The morning air was not yet hot, and there was a nice breeze blowing. Charlotte was determined to be honest with Thomas today. It was past time for that!

They walked north up the long driveway to the road and then turned west. East would have taken them toward Denver City. Thomas thought of the wonderful friends they'd made there. Before leaving, he'd told them he would be returning in a few weeks, and he was already looking forward to the next visit.

"Putting up this fencing was one of the first tasks Father accomplished when we arrived," Charlotte said, as they approached sturdy wooden fencing. "We had the two oxen with us, and Father purchased twenty head of cattle once he had a fenced-in pasture for them."

"How large is their pasture? And what's their water source?"

"Father and Brendan added to the pasture several times over the years. It now encompasses thirty of the seventy-five acres. There's a small pond towards the far end of the pasture. The cattle have plenty of grass and several areas of shade. We have about forty head now."

"That's impressive! I'll certainly have my hands full!"

"Yep. You might have to hire someone to help you out here. Maybe one of the Albertson boys would be interested."

"I've been thinking that same exact thing."

Soon, they came to a corner in the fencing.

"This is where Kerry Haven meets up with the Crawford's land."

They turned south and kept walking.

"I wonder what will happen with their property," she mused a few minutes later. "I know they had family back in Boston, but, from what Nancy and her brothers said, I can't imagine they are the sort of people to want to leave their home for life in the Wild West."

"I'm anxious to see what the clerk at the land office finds out. I think I might like to buy this land if the Crawford family members aren't interested. Then, Emily could set up house next to me if she wanted. She would have plenty of land for starting a life and family of her own someday."

"That would be wonderful," Charlotte said. Maybe this was the moment to tell him.

But Thomas continued talking.

"I feel so protective of her. It will be a miracle if any man ever meets my standards," he said, chuckling softly. "Poor Emily, I imagine overbearing older brothers are not fun."

"Brendan was super protective, too. But I kind of liked it," Charlotte countered, smiling at him. "He really was such a great big brother. Ruth had her small pony but could only ride it if someone walked alongside her and led the pony. She loved to ride, and Brendan was so accommodating. He made sure she got to ride every single day. He would lead her pony or pull Ruthie up on his horse with him and gallop all around. Riding fast was her very favorite thing to do and her laughter was Brendan's constant goal. He truly did all he could to make her happy. And me. He made us all so happy."

"He almost sounds too good to be true," Thomas offered.

"He was. I will miss him as long as I live."

Soon Thomas saw the large herd of Shorthorn cattle congregating around the pond. They looked fat and healthy, and Thomas noticed several cows with young calves at their sides. He needed to ask Charlie to teach him how to make butter. There were so many things he'd need to learn if he was going to make it here alone.

"How many calves were born this spring?"

"There were ten born. We lost one to coyotes. Father said we needed to find a good cattle dog to protect the herd."

"I'll add that to the growing list of things I need to accomplish and procure while in Denver City."

"Are you still thinking of going back at the end of the month?"

"Yes. I want to draw funds from the bank to pay you for this land and possibly purchase the Crawford's property. I'll ask around for a good dog breeder and hopefully we can bring one home with us. We can check to see if there is any mail waiting at the post office for your family. And we can inquire about travel to Ireland if you're still thinking that the best option."

"Thomas, I've been meaning to talk with you about that."

Charlotte stopped walking and Thomas turned around to face her. Charlotte took a deep breath, fully intending to tell him who she was. To her dismay, she still found herself unable to do it. Why was she acting like such a chicken?

"Thomas, I…I don't want to go to Ireland anymore. I don't want to leave my home and my family's graves. I don't want to leave these mountains, and I don't want to leave you. Over the last few weeks, you've become like family to me."

Thomas was touched. The boy seemed embarrassed by his admission.

"I feel the same way, Charlie. You've become like family."

"Well, would you possibly want to hire me on as a cook and farmhand? I know the land well, and I'd be willing do anything you needed."

"Charlie, I would love it if you stayed. But if that's the case, you should keep Kerry Haven and I'll buy the closest property I can find. We could help each other on both sites. We'd make a great team. We already do! And I don't want you selling this land if you're going to stay in America. It's yours and it should someday pass to your children and their children."

She needed to tell him! What was wrong with her?

Thomas stood still for a moment longer, thinking Charlie would continue talking. He looked as though he might. When he didn't, Thomas turned and began walking again.

"Here is where the farmland starts," Charlotte said much later when they came to the end of the cattle pasture fencing.

"What have you had success growing?"

Thomas knew nothing about farming, but he was eager to learn.

"Corn, cotton, tobacco, and potatoes, so far. Father is...was always looking for new things to try. He grew just enough wheat for our family. The cattle and other crops were where he made his money. This wheat here looks just about ready to harvest."

She stopped walking and looked at Thomas. "Over the last few years, the Crawfords helped us harvest and we helped them. It's going to be difficult with just the two of us."

Thomas noticed the anxious look on the boy's face.

"Charlie, we'll do our best and that's all we can do. If we aren't able to harvest it all, we can supplement with wheat from the general store next time we're in Denver. Remember, I'm just learning about all this, so there will most likely be lots of supplementing my first few years!"

Charlotte laughed as she remembered that Thomas had more money than her family ever had. He wouldn't have to depend so heavily on crop success.

"What is the ratio of crops to sell and crops to sustain the family?"

"I'm not sure about that. Father and Brendan were the real farmers. I just helped them occasionally. I'm sure the traders in Denver City will be able to give you that information, though."

They kept walking, each of them silently lost in their own thoughts.

"The stream you so enjoyed makes up the back edge of the property," Charlotte said when they arrived at the edge of the water. "It's definitely my favorite place. There are some really beautiful areas here along its banks."

"I can imagine many, many hours spent down here. Does the stream also mark the end of the Crawford property, or will I have to come over here to swim with you if I live there?"

"No, you'll be able to swim on your own property. The Crawfords had more acreage, but our properties have the same depth. Ours is just narrower—"

"Ah, excellent. We can hang rope swings on both properties."

She simply nodded. The thought of swimming with Thomas was not one she would soon get out of her mind.

The area along the stream was, indeed, beautiful. Thomas pointed out several shady spots where hammocks could be hung. He still couldn't believe how spectacular Kerry Haven was. The east length of the property was primarily devoted to green, lush grass. Thomas allowed his fingers to brush the tips of the tall blades as he walked. Eventually they saw the cabin up ahead.

"I'm going up to visit the cemetery," Charlotte said. "I'll be back to the cabin soon."

"Do you need company," Thomas asked. Over the last week, Charlie had gone to visit the family graves every day, and Thomas always accompanied him. He knew it was unlikely, but what if the men returned and hurt or killed Charlie? It wasn't something Thomas could even contemplate. He wondered how Sergeant Albertson's manhunt was progressing.

"I think I'd like to go alone today."

Thomas felt so proud of the boy for conquering his fear. And yet, he would miss this precious time together. There was something so calm and peaceful up on that hill where the Gallaghers were buried. Occasionally, Charlie would share another memory or two, and Thomas loved the family more and more with every story.

"Okay, I'll go work on a letter to Emily. I want to have several ready by the time we visit the post office in a few weeks."

Charlotte turned left and headed toward the hill.

Chapter Fifteen

Another ten days passed in easy camaraderie. Three days were spent harvesting as much of the wheat as they could. And, when they were both too exhausted to spend even one more day in the fields, they ended the week by butchering and processing a pig. In the evenings, they would play cards or spend time in the kitchen, improving Thomas' cooking abilities. Life out here in Colorado was such hard work, but Thomas was happier than he'd been in years; probably ever.

One night, Thomas sat alone, staring at the empty fireplace. Charlie always went to bed well before he did, and he'd quickly developed the habit of spending the last hour of his day in one of the rocking chairs on the porch or here in the living area. Tonight, he was overcome with gratitude and joy. It was still astounding to him that he had found such a perfect property and someone to help him learn its management. God had truly blessed him, and he was so grateful. He simply couldn't imagine Kerry Haven without Charlie's funny, brave, compassionate presence. Charlie kept him so amused, and he constantly went out of his way to make the boy laugh. He loved that laugh! Thomas leaned his head against the back of the tall rocking chair and closed his eyes.

The silence was broken by a distant coyote, and Thomas opened his eyes and looked around the cabin. He took in the well-built fireplace, colorful braided rugs on the floor, and sturdy bookshelves. The wide spine of the family Bible caught his attention. He felt guilty for neglecting his own Bible the last few weeks. He stood up and walked over to the shelf. The Gallagher Bible was well-worn, and Thomas could tell that the family used it often. He smiled as he imagined them sitting in this very space. Mr. Gallagher would be sitting in the chair near the table, reading aloud to the family. He pictured Mrs. Gallagher darning socks while she listened from the other chair. Where did the three children usually sit? What would they be doing as they listened to their father's voice?

Thomas gently pulled the Bible from the shelf, then sat back down in his chair; or rather, Mrs. Gallagher's chair. There was a bookmark in the Bible, and he longed to see what chapter the family had been reading. He flipped to the book-marked place. It was the twelfth chapter of the Gospel of Luke. He began reading and soon came to some of his favorite verses:

"Are not five sparrows sold for two pennies? Yet not one of them is forgotten by God. Indeed, the very hairs of your head are all numbered. Don't be afraid; you are worth more than many sparrows. I tell you, whoever publicly acknowledges me before others, the Son of Man will also acknowledge before the angels of God. But whoever disowns me before others will be disowned before the angels of God. And everyone who speaks a word against the Son of Man will be forgiven, but anyone who blasphemes against the Holy Ghost will not be forgiven. When you are brought before synagogues, rulers, and authorities, do not worry about how you will defend yourselves or that you will say, for the Holy Ghost will teach you at that time what you should say.

"Someone in the crowd said to him, 'Teacher, tell my brother to divide the inheritance with me.'

"Jesus replied, 'Man, who appointed me a judge or an arbiter between you?' Then he said to them, 'Watch out! Be on your guard against all kinds of greed; life does not consist in an abundance of possessions.' And he told them this parable: 'The ground of a certain rich man yielded an abundant harvest. He thought to himself, 'What shall I do? I have no place to store my crops.' Then he said, 'this is what I'll do. I will tear down my barns and build bigger ones, and there I will store my surplus grain. And I'll say to myself, 'You have plenty of grain laid up for many years. Take life easy; eat, drink and be merry.'

"But God said to him, 'You fool! This very night your life will be demanded from you. Then who will get what you have prepared for yourself?' This is how it will be with whoever stores up things for themselves but is not rich toward God."

Thomas stopped reading and reflected on the passage, which had always left him feeling conversely comforted and challenged whenever he read it. He thought again of his family's wealth. Had it profited his mother or father at all to have abundant wealth and property when they died? No. They died with nothing to show for their lives besides their children, who had primarily been raised by nannies and governesses. Their great wealth had never been used for charitable purposes of any kind. Thomas intended to rectify that situation.

He thought how different his upbringing had been from Charlie's. The boy's family seemed so concerned with the welfare of all those around them. From Patrick and Annie Gallagher's assistance to the Crawford family when they arrived with hardly a penny to their name, to the overwhelming generosity of Jared and Betsy Marshall to the needy in Killarney, giving seemed to be a constant practice with this family. Thomas longed to live that way. There were so many good things his wealth could accomplish.

The first altruistic project he wanted to fund was the Catholic Church Mr. Gallagher had always dreamed of. He would honor the memory of Charlie's father by carrying out his plans in this respect. This would ensure that the Gallagher legacy lived on for decades to come. The idea excited him, and he planned to post an employment flier in the post office when next they were in Denver City. He knew very little about construction, but he was sure there were men in the area who did. They would likely welcome the work, and he could afford to pay them well. He also needed to post a flier inviting all Catholics in the area to gather for a meeting at Kerry Haven to begin planning. Once he knew how many people might begin attending Mass if a nearby church were available, he could schedule an appointment with the pastor of St. Mary's to discuss the process for requesting a priest. They would need to build a residence for the priest, as well. Thomas could see it all in his mind. The hill Mr. Gallagher chose for the church location was breathtakingly beautiful and afforded a view of many miles in all directions. He imagined a tall, Gothic-style stone structure amidst the thick trees. The church might serve only a few hundred congregants when first built, but Thomas wanted to assure it would be large enough to accommodate the community as it inevitably grew. He wanted capacity for at least a thousand worshippers. Laughing silently, he imagined the reactions he might get from his fellow Catholics. Perhaps his dreams were too grand, but why should he hold back when money was not an issue?

Pulling himself back to the present, he looked down at the folded paper bookmark still in his hand. Giving in to his curiosity, he unfolded the pages and realized he was holding a letter dated August tenth; merely four days before he arrived to find young Charlie digging graves for his family.

"My dearest Betsy," the letter began in beautiful, flowing handwriting. He skipped to the end to discover its writer. "Your loving older sister, Annie." His heart accelerated as he realized it had been written by Charlie's mother. Thomas longed to know more about Charlie's parents, but he was hesitant to press the hurting boy for more information. This letter would hopefully give him a glimpse of who Mrs. Gallagher was. He felt a pang of guilt at invading her privacy, and almost folded the letter back up. But then he thought about Charlie. The more he knew about the boy's parents, the better he could help him in his grief. With a quick prayer for the deceased Mrs. Gallagher, Thomas began to read.

Thomas stopped reading. How interesting that the Gallagher family had both a Charlotte and a Charlie. Charles must be the name of a highly revered grandfather or uncle. But this description didn't match either of the females he and Charlie had buried. Was there another sister somewhere? Had she traveled in the days before Thomas arrived? Would she return home to find that her family was gone and only Charlie had survived? Or had she been taken by the outlaws? No, surely Charlie would have mentioned that to Sergeant Albertson and the other policemen. Why had Charlie not mentioned her at all? He talked so lovingly about Brendan and Ruth. Was there conflict between him and Charlotte? Had something horrible happened to cause her to leave the family? Thomas would have to ask Charlie about it tomorrow.

He looked back down at the letter, found his spot, and continued reading.

A wave of relief washed over Thomas, and he realized he didn't want Charlotte to be already attached. What a fool he was! Had he just felt a rush of relief because a woman he'd never met might be available for him to court? He chuckled softly, and then admitted to himself that he truly wanted to meet this Charlotte. She sounded like a woman with whom he could have great conversations and debates; a woman who would be so different from the boring women he'd dated in the past. She sounded like a woman of passion and opinions with whom he could build a life and a family.

Where was she traveling, and when would she be back? He imagined her deep grief at learning of the attack and deaths of her parents and siblings. He wanted to wake Charlie up immediately and get all his questions answered. But the boy deserved his sleep. Impatiently, Thomas continued reading.

Thomas' body was flooded with rage. How could someone so innocent and pure have been violated so horribly? When he thought about this tiny creature being raped by those men, he wanted to kill them with his bare hands. He comforted himself with the thought that Ruthie was now in the arms of her Creator. She was in a place where everyone was as joyful and filled with the Holy Ghost as she had been every day of her short life. She was home. He wiped a tear from his cheek and continued.

In contrast to Charlotte's loquaciousness, Ruth still possesses such a limited vocabulary. She is now able to communicate most of her daily needs, and is finally able to visit the outhouse without prompting, which is such a wonderful blessing (as I'm sure you can imagine). But I do not know her heart as I know Charlotte's. What I would give to experience one day in Ruthie's mind! It must be a lovely place if her constant smiles and laughter are any indicator.

This was exactly the impression Thomas got whenever Charlie talked about Ruthie. What an enormous impact this tiny girl had on everyone who knew her. He wished again that he had known the Gallagher family. And again, he thought how odd it was that he could miss people he'd never met.

Brendan is only fifteen and has already surpassed his father in height! He is a brawny, healthy young man and it makes me laugh when I remember that at one time he was no longer than my forearm. Oh, and those fat little feet of his! They looked just like building blocks! Do you remember? I actually despaired of him ever walking! Now, he is on the move all day long and his little block feet have grown into the huge feet of a grown man! He brings so much sunshine into my life, and I thank God every day that he was too young to go fight alongside Patrick. I couldn't have borne it if he came back with that hollow, empty look Patrick had for a while. Sister, I know I've written you about how bad those first few months were. My formerly jovial, loving husband was a shell of his former self. I shudder remembering it. But, it was so beautiful to watch the children rally around their father. They brought him back a day at a time with their humor and unwavering love. We are so blessed!
Occasionally, when he thinks no one is around, Brendan will burst into song as he chops wood or works in the field. He has his father's deep, resonating voice and it thrills my heart. Do you remember that it was Patrick's voice which first attracted me to him all those years ago? It's fortunate that he sang so freely that day, else he would have never

won the heart of so fair a wife! He said he was always too timid to sing at his own parish where everyone knew him, but felt no fear to sing aloud while a stranger visiting Killarney. How foolish we humans are in worrying about what others think! If he had attended that Mass silently, I doubt we would have even met. I still laugh when I recall how I begged our father to go introduce himself. I remember you were so embarrassed by it! Oh, sister! I was rather impetuous, wasn't I?

Patrick and Brendan have been trying their hand with different crops and have found great success with potatoes, corn, cotton, and tobacco. I still have occasional bad dreams about the potato blight and ensuing famine, as I'm sure you do. It is doubtful any Irishman our age will ever take potatoes for granted again! I'm happy to have them in such abundance here. However, corn is definitely my favorite crop to watch grow. The green and yellow are so vivid, and the stalks grow so high. There's something almost majestic about a field of ripe corn. And, it's much easier to harvest than the cotton. Brendan and Patrick tear up their hands every year bringing in the cotton. But I've developed a salve that seems to work very well in restoring their dexterity. Oh, Betsy! I look back over this last paragraph with embarrassment! When did I become such an old farmer's wife?

There had been no mention yet of Charlie. As he read about the other children, he grew more and more anxious to see how Mrs. Gallagher would describe him. Thomas wanted so keenly to know more about what Charlie had been like before the traumatic events of last week.

I miss you every single day, Betsy, and regret that our children are not growing up together. Despite my occasional homesickness for Ireland and you, I cannot regret our decision to move to America. This life Patrick and I have built together is more than I ever dreamed possible. I only wish the Gallaghers and Marshalls were on the same continent! Please tell Jared (yet again) that there is a growing community here with no general store as of yet. He could open the first one and become a very wealthy man! Imagine the legacy he would leave for your children and grandchildren. Remind him that he has a sister-in-law here in Colorado who would make his favorite pie every day in gratitude if he only moved his family to America!

With greatest affection,

    your loving older sister, Annie

Thomas went back to the beginning and read the letter a second time. How very odd that there was no mention of Charlie at all. He felt a tiny flash of indignation that Mrs. Gallagher had written so beautifully of her other three children and not once mentioned Charlie. The mother Charlie described did not seem like a woman who favored some of her children and spurned others.

A niggling thought began stirring in his mind and he quickly turned the page over to reread the description of Charlotte. The deep blue eyes. The inner fire and determination, sweetly masked by a calm and serene exterior. Could it be? No. No, that would be crazy. He would know if Charlie was actually a woman. Wouldn't he?

His mind was whirling, and he decided to go back through the last two weeks one day at a time looking for clues. When he'd first arrived that Tuesday, he'd been attacked by a filthy, feral beast with one eye. The physical appearance of the small, angry being had been so ghastly that Thomas hadn't questioned anything beyond what in hell had caused such destruction. Charlie had worked ceaselessly alongside Thomas digging the graves. It seemed unlikely a woman could have carried out such a physically grueling task for so many hours. He tried to imagine Emily doing anything like that and didn't think she would last five minutes. No, Charlie had to be a boy. He just had to be. But, if Charlotte had grown up here in Colorado working hard alongside her family, maybe she would have been used to it. He thought about the rest of that first day. After the burial, Charlie had fallen asleep on his plate and Thomas had carried him to bed. He remembered how small the boy had felt in his arms.

The delicious biscuits the next morning definitely tipped the scale in favor of Charlie being Charlotte. He thought about the way Charlie talked and how he described his family. If he were being honest, Charlie's choice of words often seemed odd for an eleven-year-old boy. He had simply assumed that Charlie's mother was an exacting educator and had imparted a spectacularly diverse vocabulary to her son. As he replayed their conversations, while considering the slight possibility that Charlie might be a woman, well, it made more sense.

He remembered Charlie's joy at meeting Big Viv, George, and the Groves and Albertson families. Charlie had seemed much more at ease with Sarah and Julia than with the Albertson boys. That had surprised Thomas greatly. When he'd been eleven, he'd had no use at all for older girls who just wanted to boss him around all the time! But for Charlotte, time spent with John David, Fulton, and Damien would have been terrifying. Of course she wouldn't want to spend more time than necessary around men, even young ones.

Then he remembered Charlie's very odd reaction when he'd shaved and had a haircut on Saturday. The reaction made much more sense if he thought of her as a young woman. Why, she'd felt comfortable and protected when she saw him as a father figure. Finding out he was only a few years older than her must have shocked her greatly. He imagined her extreme discomfort at being forced to share a room with him. How utterly inappropriate that had been, and yet, she'd had no way to get out of the situation without revealing her true identity. Marnie Albertson would certainly be mortified to discover she'd unknowingly placed an unmarried man and woman in the same room for the night!

But why had Charlotte gone to such extraordinary lengths to hide the fact that she was a woman? She'd even cut off her hair! No woman he knew would ever sacrifice their hair for a disguise!

And then the rest of the horrible truth began slowly slithering into his consciousness. If she were a woman…

No! Thomas' mind threw together a wall of protection, as if it could stubbornly prevent him from arriving at the inevitable realization. Unwilling to be deterred, he forced his way through the wall and was punched in the chest by Charlie's description of what the men did to his mother and sister. He stood up and ran to the door, jerking it open and barely making it off the porch before he vomited. His fists clenched as he tried to push away thoughts of what Charlotte had no doubt endured at the hands of those brutes. No wonder she wanted to appear as a boy. Until this moment, Thomas had thought Charlie the bravest young boy he'd ever met. But Charlotte, what she'd endured…her bravery was so immense it humbled him.

Now that he knew the truth, what was he to do? Should he admit to her that he knew her secret and admired her even more than before? Or should he just keep things as they were and wait until she was ready to talk with him about it? What would cause her the least amount of pain?

"Oh, Lord. Help me to handle this with wisdom and love," he whispered up to the bright stars and velvety night sky. He walked over to the well and rinsed his mouth with cool, clean water from the hand pump.

As he reentered the cabin, he felt an urgent need to put the Bible and letter back where he had found them. This was a conversation that needed planning and wisdom; not one that could happen before its time. If Charlotte came down from the loft and saw the letter, it would force a very awkward exchange before he, or she, were ready. Charlotte had been hurt so much already. He wanted to make sure that he did nothing to add to her pain. And this would be a big, big turning point in their relationship. He must handle it correctly.

He sank back into the rocking chair and asked himself what Emily would advise if she were here. Emily was always unfailingly kind and gentle. She was an expert at putting those around her at ease. So, how would she handle this difficult situation? He thought about it for a few silent minutes, finally determining that Emily would encourage him to allow Charlotte to maintain her dignity. She would advise him to go along with the ruse until the wounded young woman was ready to be herself again. She would advise him to support and love Charlotte until she was ready to reveal herself, on her own terms. He smiled. This seemed like a good course of action; certainly the most wise and compassionate thing to do.

Thinking of Emily brought another question to his mind. What would Emily think of Charlotte? This question was the easiest he'd been faced with tonight and it made him smile to himself again. Emily would love Charlotte. Of that, he was sure. Charlotte was funny and intelligent and could easily execute the sort of conversations Emily enjoyed; those filled with wit and strong opinions and clear reasoning to support the opinions. Those two women were going to get along remarkably well!

With all his might, he wished that Emily were here right now. Then, Charlotte would not be totally alone with him. Men had caused all her pain and grief and loss, and now she was alone with one. On nights when he was awakened by nightmares and came to sit in the living area to relax, he often heard whimpers from the upstairs loft. Oh, dear God, how she had been traumatized! How he wanted vengeance on the horrible men who had hurt her. And how he wanted to devote the rest of his life to protecting this exceptional young woman.

Thomas wondered again what the future held for her. She was intelligent and capable. He would help her keep Kerry Haven and build a new life here. He would secretly ensure that she had the finances available to do anything she liked, to build any sort of life she wanted.

He tried to imagine what Charlotte would look like if she decided to be a woman again. What would she look like if her hair grew out and she was dressed in woman's clothing? She would probably be rather pretty. Her wound was healing nicely, but he could tell it was going to leave a very pronounced scar. Thomas remembered thinking the scar would be a badge of honor for young Charlie. Not so for a young woman! It would probably cause her a lifetime of stares and questions. He wondered if any man would see past the scar to the extraordinary person she was. And then, he realized with a surge of jealousy that he didn't want any other man to see who she really was. The thought of her courting anyone else was not one that he wanted to entertain.

So, let her keep the short, uneven hair and men's clothing as long as she wanted. He had Charlotte in his life, and he would protect her secret for as long as she needed.

Chapter Sixteen

Saturday, August 31, 1867

When the sun rose bright and early the next morning, Thomas had already been awake for over an hour. He was too excited to fall back asleep, and too exhausted to want to get up from bed. He simply couldn't wait to start the day; his first day with Charlotte.

Sitting at the breakfast table some minutes later, Charlotte looked up to find Thomas smiling like a simpleton.

"What's got you so cheerful this morning," she asked, in a grumpier than normal voice.

"No nightmares last night. I got a great night's sleep and woke up ready to tackle the world!"

"Hmm," Charlotte grunted, and took another sip of her coffee.

"What's got you so grumpy today," he asked, with a smile. This made her chuckle.

"I realized last night that it's time for the haying, and there's no one besides us to do it."

"Well, how bad can it be," he asked, cheerfully. "We got the wheat done together."

"So bad. Thomas, it's much more work. There are twice as many acres of hay grass as there were acres of wheat. Usually, we go help the Crawfords bring theirs in and they help us with ours. Unlike the crops, which we can purchase in Denver if we need to, the hay will need to be done and done well. I don't think hay is sold at the general store."

"So, explain to me what happens if we don't have hay. And remember, you're talking to a city dweller here."

"In the spring, summer, and fall, our horses and cattle survive mainly on grass. It's plentiful and we can rotate the animals around so that no pasture gets too barren. But in the winter, the ground is covered in snow and dried hay is what they will need. We keep several large pastures free of animals each year, and those are our hay pastures. If we don't get the grass cut and dried out and stored in the barn before our next rainstorm, we could lose it all to mildew. And if that happened, we wouldn't even have the Crawfords to borrow from. It would be bad."

"Ah, I understand now." He stood up from the table and picked up both of their plates. "Show me what to do, and we'll get it done as quickly as we can."

Thomas hated the fact that Charlotte would be forced to do this backbreaking work. He wished he could just do it all for her.

"Would it be worth it to ride into Denver City and ask the Albertson boys to come help?"

"That might be a really good idea," she answered. "Let's see how much we can get done today, and then we can decide. It would take a full day to ride there and back, but we could work so much faster with five than with two."

Thomas realized his mistake. If the Albertsons came, it would cause a logistical nightmare. Being that Charlie was supposedly a boy, and the Albertson boys were close to Charlie's age, it would make sense for them to all sleep up in the loft together. But now that Thomas knew Charlie was actually Charlotte, he saw no way for the Albertson boys to come help without destroying Charlotte's façade.

"Well, I think you're right about today. Let's just see how much we can accomplish together."

Charlotte grabbed her father's sombrero from near the door and turned to speak to him.

"I'm heading to the barn to get the scythes. Will you meet me there whenever you're ready?"

"Sure," he answered.

Once she closed the door behind her and walked into the still-dark morning, Thomas let out a long sigh. He wondered how long he could keep up this charade. Charlie, now Charlotte, had quickly become his closest friend. They spent hours together every day. Certainly, he would slip up sooner or later and call her by her real name. He prayed she would be honest with him soon. Did she trust him enough to tell him the truth? What could he do to help build her trust?

He thought, with shame, about how he'd stripped down naked in front of her before diving into the stream. That surely hadn't helped her feel comfortable around him. He would need to be more of a gentleman now. No more boyish roughhousing.

A few hours later, every part of Thomas' body ached. Charlotte was right about haying. It was backbreaking work. At roughly eleven o'clock, he yelled over to her, "Can we stop for lunch soon? I'm dying over here!"

Charlotte nodded and mopped her forehead with her bandana. "Let me finish this row and we can head over to the lunch basket," she yelled back to him.

Thomas immediately set his scythe down and began walking toward the spot where they'd left the basket this morning. Reaching it, he collapsed onto the soft grass. Charlotte laughed heartily when she walked over a few minutes later to find him sprawled in the grass.

"Don't laugh at me. I'm a city dweller," he said, turning over onto his back. "You've got more experience with this!"

"And even I can't do it as well as Brendan and Father could. It's hard work. You're actually doing pretty well…for a city dweller."

As they sat down in the grass to eat a small lunch, Charlotte looked over at Thomas and said, "You never finished telling me how you became Catholic."

"Oh, that conversation seems like ages ago! When was that?"

"We were on our way home from burying the Crawfords. You had reached the point where you were nine years old and wanted to become Catholic, but the priests encouraged you to wait."

"Yes. They said I should keep learning and growing in my faith. They were right, of course. The more I learned about the Bible and the early church, about the sacraments and the beauty of the Mass, the more I fell in love with Catholicism. I went home each afternoon and shared with Michael and Emily what I learned that day at school. By explaining it to others, I think I grew more confident and convicted in my beliefs. Sometimes, Emily or Michael asked a probing question that no one had asked in class. I would take it to the priests the next day and we would have great conversations. There was never a question the priests shied away from. If they didn't know the answer, they would find it for me. It was a spectacular journey, Charlie!"

"I can tell you love your faith very much," she said, looking at the joy in his face.

"I do. It's the most important thing in my life. By the time I turned twelve, I would not be deterred any longer. I arranged a conversation with my parents."

Thomas chuckled. "When I asked to speak with them, it took them two days to find time for me in their busy schedules. It's funny, though, they both thought I was going to try to negotiate an increase in my allowance and had decided together on what amount they would offer!"

"Two days to find time for you," she asked in surprise.

"Yes. Like I said, that was pretty normal in our household. They were very often away from home. When I told them what I really wanted to discuss, they were pretty shocked. My mother was very upset and hurt. She'd grown up believing Catholics were superstitious and worshiped idols. I tried and tried to correct her views, but I could tell it was only making her more upset. 'Where did I go wrong,' she kept saying as she cried. By now, Michael was also attending school with me, and she threatened to pull us both out. Her threat scared me. All my friends and beloved teachers were there. So, I backed down and told them I wouldn't convert if they would just allow me to finish school there. Finally, my mother calmed down and relented. My father looked at me and said, 'Thomas, we will not discuss this again.'"

"I'm sorry. That sounds very difficult. I can't imagine being at odds with my parents—"

When she did not continue, Thomas waited for a moment and then asked, "Are you okay?"

Charlotte just nodded her head and took a bite of her sandwich. She knew if she tried to talk, she would lose control of the tears threatening to flow down her face. Damnit! Every time she remembered, it was like getting kicked by a horse.

"So, what happened then," she asked a few minutes later when she had her emotions under control.

"Well, the next day, I went to school and poured out my heart to Father Michael Rother. He was the one I'd known the longest and from whom I'd taken the majority of my classes. I told him that I was determined to become Catholic but didn't want to risk my parents withdrawing me from St. John the Baptist school. I was eleven years old and full of righteous anger! I went on and on about how unfair it was that my mother wouldn't even listen to the truth."

Thomas looked across the grass at Charlotte and his eyes twinkled with amusement. "I'm sure Father Rother thought it most hilarious to listen to a wealthy little white child talking about how persecuted he was. Now that I'm older, I see the absolute skill with which he handled the situation. He reminded me that honoring my parents was one of the most important tasks God asked of me. He assured me that there was no rush. Because I had been baptized, I already belonged to God, he explained. My heart belonged to

God, and if I chose to see this time of waiting as a time of 'courting the faith,' it could be a time of great blessing. He was right. I dedicated myself to becoming the best son and brother that I could be. Every time I felt resentful at my parents' refusal to allow me to convert, I turned my heart to prayer instead of wrath. I changed so much, Charlie. Even Michael noticed."

"I'm sure it made your eventual reception of the sacraments all the more special."

"It did. I imagine it was like when a young man must wait years for the woman he loves."

Thomas was watching Charlotte closely as he spoke and was amused to see her eyes jump to his and then quickly glance away. It took great effort to not smile with satisfied pleasure. Did she perhaps care for him? Could she ever care for a man after what had been done to her? Did he want her to care for him?

"I waited until the day of my eighteenth birthday. I was in my last year of school at St. John the Baptist. My parents and I had never spoken again of my desire to convert. Six years was a long time to wait, but thankfully, I had Father Rother and Michael as my confidants. In fact, Michael was just as determined to convert as I was."

"I suppose you received the sacraments without your parents in attendance."

"Yes. Michael and Emily were there, along with several classmates and many of my teachers. It would have been lovely to have my parents there, but it was a wonderful experience despite their absence. Michael and Emily both followed in my footsteps and converted at the age of eighteen."

"What did your parents say?"

"They never once brought it up in conversation. Not once. They attended their church, and I attended mine. We came home and ate Sunday lunches together. And no one talked about it."

"My faith journey seems so boring compared to yours. I've been Catholic since birth. Back in Ireland, we attended every Sunday and often went to daily Mass during the week. The parish priests were all dear friends. It's been difficult not having a parish nearby for these last few years, but we made do. I certainly treasure every Mass I'm able to attend in Denver City. The difficulty of attending makes it more precious."

When they finished eating, they walked over to the stream and refilled their canteens. Then they returned to their labors. Though every part of him ached, Thomas was determined not to let Charlotte outwork him. He often looked over to see if she was slowing down, but she just kept going. In fact, she did not stop until darkness fell and they could no longer see what they were doing.

With both of them too exhausted to cook anything elaborate, dinner that night consisted of leftover biscuits and hot, crispy bacon. Thomas was almost too tired to eat. As soon as the meal was finished, they each went to their room and fell fast asleep. It was the first night in a long time without conversation.

The next day was Sunday, and both of them slept well past the sunrise. When Charlotte finally climbed down from the loft, she saw Thomas sitting in one of the rocking chairs reading from her family's Bible.

"May I join you," she asked.

"Of course you may. There's coffee on the stove if you'd like some."

Charlotte poured a cup of coffee, added some sugar, and went to join Thomas. He leaned his head against the back of the chair and looked over at her.

"I am so sore today, Charlie. I don't think I've worked that hard since my first year in battle."

"What made the first year the most difficult?"

"I'm not sure. We certainly dug more trenches and cut more wood to build protective structures the first year. And, maybe I just grew stronger each year. Whatever the reason, the next few years seemed a bit less physically strenuous than the first."

He stared down into his coffee cup, and Charlotte sensed he didn't want to talk further about the war.

"Will you read aloud to me," he asked, handing her the Bible. He secretly hoped she would find the letter and be prompted to reveal her true identity.

But, Charlotte opened the book to Psalms and began reading. Thomas found her voice hypnotically alluring and closed his eyes to fully concentrate on the words. Soon, he was fast asleep.

When Charlotte realized Thomas was sleeping, she closed the Bible and simply stared at him. She had grown to love this handsome, gentle man with all her heart and wanted to take full advantage of this quiet, unguarded moment. As soon as the haying was done, she would tell him the truth and then lose him forever. Slowly, she endeavored to memorize his facial features. His gorgeous green eyes, strong jawline, and beautiful lips mesmerized her. She wanted to remember the way his wavy black hair shone in the sunshine and the way his laugh sounded. She would miss him for the rest of her life, but hopefully she would be able to remember the days they spent together. Thomas dozed for over an hour, and Charlotte treasured every minute.

Thomas was exceedingly embarrassed when he awoke.

"I'm so sorry. Your reading voice just lulled me to sleep!"

"There's no need to apologize. Once I eat some breakfast, I'll probably join you in napping."

Thomas chuckled and Charlotte's eyes grew wide.

"I won't join you. I will take my own nap. I just meant that you won't be the only one to take a nap today."

"Charlie, I knew what you meant. No need to get so flustered."

But Thomas had to admit he was very, very flustered. He imagined lying down to sleep with Charlotte in his arms. He visualized himself caressing her cheek and kissing those beautiful lips. Pulling himself back to reality, Thomas wondered where those thoughts had originated. Charlotte was his friend, not some woman to be viewed with lust.

Charlotte jumped up from her chair and practically ran into the kitchen. Her face was red with mortification and she needed some distraction.

"I'm going to make us pancakes for breakfast. Would you mind bringing the milk up from the cold cellar?"

Thomas walked out of the cabin and Charlotte almost allowed herself to sink to the floor. How could she be so stupid? She needed to stop constantly thinking about him. It was one thing to allow herself to watch him sleep. It was entirely another to accidentally imply she wanted to join him in his sleep. Her imagination was leading her into unsafe places. She needed to focus and stay alert. Another stupid mistake could lead to disaster.

That evening, a cool breeze enticed them both outside. Charlotte sat in her rocking chair, but Thomas didn't join her as he usually did. She watched as he walked down the porch stairs and turned his face up to the sky. Then, without saying a word, he lay down on his back and crossed his arms behind his head. He looked so comfortable there in the soft grass that Charlotte couldn't help walking over to join him.

"What are you doing," she softly asked.

Thomas raised one arm and pointed to the sky.

"Have you ever seen anything so magnificent?"

Charlotte looked up. The sky was breathtakingly beautiful. Slowly, she lowered herself to the grass and lay down next to Thomas. The heat emanating from his body threatened to set her aflame, and she realized that she was much too close to him. No eleven-year-old boy would lie this close to someone who wasn't a parent. She briefly thought of sitting up and scooting away, but it would just be awkward now. She resolved to lie still and focus on the stars. Hopefully, Thomas wouldn't notice her nearness.

But Thomas was keenly aware of Charlotte's presence. He concentrated on the night sky and tried to locate constellations or shooting stars. He was overcome with an urge to reach over and touch her hand. What would it feel like to lightly brush his fingers over hers? What would it feel like to kiss her? It had been years since he'd kissed a woman. Charlotte's nearness was intoxicating, and Thomas almost laughed to himself. This was the most romantic situation he could imagine. He was lying here under the most exquisite stars, with the funny, caring woman who consumed his every waking thought. And yet, he may as well be miles away. Until Charlotte was ready to admit she was a woman, he was trapped. At least this would make for a great story someday.

"Tell me about your dreams, Charlie."

Charlotte balked. Her dream was to live the rest of her life here on this property with Thomas as her friend and protector, but that was not the dream of an eleven-year-old boy. She racked her mind to think of an appropriate answer.

"I'm not sure, Thomas. Will you tell me yours?"

"I guess it's difficult for a young man like you to narrow it down. I remember having so many plans and dreams for my future when I was your age." He willed Charlotte to correct him, to tell him that she wasn't a young boy, but a nineteen-year-old woman. If she told him right now, their first kiss could be in their own backyard under this bewitching blanket of stars. Why didn't she just tell him? He decided to prompt her a bit more. Maybe, just maybe, she would break down and tell him.

"Now that I'm grown, I have just one main dream," he continued. "I want to fall in love with a smart, caring woman who makes me laugh and brings me joy. I want to marry her and have a whole passel of children. I want to teach those children to ride horses and plant crops, and how to read and even cook. Most of all, I want to live a life pleasing to God and pleasing to my family."

Thomas' words devastated her. These were all the things she had dreamed of since she was a girl. A loving husband, children, and even grandchildren someday. Now, none of those things could be hers. In a ten-minute span of time three weeks ago, all her future dreams had been destroyed. She turned her head and looked over at the man lying next to her. Their faces were mere inches apart.

"Your dreams sound like my parents' dreams, Thomas. They are noble dreams, and I hope and pray they will come true for you. You deserve every good blessing God can give."

She rose and walked alone into the cabin. Thomas cursed himself. He had not intended to be cruel or make her sad. He was tempted to follow her into the cabin to try and comfort her, but boys preferred to be alone when they needed to cry. Until Charlotte admitted she was a woman, his hands were tied.

On Monday morning, the sun rose to find them already out in the field cutting hay. Charlotte had suggested that they work until midday and then take a brief rest while the day was at its hottest. By working hard in the early mornings and again in the early evenings, she thought they could finish the hay cutting without either of them succumbing to heatstroke. That sounded like a brilliant plan to Thomas.

Charlotte found her eyes drawn to Thomas more and more often. She knew that she needed to talk with him this evening. It was time to be honest. Of course, maybe she should wait until the hay was brought in. As soon as she told him who she really was, she would have to leave. There was no way around it. And Thomas wouldn't know how to gather the dried hay. Maybe another few days of deception would be okay. Charlotte felt less guilty about things when she justified it that way. She stole one more glance at the tall, handsome man across the field. How was she going to live without him?

Thomas stopped swinging the scythe and removed his hat. He pulled the bandana out of his pocket and wiped his sweaty face. Then, he looked over and saw Charlotte staring at him. He lifted his hat in a cheerful greeting. Now that he was knew who she was, he saw her so differently. Every time he looked at her, she seemed more beautiful to him. Even wearing boys' clothes which were drenched in sweat, there was a quiet grace and dignity that called to him. Her smile was more stunning than before, her eyes more mesmerizing, and her laugh...there was nothing like her laugh! Every time she laughed, it brought him so much joy. Thomas was surprised that he hadn't slipped yet and revealed his discovery. What would Charlotte do when she realized he knew the truth? His biggest fear was that she would leave, and he knew he could not bear a life without her.

Charlotte was embarrassed that Thomas caught her staring at him. What a relief that he was too far away to see her blush. She shook her head and turned her attention back to the task at hand.

When the sun was straight above them, Charlotte began walking over to where Thomas was working.

"Are you ready for a meal break," she called.

"I thought you'd never ask," he cried, and comically collapsed to the ground.

Thomas' stunt led to her laughter. She now stood looking down at him, and her beautiful smile almost undid him. He was overwhelmed with a desire to pull her down into his arms and kiss her with all his might. But he knew that would terrify her, and terrifying her was the last thing he wanted to do. Again, he longed for her to be honest with him so that he could tell her how he felt. He loved her, and he needed her to know.

"I think I'll go take a plunge in the river before heading to the cabin," he said, as he stood up. "It's so hot out here, I feel like I could burst into flames at any moment."

Charlotte looked down at the ground and Thomas imagined she was trying to formulate an excuse to avoid swimming with him.

"I'll see you at the cabin in just a bit."

"Yes, I'll go prepare a simple lunch for us," she said, turning to walk toward the cabin.

Thomas watched her leave and then made his way to the river. How on earth was he going to survive this? Hour by hour, the situation grew more troublesome. His feelings for Charlotte were becoming increasingly difficult to hide.

Monday and Tuesday were spent haying, and Thomas noticed Charlotte grew more and more withdrawn. His attempts to make her laugh often failed. If she didn't reveal herself soon, Thomas knew he would just have to broach the topic himself. He prayed for guidance and kept working alongside the woman he loved.

On Tuesday evening, a cool breeze blew in some relief after the hot August day. Once they finished eating a cold dinner of bread and cheese, Thomas cleaned the dishes and Charlotte brewed some tea.

"I'm going to sit outside and enjoy this glorious evening. Will you join me," Thomas asked, as she handed him his warm mug.

Charlotte nodded and followed him out to the porch. This was it. This was the perfect moment to come clean. She would be brave and just get it done. They sat side by side in two of the five sturdy rocking chairs occupying the spacious porch, and Charlotte mustered her courage. But Thomas spoke first.

"Did your father build these," he asked, indicating the chairs.

"Yes. Well, we all did, Father was extremely talented at carpentry and these chairs were one of his first projects after the cabin was completed. He and Brendan gathered the wood throughout the fall months, and we worked together to build them during the winter when we couldn't spend as much time outside. It was such a fun project."

Even without looking over at her, Thomas could hear that she was smiling.

"I notice that you even made Ruthie's chair small enough to fit her tiny frame."

"Hers was the very first one Father made. Ruth loved her chair, and would spend hours out here singing and rocking. There really was something ethereal about Ruth."

Charlotte thought of all the wonderful evenings her family had spent out on this porch in their rocking chairs. The mountains in the distance provided such variable beauty each evening, depending on the colors of the sunset. And once the mountains were swallowed up by the darkness of night, the stars took over the show. There was always something beautiful to observe from this porch. Oh, how she would miss this home and this land, her family, and Thomas.

For, as soon as she told him the truth, she would need to leave for Denver City. Once Thomas knew she was a woman, the terrific impropriety of the situation would necessitate one of them leaving. And, since she couldn't be out here alone, it would have to be her. Would the Albertsons or Groves take her in until she left for Ireland? No, she wanted to leave Colorado with her reputation intact. She didn't want them to know she'd lied to them. After Thomas paid her for the land, she could easily afford to stay at one of the hotels in Denver City while she figured out what to do next.

She looked over at Thomas who was silently enjoying the sunset. "Thomas, I need to tell you something," she began. Then she froze. This revelation would mean the end of their easy friendship; perhaps the best friendship she'd ever had. She took a deep breath and willed herself to just tell him.

Thomas suddenly felt compelled to make this easier for her. He reached over and placed his hand over hers on the arm rest. The feel of her skin made his heart race. Charlotte looked down at their hands and swallowed before returning her gaze to his face.

"Charlie, do you trust me," Thomas asked, staring intently at her.

"Yes. I trust you with my life," she responded shakily. What was this? Why was he asking her about trust?

"Do you think Charlotte could ever trust me?"

She pulled her hand away from his as though she'd been burned.

"How did? When did you? How did you know?" She shook her head as if trying to dislodge unwelcome thoughts. "You know what, it doesn't matter. I meant to tell you, Thomas. I truly did."

"Charlotte," he interrupted. "I understand."

But she continued talking as though she hadn't heard him. "I only did it because I was so scared and so hurt. I never meant to hurt you. I promise I never did. And then, I began to care for you, and I couldn't bear to tell you and lose your friendship."

"Charlotte," he said again, but she continued to babble nervously.

Finally, Thomas stood up from his chair and knelt in front of hers.

"Listen to me," he instructed, taking both her hands in his. "I understand why you wanted to hide your identity. It makes perfect sense that you would feel unsafe as a woman. I'm not angry. In fact, I admire your quick thinking."

"Oh, Thomas," she cried in relief. "I was so worried that you would hate me for it. Can you even process the scandal of it all? We slept in the same room at the Albertson house. Marnie will never forgive me. I've hurt so very many people."

"Charlotte, the Groves and the Albertsons love you. They will understand, just like I do. Trust me, they will."

Thomas was surprised to find himself anxious and short of breath. His heart threatened to pound a hole in his chest.

"I pray that you are right about that."

The hint of a smile began to pull at Charlotte's lips.

"So, what gave me away? Was it the constant crying?"

Thomas smiled and shook his head.

"The soprano singing voice?"

He shook his head again.

"The cooking lessons?"

"None of that."

To her frustration, Thomas offered no further explanation.

"Come now, you must tell me what blew my cover," she insisted impatiently.

"I picked up the Bible last night after you went to bed and read a passage. Inside, there was an un-mailed letter as a placeholder. I shouldn't have read it. But I wanted so much to know more about your mother. In the letter, she wrote extensively about a daughter named Charlotte. At first, I laughed about one family having both a 'Charlie' and a 'Charlotte.' I figured Charles was a beloved name amongst your predecessors. Then, I wondered if Charlotte had been kidnapped by those horrible men, or was traveling. But the letter was written only a few days before I arrived, and your mother mentioned nothing about Charlotte traveling. And you never mentioned Charlotte at all. That was odd because you talk about Brendan and Ruth so often. Your mother also wrote about Brendan and Ruth in the letter, but there was nothing about Charlie. That seemed cruel, to completely neglect mentioning one of your children. Based on all you've told me about her, I didn't think your mother would do that. So, I started reading the letter again from the beginning, and something about her description of Charlotte's blue eyes planted a seed in my brain. You have the most vivid blue eyes I've ever seen."

Thomas squeezed her hands and flashed that beautiful smile that always made her heart race.

"The more I thought about it, the more I suspected you were not Charlie, but Charlotte. By the way, the name Charlie suits you."

"Charlie was my mother's pet name for me."

"Well, I've enjoyed getting to know you, Charlie, and now I look forward to getting to know Charlotte."

Thomas' hands felt warm and wonderful as they held hers tight. He looked at her with such intensity that she didn't know what to say. She wanted to tell him about how she loved him and longed for his embrace. About how he had saved her. About how grateful she would always be that God sent him into her life. But she just couldn't. Everything was going to change and she couldn't leave herself so vulnerable.

After a few moments, she asked, "Is Mother's letter still in the Bible? I would dearly love to read it."

"Yes, let me get it for you."

Thomas stood and walked into the cabin. Once inside, he took a deep breath and attempted to calm his heart.

"Pull yourself together, Thomas," he whispered to himself as he grabbed the letter from the Bible. Then he walked back outside and handed the letter to Charlotte.

"Would you like some privacy as you read it?"

"No. I don't think I want to be alone for this."

"I'll be right here for as long as you need me."

He wished he could tell her that he'd stay by her side as long as she needed him tonight, and for the rest of her life if she let him. Instead, he just smiled in hopes of encouraging her. This letter was going to be difficult; her mother's words would no doubt be comforting and heartbreaking all at the same time.

Charlotte looked at her mother's familiar handwriting and began to sob. She perused the letter and then set it down in her lap. Through her sobs, she laughed.

"I can't even read the writing through my tears!"

"I can read it to you if you like, or we can just sit and enjoy the silence. Whatever you want to do is fine with me."

She handed the letter to him, and he began reading. Charlotte cried, and laughed, and cried some more. When he finished the last line, he carefully folded the letter up and handed it back to her.

"I'm glad she never mailed this," Charlotte said, holding the paper close to her heart. "I will treasure it forever."

The crickets chirped and the wind whipped the leaves into a symphony. Thomas looked over at Charlotte and instantly knew he was right where God intended him to be. Jason Albertson's words rang in his ear.

"I feel that way every time I look at my wife; that feeling of being right where God wants me, of being home."

Thomas had never felt so at home in his life as he did in this moment. He saw his whole future stretching out in front of him. He and Charlotte, sitting on this porch together for many, many years to come, watching children and then grandchildren grow. His racing heart slowed and he breathed in the cool, clean air of home.

"I don't know what I should do now," Charlotte admitted a few minutes later. "Would you prefer that I move to Denver City, so we don't cause further scandal? I could try to stay with our new friends until arrangements can be made for travel to Ireland."

This was the last thing in the world that she wanted, and she felt her heart break as she suggested leaving. But she didn't know how Thomas felt about the situation. She had already promised him this land and he had so many dreams for it. Yes, she would need to leave.

"No. I hate that idea," he answered vehemently.

"I must say, I will miss this place so much. And I'll have to be a very different person when I leave the sanctuary of rural Colorado. I've recently been thinking about all that I will be giving up."

The mountains were invisible in the darkness and the sky overhead was a twinkling blanket of stars.

"You can still stay here, Charlotte," Thomas began.

She interrupted him with a bitter laugh. "A woman can't run a place like this alone!"

"Charlotte, I told you that very first evening at the gravesite that I would stay as long as you needed me. I meant it then and I mean it now. I'm not leaving unless you ask me to. I'll find some land of my own and we can work together to grow both of our properties."

"That's hardly appropriate now that you know I'm a woman."

She dropped her head against the tall back of the chair and closed her eyes.

"Oh, Thomas, this is all so scandalous! I can't even imagine what my mother would say. Or what Marnie and Clara will say. They'll be horrified by what my betrayal has caused. We shared a room, Thomas! And the Albertson children will know it. I'm so ashamed that I can't imagine facing them ever again."

Thomas reached for her hand once more.

"Charlotte, I love you and I don't think I could bear it if you left. Marry me, and we can stay here together forever, scandal-free."

She shook her head, but he continued.

"I will explain the situation to our friends. Like I said earlier, they'll understand you were just trying to protect yourself. When they see how happy we are together, that's all that will matter."

"Thomas, I can't be your wife," she said sadly. She had not raised her head or opened her eyes.

Thomas was stunned by her answer. At some point in the last few days, he had fallen deeply in love with Charlotte Gallagher. Every plan he had for the future now included her. Did she feel nothing? Did she not experience that crackle of energy every time they touched? Did she not treasure the time they spent together, talking and laughing, and just living their lives?

He tried to hide the pain in his voice. "I understand it wouldn't be the marriage you probably always dreamt of Charlotte, but I love you with all my heart. I never dreamed I could feel this strongly about anyone. Certainly you could grow to love me in time. We seem to get along well enough."

Charlotte still didn't speak, or even open her eyes.

"And I know you're very fond of my cooking," Thomas added with a laugh. He desperately needed to see her smile again, but his comment produced not even a flicker of humor on her face. Why was she suddenly so sad? It crushed him that she wouldn't even consider marrying him.

"Charlotte," he questioned and squeezed her hand. "Say something. Please."

She pulled her head up and looked over at him.

"Thomas, I don't need time to grow to love you. I already care for you so much, and the thought of no longer having you in my daily life makes me feel terribly empty."

She saw hope light up his face and shook her head again.

"But I won't marry you. I can't be a wife. Not to you. Not to anyone. What those men did to me, well…."

Charlotte struggled with a way to express her thoughts. This was not an appropriate conversation for a young woman to have with anyone, most of all a man. But she had to make him understand. She took a deep breath and forced herself to continue.

"I just could never be with a husband in the way a wife should. You deserve to have your dreams come true. You deserve children and grandchildren. It's obvious to me that you will be a wonderful father someday. I won't keep you from that."

"Charlotte, I've fallen in love with you. Even when you were Charlie, an eleven-year old boy who made me laugh uproariously and feel so protective, all I could think about was how desolate it would be here when you returned to Ireland. Now that you're Charlotte, I want to marry you. I want you to be with me always. I want to grow old with you. And if we can't share a bedroom right now, I'll wait as long as it takes."

Charlotte shook her head yet again. She seemed draped in a heavy cloak of sadness. But Thomas wasn't ready to give up.

"Charlotte, I will leave this alone for now. But I'm going to pray unceasingly that my love will slowly help heal your pain. I'm going to pray that someday you'll long for me the way I long for you."

"Thomas," she began, and then her voice trailed off. There was nothing more to say, so she just held his hand in silence. They sat together and stared at the stars. Holding hands with Thomas, Charlotte felt more complete than she had ever felt in her life. And yet, she knew she could never marry him.

When Charlotte released his hand an hour later and announced she was going to bed, Thomas stood and pulled her into his arms. His chin rested on the top of her head, and she held him tight around the waist, her cheek against his chest. She felt that she could stand like this forever with Thomas' heartbeat throbbing in her ear. Was it a few minutes or a few hours that passed as they stood in this embrace? Neither of them knew nor cared.

"May I kiss you just once, Charlotte?"

Thomas' deep, husky voice flamed the fire already burning inside her. She knew it was a mistake. She knew she should say no. She knew this would only make her want him more. But her rebellious heart paid no heed to the sensible warnings her cautious mind shouted. She gave her assent without words, raising her face to gaze up at him.

The look in Charlotte's eyes told Thomas all he needed to know. His right hand traveled up to cradle her head and he lowered his lips to hers. She closed her eyes and melted into him. Thomas had never experienced a kiss like this. When he finally pulled away and said goodnight, he knew he would wait forever for Charlotte. As much as his body longed for her, he would be satisfied with a quasi-platonic relationship if it meant he could spend every day of his life with this woman.

As Charlotte climbed the ladder to her loft, there was a smile on her face that she could not suppress. It seemed to originate from her very soul and heighten every sense. She felt guilty for being so giddy when she should be grieving her loved ones. Happiness and grief seemed such incompatible partners, and yet, since meeting Thomas they were her constant companions.

She lay in bed that night replaying the kiss over and over in her mind. She'd never been kissed before and hadn't dreamed anything could feel so wonderful and intoxicating. How she wished she could have met him under different circumstances and courted him as a whole woman. Her parents and siblings would have loved him. She let her mind wander into the world of "what ifs" and the tears began to flow. She saw Brendan and Thomas working together to put up hammocks and a new rope swing. She saw Thomas making Ruthie squeal with joy, and delighting Mother with his appreciation for her cooking. She saw the look on Father's face as he granted Thomas permission to marry her. Father would be thrilled that such a wonderful gentleman was going to become his son. Why, oh why had things turned out this way? She sobbed at the injustice of it all.

It was so tempting to accept Thomas' offer of marriage. She didn't think she'd ever wanted anything more in her life than to spend every day of the rest of her life with him. But it wasn't fair to tie him to a life without intimacy and without children. If his treatment of Charlie was any indication, he was going to be a loving, supportive father. She loved him too much to deny him that esteemed role. Thomas needed a real wife who could give him everything she couldn't. And yet, her heart rebelled as she imagined him with another woman. She wanted him so much. When she finally fell into an exhausted slumber, there were no nightmares. Instead, her night was filled with dreams of Thomas' lips on hers.

After Charlotte retired, Thomas lit a lantern and walked out to the cemetery. His heart brimmed with hope. Charlotte might refuse him now, but he knew without a doubt that she loved him. She had passionately participated in that earth-shattering kiss. She admitted she cared deeply for him. That was a great start! He only had to be patient. There was no rush. He could focus all his time and attention on getting to know Charlotte more and more each day. Their easy camaraderie was a great basis for love to continue to grow.

When he arrived at the burial site, he sat down between the two graves. After about ten minutes of prayerful silence, he spoke.

"I wish you all were still alive. The more I hear about each of you, the more deeply I long to have known you. You are the family I always dreamed of having. You are the sort of family I want to build someday. Growing up with so much love, it's no wonder Charlotte is who she is."

He paused and then placed a hand on the dirt covering Charlotte's parents. He knew this was stupid, but he felt the need to do it anyway.

"I want to ask you both for your blessing to marry Charlotte. And for your intercession, I guess. Please help her. She's hurting so badly. I can't even imagine what she's going through. Please help me. Help me to be patient and gentle with her. I know she always dreamed of a marriage like you two had. I know she wants to love and be loved, and I believe that I'm the right man for her. With your intercession, perhaps I can win her love. She already has my whole heart."

He closed his eyes and breathed in the cool night air.

"Ruthie, I wish you were here to bring some joy back into her sad eyes. And Brendan, well, I think she loved you most of all. Please put in a good word for me if you would."

Thomas stood, smiling at his foolishness. Somehow, though, it didn't seem all that foolish. He imagined Brendan and Ruth, Annie and Patrick smiling down at him from heaven. Certainly, they could see his heart and his desire to love and protect their Charlotte for the rest of her life.

He took another deep breath and then began his walk back to the cabin. It had been a very long day, and he couldn't wait to climb into bed. The bed he hoped to someday share with Charlotte.

Chapter Seventeen

Wednesday, September 4, 1867

The next morning, Thomas walked into the kitchen area to find that he was the first awake. That was odd. Every other morning, he had awakened to Charlie, rather Charlotte, already preparing breakfast. He felt a surge of panic and wondered if his kiss last night had caused her to run away. How could he have been so impulsive? She needed more time to get over her fears. He shouldn't have rushed her.

As he contemplated running to the barn to check if Meg was gone, he heard a sound from the loft. A moment later, Charlotte carefully descended the ladder. She was dressed in a blouse and long skirt. When she reached the bottom rung and turned around, Thomas' breath caught in his chest. Her short hair was slicked back and arranged in a very feminine way. The skirt and blouse fit her figure perfectly. He had fallen in love with Charlotte Gallagher before he ever knew what she really looked like. Now he was overwhelmed with desire.

"You look," he began.

Charlotte interrupted nervously. "I couldn't decide what to wear this morning! I didn't know whether to continue as a boy or show you the real me."

She was still looking at the floor and she shook her hands to release nervous energy. "I can't remember the last time I was this nervous."

Slowly, she lifted her face. Her eyes met his and heat flooded her face as she remembered the kiss. She longed to walk straight into his arms and beg him for another. Oh, but that had been such a bad idea last night. If she hadn't let him kiss her, she wouldn't know what she was missing.

Thomas couldn't pull his gaze from her.

"Charlotte, I already loved you for your quick humor and your strength of character. Never in a million years did I dream you would be so beautiful."

His praise brought a huge smile to her face. Embarrassed by her body's response, she quickly grabbed the water pitcher and turned to the door.

"I'll be right back."

She walked out into the cool morning air and was glad that she had decided to dress like a woman today. She'd used Brendan's hair pomade to arrange her hair sleek against her forehead and temples and thought it looked rather pretty. The ugly black stitches were still awful, but judging by Thomas' reaction, she'd made a good impression. She practically skipped to the well, so happy she felt.

When she returned to the cabin, Thomas had set the table.

"What are we making this morning, milady? Oatmeal, or my famous tortillas and scrambled eggs?"

A teasing smile lit up his face and she couldn't help but laugh. Would every day with this man be so fun and refreshing? Could she possibly allow herself to be his wife?

"Well, that depends. What are you in the mood for," she asked, setting the water pitcher on the table.

"Honestly, I'm in the mood for another kiss. But I promise to wait until you are, too."

Her insides did a somersault. Was he reading her mind? She crossed the room in an instant and was in his arms.

"This could easily become a habit," was her last thought before she lost all ability to think.

Long before she was ready for the kiss to end, Thomas stepped away and fell to one knee.

"Marry me, Charlotte. I want to spend the rest of my life with you."

"Thomas, you deserve," she began, but he interrupted.

"If I deserve anything, I want it to be you. I can assure you, I understand your concerns and I still want to marry you. The other dreams won't matter if I can just have you in my life. I don't need family or children as much as I need you, Charlotte."

He stood and pulled her into his arms again, looking deep into her eyes. "Please say yes, love."

Charlotte knew she should say no. She knew Thomas would regret this someday when he was older and had no children to love. She knew it was extremely selfish to allow him to enter into this ridiculous situation, but she simply couldn't stop herself. She wanted him.

"Yes," she whispered.

"I promise you won't regret this, Charlotte!"

Thomas' face was glowing with joy.

"I'm only afraid that you will."

"Never," he countered, and kissed her gently on the forehead.

She still looked concerned.

"Just think of all the biscuits I'll be getting out of this arrangement."

Thomas was thrilled when his comment made her laugh.

"You and your biscuits," she said, unable to keep from smiling.

"Let's head to Denver City tomorrow to meet with the priest. Perhaps he can marry us right away, considering the circumstances."

Thomas was brimming with excitement that Charlotte found adorable and utterly contagious. She wasn't as confident as he was about how the Groves and Albertsons would react to learning the truth, but she decided to trust him. Thomas Linz had a way of charming everyone they met. If anyone could smooth over this awful situation, it was him.

They spent another long, hot day cutting the grass for hay. Later that afternoon, when Thomas went to the barn to prepare their saddle bags for the early morning ride to Denver City, Charlotte walked alone to the hill where her family was buried. She needed to talk with her mother and father about this. She climbed the hill with a blanket over her right shoulder. In her hands, she carried all the wildflowers she could manage.

She placed flowers on each of the two graves. Then she spread the blanket and lay on her stomach, looking out over the property that would soon belong to her husband; her beloved husband, Thomas. Tears began streaming down her cheeks and she let them flow, unchecked, to fall on the blanket.

"I'm getting married soon," she whispered. The words sounded wholly unbelievable. How could she be getting married to someone her family had never met? How could she be getting married with so little preparation or planning, and without her family beside her? None of this was how it should be.

"You would have loved him so very much, Daddy. His gentleness and sense of humor remind often me of you. I wish he could have known you and asked you for your blessing."

Sobs cut off her words and anger boiled up from deep inside her.

"God, I'm so terribly angry with You. I can't understand how You would allow this! We have honored You faithfully all these years. How could You let this happen?"

She wanted to scream and pound her fists against the ground like a little child. She seethed with anger. But if she screamed Thomas would no doubt hear and come running to her. As much as she loved him, she needed this time alone with her family. She needed assurance that what she was about to do was okay with them.

"I know it's stupid to come out here and talk with you all, but I must believe you can hear me. I feel you close every moment of every day, and I must believe that you have seen Thomas and how he treats me. I love him with all my heart and I wish every day that you were here and that we could all be a family together. You would have loved him so much."

"Mother, please help me be a good wife. Please help me to love him unconditionally and to be a good and supportive spouse. I really had the very best example in you. Father, send Thomas and me guidance as we move forward with your plans to grow the farm. Neither of us know enough. Ruthie, send me some of your joy. I'm so overwhelmed with my sadness, and I wish I could be more like you. I would give anything to have you with me. Brendan, I miss you so much..." She simply couldn't continue. Thinking of Brendan was just too painful. She lay there on the ground between her family's graves and cried until she could cry no more.

When she returned to the cabin much later that evening, she was surprised to see a large mare tied to the hitching post. The horse looked familiar, but she couldn't immediately remember whose it was. As she grew closer, the answer finally came to her. This was Sergeant Albertson's horse. She looked down at her blouse and skirt.

"I guess he finds out before the rest of them," she thought wryly. As she walked the last few yards to the back porch, she realized maybe this was for the best. If he reacted poorly, she and Thomas would know to avoid visiting the Groves and Albertson homes tomorrow. Her heart ached at that possibility. These new friends already felt like family, and Charlotte needed all the family she could get!

She took a deep breath, and opened the door. Upon her entrance, both men stood from their places at the table.

"Ms. Gallagher," Jason called with jubilation, and approached her with open arms.

"I was just telling Sergeant Albertson the good news," Thomas said. Pride and excitement were evident in his voice.

"Sergeant Albertson," Charlotte asked, as she was enfolded in the man's huge bear hug. "You're not angry?"

With his arms still around her, he pulled his head back to look into her eyes.

"How could I be angry, my dear? I am just so darned happy for you both. Mrs. Albertson and I noticed how close you and Thomas were, and thought it wonderful that neither of you would have to face life alone. This is...well, it's just better than anything we could have dreamed up. You'd best be prepared because Mrs. Albertson will be beside herself with excitement!"

He released her and took a step back. He ran his fingers through his hair and looked a bit timid about something. Then he spoke again.

"Charlotte, I hope this isn't presumptuous of me, but I'd be honored to stand in for your father and walk you down the aisle."

Charlotte couldn't answer for the lump in her throat. Instead, she stepped forward, wrapped her arms around his waist, and laid her head on his chest. With tears flowing down her cheek, she thought about how sad she would be to marry Thomas without her family present. This wonderful, kind man. How thoughtful of him to offer.

"I'll take that as a yes," Albertson said, laughing.

"Yes," was her muffled response. "Yes. And thank you."

When Jason pulled away again, he gestured for her to take a seat. She pulled out her handkerchief and attempted to stop crying. Thomas and Jason visited about trivial matters until she had regained control of her emotions.

"To what do we owe this pleasure," Charlotte finally asked with a smile.

"I'm afraid this is a police visit and not a social call. There have been three more attacks in the last two weeks. All were very similar to what happened here and at your neighbor's place. I came to update you and let you know that we now have law enforcement and volunteers from all around the territory searching for these men. I've received several telegrams today and it sounds like we're getting close to capturing them. I was asked to summon you to Denver City in the next day or so to identify them."

Charlotte was suddenly terrified. She reached out for Thomas' hand and took a deep, calming breath. Thomas squeezed her hand and gave her a reassuring nod.

"How very convenient that we were already planning to travel there tomorrow," she offered, attempting to make light of the situation.

"I know you're scared," Thomas said. "But I will be with you through every moment of this. And you've got Sergeant Albertson on your side, not to mention Big Viv!"

This made them all laugh.

"Do you think Vivian would come to the jail with me? I think she could scare Fred and Dan. Really scare them. It would do me a world of good to see them afraid."

"You had that woman wrapped around your finger within minutes of meeting. I think she'll do anything you ask," Albertson answered.

The three of them began discussing what would occur once the criminals were captured and brought to the jail. Jason explained the legal process and what the trial might entail. Night had fallen by the time they were finished.

"Would you like to stay here tonight, Sergeant," Charlotte asked, "Or should we leave right now?"

"I have everything packed and ready to go," Thomas added. "Do you know what you'll need, Charlotte?"

"I can be ready in five minutes," she answered.

"There's no rush," Albertson said. "We won't actually need you for another day or two at the earliest. It's probably wiser to wait until daylight, anyway. Are you sure you have room for me?"

"Charlotte has been sleeping up in the loft, and I've been in the bedroom. Maybe we could switch since there are two beds up there and only one down here," Thomas said, indicating the bedroom behind him.

"That works for me," Charlotte said. "Are you hungry, Sergeant Albertson?"

"Call me Jason, please. And yes," he answered with a huge smile. "I'm always hungry!"

"Well, that sounds like someone else I know," she laughed and cut her eyes to Thomas who was also chuckling.

"How about I make you some of my award-winning tortillas, Jason," Thomas suggested.

Albertson was confused when Thomas and Charlotte both doubled over in laughter. Whatever the reason, their mirth filled his heart with joy. These two were going to make a great couple. He remembered his conversation with Thomas the night they met. Yes, sir! Thomas had truly found the right one. Jason quickly swiped his eye. He'd always been soft-hearted, but it would not do to cry in front of his new friends.

Thomas made fresh tortillas to eat with the pinto beans that Charlotte had prepared. The beans had been simmering all day long and the smell made Jason's mouth water. Charlotte and Jason sat at the table, visiting with Thomas while he deftly cooked the tortillas.

"You know, Thomas," Charlotte began, smiling slyly over at Jason. "When you thought I was a boy, it made sense for us to share kitchen duty. But now that I'm a woman again, it hardly seems acceptable for you to be cooking."

Thomas turned from the stove to face them. "What are you suggesting, my dear? Do you want me to give up my most rewarding chore," he asked in mock indignation. "I'll have you know that an accomplished cook like me will be hard to replace!"

The cabin was filled with laughter and Charlotte felt perplexed that she could have laughed so much since walking into the cabin, when she had been utterly devastated and angry only minutes before. For the moment, she felt like she could face anything that happened in that courtroom with strength and grace. She had good, good people on her side, and she would be just fine.

When dinner and cleanup were complete, Charlotte went to sleep in her parents' bedroom, while Thomas and Jason climbed up to the loft. Due to Jason's presence, there had been no more kissing, and Charlotte closed the bedroom door in a very disappointed state.

"I have indeed become addicted," she mused as she stripped off her clothes and put on her nightgown.

Kneeling down at the side of her parents' bed, she tried to quiet her thoughts. She was still so angry with God, and then felt guilty for her anger. Instead of her usual night prayers, she poured out her heart to her Heavenly Father.

"God, I don't know what to say right now. But You know my heart, even better than I do. You know how much I love You. And You know that I'm trying my best to trust You."

Tears were streaming down her face, and she cried in silence for several long minutes.

"I want to trust You, but I just don't understand. I know that bad things happen to good and bad alike, but I just don't understand how this could have happened? Why didn't you protect Your friends?"

Then, she realized that, while Jesus was walking the earth, God had not protected His beloved Son or those closest to Him. Jesus, and every apostle besides John, had died in horrific ways. She knew it should probably make her feel better, to know that her family hadn't been abandoned by God. But all she felt was confused.

"Please be with me, God. I'll love You through my anger, and I hope You will still love me. Just help me to trust You and help me to heal from my losses."

A few hours later, Charlotte awoke to her own screaming. Heart racing, she sat up in bed and tried to calm down. Within moments, she heard knocking on the bedroom door.

"Come in," she said, pulling the blanket up to her chin.

"Are you okay," Thomas asked. He crossed the room and struck a match, carefully lighting the candle on her bedside table. Then he sat at the foot of the bed.

Charlotte took a shuddering breath and nodded her head.

"Just another nightmare. Thomas, I'm feeling so angry with God these days. At first, I was just numb and sad all the time. Now, I spend every day confused and angry. I don't understand how He could have allowed this to happen to such a family who loved Him so much."

Her fists clenched and unclenched at her sides.

Thomas didn't speak but reached out his left hand. She placed her right hand in his and he held it tight. He knew she needed to talk and needed him to just silently listen. He couldn't fix this, but he could be here with her as she talked through her anger and pain.

"I know I need to keep trusting and praying; to keep focusing on something my mother told me once. I was probably ten or eleven and was having a hard time understanding why God didn't stop bad people. She said, 'Charlotte, if God stopped every bad thing from happening, we might like it for a while, but it would cost us our free will. God is perfect love, and He wants us to live with each other in perfect love. But He won't override our free will. Evil exists in the world not because God wills it; only because He loves us too much to control us.' I'll never forget that conversation."

Thomas could hear the admiration in her voice.

"My parents didn't just teach us about our faith, they lived it every single day. If I turn out anything like my parents..."

Her voice trailed off and she looked down at her lap. Her body began trembling with sobs and Thomas saw a tear fall onto the blanket below her downturned face.

"You are off to a very good start, Charlotte."

He reached over and placed his right hand under her chin. Gently, he lifted her face until she was looking at him.

"Your mother and father both live on through you. As do Brendan and Ruth. Their legacies will never die. You will keep them alive as long as you live."

He wanted to say that their own children would carry the memories long after he and Charlotte were gone, but he knew she wasn't ready for that. He let her cry for several more minutes.

"Speaking of legacies," he tentatively began. "With your permission, I'd like us to start by building your father's church."

Thomas heard a sharp intake of breath and Charlotte looked up at him.

"Really, Thomas?"

"I've been thinking about it for a few days, actually. I plan to post a flier at the Denver City post office inviting all nearby Catholics to join us here for a planning meeting in two months. That should give everyone time to see the flier and spread the word. Once we gather, we can all work together to determine the needs of the community. Then, I'll hire workers to begin construction."

"You would do that for him," she asked in bewilderment.

He nodded his head.

"But Thomas, it will cost so very much!"

"Charlotte," he grimaced, and seemed hesitant to go on. "It's embarrassing to talk about this. However, as my future wife you need to know."

Charlotte felt a flash of fear. What horrible thing was Thomas hiding?

"No, it's nothing scary," he insisted, shaking his head with a soft chuckle. "I should have phrased that better. I'm realizing that I haven't shared much about my past. I was born into the combined prosperity of two enormously wealthy families. The war wiped out many of my cousins, and there are very few Linzs or Pipers left. Emily and I each inherited several million dollars upon our parents' deaths."

Charlotte's face reflected her shock and surprise.

"Million?"

"Yes. Millions. I've always felt ashamed of being so rich when many others had so little. My family was generous, but we could have done so much more. I want us," he freed one of his hands from hers and motioned to Charlotte and back to himself as he said the word 'us.'

"I want us to be as generous as possible. I want us to carry on your family's legacy. Building this church is the best possible way we could begin. It will help so many families, and it will bring me the greatest joy."

Charlotte beamed at him. "How I wish you and Father could have met."

"I wish the same, every single day. But we will someday- in heaven. I'll get to meet Ruth and Brendan and your parents. And you'll get to meet Michael and my parents. I hope they will all be proud of everything you and I accomplish together between now and then."

"I know they will. And Thomas, I know my family is so thankful that I have you in my life."

Charlotte's small, feminine hand was still enfolded in Thomas' larger, stronger one. With a shy smile, she pulled him close.

"I missed my goodnight kiss tonight."

Did the woman have no idea how seductive that was? This abstinent marriage was going to be the death of him! Thomas allowed himself to lean in closer to her. He closed his eyes and laid his cheek against hers, breathing in the faint rose scent of her recently washed hair. Then he kissed her slowly and passionately. It took every ounce of his willpower to not go further. She was worth the wait, he reminded himself.

"Will that suffice," he asked when he finally pulled away.

"For now," she answered with a wink. "Goodnight, Thomas."

"Goodnight, my love." He stood up and asked, "Will you be okay now, or do I need to stay downstairs in the living room?"

"Just knowing that you are here under the same roof should be all I need. Please go back to bed."

At the doorway, Thomas turned back to her.

"Don't forget that we have a lawman for a guest tonight. We're safer than we've ever been," he added.

Charlotte smiled. In the candlelight, Thomas could see the flush on her cheeks and the glow of love in her eyes. She had never looked more beautiful. Within the next few days, this lovely creature would be his wife. His heart swelled with pride, and he stood gazing at her for several long moments.

"What's wrong, Thomas?"

"Nothing. Nothing at all."

Thomas shook his head and laughed at himself. Then he turned and walked out of the room, softly closing the door behind him. He carefully made his way across the dark cabin to the loft ladder. He didn't want to wake Jason if he'd fallen back asleep after Charlotte's scream woke them both. He silently climbed the ladder to find Jason wide awake.

"Everything okay," the sergeant asked.

"Yea, sorry about that. It seems every night she's woken by my screaming, or I'm woken by hers. Our marriage will be nothing if not interesting."

"Poor Mrs. Albertson must put up with my night terrors, too. I don't think any of us came out of that damn war intact. But at least when you're fighting in a war, you know to expect horrors. It shouldn't happen here, and to good people who were just living their own lives, hurting no one. I still can't believe all that your young lady has been through. When Charlie told us his story that was bad enough. Now that I know it was Charlotte." He rubbed a hand over his face. "Truly, I've always wondered how on earth a woman survived that kind of assault. When I think about something like that happening to Marnie or one of our girls, I just don't know what I'd do."

"I keep thinking about horrible ways those evil men should die," Thomas said with anger in his voice. Then he looked over at Jason. "But I guess it's not wise to share your vigilante desires with a lawman."

"It would be damned hard to arrest someone who was just doing what any man would want to do in that situation," Jason opined. "Damned near impossible."

"Let's hope that was our only nightmare for the night! We have a long, joyous day ahead of us."

Thomas slipped back under his covers.

"Do you really think Mrs. Albertson and Mrs. Groves and Big Viv will be okay when they hear about Ms. Gallagher? If there's a chance they might react badly, I will book rooms at the hotel. We can marry quickly and head home as soon as you no longer need her for the identification. I can't bear the thought of her being hurt further."

"Thomas, my friend, they all fell for little Charlie as soon as they met him. Their motherly instincts kicked in and they just loved him wholeheartedly. When they find out their precious Charlie is actually a woman, and then learn of all she's been through, they will love her all the more. I honestly couldn't think of a better group of women to love and support Ms. Gallagher through all this. Don't you give it another thought."

A few minutes later, Thomas was surprised to hear Jason quietly laughing.

"What's so amusing, Sergeant?"

"I was just remembering our conversation around the fire that first night we met. I knew God would bring someone wonderful into your life, I just never imagined it would happen so fast."

Thomas joined in the laughter. "And I didn't realize she was already right under my nose!"

Chapter Eighteen

Thursday, September 5, 1867

The next morning, the three friends set out early for Denver City. Charlotte felt terribly jumbled with panic and excitement, love and sadness, grief and joy all warring inside her. By tonight or tomorrow she could be a married woman. She loved Thomas, of that, she was sure. But this was not how she had ever imagined entering a marriage. For the millionth time in the last three weeks, Charlotte longed for her mother. No girl should have to be without a mother on her wedding day. And yet, that was how it would be. Charlotte wouldn't have her mother there to help her dress or do her hair. She wouldn't be surrounded by family. She wouldn't have Father to walk her down the aisle. She wouldn't get to see the brotherly pride in Brendan's eyes, or the tears of joy Mother would certainly cry. She wouldn't hear Ruth's excited noises from the pew behind her as she knelt with Thomas before the altar. She wouldn't even have a beautiful wedding dress. Remembering the many conversations she and Mother had enjoyed while dreaming of what kind of wedding dress they would someday sew together broke her heart.

"I know you're here, Mother. I know you're with me."

The thought calmed her some. She thought again about her dress. The only dress she owned right now was her worn-out, too small, Sunday-best outfit. For months, Charlotte had intended to ask for material the next time her father went into Denver City for supplies. Somehow, she always forgot. And when they went on Sundays for Mass, all the shops were closed.

Well, this dress would just have to do. She shook her head and nudged Meg to walk faster. During the ride, she had purposely fallen behind Jason and Thomas so she could have some time to think. But her solitary thoughts were definitely not improving her mood. The men's conversation would at least provide distraction from her melancholy.

"There's my beautiful fiancé! I was about to send out a search party for you."

"Oh, Mr. Linz," she sighed. "I have no hair, and I'm dusty from two hours of riding." She looked past Thomas to Jason. "Perhaps we need to ask Dr. Groves to check his eyesight when we get to Denver."

Jason laughed.

"Forgive me, Ms. Gallagher, but you are a silly goose! Not only are you beautiful, but you and Mr. Linz have just the sort of relationship he described to me the first night we met. You had fallen asleep, and we were up talking."

Charlotte didn't admit that she had heard the whole discussion.

"He said he wanted it all- love, friendship and humor. He said he was willing to wait for as long as it took. But instead, he found that love within weeks!" Jason chuckled again. "My dear, I'd venture to say you are the most beautiful woman Mr. Linz has ever met."

"You would be correct, sir," Thomas agreed. Then he turned to look at Charlotte. "Darling, I want you to always feel free to wear your hair however you like. But I must admit this short style has really grown on me. I love how it looks today. You'll soon have all the Denver City women following your lead! And I imagine it's a sight easier to take care of than long hair."

"That's very true. Maybe Mrs. Albertson or Mrs. Groves could trim it up for me." She started laughing. "Would you believe that I hacked off all my hair with Father's barn shears?"

"Now that is a funny thought," Jason said.

"What did it look like before," Thomas asked. He wanted to know everything about this mesmerizing woman who would soon be his wife.

"It was long, almost to my waist. When I washed it, it could take all day to dry out. It got horribly tangled in the wind if I ever left it loose, so I mostly wore it in two long braids."

They rode on in silence for a few minutes when Charlotte spoke again.

"Now that I think about it, that long hair really was rather difficult to maintain."

"Well, then. Short it should remain," Jason said, good-naturedly. "I recall Mrs. Albertson coming home last week surprised by all the beautiful wigs that had arrived at Larimer's Store. That is always an option if you remain too worried about your hair. I'm sure Mrs. Albertson would relish a day spent shopping with you!" He laughed. "You'd better be ready, Mr. Linz. Wives can be expensive, especially if you live near stores with new items available every week."

"My saving grace will be living three hours away from the nearest store," Thomas exclaimed, and joined in the laughter. "Of course, while we're in town, Charlie, you should buy anything your heart desires."

Charlotte was still reeling at the amount of money Thomas had disclosed to her last night. It made her happy and excited to think of all the good deeds that could be accomplished with such great wealth. They would start with a church, but maybe a school could be the next project. Most families out near Kerry Haven had no place to educate their children. Parents were the primary educators, but on a busy farm or ranch, there was generally very little time for teaching. A local school would be a blessing to so many. She let her mind wander. There were so many possibilities!

"I've been wondering," Thomas pondered as they reached the outskirts of Denver City. "Would you like for Sergeant Albertson and me to talk to the ladies first, or would you prefer to approach them all together?"

"I've been thinking about that," she admitted. The men could hear the underlying anxiety in her voice. "I know you both think that everyone is just going to be overjoyed, but I still find that hard to believe. Mr. Linz and I stayed in the same room! Mrs. Albertson is going to be so upset that we've caused a scandal in front of your children. She'll not easily get over that. I think I might prefer it if I could check into the hotel near your house, and then you could bring the women to meet me there. If they find out in private, they won't have to guard their tongues in front of the children. And I won't be so nervous if I can meet the two of them alone."

"We could do that," Thomas said. "I was already planning to book the finest room available for our wedding night."

"Mr. Linz! You shouldn't talk so," Charlotte admonished. Her face quickly turned a brilliant shade of red. "Not in front of another man!"

"I'm sorry, love. I'm a barbarian."

Thomas turned away from her to face Jason with raised eyebrows and a big grin on his face. "Please forgive me, sir."

It was all Jason could do to keep from bursting into laughter. He could tell Thomas wanted to laugh, too. But Charlotte was mortified. Now was a time to behave like grownups and not immature schoolboys. The two men looked away from each other and tried to keep sober.

"What I meant to say," Thomas began slowly, determined to keep from laughing, "is that I will book the hotel for you, and you alone, from tonight until our marriage. We can certainly bring the women to you. You're right about giving them a safe space to discuss this."

"Thank you, Thomas. I really do appreciate it," she said.

Talking about the wedding and sharing a hotel room stirred up so much anxiety in Charlotte. This was a mistake. She needed to stop this silly charade. It was not fair to marry Thomas when she knew she couldn't truly be his wife. Her stomach was churning, and she regretted eating breakfast this morning.

As soon as they arrived in town, Jason excused himself to check in at the jail and get an update on the search.

"I will meet you at your office once Ms. Gallagher is settled," Thomas informed him. "Then, you and I can go together to gather the ladies."

"Sounds good," Jason agreed. He tipped his hat to Charlotte and turned his horse toward the jail.

"I really am sorry if I embarrassed you earlier. Sometimes I don't think about things before I say them."

"It's okay. I'm just feeling so flustered today. Are you as nervous as I am about all this? I still can't believe we'll be married in a matter of days."

"No. I've never felt more certain about anything in my life, Charlotte. If anything, I'm just overwhelmed with gratitude."

"But we hardly know each other, Thomas. What if you realize in a few weeks or a few months that I'm not quite who you thought I was? What if you don't feel the same anymore? What if you find that giving up a true marriage and the possibility of children is simply too much to sacrifice?"

"Oh, my love. I cared for you even before I had any clue about who you were. You were just a sad little boy who looked remarkably like a monster," he quipped.

"A monster," Charlotte interrupted, looking at him with mock indignation. How was it that he could make her laugh even when she felt she might be sick from worry?

"You must admit you weren't looking your best that first week or so!"

"Little monster Charlie," she agreed, laughing along with him.

"But even before I knew who you were, I felt closer to you than I'd ever felt to anyone, even my dear Emily. I knew I wanted you in my life and I dreaded the idea of you going to live with family in Ireland."

Thomas was speaking passionately and none too softly. Charlotte looked around to see if others were hearing their conversation. Luckily, it was still pretty early in the morning, and not many people were out on the streets. Then she admonished herself. She needed to quit putting so much stock in the opinions of others.

"Charlotte, I loved you from the start. And every day, I've grown to love you more. Don't you understand? That isn't going to change; it will only grow as time goes by."

He was looking at her intently, waiting for a response. Finally, he asked, "Do you not feel the same?"

Charlotte saw the pain on his face. How should she answer him? She decided to be totally honest.

"I don't know, Thomas. I don't know how I feel. Ever since we met, I've been filled with the greatest sorrow, and joy, and grief, and nightmares, and laughter and excitement. Oh, and then the thrill of your touch and your kisses! Well, it's all just a tornado inside of me and I'm not sure of anything anymore."

"I understand," he said silently.

It was obvious that her words had hurt him.

"Thomas, I…I don't want to hurt you. I'm trying to be excited. I promise I am." She didn't know how to erase the pain she'd caused.

Thomas just wished he could be alone for a moment. His mind was reeling at her words, and he needed a place where he wouldn't have to pretend he was okay.

"It's fine, Charlotte," he lied. "I understand."

Charlotte nodded in relief. At the end of the next block stood the beautiful Tremont House Hotel. Charlotte had never stayed in such a grand hotel before and was excited at the prospect of a hot bath and comfortable bed. Then her face flushed as thoughts of the bed led to thoughts of their wedding night. Surely, Thomas would need to stay here with her to at least give the semblance of a real marriage. What would it be like to share a room with him again? To share a bed?

"Will you wait here with the horses while I check for availability," Thomas asked as he dismounted Trigger and handed her his reins.

He hadn't even looked at her. As she watched him walk into the hotel, Charlotte suddenly felt more alone than she had felt since he first rode into her life. Despite pretending he understood her feelings, she realized he was deeply hurt. The realization crushed her, and she immediately regretted her words. Thomas truly had been the one who saved her from just giving up. If not for his arrival she might have buried her family near the barn and then lay down near them and given up on life. Thomas' kindness and humor and love had pulled her through something she might not have survived. He'd loved her unconditionally and in return, she'd broken his heart.

Had she ruined everything? Had she ruined their chance at happiness? Why hadn't she just said what she knew he needed to hear? She could have told him she was excited and looking forward to their wedding. She could have told him she loved him. After all, she didn't know whether these things were true or false. They very well could be the truth; she was just too confused to know. What had she done?

When Thomas returned a few minutes later, she tried to apologize again.

"Thomas, I'm so very sorry. Just forget what I said earlier, please. I do love you and I am excited to spend the rest of my life with you. I'm just feeling nervous right now."

He smiled up at her and helped her down from Meg, but his smile didn't reach his eyes, and he didn't speak.

"Thomas, say something, please," she begged.

"I don't have anything to say right now, Charlotte. But we'll get through this," he added, and squeezed her hand reassuringly. "I promise."

He unfastened the carpet bag from her saddle and looped her arm through his. "Let me show you to your room, and then I'll go meet Albertson."

They walked together into the hotel lobby and Thomas led her to the gently curving staircase.

"Your room is on the second floor. I'm told it has a balcony with table and chairs. The purveyor assured me it's a wonderful place to sit and enjoy a coffee or tea."

When they arrived at the room, Thomas unlocked the door and then handed her the key.

"I'm sure Mrs. Groves and Mrs. Albertson will find it odd that we are summoning them to the hotel this morning. I'd like your permission to briefly present the situation so that they can understand why we are requesting their presence. What do you think?"

All the humor and passion were gone from his voice and Charlotte thought she would burst into tears.

"Oh, God, what have I done," she silently prayed. "You brought the perfect mate into my life, and I've ruined everything."

"I think that's a wonderful idea, Thomas. Thank you for suggesting it."

She wrapped her arms around him and raised her face to look deeply into his eyes. She needed him to kiss her and tell her everything would be okay. He kissed her swiftly on the forehead and then pulled from her embrace.

"I'll be back soon. Please lock the door behind me."

Then he was gone. Charlotte locked the door and leaned against it. She was consumed with self-condemnation. How could she have been so staggeringly stupid? All she wanted was to lie down on the big, soft bed and cry until she had no tears left.

However, Marnie and Clara both lived close to the hotel and would likely be here soon. There was no time for tears. She needed to wash her face after the dusty ride and change into something more presentable. Then, when her appearance was improved, she would spend what little time she had preparing for her discussion with the two women. There would be time later to fall apart. She was so grateful that Thomas had offered to fill the women in on some of the details before they arrived. He always thought of the feelings of others, and she greatly appreciated that about him. Silently, she prayed that Marnie and Clara would understand and still love her.

Before long, Charlotte heard a knock on the door.

"Please God. Please help this go well," she fervently whispered as she placed the key in the lock and turned it.

She opened the door to find Clara and Marnie with huge smiles on their faces. She was enveloped in their loving arms and burst into tears.

"Dear Miss Gallagher," Clara cried, once they had walked into the room followed by Thomas and Jason. "Please don't cry! This is the best news ever."

Charlotte laughed through her sobs. "I was so nervous that you'd be angry, and I'd lose your friendship!" She shook her head and swiped at her tears. "You can't imagine how relieved I am."

She couldn't stop laughing and crying at the same time. "What is wrong with me," she asked, and sniffled.

By now, all five of the room's occupants were laughing along with her.

"I'd imagine you're just overwhelmed. I'm sorry you ever worried about our reaction," Marnie said, her eyes filled with tears. "Sweet girl," she murmured, pulling Charlotte into another hug.

This kindness just made Charlotte cry even harder.

"Okay, that's enough emotion for the two of us," Jason said, clearing his throat. "I'm happy things have turned out so well, but you know we men are uncomfortable around tears."

He turned to Thomas. "Let's go have a drink or do something manly!"

"I think ten o'clock is a mite early for a drink, Sergeant," Thomas chuckled, putting his arm around the other man's shoulders.

How he would have loved a father like this, he thought. Jason truly was a big softie under his tough exterior. He thanked God for leading him to Colorado and these wonderful friends. They loved Charlotte so easily. Their love, along with his own, would help heal her deep wounds and allay her grief.

"I'd like to head to St. Mary's to set up an appointment with the pastor," Thomas said, looking at Charlotte. "And then I'll head to the land office and post office if there's time. Should we all plan to meet for dinner together?"

Marnie answered his question. "We can all meet for dinner at our house tonight. Let's say half past six."

Thomas nodded and pulled out his wallet. He handed Charlotte several large bills. "Please purchase anything you need for the wedding. And then, maybe your friends would be available for lunch here at the hotel."

He kissed her on the forehead and turned to leave the room.

"We'll take good care of your beautiful fiancé," Clara called to the men as they left.

"Of that, I have no doubt," Thomas responded, and closed the door behind them.

"I thought they'd never leave! Now, my dear Charlotte, let's sit down and get to know you," Marnie said, indicating the chairs on the balcony.

One hour, and many tears later, Charlotte had shared everything with the women. She described the tragedy of losing her family and her dear friends cried with her and took turns assuring her she was now part of their families. They promised she would never be alone again. When she finished, Charlotte was pleasantly surprised to realize how much lighter she felt. This secret had been such a huge burden, and now she could set that burden down and walk into her future.

Then, they'd excitedly asked her to tell them all about how Thomas finally discovered her, and how they'd fallen in love. She relished the telling of it. When she got to the part about Thomas confronting her on the porch the other night and then declaring his love, the women almost swooned from the romance of it all. Charlotte left out the part about not being able to give Thomas a full marriage. It somehow seemed too intimate to share with anyone, ever. Clara and Marnie were overjoyed about the upcoming wedding. Charlotte had never had a sister that she could confide in or share her feelings with. She looked at Clara and Marnie and her heart filled with love and gratitude.

"Let's go shopping, my dear," Marnie suggested, standing and motioning to the open door to Charlotte's hotel room. "A wedding! I can hardly contain my excitement!"

"I hope we can find something suitable for me to wear," Charlotte said. She entered the hotel room and crossed to the bedroom where her carpet bag lay. "All I have is my Sunday best, and it's not looking too good! Is there a shop that sells pre-made dresses? I think Sergeant Albertson mentioned Larimer's. I realize there's no time for a wedding dress to be made, but maybe I could find something prettier than this."

She pulled a rather plain looking lilac dress from her carpet bag.

Clara's eyes beamed as she spoke. "Charlotte, I understand if you want to buy something of your own, but I'd like to offer my wedding dress. We're about the same size, and I could easily make any alterations necessary," she offered. "It's really rather beautiful, if I do say so myself."

"Are you serious? I can't thank you enough!"

"It will make me so happy for you to wear it," Clara answered, and Charlotte squealed with excitement!

"Okay, then! We head to your house first," Marnie said.

"Oh, that reminds me—I would love it if Dr. Groves or George could remove these awful stitches. I think when they cleaned the wound, Dr. Groves said we should remove them in three weeks, so it's right about time. I really don't want to get married looking like a monster," she finished with a giggle.

"Yes, that's probably not the best look for a bride," Clara added with a grin.

Charlotte folded the money Thomas had given her and carefully placed it in her reticule. She couldn't remember the last she'd carried this small bag, and she'd certainly never carried this much money in her whole life. What would being wealthy feel like, she wondered. It was not something she'd ever imagined for her future.

She locked the door behind them and the three friends walked down the staircase to the lobby and out of the hotel. Within a few minutes, they arrived at Clara's house. Vivian opened the door and pulled Charlotte into the biggest hug she'd ever had. Then she led the three women into the house.

"My sweet, sweet child," Vivian crooned. "I knew you talked too well to be a young boy!"

"Thank you, Vivian," Charlotte sighed. "Thank you for understanding. Does Dr. Groves know?"

Charlotte looked anxiously between the three women.

"Yes," Big Viv answered. "Your Mr. Linz didn't share much, but everyone is at least aware of the general situation." She looked pointedly at Charlotte. "And not a one of us was angry, Ms. Gallagher. Not a single person is upset by what you did. You were just doing what you had to do to survive."

"Please Vivian, call me Charlotte."

"I'm just so heartbroken for you," Vivian said. "You poor child."

"And, please, whatever you do, don't be too kind, or I'll start crying again," Charlotte said, laughing. "Trust me, you don't want me to start that again!"

"I don't know that any of us have tears left to cry," Marnie said. "I know I've cried all mine out."

Just then, Dr. Groves entered the room. Charlotte was happy to see a big smile on his face.

"Well, I hardly recognize you now that your huge gash has healed and your face is back to its normal shape," he cried joyfully. "What a beauty you've turned out to be!"

"I don't know about beauty. However, I can tell you that I used the salve every single day until it ran out. I was hoping you could remove these stitches before my wedding. Mrs. Groves agrees that it's not a great look for a bride."

"I think the beautiful Mrs. Groves is right again," he said, cheerfully.

Dr. Groves looked over at Clara with such adoration in his eyes. Would Thomas ever look at her that way again? Her heart longed to talk with him. She had to make things right between them!

Clara and Marnie stayed in the drawing room to begin working on a shopping list, and Dr. Groves led Charlotte to the exam room. "George is simply not going to believe how well this has healed."

George looked up as they entered the room.

"Miss Gallagher, how are you today?"

"I'm doing much better than the last time you saw me," she answered as she shook his hand. "It's good to see you again, George. And please, call me Charlotte."

"George, I'll let you do the honors," Dr. Groves said.

"Have a seat, Miss Galla, I mean, Charlotte," George instructed, indicating a high-backed wooden chair.

When she sat, he pulled his stool close and peered carefully at her forehead.

"This looks great," he said as he turned to open a drawer. She watched as he removed a small pair of scissors, tweezers, and some gauze cloth.

"Here you are," Dr. Groves said, as he handed George a metal basin, partially filled with steaming water.

"Thank you, sir," George answered, dropping the gauze into the basin and setting it on the small exam table next to him. "Now, you might feel some tugging, but I want you to tell me if it hurts."

Charlotte nodded, and George began carefully snipping the stitches. He was right about the tugging sensation, but Charlotte never felt any pain. When he was done removing the stitches, George swabbed her forehead with the warm, wet gauze. She relaxed into the soothing heat. While the wound was healing, there had been such a constant itchy feeling. Now that the prickly stitches had been removed, everything felt so much better. She tentatively reached up to touch the area.

George handed her a small mirror.

"It's not too bad," he assured her.

Charlotte looked into the mirror as she gingerly ran her fingers over the scar. With disappointment, she realized the long, shiny white line would be a constant reminder of the worst day of her life. Then she shook her head. Today was a new day and she was surrounded by love and friendship. She would not dwell on the past right now. Marnie and Clara were waiting for her, and they had an exciting afternoon ahead of them.

"Thank you both so much," she said and forced a smile to her face.

She would survive this. She had, in fact, survived this. Standing up, she looked from George to Dr. Groves.

"I hope you both can attend the wedding, once we know when it is. It would mean the world to Mr. Linz and me."

"You can count on it, Miss Gallagher," George said.

"Absolutely," Dr. Groves agreed.

She walked back to the drawing room and joined her friends.

"Oh, my goodness," Marnie cried. "What a difference that makes!"

"Not a monster anymore," Charlotte asked with a giggle.

"Not a monster at all," Clara answered. "Now, I've pulled the wedding gown out and laid it on the bed. Follow me." Marnie and Charlotte followed her down a hallway away from the clinic area of the house. With just a few steps, they arrived in her bedroom.

Charlotte was awestruck by the gorgeous dress lying draped over the bed.

"I know it's probably too much for Denver City," Clara said, holding up the dress. "But you must keep in mind that this was worn at a rather lavish wedding in Wilmington, where bigger was always better. I can easily make any changes you like."

"It's the most beautiful dress I've ever seen," Charlotte said as she quickly stripped down to her chemise and petticoats. "I can't wait to try it on."

Clara and Marnie carefully slipped the beautiful ivory silk dress over her head and then helped tighten the complicated bodice laces in the back. When they were finally done, Clara turned Charlotte around to face the looking glass. Charlotte could not believe her eyes. A huge grin covered her face, and she giggled in delight.

"Is this really me," she asked in stunned bewilderment.

Clara and Marnie laughed. "It's you, dear," Marnie answered. "What a beauty you are!"

"Oh, try these as well," Clara said, suddenly remembering the gauzy veil and dainty slippers that matched the dress perfectly. "If they don't work, we can find something during our shopping."

Charlotte removed her boots and slipped her feet into the fancy slippers. They fit perfectly. Clara arranged the veil this way and that. She solicited their opinion several times until Marnie and Charlotte finally agreed on the best style.

"My goodness," Marnie said, looking at Charlotte's reflection in the mirror. "You are a vision, my dear."

"We'll need to tell Mr. Linz that he requires a very fancy suit if he wants to stand next to this beauty," Clara added. "He's going to be so proud to be your husband!"

"I still can't believe this is me," Charlotte gasped. "I've never worn anything so wonderful. Thank you so much, Clara!" Then she remembered something.

"Mr. Linz said he liked my short hair, but Sergeant Albertson said if I was still too worried about it, there are wigs to be had at Larimer's."

Clara and Marnie looked closely at her hair, and then Marnie spoke candidly.

"If this was going to be a big wedding with a great number of guests, I might suggest a wig just so you wouldn't feel self-conscious."

She walked around Charlotte and asked, "May I?"

"Of course."

Marnie smoothed her hands over Charlotte's very short, uneven hair. Now that it was slicked back and styled with pomade, it really was very flattering to her youthful, heart-shaped face. Marnie saw several uneven strands which could benefit from a trim, but altogether, it was too adorable to cover with a wig.

"This is really a cute style for you. If you'll allow me to trim a few uneven areas, I think that would be better than a wig. Especially if Mr. Linz favors it," Marnie said with a wink.

Now it was Clara's turn to walk around and inspect her.

"Are there any changes you'd like to make," she asked as she pinched the soft fabric here and there. "I plan to take in the waist an inch, and I'll need to hem the front of the dress to match your height. Two inches should be sufficient. While a train is lovely in the back, we certainly don't want you tripping on your way up the aisle."

"Oh, Clara, there's nothing else I would change. Absolutely nothing," Charlotte insisted. She couldn't stop staring at her reflection.

"Well, let's get you changed back into your shopping clothes," Marnie suggested, looking down at the list she and Clara had composed. "There's so much to do. You'll need a bouquet, perfume, some frilly nightgowns—"

Marnie's voice continued, but Charlotte heard nothing after "nightgowns." She imagined a true wedding night with Thomas and felt her heart start to race. Then, she remembered what Dan and Fred had done, and all her pleasant imaginings were squelched. She would never, ever willingly subject herself to that sort of pain.

Once the dress had been removed and was safely wrapped in tissue paper, the women left the house and began visiting various stores. Charlotte kept looking around, hoping to catch a glimpse of Thomas between his different destinations. She needed to repair things between them.

"I wonder if it's too late to find a photographer to do a daguerreotype of you and Mr. Linz on your wedding day," Marnie mused.

"It would help if we knew the date and time," Charlotte answered. "Should we try to locate Mr. Linz? Perhaps he has already met with the priest."

"The post office is right around the corner," Clara offered. "Let's see if he's been there, yet."

As the women approached the post office, Thomas exited the building. He was pleasantly surprised to see Charlotte and her friends.

"Well, look at you," he said to Charlotte. "No more stitches!"

"Oh, Mr. Linz! I hope you have a very fine suit for your wedding," Marnie exclaimed excitedly. "Your young bride is going to be a vision."

"Is that so," he asked, looking quizzically at Charlotte. "I thought you weren't very happy with your dress options, Ms. Gallagher."

"Mrs. Groves is lending me her wedding dress. And it's the most beautiful creation I've ever seen," Charlotte gushed.

"Mrs. Groves, how can I ever thank you," Thomas asked. "It looks like you've made my sweetheart very happy.

"It's my pleasure, really. I was so very happy to see her in it!"

"Were you able to meet with the priest, Mr. Linz," Charlotte asked, suddenly remembering his very important task.

"I was informed that Father Joseph was out administering last rites, but his secretary scheduled us for tomorrow morning at ten."

"For the wedding," Charlotte asked, wide-eyed.

"No. No. We're scheduled to meet with him tomorrow to simply state our intention to marry and discuss the marriage process. If he allows it, I'd like to be married on Saturday. If he requires the reading of the banns, it may be a few weeks from now. Hopefully, our unique circumstances will encourage him to release us from that requirement."

"Oh, goodness. I hadn't thought of that," Charlotte said. She felt bitterly disappointed and realized how excited she was beginning to feel about the wedding. She looked at Thomas.

"What will we do if he says we must wait?"

"If that's the case, I will leave you here at the hotel and visit as often as possible."

"I truly hope that you can be married this weekend," Clara said. "But, if not, please, please come stay with Dr. Groves and me, Charlotte. It would be like having a little sister!"

"That would certainly ease my mind, Mrs. Groves," Thomas said, in gratitude. "Of course, I'd prefer to make her my wife sooner rather than later," he added, looking over at his betrothed.

Charlotte felt as though she might catch fire from his gaze. Thomas must have noticed her blush because he quickly continued.

"Have you ladies eaten," he asked.

"Not yet," Charlotte answered.

"May I join you, then? I'll be the envy of every man around with three such beauties as my dining companions."

He smiled at Charlotte, and she thought that maybe, just maybe things were better between them. She looked forward to some time alone with him, and realized just how much she had taken for granted their time together during the last few weeks.

"I would love that," she answered, and looped her hand through his arm.

The hotel luncheon consisted of delicious breads, hashed meat, cheese, and a variety of sweets. At the end of an hour, all of them left feeling slightly more than full. Thomas stood and offered his hand to Charlotte.

"Do you have more shopping to do, or would you like to accompany me to the land office," he asked.

"Why don't you let us purchase the last few surprises, I mean supplies," Marnie suggested with a demure smile. "You go spend some time with your betrothed."

"Thank you, that would be lovely," Charlotte answered. She opened her reticule to hand her friends the remaining bills Thomas had given her that morning.

"There's no need, honey," Clara said, refusing the money.

"Please oblige me, Mrs. Groves, and let me pay for this special day," Thomas asked, bowing gallantly.

"As you wish," Clara capitulated. She accepted the bills from Charlotte, and immediately tucked them into her reticule.

Charlotte took Thomas's offered arm and wished her friends goodbye. Then, suddenly, she thought better of it and turned back toward the two ladies.

"Should I be worried about what you're purchasing," she whispered to Clara and Marnie.

"Of course not," Clara said innocently, as she winked mischievously at Marnie.

"We'll see you both at the house for dinner," Marnie added, shooing Charlotte and Thomas on their way.

"What was that whispering about," Thomas asked, good-naturedly, as they walked down the street.

"I'm embarrassed to say."

Charlotte hesitated as she looked up at him.

"They said I need some frilly nightgowns," she whispered.

Thomas began to laugh. "I guess they don't know the parameters of our marriage?"

"No! Certainly not," she insisted. "I could never talk of something as intimate as that."

He looked over to see her bright red cheeks.

"Well, I only thought that you might want some sisterly advice from two women who are obviously very happy in their marriages," he offered. "Tell me, how was your morning."

Charlotte was happy he'd changed the subject.

"I missed you, Thomas. I didn't realize how much the last few weeks alone with you have meant."

Thomas stopped walking. He looked at her and then slowly raised her hand to his lips. His brief kiss on the back of her hand sent hot white flames through her body.

"It has been wonderful, hasn't it? I kept finding myself looking around for you as I walked from place to place today. We've lived in a little cocoon of our own and I'm afraid being around others will take some getting used to."

"I find I don't want to share you," Charlotte laughed as they continued walking, hand in hand.

"Nor I, you. But I'm so thrilled that you have Mrs. Albertson and Mrs. Groves in your life. It looked like they are planning some mischief."

"Thomas, it's so wondrous! I feel like I finally have sisters I can talk with and laugh with and share secrets with. Ruth was wonderful, and I wouldn't trade her for the world, but I always longed for a sister who could understand me."

"That makes perfect sense," Thomas said, thoughtfully.

He was so thrilled by her happiness, and he felt the hurt and disappointment of the morning dissolve in her presence. They had almost reached the land office when suddenly Thomas stopped, remembering the mail in his jacket's inner pocket.

"Charlotte, I almost forgot. Your mother received a letter from Ireland. I'm guessing it's from your Aunt Betsy. Would you like to read it now, or wait until you can be alone at the hotel?"

He handed her an envelope with her aunt's distinctive handwriting on the front.

Charlotte stared at it. This would be a difficult letter to read. She winced as she thought about the fact that she still hadn't written to inform Betsy of her family's tragedy.

"Let's visit the land office and then head back to the hotel. I want to be able to focus on the letter and I want to share it with you. Will you please keep it in your pocket until then?"

"Of course," he answered, and accepted the envelope. Then, he placed the letter back in his jacket, near his heart. "Charlie, my dear, I'm so very glad I'm not losing you to Ireland."

"As am I," she beamed up at him. "I couldn't bear to leave you."

She hoped he could see how much she truly loved him. She had simply been nervous and confused this morning. The realization that she could lose him had certainly brought her to her senses.

They entered the land office and the jangling bell over the door caused the clerk to look up from his papers. His face broke into a smile as he recognized Thomas.

"Ah, Mr. Linz, it's good to see you again," he said, standing and walking around his desk to shake hands with Thomas.

"May I introduce you to my fiancé, Miss Charlotte Gallagher? We've been eager to find out what the Crawford family back east decided about the property. Have you received word, yet?"

"Indeed, I have," the clerk answered with a nod. He hurried back to his desk and pulled out a telegram. "They were devastated by news of their kin but have no intention to resettle in Colorado. The land is yours if you want it."

"How wonderful," Charlotte exclaimed, looking at Thomas with a big smile. "Won't Ms. Linz be excited?"

"I definitely want it, sir. And any other property that abuts the Crawford or Gallagher properties."

"I'm afraid that you can only apply for one parcel through the Homestead Act, Mr. Linz. If you contract for the Crawford plot, it will be the only one available to you."

"I'll contract for that parcel through the Homestead Act. But if there is more available next to either property, I would like to purchase it. Will you see what might be available?"

The surprised clerk turned to open a large cabinet on the wall, and Charlotte looked over at Thomas with a questioning glance. He merely winked at her.

"It looks like you're in luck," the clerk said. "The property to the east of the Gallagher place is available. You can choose any amount between one hundred and three hundred acres."

"I'd like the full three hundred. I have placed my letter of credit at the First National Bank. How soon can you have the paperwork drawn up?"

"I will get to work on it right away, sir. If you will kindly come back tomorrow afternoon, it should be ready for your signature."

"Excellent. Thank you, sir!"

Thomas grabbed Charlotte's hand, and they left the office for the short walk back to the hotel. Charlotte could not wrap her mind around the amount of wealth Thomas must possess.

"It feels wrong to be so excited about the property when I know it's only available due to the Crawford's deaths. But I can't help it. I'm thrilled with the prospect of having Emily so nearby. She'll be another sister-figure for you."

Thomas smiled and squeezed her hand.

"I can't wait to meet her. How soon do you think she might arrive?"

"Unfortunately, it could take up to a year. I only mailed my letter three weeks ago and it may or may not have reached her. Then, she'll have to write and inform me of her decision. There's another few weeks. And then I want to travel to Cincinnati to bring her here. I would never dream of letting her come alone. When I traveled by horseback, it took about thirteen weeks to get here. I'm hoping that traveling by train will cut that in half."

"Will I stay here in Denver City while you're gone?"

Charlotte tried to hide her disappointment. She couldn't imagine being apart from him for so long.

Thomas stopped and turned to her.

"Why, certainly not! Of course I'll want to take my wife with me, Charlotte. I want to share my childhood home with you and introduce you to Aunt Shirley. I want to take you to operas and ballets and symphonies. I long to show you everything Cincinnati has to offer."

The way Thomas looked at her made her feel faint. He must have noticed, because he tucked her hand under his arm and turned to continue to the hotel.

"I think we'd better keep walking," he said with a satisfied smile.

When they entered the hotel, Thomas led her towards chairs at the far end of the lobby. "We can stay down here for propriety's sake."

"We don't even know anyone here," Charlotte laughed. Then she sobered. "Would you mind terribly if we read it upstairs? I know I'm going to cry, and I'd rather not do that in public."

"Not at all, love."

Thomas escorted her up the stairs. He couldn't stop himself thinking about walking up these stairs soon, carrying his wife. He thought about spending a whole night lying next to her. Thankfully, they reached the room before his thoughts could go further. Charlotte pulled the key from her reticule and handed it to him. As soon as he closed the door behind him, Charlotte put her packages on the nearest chair and turned to him.

"Thomas, I want to," she began, but that was as far as she got.

He pulled her into his arms and interrupted her with a kiss. She responded desperately, clinging to him for dear life. Thomas could feel the blood pounding through his body. He wanted her. Every part of his body wanted her. After several blissful minutes, he pulled himself away and took a deep breath.

"I'm sorry," he said, running his hands through his hair. "We can't keep doing that."

He turned and walked to the balcony door at the back corner of the sitting room.

"You are far too desirable, Ms. Gallagher," he said with a rueful laugh. "I think I'll be safer over here."

"But what if I don't want you over there," she asked, in a throaty voice. "What if I never want to stop kissing you?"

She began to walk toward him.

"Charlotte, I can't," he said. Then, seeing the bewilderment flash across her face, he added, "Trust me, I want to. I want to kiss you forever, but we need to wait." He walked back over to her and took her into his arms. "We have the rest of our lives for kissing."

"Well, then. Let's read this letter."

Charlotte couldn't understand why Thomas always ended their kisses so soon. Were it up to her, they'd kiss forever. Maybe she could discuss this with Clara and Marnie tomorrow. They would certainly be able to answer her questions.

Thomas released her and pulled the letter from his jacket.

"Where would you like to sit," he asked.

Even with the open windows, the room was hot. She wished it was cooler out on the balcony, but the sun was blazing down and likely baking the outdoor furniture. Charlotte looked around the room and then indicated a settee near the door to her bedroom. They sat down, side by side, and she slowly opened the letter. Thomas noticed her trembling fingers.

"It's okay, Charlotte," he whispered. "I'm right here and I'll stay here as long as you need me."

He put his arm around her shoulders and gave her a reassuring squeeze.

"May 31, 1867
My dearest sister,

I am about to make you the happiest of women! Jared and I have finally decided it's time to join you in America! I have dreamed of this day for years, and I am bursting with joy. It will be so wonderful to watch our children get to know each other, and even more wonderful to be close to you, dear sister."

"Oh, Thomas, she's so excited."

Tears began streaming down Charlotte's stricken face.

"You will be surprised to hear that Winchester is coming, too! He insists that he's ready for adventure and that we'd never survive the journey without him. However, I suspect that he knows he'd be lonely without his nieces and nephews around. I've

never seen someone so invested in children that aren't even his. Growing up, I always thought he'd marry and have a huge gaggle of children. It always makes me sad when, after a day or two with us, he packs up and returns to Killorglin all alone. Sometimes, William and Henry beg to go with him, and he takes them for a week. They love working with the sheep and feeling the freedom of the great outdoors. They are not built for city life. Oh, Annie, I'm so very excited about the life we'll have with you in Colorado!

What I'm not excited about is the voyage. What you described in your first letter sounded absolutely horrible. I thank God the new steamships can make the trip in mere days. I fear I could not have survived weeks in the conditions you described. I think that now is the perfect time to come.

You might wonder what led to this decision. Well, several things have played a part. First, the soup kitchen is no more! Halleluiah! There is no longer any need for such a large operation, and Father Peter at St. Mary's has enthusiastically offered to take over the endeavor. This allows me to move away without worrying about all those who needed the food you and I distributed for so many years.

Secondly, Grandpa Marshall has died. Fortunately, he died peacefully in his sleep without ever having to suffer through brain congestion or loss of bodily functions the way our dear mother did. Those years before her death were so painful for her and for all of us who loved her. No, Grandpa Marshall had the sort of death for which we all pray! His passing made it possible for Jared to finally consider emigrating. He and Darren talked about it for a few weeks, and Darren feels fully capable of running the two stores with his sons. All three of his sons are now in their twenties and have grown up training for this. The north and south stores are both thriving, and Jared and Darren are developing a plan to incorporate the new store we will eventually open at Kerry Haven.

We hope your very generous offer of five acres of your land is still good. Jared loves Patrick's idea of opening the store right at the front edge of Kerry Haven on the main road. Your frequent descriptions of the difficulty involved in procuring supplies have excited Jared. He is looking forward to being the first dry goods purveyor in the area. And I'm just so excited to be near you! We will be close enough to see each other every day again, sister! Can you even imagine?

Winchester hopes to find acreage nearby where he can raise sheep, and he is looking forward to trying his hand with a herd of cattle. You should see our brother—he's practically giddy with excitement. Of course, he tries to hide it, and says he's just coming for our protection, but I see the truth. Annie, I still miss Will every single day, as I'm sure you do. But I think the loss somehow affects Winchester even more than you or I. No one should have to lose a sibling like that, especially one so young.

Having the three remaining siblings all together again- it will be healing for all of us, I think.

I hope this letter reaches you quickly. We have planned to not leave until the first of September so that you receive the letter at least a few days before receiving us! Please leave a map with directions to your land at the Denver City post office. We will report there first.

I cannot wait to see you and catch up on the last six years. I have missed you so!
Your little sister,
Betsy"

"She is going to be utterly devastated, Thomas."

Tears were still streaming down Charlotte's cheeks.

"I can't imagine leaving everything you've ever known to join your sister and then arriving to find out...." She shook her head and looked at the date of the letter. "And I can't even stop them because they've already left Ireland. I wish I would have thought to check for mail the last time we were here in Denver City. Maybe I could have stopped them from coming."

Thomas let out his breath and chose his words carefully. He wanted to make sure they didn't further upset her.

"You're right. Telling them what has happened will be awful. But Charlie, I can't help thinking the move will still be a good decision for them. It sounds as though your uncle Jared is ready to branch out with a new store, and your aunt wants her boys to grow up away from the city. She wants them to enjoy the freedoms we have out here in the great wilderness. And surely, they will prefer to grieve here with you, rather than hear about the tragedy in a letter while separated from you by a great ocean."

Charlotte didn't speak, so he continued. "It's odd for something to be so wonderful, and yet so awful, at the very same time."

"Wonderful and awful perfectly describe the last few weeks of my life. Happiness and grief seem such opposite emotions, and yet, since meeting you, Thomas, I feel them together almost daily. I've felt so devastated and so elated lately, and sometimes I feel like I'm going crazy. When my family was killed, I thought I would never smile or laugh ever again."

Charlotte smiled up at Thomas. "But then you came into my life. You came into my life, and within a few days, I was smiling and laughing and receiving cooking lessons from the most accomplished artisan."

Thomas laughed loudly at her humorous remark, happy that she could still make jokes.

Then she sobered. "I even fell in love, Thomas."

"Oh, Charlotte."

Thomas pulled her even closer as she continued to cry. He removed a fresh, white handkerchief from his pocket and cleared her tears away.

"I can't promise you will never hurt like this again, but I can promise a lifetime of laughter and baking, and my undying love."

Moments later, Charlotte stood and walked to the small side table with a water pitcher and glasses.

"Would you like some water? I'm parched."

"No thank you."

Thomas pulled out his pocket watch and stood up from the settee.

"I've been told that I need a much nicer suit if I'm to approach the altar with you, so I need to rush to the tailor's shop and see what is possible! I'll be back soon to walk with you to dinner, but I think you might have time for a short nap if you're interested. I imagine we'll be up very late visiting with our friends and celebrating our engagement, and we've got that meeting tomorrow morning at the church."

"A nap actually sounds perfect right now," she agreed.

She quickly finished her water and met Thomas at the door. Then, she flashed her most charming smile.

"One more kiss before you go?"

"How could I refuse?"

Chapter Nineteen

Thursday, September 5, 1867

Thomas arrived at the nearest tailor shop within minutes.

"Good afternoon," the proprietor greeted him. "How can I help you?"

"Can you work miracles," Thomas asked, laughing.

"My name's Ephrem Fuchs, and I'm surprised you heard about me. I normally try to keep my miracles secret."

Mr. Fuchs laughed, and reached out to shake Thomas' hand.

"What seems to be the problem?"

"I'm hoping to be married this Saturday," Thomas began.

"And the miracle you're needing is a 'yes' from the lady?"

"Fortunately, I have my 'Yes.' My problem is that I thought the suit I had would be sufficient. However, my fiancée's dear friend lent her a proper wedding gown. I've been told that it's simply gorgeous and I will need a much better suit if I want to stand next to her!"

"Ah, I see," Ephrem nodded.

"I know this is very short notice and probably not a possibility, but I must try. Now, please don't take offense, or think I'm being a braggart, but money is no problem. If you think you can have something done in time, I will pay whatever you think fair."

"No offense taken, sir. I understand your urgency. No man wants to disappoint his bride. I can't promise anything, but it might be possible. I'm recalling a bolt of fabric...." His voice trailed off and he asked, "Will you excuse me for just a moment while I look through my supplies?"

Before Thomas could answer him, the man had disappeared through a narrow doorway behind the counter. He returned a few moments later with a sparkle in his eyes and some black material under his arm.

"We are in luck! I have a small amount of this lovely black silk left over from a suit I finished last year. What do you think of it?"

Ephrem unrolled a few feet of the silk so that Thomas might inspect it.

"I think it's perfect," Thomas said, admiringly. "The sheen is quite elegant. Do you know where this fabric was made?"

"The gentleman who brought it in said he bought it in London. He insisted it was easier to travel out here with a parcel of fabric than with a finished suit and I tend to agree, although it's been years since I traveled far from here. I purchased the remaining fabric from him once the suit was complete. I figured it would come in handy one of these days. Okay, then, let's take your measurements and see if I have enough of this."

Fuchs motioned Thomas to a small platform. The gregarious tailor talked as he took measurements and wrote them in a small notebook.

"You'll want to keep the lines simple, so as to not upstage your bride. Silhouettes in menswear are slimming down somewhat from years past. Jackets are also shorter, so that might save us. I just hope we'll have enough. You'll also need a plain white shirt, but I suggest that you buy one ready-made from Larimer's down the street. I will be focusing exclusively on working this miracle and won't have time for trivial things like shirts."

Thomas chuckled at this. He really enjoyed this man's sense of humor.

"A miracle worker. We might have to add that to your advertisement out front, Mr. Fuchs."

The tailor tsked and shook his head.

"Oh, no sir! I keep busy enough without offering more enticement. Now, back to the shirt. I don't know if you follow fashion, but collars are not being worn as high these days, so please ask if they have one with a collar that folds down. It's also customary to wear a white tie and cravat to be married. Colors are not really the thing for weddings."

The gentleman talked on and on, and Thomas thoroughly enjoyed the monologue. Within a half hour, all measurements had been taken, and Mr. Fuchs was fairly certain that he had enough of the silk to put together a spectacular suit.

"I was worried because you're so tall, but you're also rather thin around the midsection and jackets are shorter now. That will leave more material for the shoulders and length."

Thomas just nodded his assent, not at all sure what answer would be appropriate. He knew nothing about the craft.

"Check back with me tomorrow morning and I should know for sure."

Having completed his monologue, the tailor abruptly disappeared through the hallway door again without a goodbye.

"Well, goodbye," Thomas said to himself as he turned to leave.

He fervently hoped there was, indeed, enough material. Now that he had seen the fine silk, any other fabric would look shabby by comparison.

As he walked back to the hotel, Thomas thought about all that needed to be done tomorrow. First, he and Charlotte would meet with Father Joseph at St. Mary's. He offered up another silent prayer that they would be allowed to marry right away and not wait for weeks or even months. Charlotte would be well taken care of if she lived those days with Clara and Dr. Groves, and it might be beneficial for her to have time away from Kerry Haven's constant reminders. But he did not relish the thought of returning to his new home without her.

After the meeting at the church, Thomas would check in with the tailor to see if there had been enough material, or if he would need to try to find something ready-made. Then he would visit Larimer's Store for new suspenders, and a white shirt, tie, and cravat. He remembered Fuchs advice about not upstaging his bride with colorful options. If his new friend couldn't make the suit, he prayed Larimer's would have suits available.

Once he procured his wedding clothes, he would go to the land office and sign documents to take possession of the Crawford's property. And then, he would return to the blacksmith he'd visited this morning. He had taken his mother's beautiful amethyst ring to be sized down to fit Charlotte's small hand. Ever since he was a child, Thomas had admired the purple stone. When their mother died, Emily insisted that Thomas keep the ring to give his future bride someday. He hoped Charlotte would like it as much as he did.

He also wanted to locate a lumberyard and inquire whether Denver City had an architect. He also needed to find trustworthy, experienced carpenters. During the long weeks of traveling west, he'd dreamed of the houses he would build for Emily and for his future family. Now that the Marshalls were coming, it really pushed his timeframe forward. He felt sure he would love the Marshall family if their letters were any indication. And it would be so convenient to have a dry goods store closer than Denver City. He imagined that Jared Marshall was going to be wildly successful in this endeavor.

Yes, tomorrow was going to be a long, but exciting day. By this time Saturday, he might already be a married man! Try as he might, he could not erase the smile on his face; that same entranced smile that Jasper and Jeb had ribbed him about all those weeks ago. Thinking of the two old men reminded Thomas of one more thing he needed to do tomorrow. He would visit his friends at the barbershop and get a proper shave and trim. Wouldn't they have fun with news of his love life? Jasper and Jeb would probably be as giddy as Clara and Marnie had been. He chuckled as he entered the hotel lobby.

He stopped at the hotel bar and ordered a whiskey. He wanted to allow Charlotte a bit more time to rest. What an emotional day she'd had! First had been their little spat this morning, then the relief of finding out Marnie and Clara weren't upset, and lastly the emotional letter from her Aunt Betsy. He stared into his glass and thought about how hurt he had been when she said she didn't know if she loved him. In that moment, he'd felt he couldn't breathe. But a few hours apart had helped to put things into order in his mind. Charlotte had been through more than any person should ever have to endure, and although she carried herself well, she was still very young. He tried to remember himself at nineteen. He had been a rich, irresponsible brat. No, he'd never been cruel or hurtful, but he'd been self-centered; solely focused on fun and pranks and anything that brought him a good time. That had been before the horrors of the war. How quickly his outlook had changed. He tried to never think of the things he'd seen and done, but sometimes the thoughts would not be easily banished.

He closed his eyes, and let the images flood his mind. So many men lost, some of them merely boys who were much too young to be fighting. He prayed every day for the souls of the departed and for their families.

"Please God," he prayed every night, "may we never experience anything like that again."

This nation could not survive another horror of that magnitude. He thought of the hundreds of thousands of men, women, and children who had been affected by the damned Civil War. It could not happen again.

Opening his eyes finally, he looked at the stately old clock in the corner of the room. It was time to wake Charlotte. He didn't know how much time she might need to get ready and didn't want her feeling rushed. As he walked up the staircase, he realized he'd grown up in a household with several paid servants. Never once could he recall Emily or Mother needing to dress themselves or do their own hair. He wondered how ladies out here in Colorado managed all that. It didn't appear that the Groves or Albertson families kept many servants. If Emily moved here, would she bring someone with her? Would they need to hire someone once she arrived? So many questions he must ask her.

Men had it much easier. Thomas had not maintained the services of a valet since he finished college and went off to war. But it was different for women, whose clothing was so much more complicated. He imagined what it would be like to assist Charlotte with dressing and undressing. Nope, that was not a safe thing to imagine! Now that his sweet Charlotte had developed such a fondness for kissing, he was going to have to stay on guard.

Charlotte had agreed to marry him only on the condition that they never engaged in marital relations. He understood her fear and aversion based on the trauma she'd experienced and swore to himself that he would never, ever push her into it. However, if her passionate kisses were any indicator, they would likely not remain celibate for long! If he were patient and strong, the rewards would be beyond belief. She just needed more time to get over her trauma. She needed to be the one to initiate intimacy. He would be a patient man, but not a stupid one. Only a fool believed he could kiss a woman passionately without it leading further. He must be smart and keep strong boundaries if he were to prevent something from happening that she wasn't ready for. Taking a deep breath, he knocked on the hotel room door.

Dinner that night was a boisterous affair. Thomas and Charlotte sat next to each other at one of the big dining room tables. The room was filled with loud laughter and multiple competing conversations, along with numerous toasts and well-wishes. Every time Charlotte looked over to find Thomas gazing at her, she couldn't help but smile. At one point, he reached over and grabbed her hand from her lap. Her body burned as his hand accidentally brushed her thigh. Holding his hand under the table felt clandestine and intoxicating, and she could hardly breathe.

When dinner was over and the night's card games were winding down, Clara and Marnie disappeared from the drawing room for a moment. They were each holding a small gift box when they returned.

"Before you go back to the hotel, Miss Gallagher, we have a gift for each of you," Clara announced.

Thomas rose from his chair and accompanied Charlotte over to where the two ladies stood.

"This first box is for you, and it's only on lend," Marnie said, handing it to Charlotte. "All the women in my family have worn this on their wedding day. I was hoping you might want to, as well. You are like a sister to me now, and I'd love for you to participate in the family tradition."

Charlotte's eyes flooded with joyful tears, and she opened the box. Inside was a beautiful pearl necklace. Marnie moved behind her to fasten it around her neck. "My great-great-grandfather gave these pearls to his wife on their wedding day back in 1759. I can't even tell you how many of us have worn this necklace since then. Welcome to the family, Miss Gallagher."

Wordlessly, Charlotte pulled Marnie into a hug. "You will never be alone," Marnie whispered, as the young girl's body began to shake with sobs. "You are a part of all of us, now; over one hundred years of strong, feisty women."

Again, Charlotte found herself laughing through her tears.

"Your kindness is dangerous," she joked as she attempted to control her tears. "You all need to stop being so kind."

Charlotte looked around the room at all these wonderful new friends. Some were misty-eyed, but all joined in her laughter.

"And this one is for Thomas," Clara said, handing him the second small box. "I pray it won't make you cry like that," she joked, with a wink at Charlotte.

Thomas carefully opened the box to find an exquisitely embroidered pair of suspenders made of leather and silk. As he pulled them out to show everyone, Clara continued.

"It's supposedly very good luck for a groom to wear decorated suspenders on his wedding day. Of course, your marriage will be built on love, not luck, but those suspenders were just too grand to pass up. Best of luck to you both!"

The room erupted in cheers and well-wishes. Half an hour later, the two married couples accompanied Charlotte and Thomas to the door.

"As soon as I get Charlotte settled at the hotel, I'll head straight over to your house," Thomas said to Joseph and Clara. "And we'll see you all tomorrow," he said to the Albertsons. "Thank you for another lovely evening."

"I can't thank you all enough for everything you've done," Charlotte said as she stood in the doorway. "I am so sad about not having my parents, or Ruth, or Brendan by my side as I marry Mr. Linz. Thank you for being family to us both. God has truly blessed us through you."

With that, Thomas and Charlotte walked down the sidewalk, hand in hand. They walked almost to the end of the block before Charlotte spoke.

"What are you thinking right now?"

"Nothing much. I'm just enjoying the cool temperature and the feel of your hand in mine," he answered smiling down at her.

"It has gotten rather chilly, hasn't it?"

Thomas stopped walking and removed his jacket. He put it over Charlotte's shoulders.

"Sorry, love. A true gentleman would have offered you this as soon as we stepped outside. By the way, when I was at the tailor's today, I wondered if you might want some new clothes made. I know there's not much need for anything fancy out on the farm, but I thought I'd offer."

"I've been thinking about that since we discussed the church last night. For the last few years, we were only able to come into Denver City for Mass every month or so, and I always just wore the same dress. I'd like to have something nice to wear when we host the gathering in November, and once we have weekly Mass available, it would be wonderful to have a few dresses to rotate through."

She laughed and looked up at Thomas. "It's been years and years since I worried about how I looked! But if I'm marrying a millionaire, I must look the part."

"Don't you dare go change yourself to try to fit some part! I love you for you, and I have never wanted the sort of woman who would love me for my money. In fact, I hope you won't tell anyone about that. It's sort of... well, people might think less of me, you know."

"Thomas, I won't say a word. You can be just another farmer and rancher making his way in this wild land. However, once you start building churches and such, people will likely start to wonder!"

"You're probably right, but maybe we can hold on to that knowledge for a while ourselves." Thomas wasn't sure why he felt so odd about being wealthy, but he just didn't want Jason and Joseph to find out, yet.

"Now, let's return to the clothes conversation. While I would find you beautiful no matter what you wore, I want you to have fun with your friends and have as many outfits made as you like!"

"That will be fun such fun! I enjoy spending time with them, and they'll know what sort of items I need. Is there any particular color you're partial to, Mr. Linz?"

"I always thought Emily looked especially pretty in pinks and purples, but your coloring is so different from hers." He thought for a moment. "I imagine blues and greens would really bring out the color of your eyes. It's funny. Earlier today, I found myself wondering if it was difficult for you to return to women's clothing after those weeks dressed as a boy. We men seem to have it so much easier with our simple trousers and shirts. I remember it always took an abundant amount of time for my mother and Emily to dress, even with maids assisting them."

"Yes, it has been rather an unpleasant adjustment to get used to the restrictive clothes again. Of course, life out here in Colorado doesn't demand the same rigorous wardrobe requirements that Emily and your mother faced. Ridiculous clothing was one of the things I was dreading about moving to Ireland and living in Killarney. I would have to be corseted tightly like this every single day."

Suddenly, she looked at Thomas and couldn't hide her mirth.

"Oh, my goodness! That is not at all appropriate to discuss with a gentleman."

Thomas laughed and squeezed her hand.

"I hope you will always feel free to discuss anything with me. One of the best parts about getting to know you as Charlie was the lack of societal restraints. If we'd met in a ballroom in Cincinnati, we might still be using each other's proper names at this point, Miss Gallagher! I've always been frustrated by the ridiculous rules one must adhere to when talking with young ladies. There are just too many guidelines about what is and isn't allowed. These past few weeks together, I have loved how easily we can talk about anything. I look forward to decades and decades of interesting conversations with you. Even when we're old and don't know who we are anymore, we'll still have fun together!"

"How happy I am that you found other young ladies frustrating," Charlotte observed with a laugh. "I wonder if we'll still be sitting on those same old rocking chairs watching the mountains."

"That's my plan, love. Something about those mountains calls to my soul."

They'd reached the hotel now, but he didn't want to say goodnight, yet. He wanted his time alone with her to last forever.

"If you're not too tired, Charlie, maybe we can keep walking for a little while," he suggested.

"No, I'm not tired at all. Let's keep going."

"Your mention of the porch and rocking chairs brings me to another question. When I was traveling out here, I imagined building a rudimentary structure to protect me from the elements while I had a proper house built. Unlike your father, I have no construction experience at all. I planned to contract a team to build a large wooden or stone house with several bedrooms for my future family. And, of course, it would have room for Emily to stay until she was married and moved to a house of her own. Even though it has transpired that I am marrying into land with an existing cabin, I'd still like to build us a larger house with indoor plumbing. How would you feel about that? I know your family built your cabin, and I certainly don't want to tear it down. It would make a lovely place for Betsy and Jared to start their lives. But, how would you feel about having a house built for us?"

"That would be marvelous, Thomas! I honestly never dreamed of living in a house where water comes in from the well by itself. It's been so wonderful to use it at the Groves and Albertson homes. Just think of all the time that can be saved when hauling water from the well is no longer necessary!"

"It was already fairly common in the northeast. My parents had our house updated back in 1856 and it was certainly a welcomed improvement. Just think how an upgraded kitchen with running water will improve my newfound cooking abilities."

Charlotte burst into laughter at his last comment and he was relieved by her response. He'd been so worried that she might feel sad or resentful if he started introducing too many changes all at once, but she seemed excited by this idea. How fun it would be to design their home together.

"In that case, I will ask around for architects and builders tomorrow. I want to have lots of porch space for our rocking chairs. And upstairs balconies, as well. We can add anything you like, darling."

"How exciting this will be, Thomas! I can't wait to start planning. Where do you think we should build it?"

"That's a good question. I agree with your father and Jared that the store should be built at the front of the property on the main road. I predict it will quickly become a very busy store, so your uncle will want to leave room for future growth. We already know where the church and rectory will be built. Betsy and Jared will eventually have our cabin to themselves, and I know you'll want to stay close to them. So, I guess it's up to you. Between Kerry Haven and the new properties we'll acquire tomorrow, do you have any favorite spots?"

"Let me think about that over the next few days. How long do you think it will take for the house to be built?"

"That depends on what I find out at the lumberyard tomorrow. Most of the experienced builders are working diligently to rebuild Denver City, but I'm hopeful that there are still some looking for work. It could be done as soon as early November, or it could take until the spring."

"If the Marshalls are traveling by steamship and then train, I wonder when they will arrive. It took us a little more than six months from the time we left Killarney until my parents were choosing property here in Colorado, but I imagine it will be so much quicker for them."

"The steamer voyage will be the quick part. Unfortunately, train travel out here is not an easy, straight journey. I researched it myself when I decided to come west, and realized that, although there are many rail lines, none were a straight shot from Cincinnati to here. When I realized how many times I would have to disembark one train and switch to another on a different line, I decided that it might be quicker on horseback.”

“Is it really as bad as all that?” Charlotte was shocked. “I thought travel back east would be quick and easy now that there are trains.”

“It probably will be in another ten years. We’re just not there, yet. I would hazard a guess that the Marshalls won’t be here until at least mid to late November.”

“Well, that gives us more time to get our house built,” she said, cheerfully. “Thomas, it makes me so happy every time I say ‘our.’”

Charlotte looked up at him and, although it was dark all around them, Thomas could feel the love in her gaze. It took all his control to resist kissing her, right here in the middle of town.

“I’ve noticed that very same feeling. I thrill to imagine my future with you.”

They walked on in silence for a few more moments.

“Tomorrow is going to be a long day, Charlie. I think it’s time to get you back to the hotel.”

They turned around and were soon back in front of the Tremont House Hotel. When they reached the room, Charlotte hoped he would come in and visit for a while. She unlocked the door and walked in, but Thomas lingered in the hallway.

“Please lock the door behind you. I’ll be back to meet you at half past nine tomorrow. I love you, Charlie.”

And with that, he was gone. Charlotte knew this was exactly what a gentleman was expected to do, but she still felt disappointed as she watched him walk down the hallway and turn toward the stairs. When he disappeared around the corner, she closed and locked her door. Only one more night, and then she would have him with her forever. She remembered the two times she’d woken up in his arms and smiled dreamily as she allowed herself to imagine a lifetime of mornings with Thomas in her bed.

Chapter Twenty

Friday, September 6, 1867

Thomas woke early the next morning and decided to complete at least one of his many tasks before meeting Charlotte at the hotel. He declined Big Viv's offer of breakfast, but soon found himself seated at the table with a full plate in front of him. How it happened, he did not know! Shaking his head, he dug into the huge mountain of food on his plate. Vivian Lincoln was certainly a force to be reckoned with.

As soon as he finished the large meal, he thanked Vivian and hurried over to the lumberyard. Although most businesses were still shuttered up due to the early hour, the lumberyard was a beehive of activity. Entering the small office, he was immediately greeted by the tallest, thinnest man he'd ever seen.

"Good morning, sir," the man said with a slow, southern drawl. "My name is Edward Brown. How may I help you?"

"Thomas Linz," he answered, and shook the man's outstretched hand. He was shocked by the huge hand and long, bony fingers. The man looked not exactly real.

"I recently purchased some property about three hours west of here and I'm looking to have a house built. I wondered if you could connect me with an architect and some experienced builders."

"Well, sir," the man slowly began. "I'm afraid we don't have an architect in Denver City at this time. But Hercules Wilson is the best builder I've ever seen, and he draws up all his own designs. Folks just describe what they want, and a few days later, Hercules has it all drawn out for them."

Thomas could have sworn it took Mr. Brown five long minutes to speak those few sentences. Would he even have time to get the information he needed?

"Where can I find Mr. Wilson," he quickly asked. Maybe if he spoke at a brisk pace, it would hurry Edward along.

"Oh, he never goes by Mr. Wilson. He likes to be called only by Hercules."

"Okay, where can I find Hercules," Thomas asked.

"Lord, grant me patience," he thought to himself.

"He always gets an early start," the man said, completely ignoring Thomas' question and talking even more slowly if that was possible. "He's rebuilt most of Denver City. You know, we lost much of the town in that big fire April of sixty-three. It just raged through all those wooden buildings and destroyed everything. Almost the whole city was burned."

"Yes, I had heard about that. Horrible business." Thomas tried to sound as polite as he could. "Mr. Brown, I'm in a bit of a hurry. Would you know where I can find him today?"

"Hercules," Edward asked.

Thomas nodded his head.

"He's most likely working on the courthouse today. Do you know where that is?"

Yes sir, I do. Thank you so much for your help," Thomas said and left the office.

As he walked back toward the main part of town, he realized he hadn't asked anything about materials or hiring workers. Why had he been so frustrated by the man? Edward was nice enough, helpful enough; but Thomas felt his head would explode if he spent one more minute in the man's presence.

He pulled out his pocket watch, wondering if he had enough time to look for Hercules before meeting Charlotte at the hotel. It was already a quarter past nine. He would have to locate Hercules later today.

By half past nine, Thomas was knocking on Charlotte's door. She unlocked the door, and he stepped into the sitting room. Charlotte flew into his arms.

"It was so difficult to sleep away from you. I had one of my nightmares, and you weren't in the next room."

"Oh, Charlie," he said, and held her close. "Would you prefer to stay with Dr. and Mrs. Groves tonight and I could stay here? Hopefully tonight will be our very last night apart."

"I hope it is. I don't like being apart from you."

She turned to grab her reticule, and they made their way out to the hallway. She locked the door and dropped the key in her bag.

"It might be nice to stay there tonight so that Clara can help me dress without having to transport everything here."

"Good idea. I can swap out our things today. Are you hungry," he asked as they walked down the staircase.

"No, I had the most wonderful coffee and pastry in the dining hall this morning. I've been awake since before five. I guess I've become dependent on having you around, Mr. Linz."

Her smile dazzled him, and he prayed again that they would be allowed to marry the next day.

A few minutes later, they were being ushered into a small office and formally introduced to Father Joseph P. Machebeuf, the pastor of St. Mary's Church. Once introductions had been made, Father Joseph offered them each a chair and got right to the point.

"I understand you're planning to be married," he said, with a kindly smile.

"Yes, Father," Thomas answered. "We live about three hours away and don't often make it into Denver City. We were hoping very much to be married tomorrow."

The priest looked from one to the other. "You're hoping to be married tomorrow? What do your families think of this?"

"We are in a rather peculiar situation, Fr Joseph."

Thomas looked at Charlotte and she nodded her head. It would be best to simply start with the whole truth and not make the priest drag it out of them bit by bit. Once Thomas had finished an abbreviated version of the last three weeks' events, Father Joseph sat in sorrowful contemplation for a few moments.

"I thought I recognized you, my dear. The short hair and awful wound threw me off, of course, but I remember your family. I am so very sorry for your loss. Would you like for me to come by and say a funeral Mass the next time I'm in the area."

"Oh, that would be wonderful, Father Joseph! I've been so sad that they didn't have a proper Mass and burial. As it turns out, we will be having a community meeting at our land in early November and would be so thrilled if you could join us. Maybe we could hold the funeral Mass then. Mr. Linz and I want to donate land and begin construction on a Catholic church for our community. It was my father's dream, and we want to honor that. Once a church and rectory are built, we will request a priest. It will be lovely to attend Mass weekly, or even daily!"

Father Joseph noticed the way Mr. Linz watched the young woman as she spoke. There was so much love evident between these two. Despite his own vow of celibacy, or perhaps because of it, he was always overjoyed to see young couples so in love. The Church would not exist without both married couples and priests. It was a beautiful, necessary partnership.

"The Catholic population is growing rapidly out here, and I know that many people are unable to come to Denver City for Mass. A new parish would be very exciting. I will reach out to Bishop Jean-Baptiste Lamy in Santa Fe to let him know of your interest. Now, to your more current situation. I will begin by answering your first question: 'Is a Catholic marriage valid if it is never consummated?' Canon Law declares that consummation is not required, and a non-consummated marriage is a complete and valid sacrament. However, the marriage is not absolutely indissoluble until it is consummated."

Thomas and Charlotte shared a relieved glance.

"Now, to your second question, I'm sorry, but the only way there can be an exception to reading the wedding banns is if permission is granted by the bishop. Bishop Lamy is the nearest Catholic bishop, and he's nearly four hundred miles away. We worked together in Santa Fe for several years before I was assigned to Denver City. By the time you traveled there to plead your case and came back to Denver City, Mr. Linz, many more than three weeks would have passed. If I make the first announcement tomorrow at all the Masses, then you can be married on…" He walked back to his desk and looked at his calendar. "You can be married on September 28."

"I understand," Thomas said. "Thank you so much for your guidance, Father. And our community meeting will be on Saturday, November 30 if you would like to put it on your calendar. We would be so happy to have you, and we have a room where you can stay overnight."

Father Joseph made note of it in his calendar and then smiled at each of them while he decided on the gentlest way to speak the truth.

"You certainly may not remain under the same roof now that you know the truth, my friends. Whether or not you were having relations, there would be great scandal involved. What arrangements can be made?"

"Miss Gallagher will remain here with our friends, Dr. and Mrs. Groves, while I return to our homestead. I will come back each weekend for Mass and to visit her. I can stay at the hotel or with our other friends, the Albertsons."

"Very good," Father Joseph said. "That will be just fine."

Thomas and Charlotte stood and thanked him again.

"I look forward to celebrating the sacrament of marriage with you," Father Joseph said as he walked them to the door. "It does my heart good to see young people who love each other and love the Lord. You are the future!"

"Will you bless us, Father Machebeuf," Thomas asked.

"It would be my great pleasure."

Thomas and Charlotte bowed their heads.

"May the Lord bless you and keep you. May the Lord make His face shine upon you and be gracious to you. May the Lord turn His face toward you and give you peace. I bless you in the name of the Father, the Son, and the Holy Ghost. Amen."

Neither Charlotte nor Thomas spoke as they made their way down the stone walkway from the rectory to the road.

"I'm sorry, love," Thomas said and reached for her hand. "I know this isn't what we wished for, but we'll manage. I can tell Father Machebeuf is a good priest and would have married us tomorrow if he could."

"I'm trying to not be disappointed. I know that banns are required for good reason, but I'd hoped our circumstances…" her voice trailed off.

"Just think, this will give you three weeks to get to know your friends better, and have clothes made, and daydream constantly about your future husband," Thomas suggested with a smile.

"But I'll miss your delicious cooking," Charlotte whined playfully. Laughing together felt good.

"I know we will get through this and be better for it," she said when their laughter faded.

"You're right. Well, suddenly my very busy schedule has significantly cleared. I need to let poor Mr. Fuchs know that he no longer needs to rush, though. Would you care to accompany me?"

"I'd accompany you anywhere, Mr. Linz!"

When the couple entered the tailor shop, Mr. Fuchs was sitting at a sewing machine busily working on Thomas' suit. He looked up and smiled widely.

"Mr. Linz, I assume this must be your future bride," he said, putting aside his work and rising to greet them.

"Oh," he moaned, as he stiffly stretched himself into a standing position.

"How long have you been sitting there, good sir," Thomas asked with a laugh.

"Well, I started on it right after you left, and the next thing I knew, my dear Rebecca was bringing my breakfast! I often get carried away in my work."

"Find a job you love, and you," Thomas began.

"Will never work a day in your life," Fuchs joined in.

"I've heard that attributed to both Mr. Twain and Confucius," Thomas said shrugging his shoulders. "No matter who said it, it's how I plan to spend the rest of my life! Mr. Fuchs, this is Miss Charlotte Gallagher, my fiancé."

"So pleased to meet the young lady who has stolen this man's heart." Ephrem said with a slight bow. Then he turned back towards his work area. "I am happy to announce that the material was sufficient, and you will have your suit in time for the wedding tomorrow!" He picked up the jacket he was working on and held it out for them to see.

"You have truly worked a miracle," Thomas said in admiration. "However, our hopes have been dashed. We will have to wait the full three weeks for the required reading of the banns. I'm obviously very disappointed, but there's nothing that can be done. I'm sorry that you rushed for nothing."

"No need to apologize. Rebecca fusses when I work all night, but I love new, challenging projects. One can only make so many boring skirts, dresses, shirts, blouses, and trousers before he feels his creativity drying up. This jacket awakened my artistic sensibilities. Now, try it on for me. Try it on!"

Mr. Fuchs was fairly shaking with pride and excitement.

"Do you mind," Thomas asked Charlotte. "I'll only be a moment."

"Please do," Charlotte insisted. "I'd love to see it. That fabric is lovely!"

Thomas turned and allowed Mr. Fuchs to carefully assist him into the jacket. When he turned back toward her a moment later, Charlotte could hardly believe her eyes. Thomas had always looked handsome to her, at least since removing the overgrowth on his face, but he was absolutely breathtaking right now. What a difference a nicely tailored jacket made! She felt herself blushing.

"I think Miss Gallagher approves," Mr. Fuchs quipped, directing Thomas over to stand in front of the looking glass.

Charlotte's eyes beamed as she smiled at Thomas in the mirror.

"Yes, Miss Gallagher definitely approves," she agreed.

"Let me see," Mr. Fuchs said, grabbing his straight pins and walking slowly around Thomas several times. He pinned here and marked there, and then asked Thomas to carefully remove the jacket.

"Now that no miracles are required, I can take my time and add some extra touches," Fuchs said happily. "What is to be the new wedding date?"

"September Twenty-eighth," Charlotte and Thomas answered at the same time.

Mr. Fuchs laughed good-naturedly. "Ah, young love. I remember when my lovely Rebecca and I first fell in love. We'll be married twenty-five years next month, and it seems like only yesterday. I hope that you two will be blessed with as much happiness!"

"Thank you," Thomas answered. He pulled out a several bills and placed them on the counter. "Please let me know how much more I owe once you're finished. I will be heading back to my home at Kerry Haven, but Miss Gallagher will be staying here in town with Dr. and Mrs. Groves for the next three weeks. She will be able to pay the balance. Oh, I almost forgot!" He turned to Charlotte. "Miss Gallagher will require several new items before the wedding. Now that there is more time, would you be willing to assist her in putting together her wardrobe, or refer her to another tailor? She and her friends could come by next week."

"It would be my great pleasure. We'll have you fully outfitted before your beloved returns to wed you!"

"But nothing boring, correct? Should we include peacock feathers on everything," Charlotte asked with a humorous smirk.

"Oh, that's no challenge. I'm going design a whole wardrobe of truly outlandish pieces!"

Then Fuchs turned to Thomas, who seemed a bit nervous by their ludicrous suggestions.

"You have already found a beautiful young bride. I promise to design simple pieces that will only enhance her natural beauty."

He waved goodbye as the couple left the shop.

"What should we do next," Charlotte asked as they stepped back into the bright sunshine.

"I can take you over to the Groves house if you like."

"I'd rather have a bit more time with you."

"In that case, would you rather accompany me to the blacksmith, or assist me in finding Hercules at the courthouse?"

"Hmmmm.... both very mysterious options, I must say. But I'll need more information to make my choice. Please tell me more, dear sir."

"I've been told that Hercules is the artisan responsible for most of Denver City's new buildings. I'd like to speak with him about drawing the plans for our new home."

"That sounds very exciting, but I must carefully weigh both options. What business do you have at the blacksmith shop?"

Thomas couldn't keep from smiling. "At the blacksmith shop, I will be picking up an exquisite ring for my love."

"Oh, Thomas, really?"

She looked like an excited child and Thomas couldn't contain his amusement.

"I guess we have our decision," he said, and offered her his arm. As they walked to the blacksmith shop, Thomas continued. "This ring belonged to my mother and, although she had many, many rings, this one was always my favorite. When she passed, and we were going through her jewelry together, I encouraged Emily to take it all. 'What use does a man have for women's jewelry?' I asked. But Emily was adamant that I should take this ring and save it for my future wife someday. I must say I'm happy she persisted. I think you'll like it."

Charlotte reached to touch the locket she now wore every day. "Oh, Thomas, I'm sure I'll love it because it's from you!" She paused and then added, "Besides Mother's locket, I've never had any sort of jewelry. But why is the ring at the blacksmith's shop?"

"You're so tiny, and I knew it would fall off your finger. So, I requested that it be reset and sized down. I had to estimate a ring size, but now that you're available to try it on, we can make sure it fits and have him make more adjustments if needed."

They could hear loud metallic clanging long before the blacksmith shop came into view.

"You might want to wait right here," Thomas yelled, pointing to a bench on the sidewalk. "It's very sooty and filled with clutter inside the shop. I wouldn't want you to ruin your dress."

"Good idea."

Charlotte brushed off the dusty bench before sitting down. Thomas could tell she was eager to see the ring.

"I'll be right back," he yelled, as he opened the shop door.

Hot, dry heat punched him in the gut, just as it had yesterday when he visited for the first time. How men could work in this heat, he did not know. Farming and ranching were hot, exhausting work, but nothing compared to this!

For several long, blistering moments, Thomas tried unsuccessfully to catch the attention of the men hammering away at their projects. Finally, one of them looked up from his anvil and noticed the customer. He let out a loud whistle, and the other two men ceased their hammering. The youngest of the blacksmiths wiped his brow and maneuvered through the clutter toward Thomas.

"Well, good morning, Mr. Linz! The ring cooperated with me, and I think you'll be pleased with the result."

He walked past Thomas to a small cabinet at the edge of the shop. Taking a key from his apron, he unlocked the cabinet and pulled out Thomas' ring box. Thomas opened the box and was again impressed with the mesmerizing purple gem.

"This new setting is stunning! You really did a stupendous job."

"Thank you. Do you think it will be small enough?"

"My fiancé actually waits right outside. I'll have her try it on, and we can see what you think."

The big, soot-covered man followed Thomas out of the shop. Thomas noticed he took a deep breath of the fresh air outside. Before entering the shop, Thomas thought today was starting out to be a hot one. After being in the blacksmith shop for less than five minutes, it felt like it might snow out here! He walked toward Charlotte, and she stood up from the bench.

"I don't know whether to kneel and propose again, or just," he began.

"Don't you dare!"

Charlotte's vehemence made him laugh.

"Okay, okay. I won't embarrass you." He handed her the box. "Will you please try it on?"

Charlotte carefully opened the box and squealed with delight.

"Thomas, it's so beautiful!"

Thomas looked at the blacksmith who was grinning almost as happily as he was.

"I think the lady likes it," Thomas said to him.

"I'd say you are correct!"

Charlotte removed the ring and slipped it onto her left ring finger. Thomas could tell it was a perfect fit. She looked from the ring to him, and back at the ring again. Her joy was evident.

"Let me step back in and settle my bill. Don't go anywhere!"

When Thomas returned a moment later, Charlotte was still staring at the ring. She moved her hand this way and that, sending purple light jumping around the dusty road. He didn't need to ask if she liked it.

"If you're about finished admiring your new ring, we should start walking, milady."

"What will I do without you for three weeks," Charlotte asked as she looped her hand around his forearm, and they began walking.

"It won't be three weeks," he assured her with a smile. "I find I'm growing rather fond of Denver City and will be visiting as often as possible."

She looked up and batted her eyelashes at him. There was a pout on her pretty face.

"So, Denver is all you'll miss, Mr. Linz?"

He threw back his head and laughed.

"Actually, if we're able to locate a good cattle dog like we talked about last week, I might just be perfectly content to stay out at Kerry Haven indefinitely!"

"In that case, I hope we shall find none."

"I think I might like this new, perturbed Charlie," he teased. How he loved their easy banter and the sound of her laughter. "Perhaps we should focus on finding Hercules, right now. I've been told he is working on the courthouse today. I guess a dog can wait."

On the walk to the courthouse, Thomas and Charlotte talked about the styles of homes they most liked. Thomas eschewed the Federal Style homes which were so prominent in the neighborhood where he'd grown up, favoring the stately look of either Gothic or Greek Revival architecture. Charlotte preferred the fanciful appearance of Victorian and Queen Ann homes. They both heartily agreed they wanted a design with plenty of porch space where they could sit and watch the sun set over the mountains in the evenings.

When they neared the courthouse, Thomas quickly realized he would not even have to ask after Hercules. There was no doubt that the tall Negro standing near a makeshift drafting board was the man in charge. Authority exuded from him in an undeniable way.

Thomas and Charlotte approached him. "Good morning, sir. Are you Mr. Wilson," Thomas asked.

The large man looked up from his drawing. "No, sir. Mr. Wilson was laid to rest on his plantation ten long years ago. I am Hercules."

"I'm Thomas Linz, and this is my fiancé, Miss Charlotte Gallagher."

Thomas extended his hand.

"Nice to meet you both," Hercules said warily. After the briefest of pauses, he grasped Thomas' hand in a firm, strong handshake. "What can I do for you?"

"I've been told that you are the best designer in the territory," Thomas began.

Hercules nodded without a hint of pride.

"Obviously you are much sought after in the rebuilding of Denver City, but Miss Gallagher and I wondered if you might have availability to design a home for us."

Hercules looked at the drawing board while considering this. "What did you have in mind," he finally asked.

Thomas found the man fairly intimidating. While so many of the Negros he'd met in his life attempted to make themselves smaller, possibly in order to avoid conflict with whites, everything about Hercules seemed unapologetically large. He possessed enough strength of character for ten men.

"We haven't decided upon a style yet. I wonder if you might have a portfolio of your past work that we could study."

"I do," Hercules answered, and Thomas waited for him to continue.

When he didn't, Thomas asked, "When might we be able to view it?"

"I finish my workday at dusk. I can go clean up and grab my portfolio. Where would you like to meet?"

"I have a room at the Tremont House. There are several nice tables in the lobby where we could spread out the drawings. What time works for you?"

"I will meet you in the lobby at nine this evening," the big man said, and returned to his drafting board. Thomas and Charlotte looked at each other. Had they been dismissed?

"Thank you," Thomas said to the man's broad back. Then he offered Charlotte his arm and they turned to go.

"That man seemed like neither bullet nor sword could hurt him," Charlotte said, when they were a safe distance away.

Thomas could hear the awe in her voice as she continued.

"There was something so powerful about him. I wonder if he's ever felt fear a day in his life."

"I'd be willing to bet Hercules has known more fear and pain than either of us can imagine. Maybe that's what made him so powerful."

He chuckled a moment later and added, "I don't know which I'm more hoping; that he will be able to design our house, or that he'll be too busy. I only know I'd never want to cross him."

"Oh, no," Charlotte cried a few moments later. "We forgot to tell the Groves and Albertsons about the change in plans. They're probably hard at work preparing for tomorrow."

"I feel like a fool," Thomas said. "I got carried away in the excitement of the day. Let's hurry. We can visit the Groves house first and let everyone there know. Then I'll leave you to visit while I go inform the Albertsons."

Luckily, Marnie was at the Groves house when the couple arrived. She and Clara were working together in the drawing room. Clara altered the wedding gown while Marnie added some finishing touches to the veil.

When Big Viv showed them in, Clara looked up from her needlework and excitedly asked, "Ah, what news have you to share?"

"I'm disappointed to tell you that we will have to wait until September twenty-eighth to be married," Charlotte answered. "I'm so glad you're both here, though, because we were going to head to your house next, Marnie."

"By the way, Mrs. Groves," Thomas said. "Miss Gallagher would like to take you up on your offer of staying here until the wedding."

"Wonderful," Clara cried. "I mean, I'm sorry for your disappointment, but this is going to be great fun for Marnie and me."

"Thank you so much," Charlotte said. "Time spent here with you two will help curb my disappointment about sending Mr. Linz back home alone."

"I know this isn't what you wanted to hear, but it will certainly give you more time to make preparations and get things ready for your life together at Kerry Haven," Marnie proposed.

"Yes," Thomas agreed. "We certainly do have a long list of things yet to do. We want to find a good dog breeder in the area and ask about acquiring a cattle dog. And, this evening, once he finishes working on the courthouse, we're meeting with a gentleman named Hercules Wilson. We're going to have him design a house for us."

"You've met my Hercules, then?" Big Viv smiled and shook her head as though lost in memories.

"You know him," Charlotte eagerly asked. "What an interesting man!"

"You don't even know the half of it," Big Viv responded. "Hercules is the son of a niece of mine, named Sena. He and his mother lived on the Wilson plantation, only about two miles down the road from where I was living with the Anderson family; Miss Clara's people."

Vivian smiled lovingly over at Mrs. Groves, who returned the smile with one of her own.

"Now, every Sunday, all the slaves in the area would gather on our plantation for worship. The Andersons were kind and generous and took good care of us slaves. Everyone liked to gather there because, for at least a few hours each week, they could feel safe and at peace. And, oh, the food Mrs. Anderson let me prepare for those Sundays! It was a delight."

"My mother is a truly remarkable woman," Clara said, nodding her head. "Her mother died when she was only three, and Big Viv raised my momma with all the love in the world. As she did with me."

Clara's love was evident as she looked back at Vivian.

"Oh, you stop it now," Vivian said, shaking her head to hide her emotions. "Well, anyway, it was obvious to me every time I saw Hercules and Sena, that things on the Wilson Plantation were not good. Sena grew thinner and thinner and her clothes were just rags. Mrs. Anderson let me give Sena some of Miss Clara's old dresses, and Sena was so happy about that. The next Sunday, though, she was back in her rags and told me Master Wilson tore up them clothes and said she should 'quit giving herself airs.' He was a mean old devil. Hercules grew up with Master Wilson's children and he was a great favorite with them. Even when he was a little boy, he was much bigger and stronger than any other children they knew. Yes, the Wilson kids were real taken with him. When Hercules was about ten years old, one of the master's older boys must have snuck him a pencil and some paper. He drew those Wilson boys a picture of their house and they were so excited. Sena said they hung it up in their room. Master Wilson saw it a few days later and thought one of his boys had done it. He was right proud! Those poor babies told him that Hercules had done it. They were so proud of their friend, and never dreamed their father would react so harshly. But Master Wilson, he went right out and had the boy beaten."

At that, the women in the room shuddered, and Thomas grit his teeth together.

"A ten-year-old boy, beaten with a whip," Vivian continued. "It was shameful."

"I still remember how angry my father was when Sena and Hercules came to Sunday service that week," Clara recalled. "Hercules was moving so awkwardly that it was obvious he was in pain. My father asked him if he was okay. Hercules insisted he was, but Sena told him what had been done to the boy. I've never seen my father so enraged."

"He went over that very evening and tried to buy Hercules and Sena," Vivian said. "But Master Wilson wouldn't hear of it. Within a week, that horrid man began hiring Hercules out to do drawings for other white folk. Over time, Hercules made more and more drawings of the fine plantation homes all over the area. Everyone in the county wanted a drawing to frame and hang over their mantle. A 'Hercules drawing' became a very popular sign of wealth and gentility. I guess someone finally asked him to design a new building, and he's been doing that ever since. Sena died when Hercules was around thirteen years old. That old Master Wilson, he was just a horrible creature. That's all that's proper to say about him. At the end of the war, when the slaves were all freed, Hercules asked if he could join us on our journey out here. I was right happy about that. The boy is…well, he's like a grandson to me in some ways," Vivian chuckled. "He talks less than anyone I've ever met but he's got some terrific brains in that big 'ol head of his."

"I told Thomas that Hercules had the most powerful presence of anyone I'd ever met, Miss Vivian. Thomas said it likely came from pain. I guess he was right," Charlotte said. She shook her head. "I still don't understand how anyone could ever think owning another person was acceptable."

Chapter Twenty-One

Friday, September 6, 1867

The conversation about slavery flowed freely, and a few minutes later, George entered the room.

Charlotte smiled and asked, "How are you today, Mr. Groves?"

"I'm doing well. What did you find out about the wedding? Will it be tomorrow?"

Thomas and Charlotte filled him in on the meeting with Father Joseph. Then Thomas asked George if he might know anyone who trained cattle dogs.

"I certainly don't. But let me ask around. With all the farmers and ranchers out here, there must be someone who knows where the best dogs are to be had."

"Thanks, George. I really appreciate you checking on that," Thomas said. "Mrs. Albertson, do you know if the Sergeant had any updates on the manhunt?"

"When he left the house this morning, he seemed confident that today would be the day they were apprehended. Do you have time to check at the jail before your meeting with Hercules," Marnie asked.

"Oh, yes. The sun stays up so late in August that Hercules can't meet us until nine. We have plenty of time. Would you like to accompany me there now, Charlotte? If not, you could stay here with your friends, and I'll bring any updates."

"I actually need to be heading home to my wild brood, so I may walk at least part of the way with you two," Marnie said. "That is, if you're going, Charlie."

"Yes, let's go. If I become too nervous to visit the jail, I can always wait at your house until Thomas returns."

Goodbyes were said, and Thomas accompanied Charlotte and Marnie down the road to the Albertson house.

"Who did you and Sergeant Albertson employ to build your house, Mrs. Albertson," Thomas asked as they stood at Marnie's front gate.

"Oh, that was a crazy time right after the big fire! Most of the buildings that burned were businesses and warehouses. But, because we lived so close to the business district, ours was one of the few houses that was consumed. The city council passed an ordinance the very next day that prohibited anything but brick buildings inside the fire zone. I thought perhaps we should move further out, however, since my husband can be called in to the jail at any time of day or night, he wanted to stay close. Luckily, builders from all around the area poured into Denver to begin rebuilding. We only had to live with friends for a few months before this house was built. It was designed by Hercules and built by some of the visiting laborers."

Marnie smiled and added, "While the fire was traumatic, and the rebuilding inconvenient, I did find one aspect to appreciate. Our previous house did not have indoor plumbing, so I can be very thankful for that enhancement."

"I'm so excited that Mr. Linz is planning to have indoor plumbing in our new house! I always figured I'd live my entire life in homes with wells and outhouses," Charlotte said.

"I'm already spoiled and don't imagine I could easily go back to hauling water! Please tell the Sergeant hello from me," Marnie added, as Thomas and Charlotte turned to go.

Just a few blocks away, they stopped in front of the jail.

"How are you feeling, Charlie? Are you up for this?"

"I am," she said, nodding her head as though to convince herself. "I've got you with me. What could happen?"

"I'm honored by your extreme trust, Charlie," Thomas said, laughing. "But, now that I've met Hercules, I realize I'm not the tough character I once thought I was!"

Charlotte shuddered. "What a horrible story that was! I cannot imagine a full-grown man being whipped, much less a young child like that."

"I was forced to witness one public whipping during my years in the army and I hope to never see anything like it again. It still gives me nightmares."

Thomas opened the door, and they entered to find Sergeant Albertson putting on his jacket, as though to leave.

"What perfect timing," he cried. "I was just on my way to find you." He hung his jacket on the coat rack and invited them to sit down on a bench near his desk.

"You have news," Thomas asked.

"Yes, a courier just brought a telegram over. Two men identified as Dan Miller and Fred Clark have been apprehended in Blackhawk and will be transported here for trial. They are being credited with several more massacres between here and Blackhawk, but you are the sole survivor. If travel is uneventful, and they are not lynched by mob on the way here, they should arrive in a couple of days."

He watched Charlotte as he spoke to see how she would handle the news.

"And then I'll need to identify them?"

Both Thomas and Jason felt relief as they noticed the calm strength in her voice.

"Yes," Jason answered. "Ideally, we will put together a panel of twelve jurors and get Judge Moses Hallett to preside over the trial."

"Once I identify them, am I done, or will I need to speak during the trial?"

Charlotte moved closer to Thomas, and he put his arm around her shoulders.

"Well, if you identify them and they decide to plead guilty, it will be over and done with. Judge Hallett will determine their sentence, and you will not be needed to testify. However, I doubt that this will happen. Most criminals crave the attention of a trial. If that is the case, you will sit up front and tell the jury what happened. Then, Mr. Miller and Mr. Clark will have a chance to defend themselves and present their case to the jury. The jury will deliberate and determine guilt or innocence. I'm sorry to say that it can be a long, drawn-out process. Especially if they decide to be tried separately."

Charlotte took a few moments to process this information. Then she turned to Thomas.

"You're a lawyer, right Thomas?"

"Not really. I attended law school at Columbia for one year before the war broke out. My father always imagined I'd follow in his footsteps, and I'm sure I would have if it hadn't been for the war. Why do you ask?"

"I just want to be prepared. This is going to be…very uncomfortable, to say the least." She shook her head. "I want you both to make sure I know what to do. These men cannot be allowed to go free and keep killing people."

"Yours will not be the only testimony Miss Gallagher," Jason assured her. "The officers who have been involved in the manhunt will also describe the horrors they have found at each new crime scene. I don't think there is any way that Mr. Miller or Mr. Clark will ever have another day of freedom in their lives."

"And you can be assured that we will provide whatever assistance you need in order to feel prepared," Thomas said.

"Don't forget," Jason added with a smile, "you've got Big Viv on your side!"

This brought laughter to both Charlotte and Thomas.

"I'm going to be alright."

As Thomas and Charlotte prepared to leave the office, Charlotte turned back to Jason.

"Sergeant Albertson, your sweet wife sends her greetings!"

"Ah, and now my day is made!"

Jason's face lit up, and it was easy to see that he still adored his wife. Thomas nodded to his friend. How beautiful it was that they'd both found such perfect partners.

Upon arriving at the hotel, Thomas and Charlotte entered the dining room for dinner. The smells were mouth-watering, and Charlotte looked forward to dining alone with Thomas. The family dinners with the Albertson and Grove families were wonderful, but this was much more intimate.

Thomas ordered a bottle of white wine, and they perused the menu. When the waiter returned with the bottle, he filled their crystal wineglasses and then waited for them to order.

"I will have the roasted pork with apple sauce," Charlotte said, and handed the printed menu to the waiter.

"And I will have the beef steak with sautéed vegetables and mashed potatoes, please."

The waiter nodded his head and disappeared.

"I'm glad that there are a few days before you'll need to make your identification. I plan to ask Albertson if I may take John David and Damien back with me on Monday to finish cutting and drying the hay. I hope we can get it all into the barn before the next rainfall."

"Thank you, Thomas. I would hate for all our work to be wasted."

"While I have help, would it be a good idea to try to cut and gather some of the Crawford's hay? We have more livestock now and I don't want to run out this winter."

"Oh, I hadn't thought of that. Yes. Gathering theirs would be a good idea." She paused for a moment and then added, "It's probably time to expand our cattle pasture, as well. With the new additions from the Crawfords, I worry that we will see exponential growth this year."

"Maybe we should separate the cows and the bulls."

Charlotte just shrugged her shoulders.

"I really wish we had someone who knew how to manage these things."

"Yes, I'm afraid I won't be much help in that area," Charlotte said, with a chuckle. "We may have some interesting years until we get it all figured out."

Their meals arrived and, after blessing their food, they each took a bite. It was delicious!

"Well, Thomas, it's nowhere near the level of your cooking, but...it's edible."

"Very funny!"

Thomas pulled out his pocket watch and grimaced before putting it back.

"What's wrong?"

"I'm excited to meet with Hercules, and find the time is dragging by. You will undoubtedly discover that patience has never been a strength of mine."

Charlotte laughed.

"Oh, no! I struggle with that, as well. We'll be horrible together! I've been thinking about houses all day, too. I still haven't been able to think of the best location, though. Hopefully, once we see some drawings, we'll have more clarity about where we want it."

After the meal, they had time for a short stroll. Returning to the hotel lobby at a quarter till nine, Thomas looked around and located a table far removed from the bustle of the busy hotel. There were four chairs surrounding the wooden table, and it seemed a good, private place to look over the drawings.

Hercules arrived right on time. Without preamble, he began to extract the contents of his battered leather satchel. Thomas was genuinely impressed with the sheer quantity of drawings.

"Why, you must have more than a hundred designs here," he cried in amazement.

Hercules did not respond.

"Before we discuss style, can you give me an approximate idea of the area and number of rooms you want," Hercules asked.

"Of course," Thomas said. "I would like it to be between thirty-five hundred and four thousand square feet with at least five bedrooms."

"Okay, for a house of that size, one of these styles will probably work best."

Hercules searched through his stack and pulled out the six drawings he wanted. He placed them down one by one on the table.

"What are some of the most important features you're looking for," Hercules asked.

"We both want big porches and balconies," Thomas answered. He noticed that Charlotte's gaze was on the drawing of a large two-story house with upper and lower porches wrapping around the whole exterior.

"That means we can eliminate these three designs," Hercules said, picking up three of the drawings and returning them to his satchel. "The Georgian and Colonial Georgian do not have porches. Federal style homes do not lend themselves well to porches, either. Your largest porches will be found on the Greek or Gothic Revival houses."

Hercules rearranged the remaining drawings on the table. Thomas noticed Charlotte was still entranced with the same one.

"What can you tell us about each of them," Thomas asked.

Hercules picked up the first drawing. "The Gothic Revival style is characterized by its pointed arches and steep rooflines. This style is somewhat reminiscent of medieval castles and is a bit more fanciful than the Greek Revival." He set that drawing down and picked up the middle drawing. Holding it where Charlotte and Thomas could both easily see, he pointed to several features. "The Greek Revival is very symmetrical and has simpler details than the Gothic Revival. You can see how different the windows are here. We can do large porches and balconies on either of these." He set the drawing back on the table and picked up the last of the three.

"I can tell this one is your favorite," he said to Charlotte.

"I can't stop staring at it! It's so beautiful!"

"This design is in Gothic Revival style, but I added a porch that wraps around the whole house. I designed this one while still back in North Carolina. If I'm honest, it is one of my favorites, as well."

"May I," Charlotte asked.

Hercules handed the drawing to her.

"You are enormously talented," she said, looking slowly over every detail in the drawing.

Hercules didn't smile, but Charlotte sensed that perhaps he was warming up to them.

"Tell me, would this design work well here in Colorado," Thomas asked, as Charlotte handed the paper to him.

"I think it would work just fine. We can make any changes you need. It could be built of wood or bricks, depending on your preference and what materials are available. Tell me about the setting. What sort of landscape surrounds your homestead?"

"So, Kerry Haven is the name of the property," Charlotte began. "One of the main reasons my parents picked this area was the beautiful view of the Rockies in the distance. There are heavily wooded areas and grassy plains areas. We haven't exactly decided where the best place for the house would be," she added, looking over at Thomas. "But we want to be able to continue sitting on the porch in the evenings and staring at the mountains."

"Will you want to build near your parents' house or is some distance better? Or perhaps they will be moving in with you," Hercules suggested.

"My parents and siblings were killed last month," Charlotte answered.

At Hercules' embarrassed apology, she continued. "You couldn't have known."

"The only other structures currently on the property are a log cabin and barn. There will soon be a general store built where the property meets up with the main road through the area. We are also planning to commission a large Catholic church in the next year or so, but we have already dedicated the spot for that construction," Thomas said. Then he paused for a moment and asked, "I don't suppose you would consider traveling out to the property with us and taking a look around?"

"That would be preferable, actually. I find it much easier to design a home when I can take in the surroundings and let them guide me. A well-designed building has a spirit of its own and draws from the world around it."

Hercules became animated as he talked, and his passion for building design was obvious.

"It sounds as though you are laying the groundwork for a thriving community. That makes planning all the more important. It's much easier to take your time and plan well at the beginning than it is to make multiple changes once buildings are already present. I think a trip to Kerry Haven is a good idea."

"How lovely," Charlotte said, excitedly. "We could plan a picnic lunch and invite the Groves and Albertson families to join us."

"You know the Groves," Hercules asked.

"Yes. And Vivian Lincoln tells us that you are like a grandson to her," Charlotte answered. "She thinks very highly of you, Hercules."

"Sometimes I question if I would have made it to adulthood without Big Viv." Hercules' face betrayed nothing of his feelings. "When would you like to make the trip?"

"What is your work schedule here," Thomas asked. "Do you get Sundays off?"

"Mr. Linz, I am my own master," Hercules said, proudly. "I've never missed a timeline, and usually complete projects well before the agreed upon deadline, but my hours are my own. I can make this trip on whatever day is convenient for you and Miss Gallagher."

"Excellent! Let me find out when she might be needed by Sergeant Albertson and I will come find you tomorrow," Thomas said. "Kerry Haven is three hours away. On the day we go, we can leave early, eat a picnic lunch at the property, and head back the same evening."

"That sounds good, Mr. Linz."

Hercules carefully returned his drawings to his satchel. He paused, looked at each of them, and then said, "I am looking forward to working with you both. Good evening."

With that, he turned and made his way out of the hotel.

"Well," Thomas said, letting out a long sigh. "This will be interesting."

"I like him. I wonder if we'll get to know him better through this project, or whether he'll forever remain aloof."

"I definitely like him, I just don't know if he likes us," Thomas laughed. "Let's retrieve your things and head over to the Groves house. I don't know about you, but I'm exhausted!"

"I'm tired, but I think I'll be too excited to sleep. His designs were all so beautiful! And that one with the porches all around; Thomas, I've never seen such a beautiful home."

Despite her excitement, Charlotte fell quickly asleep once Thomas left her with the Groves. Her dream that night was not a nightmare, but a lovely experience of sitting on the porch with Thomas, gazing at their beloved mountains, while several delighted children played in the yard in front of them.

Chapter Twenty-Two

Monday, September 16, 1867

It was half past eight on Monday morning, when Thomas arrived at the jail.

"Thanks for coming in, Thomas. I didn't want to discuss this in front of Miss Gallagher," Jason said as he walked to his desk and pulled out a chair for Thomas.

"I received a telegram at six this morning notifying me that the men bringing in Clark and Miller were held up in Golden. Then, about thirty minutes ago, a rider arrived to tell me the details. It's pretty horrific, Thomas. The posse stopped for the night at an already established campsite right outside of Golden, and the officers began caring for the horses. The two outlaws were sitting by the fire with their hands tied in their laps. Apparently, Dan spent the first day in captivity spilling his guts about all they'd done and repenting to God for his evil deeds. I guess Fred had reached his limit. Suddenly, he grabbed Dan and began smashing his head into one of the large stones making up the fire ring. Before the officers could get over to stop him, he'd opened Dan's skull. There was nothing they could do at that point."

"Good heavens," Thomas shuddered. "There is no limit to this man's evil!"

"While I cannot be happy about the gruesome death, Fred's latest murder may keep Charlotte from having to testify in a long, complicated trial. There were at least five officers who witnessed Fred kill Dan. If Fred is convicted of murdering a captive in law enforcement custody, Judge Hallett will most likely recommend the death penalty."

"Jason, I would be so relieved if Charlotte didn't have to testify. How soon might we know?"

"I'm not sure," Jason answered, running his hand through his hair. "Judge Hallett is almost at the end of his circuit and should be returning to Denver any day now. I plan to meet with him as soon as possible to discuss this case. You can count on my recommendation to try Fred for this latest murder before looking at any of the rest. Judge Hallett is a very fair, honest man and I imagine he'll agree that it would be best to spare Miss Gallagher the ordeal."

"Thank you, Sergeant. I won't mention this to Charlie."

Thomas stood up and began making his way to the door. "I'm heading to your house now to pick up the wagon and your sons. I can't thank you enough for lending them to me. I hope we'll have a great time despite all the work that needs to get done!"

"All you had to say was 'swimming,' and they were ready to leave! I often wish they were growing up on land, like I did. City living has its conveniences, but there's something about having the freedom to roam and hunt and get into good-natured mischief. Denver City doesn't offer that."

"Oh, I almost forgot," Thomas said, turning around to face his friend. "Hercules would like to see the property and help us determine the best site for building the new house. I told him that I would find out when you needed Charlotte for identification and then plan around that. Do you think you'll still need her after this latest murder was witnessed by so many?"

"So much is undecided right now. But, even if we do end up needing her identification, it won't be right away."

"Charlotte is excited to show all her friends the property. She wants to invite your family and the Groves, and is planning a big picnic for everyone. The children can swim and run around while the adults look for building sites. Do you think you could take a day to do it? Maybe we could go on Saturday, or on Sunday after Mass. We're planning to leave in the morning and come back the same evening."

"Now that would be a welcomed diversion from this stifling heat! I can't remember the last time Marnie and the children and I took a day trip anywhere. I could take a day on Saturday or on Sunday. Count us in!"

"Sounds good. If you can take either day, let's do Saturday. That way, we can leave early and have the whole day available. I'm worried that if we left after Mass on Sunday, we'd be rushing the whole day."

With that, Thomas turned and left the office. Jason found himself looking forward to a day away from the office and the city. It would be good to be out in nature again. Denver City was growing rapidly, and he missed the scents and sounds of life on a ranch.

After leaving the jail, Thomas went to the Albertson house first. The boys helped him hitch the wagon up and Marnie loaded them with food and supplies.

"Mrs. Albertson, I'm already borrowing your boys. I didn't intend to take half your pantry, as well," he laughingly exclaimed as she brought out more food. "I was planning to stop at the general store before we left town to pick up provisions."

"Perhaps you have forgotten how much food you required at this age, Thomas. I doubt the whole general store could keep these guys fed. Besides, this is how I show my love to these giant nuisances!"

The boys each hugged their mother and the group departed for the Groves residence.

"I just need to say goodbye to Miss Gallagher," Thomas informed them. There was much snickering and whispering from the back of the wagon where Fulton and Damien sat.

"They're so immature," John David said, and shook his head.

Judge Hallett returned to Denver City on Wednesday, and Sergeant Albertson immediately sent a messenger to his residence with a meeting request. Within an hour, he received word that Judge Hallett could see him at four that afternoon. Jason showed up right on time, and, after the men spent a few moments discussing the young judge's recent travels and the well-being of Albertson's family, Jason shared the reason for his meeting request.

"Your Honor, I'd like to discuss the Fred Miller case with you."

"I've only heard the barest details. Can you catch me up on the specifics?"

"The manhunt began over a month ago, on August 15. That morning, Thomas Linz and Miss Gallagher arrived at the jail and informed Whiteley, Phillips, and me about two massacres. Miss Gallagher's parents, brother, and sister were murdered. She was the only survivor. Mr. Miller and Mr. Clark then moved to the next property where they murdered everyone and burned the buildings." Jason took a deep breath and continued, "This, of course, is not common knowledge, Your Honor, but Miss Gallagher was brutally raped by both of the men. We do not know if the women of the Crawford family were abused in the same manner."

"How ghastly," Hallett murmured.

"Miss Gallagher was then knocked unconscious, and the outlaws must have presumed her dead. After she regained consciousness, Miss Gallagher-her name is Charlotte, cut off all her hair and dressed in some of her brother's clothing. When Mr. Thomas Linz showed up on her property, he thought her a young boy. For a few weeks, everyone thought she was an eleven-year-old boy named Charlie. Only a couple of weeks ago did Mr. Linz discover her identity."

"I can certainly understand why she would try to hide as a man," the judge said. "A woman, all alone out there…she must have been terrified."

"She was. Luckily, Mr. Linz is an honorable young man. He kept her safe and allowed her to recover enough to live as a woman again. Mr. Linz is planning to settle in the area, and, in an odd twist, he and Charlotte have fallen in love and are getting married on the twenty-eighth of this month."

"Getting married? How interesting."

Hallett smiled. Though still unmarried at thirty-four years old, Moses Hallett was a man who loved a happy ending.

"Yes, Your Honor. They have spent a substantial amount of time with my family over the last month, and I will say, they are a very compatible couple. I imagine they will be exceedingly happy together."

The judge nodded his head as he said, "It sounds like the young lady deserves all the happiness in the world. Do you think she'll be able to survive the horrors she's experienced?"

"I think she will, Your Honor. She is, of course, grieving deeply, but a strong, protective support system has formed around her. Everyone loves her so much, including me. She has become family to all of us. In fact, I'm standing in for her father at the wedding. But that's part of the reason I wanted to speak with you. See, Your Honor, these men attacked several more homesteads and killed many more people. Charlotte is the only known survivor, so I informed her that it was going to be necessary for her to play a large role in their trial."

"Oh, that poor young lady."

"Yesterday I received word that, while in police custody, Mr. Miller murdered his accomplice, Mr. Clark. They had stopped for the night, and the officers were getting everything prepared for camping. Clark and Miller were sitting near a fire pit lined with rocks. Miller grabbed Clark and began dashing his head on one of the big stones. Before the officers could stop Miller, Clark was dead. The attack was witnessed by several of the officers who were transporting the men here to stand trial. It has me wondering, Your Honor, if Mr. Miller could be tried for this most recent murder, and Miss Gallagher could be spared having to go through a trial where she would be forced to discuss all the details of her family's massacre."

"It sounds like the murder of his accomplice would be an easy charge to prove," Judge Hallett said. "If he is convicted on this charge, my options for sentencing would be life in prison or hanging. There would be no need to charge him for the other massacres, and no need to involve Miss Gallagher.

The only instance in which she would be required to testify would be if Miller were not convicted for Mr. Clark's murder."

"Hopefully, we won't have to deal with that. This is a clear case of murder of a prisoner in custody."

"I would very much like to meet with Miss Gallagher, Albertson."

"I can arrange that, Your Honor."

"Since you are well acquainted with her, I'd like your advice. Do you think it advisable to inform her immediately of this possibility or would that just set her up to possibly be disappointed later?"

"I'd like to tell her now, Your Honor. I will, of course, make sure she understands that she still may have to testify if Miller is unable to be convicted on the most recent charge. But I think it will bring her some relief to know that there is even a possibility that she won't have to."

"Then, I give you permission to let her know, Sergeant. I hope it brings her some relief. And please ask her if I may call upon her tomorrow morning. Where is she staying?"

"She is staying with Dr. and Mrs. Groves. Like I said, everyone just loves her, and the Groves are happy to have her there until the wedding. I will ask her if you may call upon her there. What time would work for you?"

"Let's say ten o'clock."

"If she cannot meet at ten, I will come let you know. If you don't hear from me, plan to meet with her tomorrow morning. Thank you so much for your time, Your Honor. I hope and pray that circumstances will work out to spare her the pain of testifying."

"I will be praying as well, Sergeant Albertson. Good evening!"

Chapter Twenty-Three

Thursday, September 19, 1867

At ten o'clock the next morning, Judge Hallett knocked on the Groves' door and was shown in by Big Viv.

"My name is Moses Hallett, and I'm here to see Miss Gallagher."

"Yes, Your Honor. We've been expecting you. Please, come this way."

Judge Hallett entered the drawing room to find a petite young lady waiting for him. "I'm Judge Moses Hallett," he said, bowing to Charlotte before taking the seat Vivian offered.

Big Viv moved to sit on the couch next to Charlotte. She was not going to leave her little Charlie to do this alone.

"And I'm Miss Charlotte Gallagher."

"I'm very pleased to meet you, Miss Gallagher," Judge Hallett said. There was admiration in his voice. "Let me start by offering my condolences on the loss of your family, and my congratulations to you on your upcoming marriage. I've always had a soft spot for stories with happy endings."

"Thank you, Your Honor."

"Sergeant Albertson met with me yesterday and told me about what you've been through. I'm so sorry this happened to you and your family."

Charlotte nodded her head, and Judge Hallett continued.

"Has Sergeant Albertson discussed our plan with you?"

Again, Charlotte nodded. "Yes, Your Honor. I am thankful for your efforts to keep me from having to testify. I understand this is all contingent on Miller being convicted for killing Clark, but it already takes such a weight off my shoulders."

"I'm so happy to hear it, young lady. I'm cautiously optimistic that you'll never have to set foot inside the courtroom."

"I have a question for you, Judge Hallett. Would it still be possible for me to see him when he's brought in," Charlotte asked.

Vivian gasped in surprise.

"I don't see why not," Hallett said, but his facial expression made it clear that he didn't understand why she would want to do that.

"I know it doesn't make any sense. But, you see, in these last few weeks, he's grown and grown in my mind. I have nightmares almost every night, and I can't keep him out of my mind during the day. I think that if I could perhaps see him in handcuffs and behind bars, my mind might accept that he can't hurt me anymore. Maybe I could quit feeling so scared all the time."

Her words broke Vivian's heart, and she reached for Charlotte's hand.

"I guess I didn't realize how scared you still feel. You put on such a brave face all the time."

"I will make sure that you're able to get a good look at him, Miss Gallagher. And I give you my word that Fred Miller will never, ever hurt you, or anyone else, ever again."

Judge Hallet placed his hand over his heart in a sort of oath. "I swear it on my life. He will never hurt you again. You are safe now."

A few moments later, the conversation finished, Big Viv walked the judge to the door and then returned to sit next to Charlotte.

"Charlie, I'm so sorry. I hate it that you haven't been feeling safe. Why didn't you tell us? What can I do to help?"

"Oh, Vivian! You and the Groves and the Albertsons have all been so wonderful and supportive. My head knows that I'm safe and surrounded by people that love me. It's just my body that hasn't yet received the message. Sometimes, I don't know if my body will ever truly feel safe again. I can be sitting amid all of you, having a great time, when suddenly I'm back in the moment. I see Brendan staring at me in horror, and I smell the stink of Miller's breath and hear the gunshots. It's horrible. I feel trapped inside my own body, and I can't even cry out to you all. But you are doing everything right. Big Viv. Everything."

"Well, I want you to make me a promise that you will always tell me if you need something more. Promise me that you won't try to handle this all on your own."

"I promise, Vivian," she said, and squeezed the large, black, work-worn hands holding hers. "I promise."

Fred Miller arrived in Denver City that afternoon, accompanied by almost twenty officers and volunteers. Word had traveled of his ghastly deeds, and the men of Colorado Territory were taking no chances on his escape. More and more of them joined the transport as it approached Denver. Jason Albertson was surprised that the man had brought Miller in alive. These large posse groups frequently got carried away and vigilante justice was a common occurrence.

When Miller was safely locked in a cell, the crowd slowly dispersed. Judge Hallett sent an officer to the Groves house to notify Charlotte. Big Viv answered a knock on the door to find a young police officer on the front porch with a paper in his hand.

"Good afternoon, ma'am," he said with a smile. "I have a message from Judge Hallett for Miss Gallagher."

Big Viv let out her breath and smiled back at him. "I guess that evil man has arrived, huh?"

The officer nodded.

"Come inside, please."

With another quick nod, he removed his hat and entered the foyer. As she shut the door behind him, Vivian introduced herself and asked, "Are you to wait for a reply?"

"Yes ma'am, I am."

"Then, please wait here while I take this to her," Vivian began.

At that moment, Charlotte entered the foyer.

"I was in the kitchen and couldn't help but overhear you. I am Miss Gallagher."

"I'm pleased to meet you, ma'am. My name is John Porter."

He seemed taken aback by her glaring scar and short hair. Charlotte felt a moment of self-consciousness, and reached up to nervously smooth the hair along the nape of her neck.

Vivian handed her the paper and Charlotte quickly opened and read it. Then, she looked back up to the officer.

"If I can be ready in ten minutes, will you accompany me?"

"Yes ma'am."

Vivian indicated that he should have a seat in the drawing room.

"Miss Charlotte," Vivian called, as Charlotte made her way up the stairs, "I know Mr. Thomas isn't here. Would you like me to go with you?"

Charlotte saw the concern in the woman's face.

"Oh, Vivian, thank you! I would really appreciate your company. Do you think Clara can manage without you for a little while?"

"I'll go ask her," Vivian said.

A few minutes later, Charlotte came back downstairs with a hat on her head and a small reticule in her hands. As the officer escorted the two ladies down the street toward the jail, Big Viv took Charlotte's hand.

"This old devil can't hurt you anymore, Miss Charlotte. You are safe and surrounded by people who love you."

"Vivian, when I first found out I might need to identify him, I immediately asked Sergeant Albertson if you would accompany me. I knew I wouldn't fear anything with you by my side." She turned and smiled at the large black woman next to her. "You are an extraordinary woman, you know, and I'm very fortunate to call you my friend."

"Oh, why you always gotta make me cry, Miss Charlotte," Big Viv said, and pulled out her handkerchief. "It's like you enjoy it or something!"

Way too soon, they arrived at the jail. The young officer held the door as Charlotte and Big Viv entered.

"You're really gonna do this," Sergeant Albertson asked, giving Charlie a big hug.

"I need to let go of the images in my mind, Sergeant. Every day, Mr. Miller grows larger and scarier in my imagination. I need to see that he's just a man and that he's behind bars where he belongs."

"And I see you've got Big Viv at your side," he said with a laugh. "Good choice!"

He unlocked the door that separated the office from the jail cells.

"You've got a visitor, Miller," he said as he swung the door open. "I will stand here while you approach him. Please do not get within arm's distance. I don't want him reaching through the bars."

Charlotte stood at the door for a moment before entering. Fred Miller pulled himself up to standing and stared at her with bewilderment on his face.

"Do I know you, missy?"

"You don't recognize me, do you?" Charlotte was surprised that there was no fear in her voice.

"Can't say I do." Miller looked her up and down. "But I'd sure like to."

Big Viv was disgusted by the suggestive tone in his voice.

"You vermin! You disgusting piece of filth! How dare you talk to a lady like that?"

"She don't look like much of a lady to me. What happened to your face, missy?"

Charlotte had seen enough.

"I think I've accomplished all I needed," she said to Vivian. "Are you ready to go, my friend?"

"Wait," cried Miller. "Don't go! Tell me how you know me! Wait!"

They walked out the door and Sergeant Albertson locked it.

"Did you get what you needed," he asked.

"I did. I sure did. He's nothing more than a pathetic shell of a man. I don't need to be afraid anymore."

Charlotte's relief was evident to both Vivian and Jason.

"Thank you, Vivian, for coming with me. I couldn't have done it without you!"

"Well, I'd like to meet that rat in a dark alley," Big Viv said. "He may have been a tough man when he had a gun, but he's nothing more than a scrawny, dirty fool now. I'd love to give him some of what he's got coming."

"Thankfully, Miss Vivian, Judge Hallett will see to that," Jason assured her.

Thomas and the Albertson boys returned to Denver City that evening in high spirits. Dr. and Mrs. Groves sent word that everyone should meet at their house after dinner for music and singing. Thomas bathed and shaved at the hotel and then made his way over. The Albertson family showed up soon after him.

As the evening wore on, Charlotte could not keep her eyes off Thomas, and everyone in the room noticed their stares and smiles. Dr. Groves thought about the early years when he and Clara had been like that. The last few years had been tough. They both wanted children so badly, but no children had yet come from their union. He felt like less of a man, and certainly less of a doctor, for not being able to give Clara her heart's greatest desire.

When Jason and Joseph tired of playing their fiddles, Thomas walked over to the piano and asked, "May I?"

"Of course," Clara answered. "I had no idea you played!"

"Not well, but I do enjoy it whenever I get the chance."

Thomas sat down and pulled the bench close under the piano. He began the haunting Piano Sonata Number 14 by Beethoven. Charlotte closed her eyes and let the music carry her away. She remembered taking piano lessons from the nuns when she lived in Ireland, but it had been so many years since she'd played. In her week here, with the Groves, no one had touched the instrument. Thomas' playing was intoxicating to her.

"We must have a piano in our new home," she thought to herself. She imagined many evenings spent listening to her handsome husband play.

When that song ended, Thomas immediately began something lively. Soon, everyone was clapping and singing along. Charlotte looked around her. There was so much love in this room. She briefly thought of past evenings like this at Kerry Haven. In her mind, she could see Mother and Brendan dancing as Father played his fiddle. She remembered twirling Ruthie around to the music. Yes, she'd been blessed then, and she was blessed now. George caught her gaze and smiled. She smiled back at her new friend and joined in the singing.

Chapter Twenty-Four

Friday, September 20, 1867

Charlotte and Vivian spent all day together in the kitchen on Friday preparing delicious picnic foods, and Charlotte was excited when Big Viv announced that she had invited Hercules' wife and children.

"As quiet as he is, we would probably have never even found out he had a family," Charlotte said. "I can't wait to meet them."

"Hercules and his sweetheart, Martha, jumped the broom about seven years ago. They were so young, but Hercules knew his heart and Martha had always loved him for as long as I could remember. They have three precious sons, Jack, Benjamin, and Fischer, who are six, four, and two years old. I don't get to see them as often as I'd like, but they are such a joyous bunch!"

"It's been years since I was around young children," Charlotte said, wistfully. "My sister Ruth was like a child, though. I miss her joy and laughter. Never did a day go by when she didn't make me laugh in some way or other. God blessed us when He sent Ruthie. She was like an angel living among us."

Big Viv wiped her flour-covered hands on her apron and walked over to Charlotte.

"I know you miss them all, dear. But they're with you every single day, you know. Right here," she said, tapping Charlotte over her heart. "They're never far."

A few tears fell down Charlotte's face, and she wiped them with her apron. "It will be nice to spend some time at Kerry Haven tomorrow. I feel closer to them there. And, I can't wait to show you all around my home. I hope we can arrange for regular visits even after I'm married."

"Well, I'm extending an invitation for Sunday lunch every time you and your mister come into Denver City for Mass. I'm going to miss not having you here each day."

Before the sun rose on Saturday morning, Dr. and Mrs. Groves were both called out of their beds to assist others. Dr. Groves was at the Martin house attending to a young man with an accidental gunshot wound, while

Clara was over at the Lamar house helping deliver a first baby to a young wife.

At seven o'clock, George and Charlotte met in the front hallway and walked from the Groves house to the Albertson house. There, they found Jason and Hercules already waiting with their loaded wagons. George climbed up to the driver's seat with Hercules, and excited squeals were heard from the three children inside the wagon. Thomas placed both hands around Charlotte's waist, picked her up, and gently settled her into the Albertson wagon. Then, he climbed up to sit next to Jason on the driver's seat. Excitement filled the air as the horses pulled their covered wagons out of town and towards the country. It wasn't long before Thomas began a song and the occupants of both wagons joined in. Charlotte hated that the covered wagons didn't allow the occupants of the two wagons to see each other as they traveled. However, she could appreciate that the stiff canvas covers made for a cooler, less dusty ride.

Between the singing and the constant conversation in the wagons, the journey flew by. Before long, the travelers reached Kerry Haven and pulled in through the gate. Charlotte's heart soared as she looked at the mountains and the land that she loved. The land that she would share with Thomas now. The land where she and her husband would welcome the Marshalls and watch a house, a store, a church and a community grow.

As soon as the wagons stopped behind the cabin, their occupants began pouring out like ants. The Albertson boys were looking forward to swimming again and could hardly wait to show their parents the stream. George hopped down from his seat and assisted Sarah and Julia down from their wagon. Hercules helped a tall, beautiful woman from his wagon and then began removing one cute little boy after another and setting them on their feet. The boys were shy around all these strangers and clung to their father's legs.

Charlotte approached the family. "Hello, Mrs...."

She stopped mid-greeting and looked quickly at Hercules.

"I realize I don't know what your wife would prefer to be called," she said, laughing. "I know you don't like Wilson, but I can hardly call her Mrs. Hercules!"

For the first time since she'd met him, Hercules smiled. He had brilliant white teeth, and his smile changed his whole countenance. While still a powerful man, the smile rendered him more human and approachable.

His wife held her hand out and said, "You can call me Martha. I'm very pleased to meet you, Miss Gallagher."

"Call me Charlotte, please. I am so happy that you and the children could join us. Will you introduce me?"

"Come here, boys."

Reluctantly, the oldest of the boys let go of Hercules' leg and came to his mother.

"Now, how do you introduce yourself," she prompted.

"Hello, ma'am. My name is Jack," the boy said, and held out his hand. Charlotte was impressed with his firm handshake.

"What a nice, strong handshake you have, Jack."

Jack stepped back, and the next boy approached her.

"My name is Fischer," this one said with a formal bow. "I'm pleased to make your ak— aqu—"

Fischer looked to his mother. Out of the corner of her eye, Charlotte saw Hercules shaking with laughter and it took all her strength to not join in his mirth. The boy was just too cute!

"Acquaintance," Martha said.

"I'm pleased to make your acquaintance," Fischer said, bowing even deeper this time.

Charlotte curtseyed to the young boy and said, "The pleasure is all mine."

Hercules picked up the youngest boy and brought him over to Charlotte.

"My name is Benjamin," the little boy said with a huge smile.

"Very nice to meet you, Benjamin. What lovely boys you have, Martha!"

Hercules smiled at his wife and asked, "Where should we begin, Mr. Linz?"

"Call me Thomas, please. I know that these young Albertson men are eager to go swimming. Do you all like to swim," he asked Hercules' sons.

"Yes! Yes," they cried. "We love swimming!"

"We can help them, sir," Damien said to Hercules. "It'll be fun!"

Hercules looked at Martha.

"I can sit by the stream and keep watch over the swimmers," Martha offered. "That will allow you all to look for home sites without all my husband's little helpers. Hercules is a devoted father, and these boys stay glued to his side all day long."

Thomas was seeing a whole new dimension to this formidable man. And he liked what he saw. It made him happy to realize that, despite a childhood filled with injustice and pain, Hercules had built a life of love and happiness. The private Hercules, who loved his wife and children openly and with all his heart, was so different from the professional Hercules he'd met last week.

"I'll stay with you, Martha. I ain't got no intention of traipsing all around in this heat," Big Viv said. "And besides, I can't get enough of these little rascals."

Everyone else wanted to be a part of the expedition to find the best home site, and so it was a group of eight that began discussing where to start.

"It would be too much to try to walk the entire property today, so Miss Gallagher and I have narrowed it down to three spots we'd like to show you."

Charlotte was glad the morning air was still cool as they began their quest. Mr. and Mrs. Albertson, Sarah and Julia with George, Charlotte, Thomas, and Hercules made their way from the cabin towards the mountains to the west. Hercules carried a sketchpad and several pencils.

The first spot was located amidst a grove of trees near the base of the hill where the cemetery was, and the church would eventually be built. It took about fifteen minutes for the group to walk there from the cabin. Charlotte liked that this site would have them so close to the Marshalls. Hercules looked this way and that and made notations in his notebook.

"You would have good shade cover from all these trees. We might have to clear a few here," he indicated with his arm, "so that you'd have an unobstructed view of the mountains. This looks like it may be a low point, though. See the way the land swells here and here? You might be at risk for flooding."

"I thought this would be far enough away from the stream to not have to worry about flooding, but I see that you're right. That looks like water may have run through it in the not-so-distant past. I will show you where the stream is as we walk towards the next site. The major benefit of this site would be proximity to the current cabin. Miss Gallagher's aunt and uncle and their children will be arriving from Ireland in the next few months, and I'd like her to be able to visit them daily if she wants."

Charlotte smiled happily at Thomas. The other members of the party walked around and visited quietly as Hercules made a few drawings.

"I'm ready to see the next one," he said shortly.

They soon came to the stream. The Albertson boys and Hercules' sons were having a very fun, very noisy time swimming together. Hercules smiled broadly as he watched his little ones playing freely with the older boys. It was a beautiful site, and brought to Thomas' mind his fervent dream for the whole country; blacks and whites living together in equality, camaraderie, and joy.

Once Hercules acknowledged each boy and kissed Martha on the forehead, he walked down the bank and looked closely up and down the stream. Then he looked up to where Thomas and Charlotte stood with their friends.

"If you look here, you can see debris from past water risings. It looks like the water stopped at this level during the most recent flood. But it reached as high as this at least one time," he said, pointing to a much higher area on the bank. "I think the first site would be too risky. You want this house to stand for decades. In twenty years, I'd be willing to bet you would be flooded at least once. It's a risky site, in my opinion."

After about thirty minutes walking due west, they came to a flat, grassy field with clear views in all directions.

"I like this one because it's just so open. I think that we would get good air flow when we opened the windows of the house," Thomas said. "We still have a great view of the mountains and are slightly distanced from where the church and store will be. As the community grows, we may find we want a bit more privacy."

Again, the group visited as Hercules gathered all the details he needed. Charlotte noticed that Sarah and Julie were enjoying their time with George. She heard laughter and gaiety from the trio and remembered how Sarah and George interacted on her first night at the Albertson home. There was such a connection between the two. Did Sarah's mother notice it, Charlotte wondered as she looked over at Marnie. And if she did, was she excited by the budding romance, or scared by it?

Having spent most of her life in Ireland, or secluded out at Kerry Haven, Charlotte had been given very limited opportunities to observe the interactions of blacks and whites. During her time in Denver City, though, she had quickly realized that maybe her thoughts about equality and racial harmony had been naïve. Though the Groves and Albertsons saw Big Viv and George as family members, some of the other townspeople were decidedly cold to their black counterparts. If George and Sarah were in love, it would likely be more difficult for them than she had initially imagined.

Before she knew it, Hercules had again finished his notes, and Thomas led them to the final spot. This one was located on the Crawford's former property. While she and Thomas had not had a chance to look over the land recently purchased across the road, they had discussed home sites at length. They eventually decided that if a community or small town were to grow around the store, they would not want to be on the other side of it. They preferred to stay closer to the mountain range.

This final location was on top of a small hill and, like the last one, offered great views in all directions. There were several trees around it, but not enough to reduce desired air flow in the hot summer months. No trees obstructed the mountain view, so they would be saved from the arduous task of tree removal. The elevation of the house would prevent it from ever flooding. The only downside, in Charlotte's opinion, was its distance from the current cabin. It would be a thirty to thirty-five minute walk each day to see the Marshalls. But she wasn't sure that small inconvenience made up for the superiority of this location. This location offered seclusion that the closer location would forfeit when the church was built. And, once Betsy and Jared decided to build their own home, they could build it closer to hers and Thomas'.

"What are your thoughts, Hercules? I certainly have been impressed with your insight and feel like this is a decision you should help make."

"If you don't mind, Thomas, I think we should discuss it on the way back to the cabin," Charlotte suggested. "I imagine you all are ready for a drink and some refreshment."

"Great idea, dear! We men can be such brutes when it comes to hospitality."

As they made their way back to the cabin, Hercules gave his opinion.

"I think the second and third sites are the best. The first site was beautiful, but the hill in back and the trees surrounding it would cut off most air flow through the house. That would make the summers more difficult. The church and cemetery should never flood because they're at the top of the hill. However, I don't feel comfortable with the house being built in a low-lying area. And, once the church and general store are built, I think you will be surprised by how quickly a community grows. I don't think you'll want your house to be so close to everything. I know that the third site is furthest from where you said your family will be, but apart from that, it is the best of the three locations for building. I think you'd be happy with either of the last two sites, though. What are your thoughts?"

Thomas looked at Charlotte, but she indicated he should go first.

"I like the third site the best."

"Well, that makes it exceedingly easy," Charlotte remarked with a big smile. "The first site was certainly my favorite, but I agree about its potential flood risk. Let's go with the third site!"

With the heavy decision made, the party made their way back to the stream. George, Jason, Hercules, and Thomas joined the boys already swimming and the ladies focused on setting out the lunch. Marnie looked around and sighed.

"What I wouldn't give to live out here. I miss the green and the trees and the wide, open spaces. Life in Denver City is convenient, but I was raised on a plantation. I crave the outdoors."

"Do you think you and Sergeant Albertson will remain in Denver forever," Martha asked, as she pulled potato salad and fresh rolls from her hamper.

"I'd leave in a heartbeat, but I don't think Jason would relish returning to farming. Law enforcement is in his blood."

Suddenly, Marnie laughed and turned to Charlotte. "How long before your new community will need a police force?"

"Oh, what a capital idea! Marnie, I would love having you here more than anything."

"Maybe I'll subtly bring it up to my husband over the next few weeks." She looked over to where her husband and sons were splashing and taking turns on the rope swing. "I certainly think they'd be happy here!"

"They do look to be having a grand time," Martha agreed. Each of the Albertson boys had a squealing, laughing youngster hanging on their arms. The scene was so joyful that the ladies couldn't help but laugh along.

"And Martha," Charlie said, excitedly. "If Hercules decides to be involved in building the church, the design and construction could take years. Maybe you and your family could live out here, too. Even if it were a temporary arrangement, it would be so wonderful!"

"Well, now," Big Viv interjected. "I don't relish the thought of being left behind in Denver!"

"If this community grows as fast as I'm imagining," Marnie began, "I think Dr. Groves and Clara will be needed long before Jason is."

"And what would I do without you, Big Viv," Charlie asked with a big smile.

Chapter Twenty-Five

Tuesday, September 24, 1867

The visit to Kerry Haven with all her friends had done Charlotte a world of good. She was so excited by all the future possibilities that had been discussed among her friends. She spent the whole day Sunday talking excitedly with Thomas about all that he'd missed while swimming.

"Thomas, within a few years, we may be surrounded by all our wonderful friends! And just think about the new businesses and services our community could have! A church, and a general store, possibly a school, and a police station."

Thomas just smiled and enjoyed her excitement. He knew that she was probably correct about how fast the community would grow, but there was so much that needed to be accomplished in the meantime. Right now, he planned to focus on getting their house built and expanding the pasture for their newly adopted cattle.

The house plans were in good hands. Hercules left Kerry Haven on Saturday full of ideas for the house and for the future growth of the community. He informed Thomas that he would get the designs to him by Friday. Thomas was amazed by how much he liked the man after spending a day having fun with him and his sons. Those little boys were so joyful, and Thomas hoped that they would spend a great amount of time together as Hercules worked on the house. It hurt his heart to think that, if Charlotte remained trapped by her fear, he might never have children of his own. But he'd promised her that he would choose marriage to her over the possibility of children. He knew that it was a sacrifice he was willing to make.

On Monday, Thomas and the Albertson boys returned to Kerry Haven to put up more fencing needed to expand the pasture space. He assured Charlotte that he would be back on Thursday, excited and ready for Saturday's wedding. She kissed him passionately and urged him, "Just come back safely to me, my love."

By Tuesday, Charlotte's joy had greatly dimmed. What had been merely a vague sense of unease in her mind for the last few weeks suddenly became glaringly apparent. She sent George to the Albertson home with a message asking Marnie to come over as soon as possible. Thirty minutes later, Charlotte sat in Clara's drawing room with her two closest friends.

Thank you so much for meeting us here, Marnie. I'm so upset, and I need you both to help me. I think I might be with child."

"Oh, Charlotte," exclaimed Marnie. This was a horrible, horrible position in which to find oneself. Pregnant and unmarried! In a larger, more established city, Charlotte would be a ruined woman. Hopefully, the remoteness of Kerry Haven, and the fact that she would be married this weekend would save her reputation from being tarnished. However, Mrs. Albertson felt quite disappointed in Mr. Linz. She had imagined him more of a gentleman.

"What a blessing," cried Clara, deciding to make the best of a bad situation. She pulled Charlotte into a hug. "I am so happy for you both! This may be happening out of order, but with the wedding this weekend, no one ever needs to know."

Charlotte's expression was pained as she looked again from one lady to the other. Her eyes filled with tears.

"If I am, in fact, expecting, it's not Mr. Linz's child. The one and only time I've ever," she couldn't finish the sentence.

"Please come sit down, dear," Clara instructed Charlotte. "Would you like me to ring for some tea?"

"No thank you. I just really need to figure this out, and I hope you both can help me."

"Well, of course, dear," Marnie said, leading Charlotte to the couch. She glanced at Clara. This was more serious than they could have anticipated.

"Now, how long has it been since you had your courses," Clara gently asked. The competent midwife knew how important it was to remain calm, especially when clients were distressed.

"My last one was in late July. Then the attack was on August twelfth. I began feeling slightly nauseated a couple of weeks ago but attributed it to wearing tight corsets again. Last week, I was violently ill for five days in a row. It usually abated mid-morning, but sometimes it lasted all day. I was relieved when I started feeling better. But then, this morning, a sudden realization crashed upon me. I think I'm expecting."

"How much do you know about pregnancy," Clara asked.

So many young women went into marriage with no idea about how their bodies worked. If it were up to Clara, women would be taught much earlier about their cycles and fertility. They would not be surprised by puberty, and they would be better prepared for the marital act. The prim propriety of current society was just not fair to young women.

"Not much, I imagine."

Charlotte dissolved into tears, and Marnie moved over on the couch. She put her arm around Charlotte's shoulders, handing her a fresh handkerchief.

"I'm just so upset about this! I haven't said anything about it to Thomas. When he first asked me to marry him, I said no. I told him that I could never…That I'd never be able to…be a real wife to him."

Charlotte looked imploringly at the women, willing them to understand what she meant.

"So, you and Mr. Linz will not have intimate relations," Clara asked, keeping her voice as neutral and clinical as possible.

"No," Charlotte was crying so hard now that she could barely breathe. "I don't know how women can bear it! It hurt so badly, and it took several days to stop bleeding. I never want to feel that way again. How do you endure it?"

"Oh, sweetheart!"

Marnie put her other arm around the sobbing girl. Charlotte leaned fully into her and cried even harder. Over Charlotte's head, Marnie looked imploringly at Clara. Clara discreetly nodded her agreement. They needed to help this poor girl.

"Charlotte," Clara began. "I wish your mother were still here. She could have talked you through all this hurt and misunderstanding. But I will do my best."

Charlotte lifted her head and used the handkerchief to dry her eyes. She was so thankful to have a mother of five and an experienced midwife to talk her through this catastrophe.

"Based on what you've told me, I'd say you are definitely pregnant."

Charlotte swallowed, and then nodded stoically. While this was not what she'd hoped to hear, it was, unfortunately, what she'd expected to hear. She took another deep breath and slowly exhaled.

"Charlotte, we will be with you every step of the way," Marnie assured her.

"Now, you need to hear the truth about marital relations," Clara started tentatively. "While the mechanics may basically be the same, what those men did to you is nothing at all like what would happen between you and your husband. Nothing. Making love with your husband is really quite wonderful."

"It truly is," Marnie agreed. "With someone you love, it can be…" She found herself at a loss for words. Then, a thought struck. "Have you and Thomas kissed?"

"Yes," Charlotte said. A smile overtook her face, and her cheeks began to glow.

"Okay, that's a good place to start. Tell me about how it feels to kiss Thomas."

"Tell you about it," Charlotte asked, in confusion. "I don't…"

"Charlotte, this is us," Clara said, indignantly. "You can talk about anything."

"Okay. If you must know, it's the most amazing thing I could have ever imagined! I find myself wanting to kiss him all the time. And every time he looks at me, I feel I might catch fire!"

Then, realizing how inappropriate her admission was, Charlotte clapped her hand over her mouth as her face turned bright red.

"Please don't be embarrassed, Charlie. In a perfect world, every woman would feel that way about her husband. Now, focus on the feelings you have when kissing Mr. Linz. Then multiply those feelings about ten times or a hundred times and you'll come close to knowing how lying with your husband can be."

"That's a very apt description, Marnie," Clara said.

The women realized Charlotte still looked acutely uncomfortable.

"Why should we be embarrassed to discuss this," Clara questioned with passion in her voice. "Marital love is a beautiful thing. Maybe if we married women discussed it more freely with young ladies, they wouldn't be so terrified on their wedding nights!"

Charlotte looked disbelievingly between the two married women. She opened her mouth as though she wanted to ask a question, but then just shook her head.

"There's nothing you can't ask," Clara assured her again. "Trust me, in all my years assisting women, there isn't anything I haven't heard."

"Yes, and Clara would love nothing more than to be able to educate all young women about their fertility and cycles," Marnie joked good-naturedly.

"You know I'm right," Clara insisted with a big smile.

Charlotte loved the deep friendship evident between these two women. It reminded her of how her mother and MaryAnne Crawford had always laughed with each other. Oh, how she missed Mother. Every single day, Charlotte wished her mother was still here with her, but now more than ever. Together, they'd dreamed of the day Charlotte would meet her future husband, and of her wedding day, and of the day Charlotte would turn her parents into grandparents. Now, she was pregnant with a child she didn't want. She didn't even know which of those evil men might be the father. Charlotte couldn't bear the thoughts racing through her head.

"Will this baby be evil like its father," she sobbed.

"No! Absolutely not," Clara exclaimed. "Charlotte, your baby will have amazing parents. It will grow up surrounded by so much love, not only from you and Thomas, but from all of us. Your baby will grow up knowing God's love and mercy. He or she will grow into a spectacular person. Please do not think otherwise. It will only break your heart."

"Sweetheart, your baby will be a reflection of you and Mr. Linz, not of a man he or she will never meet," Marnie agreed.

"Thank you both so much. I still don't know how I will survive this, but it helps knowing I have you both to guide me."

"And, more importantly, you'll have Mr. Linz beside you," Clara added. "Charlie dear, I've never seen a man so besotted with a woman! Well, except maybe Sergeant Albertson."

"Or Dr. Groves," Marnie quipped.

Charlotte smiled at the women. They loved their husbands with all their hearts and were so happy in their marriages. But were they being honest about the marital act? Charlotte felt sure they were just trying to ease her mind. Of course, now that she thought about it, she realized it would be difficult to stay happy in marriage if things in the bedroom were as painful as she imagined.

"Seriously, though, let's talk about your marriage," Marnie said. "How can we help you prepare to speak with Thomas about the baby?"

"He's so wonderful and I know he'll pretend to be happy about being a father. I just don't think either of us will ever be able to love this baby. I know I won't. He or she will be a constant reminder of the worst moments of my life."

Charlotte saw the women exchange a meaningful glance.

"Do you want to tell her, or should I," Marnie asked Clara.

"Go ahead," Clara said.

"The very first time you see that baby, you and Mr. Linz will both fall madly in love with him or her. Your heart will explode with love. You will realize that you never knew love this powerful before, and you will even love your spouse more than you ever imagined possible. A baby changes everything."

Suddenly, Marnie gasped and looked at Clara. "I'm so sorry, dear. I didn't mean—"

Clara interrupted her. "Marnie don't do that. Don't feel bad. Everything you said was absolutely correct. I've seen it happen hundreds of times," she said, smiling reassuringly at Charlotte. "And I truly believe that it will happen for the doctor and me someday; in God's good time."

The room was silent for a moment too long.

"Please don't pity me," Clara begged. "I'm blessed in so many ways. I have Joseph and he has me. We are happy, I promise."

Charlotte didn't have the heart to tell them that she wanted nothing to do with the baby and would be putting it up for adoption as soon as it was born. How unfair that Clara and Joseph longed for a baby and had not conceived, yet she had conceived against her will, in the most horrible way possible?

Marnie recovered from her embarrassment at possibly hurting Clara and turned back to Charlotte.

"Now, Charlotte, what questions do you have about the bedroom? You've got two experts here. Ask us anything."

"So, it really doesn't hurt?"

"It was slightly painful on our wedding night," Marnie admitted. "Not excruciating, but painful. After our first few days of marriage, it never hurt again. And now, I find I truly look forward to it. I long for my husband's embrace."

"As do I," Clara agreed with a smile. "Sometimes I find myself daydreaming all day about the hour we will close the doors and finally be alone."

"Does it happen every night?"

This made the married women laugh.

"No, sweetheart. A good husband will follow your lead. Trust me, Mr. Linz does not seem like the sort of man who would ever force or manipulate," Clara answered. "I can almost guarantee that you will want it as often as he does now while you're young. The frequency tends to lessen over the years."

"You act as though you're an old woman, Clara! Twenty-two is still very young in my opinion," Marnie insisted.

"I'm sure I'm only speaking of what clients have shared," Clara quickly said, and burst into laughter.

As she watched the women laugh together, Charlotte grew hopeful. Maybe it wouldn't be so bad. Women wouldn't laugh about something that was as horrible as she feared. It must be something wonderful and desirable. She decided she was going to trust her dear friends and be a true wife to Thomas, in all ways.

"Okay, ladies, what will I need to do?"

❧

Chapter Twenty-Six

Thursday, September 26, 1867

Thomas arrived in Denver City on Thursday afternoon and came directly to the Groves residence. Big Viv greeted him at the door with a wide smile.

"Mr. Linz! How are you doing today?"

"I'd say I'm about as happy as I've ever been, Miss Vivian. But I can hardly wait to see Miss Gallagher again!"

"Well, I'm glad to hear that. I'm sure your young miss is just as excited to see you. She's in the sitting room with Mrs. Albertson right now. Oh, and your suit has been delivered. I hung it here in the hall closet so you can take it back to the hotel with you tonight."

"Thank you, Vivian."

In the drawing room, the ladies heard Thomas' entrance and ensuing conversation with Big Viv. Charlotte looked over at Clara, her face filled with worry.

"Don't worry, my dear. Everything is going to work out just fine," Clara said softly, as Thomas appeared in the doorway.

"Good afternoon, ladies. How I have missed you, Miss Gallagher!"

"Welcome back, Mr. Linz," Clara greeted him. "It is so lovely to see you again. How was your trip?"

"Uneventful," Thomas said with a laugh. "And I like uneventful these days!"

He couldn't tear his gaze away from Charlotte. It had only been a few days since he'd seen her, and yet it felt like years. He was happy to see that she was wearing a beautiful new dress. Clara and Marnie had really taken Charlie under their wings and helped her assemble a great wardrobe. If his sister Emily was any indication, Thomas knew that pretty clothes did great things for a woman's image of herself. While Charlotte was the most beautiful woman he'd ever met, he knew she was struggling greatly to get accustomed to her scar.

Clara excused herself as soon as was politely possible.

"I will have Vivian prepare some tea and cakes. Please join us in the drawing room whenever you are finished talking."

As soon as Clara left the room, Thomas sat down next to Charlotte on the couch. He pulled her into his arms and kissed her soundly.

"How I've missed you, love." He pulled back to look deeply into her beautiful blue eyes. "Charlie, what's wrong?"

"I must tell you something."

The tone of her voice sent shockwaves through him. This didn't feel right. The whole room buzzed with nervous energy. He sat back from her and Charlotte turned so that she was facing him. Thomas was concerned that she wasn't crying. She looked so distraught, and he was accustomed to her easy tears. It was one of the many things he loved about her; her passionate nature. No matter how she tried, she could never hide her emotions.

"Thomas, there's no easy way to say this," she began.

Thomas panicked. Certainly Big Viv would have warned him if Charlotte was breaking off their marriage. He quickly thought back over the last week. Their visit had been full of easy friendship and plans for their future together. What had happened in the last three days? His anxiety rose as he waited for her to speak.

"I'm with child," she finally whispered. "Mrs. Groves estimates the birth date will fall in the middle of April."

Thomas swallowed. Of all the possible things he was dreading to hear, this was, well, it wouldn't have ever crossed his mind. He knew his response was critical. How he reacted to this news would shape the rest of his and Charlotte's lives. He smiled and took both of her hands in his. A million responses raced through his mind and he had difficulty choosing one.

"How are you feeling?"

"I'm feeling a little better this week."

A harsh chuckle accompanied her grimace. Her face was a portrait of anxious anticipation. He knew she was trying to determine how he felt about what she'd told him. But how should he handle this? If he had a few hours to think about it, he knew he would handle it just fine. But he couldn't seem to form coherent thoughts, and fear of saying the wrong thing left him tongue-tied.

"Charlotte," he began, needing to buy some time. He was sure her worry grew every second. He needed to speak!

"Charlotte, I love you."

"And I you, Thomas."

Her gaze was unwavering. He could feel her pulse pounding through her hands. Her heart raced like a galloping stallion.

"I'm so sorry this has happened to you. You've had to deal with so much already. This is another tough blow, I'm sure, but it doesn't change my desire to spend the rest of our lives together."

A flicker of hope flashed quickly across her face.

"And I know I will love this child you're carrying just as though he or she were my very own."

The hope disappeared from her eyes, replaced by what looked like anger.

"Thomas, its father was one of those…" her words trailed off and she dropped her head. "What if the baby looks like its father? And even if it doesn't, I don't think I can bear the constant reminder of that day; not just the rape, but the loss of everyone I loved. As soon as it is born, I plan to put it up for adoption."

Thomas felt a stab of pain. This was, of course, her choice to make. He was just surprised by the strong reaction he already felt at the thought of "losing" this child of Charlotte's.

"I will be by your side and support you in whatever you decide, Charlie."

He pulled her close and relished the feel of her head on his chest. How he hated the men who had done this to her. The violation of her womanhood and loss of her family were already going to leave life-long scars. But this; this was just too much for a woman to bear.

"I'm here, my love. I'm here," he whispered into her hair as he continued to hold her close.

They sat that way for a long, long time. When dusk had fallen outside and shadows danced around the room, Clara appeared in the doorway. Charlotte had fallen asleep with her head on Thomas' chest. Thomas met Clara's imploring look and gently shook his head. Clara's worry deepened when she saw the sadness in his eyes.

"Supper is ready," she said, and turned to walk to the dining room.

"Charlotte, dear," Thomas softly said, attempting to rouse the sleeping woman. "It's time to go in for supper."

She raised her head but didn't make eye contact with him. She still hadn't cried, and that worried him substantially now.

"I'm not feeling very hungry, Thomas. I think I'd like to go to sleep. Please give them my regrets."

Before he could answer, she stood and made her way up the stairs. Who was this woman, and where was his dear Charlotte? Thomas stood, helpless, for several moments before he walked into the dining room to join his friends.

After a very somber dinner that night, Joseph accompanied Thomas back to the Tremont House Hotel. As much as he appreciated the gesture, Thomas would have vastly preferred to have time alone with his thoughts. Charlotte was fading away, right in front of him, and he didn't know what to do about it.

Joseph did not waste time with any mundane, trivial conversation, but got right to the point.

"Thomas, I wanted to let you know that Clara has made me aware of Charlotte's condition."

Thomas looked over at his friend in shock.

"Before you get angry at her seeming betrayal, let me explain. Clara is very, very worried about her young friend. For the last two weeks, we've both noticed that Charlotte has not exactly been herself. She was sick and trying to hide it. She became more and more withdrawn. Then, once Clara confirmed Charlotte's suspicions Tuesday night, things deteriorated rapidly. It is as though this last blow is more than her already overwhelmed mind can handle. I'm greatly concerned and want to talk with you about my observations."

Thomas nodded solemnly. "I feel like I'm losing her, Joseph."

"During my years serving wounded soldiers at the Confederate Hospital in Wilmington I began to notice a troubling pattern. Soldiers who had fully recovered from their physical wounds were sometimes determined unfit to return to battle due to curious symptoms of mental incompetence. Initially, we attributed these to weakness or lack of character. However, as the years passed, I began to see more and more soldiers afflicted with the same symptoms; quiet withdrawal, nervousness, shaking, compulsive repeating of words or phrases that didn't make sense. They were easily startled and constantly irritable."

Joseph turned to look over at Thomas. He could see that his friend was hanging on every word.

"I even witnessed one man go suddenly blind for no discernible reason. One minute he was recuperating valiantly and the next, he lost his vision and seemed to go mad. It was so frustrating! My fellow doctors and I tried everything we could. Although these soldiers passed their physicals and seemed sound in body, their minds seemed to be...well, as I said, deteriorating in a rapid manner. I became increasingly curious and set out to research every document I could find related to historic wars and their aftermaths. I remembered studying *The Iliad of Homer* and *The Odyssey* as a boy and went through them again with more discerning scrutiny. Even all those years ago, there were references to gallant soldiers broken by the horrors of war."

Thomas recalled some of his fellow comrades who were now just shells of their former selves.

"As our American war raged on, it was no longer only soldiers who exhibited these symptoms, but civilians and even women. In the rare instances when I had time to interview them, they all shared stories of unbelievable terror." He shook his head in sad resignation. "I doubt there exists in this country a single person under the age of ten who was not adversely affected by this horrible war."

"You are probably correct."

They had arrived at the hotel and Thomas turned to face Dr. Groves.

"So, you think that Charlie is suffering from these same symptoms?"

"I'm not sure, my friend. There's no definitive way to diagnose this. My intent is not to alarm you, but just to make you aware of what Charlotte is likely experiencing. She may come to terms with this pregnancy in a few days and be just fine, or she may continue to become more and more withdrawn. If you are paying close attention, you will notice even the most subtle of changes. If at any point you feel worried for her safety, or just need advice on how best to handle the situation, please don't hesitate to come to me. Clara and I care for you both very much and want to see Charlotte happy."

"Thank you, Joseph." Thomas sighed, running a hand through his hair. "How can one young lady bear so much pain?"

"She has faith in God, and she has you, Thomas. She has a new group of friends who care greatly for her. Charlotte is a strong person and she will get through this." Joseph reached out and placed a reassuring hand on Thomas' shoulder. "Good night, Thomas."

Rather than entering the hotel and climbing the stairs to his room, Thomas turned and walked to the church. He needed to sit with the Lord, the only one who could strengthen him for what lie ahead. Slipping quietly into the church, he noticed Father Joseph kneeling in front of the tabernacle. The priest seemed to be in another world. Thomas didn't want to interrupt this intimate communion and briefly considered going for a walk, instead. He turned to go, but his heart was inexorably drawn back into the peaceful space. Without a sound, he made his way into the church and knelt out of the priest's line of sight. He really didn't want to bother the gentle man.

As it had been the last time he visited, the church was dark except for the soft red glow from the tabernacle candle. Thomas closed his eyes and tried to pray, but he couldn't quiet his racing mind. Eventually, he opened his eyes and looked across the church at Father Joseph. Thomas couldn't recall ever seeing someone so deep in prayer. He stared at the quiet scene in awe. Thomas' heart was filled with a desire for that sort of a relationship with God. The priest before him was a model of absolute trust and patience, whereas Thomas felt consumed with doubt and hatred. Doubt in a God that could allow such evil to befall his precious Charlie, and hatred for the men who'd hurt her and killed her family.

He was surprised to feel hot, wet tears sliding down his cheeks. Well, this was just perfect! Charlie was no longer showing any sort of emotion, and he was kneeling here alone, crying. He closed his eyes again, and let his head fall into his hands. Silently, he allowed all the helplessness and anger and horror and sorrow of the last five years to escape his heart and flow from his eyes.

"Please God," he whispered, desperately. "Please God, help me."

"Can I help you, my son?"

Thomas jumped at the quiet voice. His eyes flew open and he was shocked by the sight of Father Joseph kneeling next to him.

"I'm so sorry, Father. I didn't mean to disturb you."

"You didn't," the priest whispered back with a reassuring smile. "I had just finished my prayers when I felt a nudge to look around the church. I was actually surprised to see you, since I hadn't heard a sound."

Thomas was relieved he hadn't upset the beautiful communion between Father Joseph and his Lord.

"Would it help to talk about what's upset you?"

"It's so late, Father, and I don't want to keep you," Thomas answered. In truth, he wanted nothing more than to pour out his heart and get advice from this holy man.

"Son, when I was studying for the priesthood, I desired only to spend my whole life serving God. I longed to be His hands and feet in this broken world; to give food to the hungry, clothes to the poor, and be a listening ear to those who were heartbroken. I promised myself that I would never be too busy for a hurting soul."

Father Joseph seemed lit from the inside, as though by a candle, and Thomas was drawn to the love shining from the priest's face.

"It is my greatest honor to serve my beloved Jesus in every person I meet. There is no greater gift. So, how can I serve you, Mr. Linz?"

Father Joseph already knew the whole, horrific story of the attack at Kerry Haven, so Thomas just shared the latest news. At the end, he added, "I'm so glad now that we weren't married three weeks ago, before she knew. She would forever feel that I was trapped into marrying her. And nothing I did or said would convince her otherwise."

Thomas looked at the priest, and Father Joseph saw the anguish in the young man's countenance.

"Father Joseph, I don't understand how this can all be happening to her. Where is God?"

Father Joseph sat silently for so long that Thomas began to wonder if he was okay. He considered reaching over to check the priest's pulse, when finally he spoke.

"Mr. Linz, may I call you Thomas?"

"Of course, Father."

"Thomas, this is a very heavy topic, and one that I'm often asked to discuss. As you are keenly aware, there is so much suffering, so much evil in the world. There's physical evil- people getting sick and dying, and then there's moral evil, such as our country's recent war, and what was done to the Gallagher family. If God is good, why doesn't He take it away? Why does He allow evil to remain with us? Why does He even allow evil people to live? He is powerful enough and strong enough and wise enough to permanently eliminate all evil. But, what would happen if He did? What if God reached His limit of patience and used His unlimited power to stop bad things from happening?"

He paused to let Thomas think about this.

"If God did this, He would cease to be all good because He would take away our freedom. Without the freedom to choose good or evil, we humans would lose the ability to be great. And God has created us to be great. He created us in His own image and likeness and longs for us to be with Him forever in heaven. Taking away our freedom would prevent that heavenly union."

The priest looked lovingly over at the tabernacle, and Thomas spoke.

"But, what if God just fixed it, Father? What if He took us back to the Garden of Eden and gave us all a second chance?"

Father Joseph smiled and then chuckled softly.

"Thomas, how long do you think it would take for mankind to mess things up again? Anyone with small children will tell you how this works. The parent fixes the damaged plaything, and the child breaks it again. The parent fixes it once more, and the child breaks it yet again. It can be an unending cycle until the toy is irreparably destroyed. That is one of the reasons Our Lord allows this world to remain broken. He created this world good, and then we broke it. He allows it to remain broken so that we can be free, so that we can be like Him. This doesn't mean that God is distant, or that He doesn't care. In fact, it is the exact opposite."

"What do you mean?"

Father Joseph pondered the best way to enunciate his thoughts.

"The entire story of Christianity, every story about Christ, is partly an answer to the question, 'Why is there evil?' In every story of Christianity, we see not a God who keeps His distance, but a God who comes close. Far from being uncaring, He enters into our lives and allows what overwhelms us to overwhelm Him. Right now, your heart is overwhelmed with concern for Miss Gallagher. Well, God's heart is experiencing that with you. So much does He identify with us that He became one of us and allowed Himself to experience incredible betrayal, incredible suffering, incredible loneliness and incredible isolation. Christ became man and experienced having everything stripped from Him to the point where He hung naked on a cross. All He had to give was His spirit. All He could give was forgiveness, and so He gave it. Then He descended to the realm of the dead, and rose again to free us from death."

Thomas felt that Father Joseph was looking directly into his soul.

"Jesus did all of this to free you from death, Thomas, and to free your young fiancé from death. God is not impassive in the face of her pain. He is not distant from it. He experienced the Passion, and He is experiencing Charlotte's pain. But He will not take away her suffering. Instead, He will enter into it, transform it, and redeem it so that now, her suffering has great power. Now her suffering has meaning behind it. Now your suffering has meaning."

When Thomas didn't speak, Father Joseph continued.

"We who have been baptized in Christ now live as members of the Body of Christ. One of the things St. Paul said is, 'I rejoice in my sufferings for your sake. In my body, I make up for what is lacking in the suffering of Christ for the sake of His body, the Church.' Does this mean Jesus left something undone? Does it mean He did not complete the process? No, it doesn't. Jesus did it all. He paid the full price. But He gave Charlotte, and all of His followers, a sliver of His cross. So that in your suffering and in my suffering, as members of the Body of Christ, we take part in the act of redemption. We are still fighting, still suffering. And that suffering still does something. Your suffering still matters. Charlotte's suffering still matters.

God didn't prevent her pain because He was not willing to take away her freedom. God would not force Charlotte to love Him any more than you would force her to love you. True love cannot exist without freedom."

Tears were flowing down Thomas' face again. In that moment, he was no longer hearing Father Joseph's words, but words straight from the heart of God. He sensed that Father Joseph was simply the translator.

"So, how do I do this? I mean, how do Charlotte and I unite our suffering to Jesus?"

"While it's not easy, Thomas, it really is very simple. Because you and your betrothed are members of the Body of Christ, you are called to follow His example. On the cross, in the midst of the greatest suffering, Christ said, 'Father, into Your hands, I commend my spirit.' He made the decision to give everything to God. You and Charlotte are made in His image and are temples of the Holy Ghost. All you have to do in the midst of any type of suffering is say, 'Lord, use this. Father, I don't want this to happen, but use it.' This is how you and I unite our suffering with Christ's. Nothing given to God is ever wasted. If your suffering, or Miss Gallagher's suffering, can return even one soul to the Father, it will be worth more than all the riches in the world."

"Oh, Father Joseph. I wish that Charlotte had been here to hear this. I'll never be able to remember it all, and she desperately needs to hear it. If I bring her tomorrow, will you tell her?"

"Thomas, do you remember a few moments ago when I told you that serving Christ through others was my greatest joy?"

Thomas nodded.

"I think that you are the one who is to serve Christ in Charlotte right now. She loves you more than anyone else in the world. God's healing will not come through me, but through you. Trust me in this."

"But, Father, I won't know what to say. I won't remember how you explained everything."

"That's the most beautiful part, my son. You don't have to. In the Gospel of Luke, we read, 'When you are brought before synagogues, rulers, and authorities, do not worry about how you will defend yourselves or what you will say, for the Holy Ghost will teach you at that time what you should say.'"

Thomas could not believe his ears. This was a Gospel verse he'd always loved. The one he'd read right before discovering Charlotte's true identity. This was not a mere coincidence!

"God will give you the right words, Thomas, just as He gave them to me. I don't even recall what He just said to you through me. I was merely a channel through which His love flowed."

Father Joseph stood and placed a hand on Thomas' shoulder. "Just think, Thomas. You have the great, great blessing of living the rest of your life as a love letter from God to Charlotte; from God to every person you meet."

"Thank you, Father Joseph. Thank you and God bless you."

"And you, my son. Goodnight."

When the priest left his side, Thomas stood up and walked closer to the tabernacle. He knew he would remember this night for the rest of his life. He couldn't stop the smile that was spreading across his face.

"Thank you, Father," he said once again.

This time, Thomas spoke not to Father Joseph but to God the Father, present in the Eucharist. He made the sign of the cross and reluctantly left the church. He returned to the Tremont, unlocked his room, and fell into a peaceful sleep moments after his head touched the pillow.

A few blocks away, in her room at the Groves house, Charlotte was not enjoying peaceful slumber. She tossed and turned. Each time she managed to fall asleep, she was plagued with nightmares of infants born looking exactly like Dan or Fred, but infinitely smaller. In each nightmare, the ugly babies grabbed weapons and began killing everyone she loved. And each time she awoke, panting for breath, her hatred of this future baby grew. She prayed it would die. She prayed her body would reject the horrid thing. Then, as night turned into dawn, and her torments grew worse, Charlotte prayed she would die.

Chapter Twenty-Seven

Friday, September 27, 1867

The next morning, Thomas noticed fresh flowers throughout the hotel lobby and asked the footman where he could find some for his betrothed. The young man seemed only too happy to help him.

"I pick them up a couple mornings a week from the widow Johnson. She lives a bit further down Larimer Street. It's a large brick house with wide porches, one of the few left on that block. You can't miss it."

"Thank you, kind sir."

Thomas flipped the man a coin as he exited the hotel. He made his way down the street with an excited spring in his step. He was marrying Charlotte tomorrow! Within minutes, he'd arrived in front of the large brick home the footman described. As he opened the front gate to make his way up the sidewalk, he caught sight of a woman trimming roses to the side of the house.

"Good morning. I'm looking for Mrs. Johnson."

The woman stood up and turned around.

"I'm Mrs. Johnson. How can I help you?"

The woman smiled kindly and Thomas was shocked at how much younger she was than he'd imagined. It was difficult to remember that widows were no longer old women. The war had given far too many young women this distinction.

"I'd like to buy some flowers for my sweetheart."

Mrs. Thomas walked toward him, slipping her trimming shears into the pocket of the apron she wore.

"What kind of flowers does she prefer? I've roses and magnolias, and even a few wildflowers remaining in the side yard."

"I'll take wildflowers today, and could I pick up some roses tomorrow morning for my wedding?"

"Oh, would your sweetheart happen to be Miss Gallagher?"

"Yes! How did you know?"

"She came by here last week with two friends. They requested a bouquet for her wedding tomorrow. You seem almost as excited as she was, sir."

Thomas' smile grew exponentially, and Mrs. Johnson began to laugh.

"Oh, to be young and in love again! Your fiancé is a fine young lady. She'll love these wildflowers. Follow me, please."

Thomas left the Johnson house after paying for his wildflowers and the bridal bouquet order and made his way to the Groves home. He was longing to see Charlotte, and hoped that she would be feeling better today.

"God, I'm trusting You to send me the words," he silently prayed as he knocked on the Groves' door.

It was a somber Vivian who answered his knock.

"Morning, Mr. Linz. I sure am glad you're here. Miss Charlotte still hasn't come down from her room; not since last night before supper. Mrs. Clara and I have both checked in on her, but she says she doesn't want to come down." The woman's worried expression did not sit well with him.

"Dr. Groves is out on a call and Mrs. Groves is over at the workhouse helping deliver a baby and I don't know what to do. Maybe you could go up and talk to her, Mr. Linz."

"Would that upset Dr. or Mrs. Groves? I know it's highly improper."

"Mr. Linz, this is no time for prim propriety. We're all worried, and Charlie needs you, now, sir."

He handed Vivian his hat and quickly made his way up the stairs. He stopped outside her door and prayed again. "Please God, bring her back to us."

Then he knocked. When there was no response to his knock, he leaned against the door and said loudly, "It's me, Charlotte. May I come in, love?"

There was only silence. Thomas felt icy cold fear take residence in his chest. He slowly opened the door. Charlotte was sitting in an armchair staring out the open window. Thomas quickly closed the distance between them. He fell to his knees in front of her chair and took her hands in his. They were still warm to the touch. He checked her pulse and was glad to feel it strong and steady under his fingers.

"Charlie," he said, and gently shook her.

There was no response. Her open eyes did not blink or look away from the window. He set the flowers down on the floor and rose to his feet. Then he took her into his arms and carried her down the stairs, yelling for George Groves.

George came running towards him, alarm showing in his face as he took in the sight.

"Follow me."

George turned and ran down the hall toward the exam room. Once in the room, Thomas laid Charlotte gently on the table.

"She's still breathing, and has a strong pulse, but she's not responding at all," Thomas quickly explained. "Do you know when Dr. Groves will be back?"

"I don't. May I take a look?"

At Thomas' urgent nod, George turned and washed his hands. Then he placed his palm under Charlotte's nose for a few moments and moved to check her pulse. He looked up at Thomas.

"You were right, nothing wrong with her breathing or heart beats." He carefully tapped Charlotte on the shoulder.

"Miss Charlotte," he loudly called. "It's George. Can you hear me?"

When there was no response, he ran two fingers back and forth in front of her open, staring eyes. They did not even flicker. "I know that there are things that can be done, but I don't want to try them myself. I'm going to run fetch Dr. Groves."

George quickly left the room and Thomas lifted Charlotte off the table and into his arms. He sat on the doctor's stool and gently rocked her back and forth. Tears were streaming down his face. Even in the midst of battle, he'd never felt such fear. He kissed her forehead and her cheeks.

"Charlie, come back," he whispered over and over again.

Thomas had felt such peace and such hope after talking with Father Joseph last night. Now all he felt was sheer terror. Precious Charlotte was trapped in her mind and, for all he knew, might be reliving the worst moments of her life while here he sat, unable to reach her. She was hurting and there was nothing he could do to help. It seemed like forever before George and Dr. Groves returned to find Thomas still rocking and whispering to Charlotte.

"Will you place her here on the exam table, Thomas? I need to determine what we're dealing with," Dr. Groves said, as he washed his hands.

Thomas stood and walked back to the table but found he couldn't put her down. His silent tears turned into loud sobs. He squeezed her small body to his chest.

"Thomas, please let me examine her," Dr. Groves prompted.

Thomas kissed her firmly on the lips and then laid her back on the table. She was wearing another beautiful gown that he hadn't seen before, this one a soft green color. Thomas thought she'd never looked lovelier.

"George, will you please go and ask Father Joseph to come," Thomas asked through his tears. "I'm so scared."

George looked at Dr. Groves, who nodded his assent. As he watched George leave, Thomas noticed that Big Viv was now standing in the doorway, her cheeks streaked with tears. Without thought, Thomas walked over and hung his head. The large black woman enfolded him in her arms and they cried together.

"She's gonna be alright," Vivian whispered. "She's gonna be alright. Our baby's gonna be okay."

Thomas didn't know whether Vivian was talking to him or to herself, but her soft voice brought a measure of comfort. Soon, Vivian and Thomas heard Clara's cheerful voice.

"Hello! Is anyone home?"

Vivian pulled away and swiped at her cheeks. "We're in here Mrs. Groves."

Thomas heard Clara's hurried footsteps in the hall. "What's happened," she asked as she reached the doorway and saw Charlotte lying on the table. "Joseph, what happened?"

"I'm not sure, dear. Have you spoken to Charlotte at all today?"

"Not this morning, I checked in with her briefly before leaving for the delivery late last night and she was in her bed. She said she felt sad and thought a good night's sleep would help. I asked Vivian to check on her this morning."

Everyone in the room looked over to Big Viv. Everyone except Charlotte.

"I went in first thing and spoke with her. I asked her to come down for breakfast, and said she wasn't hungry. When I told her it had been too long since yesterday lunch and she should come eat something, she said, 'No thank you.' She told me she'd get dressed and wait for Mr. Linz to come over. She still seemed sad, but nothing like this. Then I checked in again around eight and she was dressed and sitting looking out the window. I asked if she was still going to come down to the drawing room to wait for Mr. Linz. She said she was watching for him out the window. That was the last time I talked with her. I knew something was terribly wrong."

Vivian pulled up the corner of her apron and dried her eyes.

"I arrived at half past eight and went almost immediately up to her room. Sorry about that, but Vivian said Charlotte needed me."

Thomas looked from Joseph to Clara, neither of whom looked the least bit concerned about propriety now.

"What are you thinking, Joseph," Clara asked her husband.

Thomas found himself grateful for her calm demeanor. It brought him some sense of peace.

"I'm not really sure, dear. Vivian, will you please prepare some strong tea and perhaps bring a few biscuits? Maybe we can rouse her with some tea."

Vivian left the room immediately, closing the door behind her.

"I didn't want to speak in front of Vivian or George. This unwanted pregnancy is not something that I think Charlotte would like for too many people to know about. I talked with Thomas last night about my suspicions."

Clara nodded at him.

"Charlotte's current state confirms my fears. She's suffering from some sort of cognitive failure. Physically, her body is fine. But she seems to be trapped somewhere in her mind. The pregnancy was likely her breaking point. I've tried smelling salts to no avail. Now, I'm going to try to see if a pinch or a needle prick will bring her back. Occasionally physical pain can bring someone back. Do either of you need to leave the room?"

Thomas moved closer to Charlotte and took her hand.

"I want to stay."

"Yes, I'll stay, as well," Clara said, and took Charlotte's other hand.

She looked at Thomas with an encouraging smile. He tried to smile back at her but couldn't quite manage it. Dr. Groves pinched Charlotte in the sensitive skin near her elbow and then on the inside of her upper arm. When that produced no reaction, he tried the fold of skin between her nose and upper lip. Charlotte did not even flinch. He grabbed a thick sewing needle from his top drawer and ran it through candle flame to sanitize it. Then he pricked the needle into each of the areas he'd pinched. Thomas could see Joseph's hope fading as Charlotte remained unaffected by the pain.

"What next," Thomas asked, desperately. "What else can you try?"

"I don't want to hurt her needlessly. Let's just keep her safe and comfortable for now. I will continue to look for remedies."

Just then, the front door opened, and footsteps were heard in the hall.

"Thank goodness you're here, Father Joseph," Dr. Groves said. "I think we could all use your comfort, and Miss Gallagher could certainly use some healing. I'm at a loss here. Her vital signs are good, her pupils are not dilated…" His voice trailed off.

Father Joseph could sense the fear in the room. It was evident that Dr. Groves needed someone else to take control for a while so he could think. Even though she was surrounded by loved ones, young Charlotte looked so cold and lonely lying there on the table.

"Pick her up, please Thomas," Father Joseph instructed. "I want her to always feel the presence of one of you with her. Please don't leave her alone. I'll even come sit with her if needed."

Thomas gladly picked Charlotte up. He wanted her in his arms. He needed the feel of her breathing to assure him that she was still alive.

"May we move into the sitting room, Dr. Groves," Clara asked her husband. "Everyone will be able to sit and pray together there."

"That's a good idea, dear. I will stay here and keep looking through my medical books. There must be something I haven't thought of."

Dr. Groves suddenly looked weary. Thomas thought of how difficult this must be for him, as well. He was a man accustomed to healing wounds and fixing broken bones. He was a man accustomed to solutions. From their conversation on the walk to the hotel last night, Thomas knew that Dr. Groves' inability to solve these cognitive situations was a source of great frustration. As the others began filing out of the exam room, he spoke.

"Dr. Groves, thank you, I know you'll do what you can."

Joseph looked solemnly at his friend. Then, he nodded and Thomas left the room carrying his love, his heart, his whole future, in his arms.

When he and Charlotte joined George, Clara, and Vivian in the sitting room, Father Joseph was pulling his stole from his bag. Thomas sat down on the settee, holding Charlotte tight to his chest.

"Stay with me Charlie," he pleaded silently. "Please stay with me."

After kissing the stole and placing it on his shoulders, Father Joseph pulled his prayer book and a small jar out of his bag.

"Let us join in prayer."

Everyone except Thomas knelt on the floor.

"In the name of the Father, and of the Son, and of the Holy Ghost, Amen. Almighty God, who hast given us grace at this time to make our common supplications unto Thee; and dost promise that when two or three are gathered together in Thy name Thou wilt grant their requests: fulfill now, O Lord, the desires and petitions of Thy servants, as may be most expedient for them, granting us in this world knowledge of Thy truth, and in the world to come, life everlasting. Amen."

Father Joseph dipped his thumb into the holy oil of the sick and made the sign of the cross on Charlotte's forehead. "We ask you, heavenly Father, to heal Your daughter Charlotte, and bring her back to us."

He turned the page in his prayer book, and continued.

"O, loving Lord and Savior, in Your arms we are safe. Keep us, and we have nothing to fear. Give us up, and we have nothing to hope for. We do not know what will come upon us before we die. We know nothing about the future, but we rely upon You. We pray that You would give us what is good for us. We pray that You would take from us whatever would imperil our salvation. O Christ, You died on the Cross for us, sinners that we are. Help us to know You, to believe in You, to love You, to serve You, to always aim at bringing You glory, to live to and for You, to set a good example to all around us."

Once more, Father Joseph dipped his thumb into the oil and made the sign of the cross on Charlotte's forehead, saying, "Lord, I am not worthy to have You enter under my roof; only say the word and my servant shall be healed."

"Loving Father, we bring Your wounded, hurting daughter, our dear friend, Charlotte for Your healing. Fill her heart with Your everlasting love and bring her out of her pain and into our loving embrace."

One last time, he dipped his thumb into the oil and, as he traced the cross on her forehead, he said, "We ask this in the name of the Father, and of the Son, and of the Holy Ghost."

"Amen," answered everyone in the room.

Father Joseph sat down next to Thomas.

"Would you like me to stay?"

"No, Father. Thank you for the offer, but I know you have so many to serve, and we may need you again soon."

"Thomas, please don't forget our conversation yesterday," Father Joseph entreated. "Now is your time to serve Christ in Charlotte. 'Whatsoever you do for the least of these brethren, you do it for me.' You will get to live that scripture this week, my son. May God bless you and keep you. I will check back with you tonight to see if there is any improvement."

"Thank you, Father Joseph."

The priest rose, and Clara walked him to the door.

For the rest of the day, Thomas sat on the settee, holding Charlotte in his arms. He talked with her, and read to her, and, remembering how much she loved to sing with him, he occasionally sang to her. But most of all, he prayed.

"Father God, I unite Charlotte's suffering and mine to Your most precious Passion. Please allow us to help You save souls."

Every few minutes he prayed it again. And every hour or so, Vivian or Clara would come in to bring him a drink or something to eat. George and Dr. Groves visited a few times, checking her vital signs and discussing several new ideas. Twice they tried to pour at least a small amount of water into her mouth in the hopes she would swallow it. Both times, the water just ran out of her mouth and down her chin. Thomas could sense the growing concern they were trying to hide.

That evening, Sergeant and Mrs. Albertson came over, and Father Joseph returned to check on Charlotte. They all knelt and prayed the Rosary together. As it was Friday, they prayed the sorrowful mysteries. Thomas found it fitting that they were meditating on Christ's Passion as Charlie passed through a sorrowful passion of her own. Her constant heartbeat against his chest was the only sign she still lived.

Everyone offered to sit with Charlotte so Thomas could take a break, but he couldn't bear the thought of leaving her. When she awoke, he wanted his to be the first face she saw. And, if she didn't wake, but instead passed away, he wanted her to die in his arms, surrounded by his love. When Clara and Joseph walked all the guests to the door and wished them goodnight, Thomas realized that tomorrow morning would have been his wedding day. He wept.

Early the next morning, George and Dr. Groves approached Thomas with their most critical concern.

"Despite your best efforts, Thomas," Dr. Groves began, looking at the cup of water on the table next to where Thomas held Charlotte tight. "It's now been more than a day since Charlie had any water. This is not something that her body can sustain. Water is the most essential requirement of the human body. We'd hoped that she would swallow some fluid on her own, but, as that is not working, we'll need to find another way."

Dr. Groves looked to George and encouraged him to explain their research.

"There are two scientists in Germany who have been working on something called rectal feeding. The results haven't been remarkable, but patients in similar states to Charlie have been kept alive for several weeks."

Thomas wanted to ask what happened after several weeks; did the patients come out of the state, or did they die. However, he had not the courage to find out. George continued.

"The other option, which we prefer to try first, involves a hollow tube made from leather which we would carefully run down her throat. This technique was developed by a Belgian chemist over two hundred years ago and seems to be moderately successful. It would allow us to administer the water she so desperately needs, and, if need be, food that has been mashed into a thin liquid form."

When George finished speaking, he looked over to Dr. Groves.

"With your permission, we'd like to begin this as soon as we can fashion the tube."

"Is it dangerous," Thomas asked.

"It will be extremely uncomfortable for Charlotte as we position the tube, but it's considered a very safe procedure."

"Yes, please do it, then. I can't lose her, Joseph."

George placed a solid hand on Thomas' shoulder.

"We will do everything we can, sir. We have all grown to care for Charlotte. She is a strong woman, and if anyone can pull through this, it's her."

"Thank you both for everything," Thomas said.

The two men nodded and left the room.

"Please come back, Charlie," Thomas whispered over and over.

Within a couple of hours, Joseph and George had fashioned the leather tube and soaked it in water to soften it enough for insertion. Joseph recommended that Thomas move Charlotte back to the exam room and then step out into the hallway so that Clara and Vivian could clean her and remove her restrictive clothing. It would be the first time in over a day that Thomas spent more than a few moments away from her. George led him to the kitchen where Big Viv had a hot meal waiting.

"I know you likely don't feel hungry, Thomas, but it's important," George encouraged. "Charlie needs you to be at your best, and you can't keep strong without eating."

"Thank you, George. You're a good friend. I'll do what I can."

Just then, Dr. Groves entered the room. "May we have a moment, George?"

"Yes, Doctor. I'll be waiting outside the exam room for the women to finish."

"Thank you. Thomas, I'm going to be honest with you. Charlotte's pregnancy really complicates this situation. A woman's body will go to great lengths to sustain a pregnancy, often at its own risk. I feel very confident that this feeding tube will buy us time, but we need her to wake up. You're doing everything right. Whether or not she is responding to us, I believe Charlie is at least partially aware that she's not alone—that she's surrounded by your love."

Thomas nodded through his tears, and Dr. Groves continued.

"Now, that being said, I am going to insist that you remain outside the exam room while we are positioning the tube. It will be very uncomfortable for her, and she's likely to gag and might vomit. Your absence will allow us to maintain her dignity. We will bring you in as soon as we are done and have cleaned her up, if needed."

Thomas nodded again.

"I understand."

"Do you have any questions for me, Thomas?"

"I can't think of any. I just…I just keep praying she'll wake up soon, Joseph."

"George and I are doing everything we can, and we are not going to give up. It's in God's hands now, friend."

With that, the doctor stood and left Thomas alone in the kitchen. With great effort, he finished half of the food. He gulped the now-cold coffee and walked down the hall to join George and Joseph. Soon, Clara and Big Viv stepped out of the exam room carrying a basin and the dress Charlotte had been wearing for the last twenty-something hours.

"She's ready, Doctor," Clara said, and squeezed her husband's hand. "I'm praying that God will guide you both."

"We'll let you know as soon as you can come in," Dr. Groves said to Thomas.

Clara handed Charlotte's clothes to Vivian and turned to Thomas.

"I'll wait here with you, Mr. Linz."

"And I'll go put the clothes in the laundry and then prepare Miss Charlotte's room," Vivian said. "I may even run over and get more flowers from Mrs. Thomas. I want it to look bright and cheerful when she wakes up."

"Oh, can she stay in the drawing room, so I can stay with her," Thomas asked quickly. "It wouldn't be proper to stay in her room, but I don't want to leave her side."

"Thomas, once the tube is in place, Charlotte will be much more comfortable in her bed. I will need to speak about this with Joseph, but I imagine it would be okay if you—"

She was unable to finish her sentence as they were interrupted by garbled screaming from the exam room. Thomas reached for the doorknob and was about to burst into the room when a surprisingly strong hand grabbed his wrist.

"Please let my husband and George do their work," Clara insisted in a calm, gentle voice.

Thomas looked down at her hand on his wrist. How did such a genteel woman have this astonishing strength? He was about to argue with her when the screaming abruptly stopped, and he heard Charlotte's voice.

"Stop! Please stop!"

There was a splashing sound, a loud thud, and a metallic clatter. Thomas looked anxiously to Clara. She nodded her head and he burst into the exam room.

The moment Thomas entered the room, Charlotte leapt off the table and ran into his arms. Holding her tight to his chest, he tentatively looked around the room. Dr. Groves was lying on the floor to the left of the exam table as George tried to rouse him. A puddle of water and a metal basin lie on the floor to the right of the table. Clara dropped to her knees beside her husband. She and Thomas spoke at the same time.

"Will he be okay, George?"

"What happened? How did you save her, and what's wrong with Dr. Groves?"

Charlotte turned her face to take in the scene before her. She wasn't going to leave the safety of Thomas' embrace, but she wanted to hear George's answers.

George chuckled, and answered Clara's question first.

"I'm sure he's going to be fine."

Then he looked up to where Thomas stood. "Once Dr. Groves wakes up, this is going to make for a great story!"

As though playing into the narrative, Joseph Groves slowly opened his eyes and looked around the room. He reached up and gingerly rubbed the growing lump on the side of his head.

"I guess that was one way to wake you, Charlie." He smiled ruefully. "Remind me to never make you angry!"

"Did I do that to you," Charlotte asked.

Joseph nodded his head, winced, and then grinned at her.

"I'm so sorry, Dr. Groves. What happened? I have no recollection."

"You've been non-responsive for almost twenty-six hours and we needed to introduce water before you became sick," Joseph said. "We talked with Thomas and decided to try a feeding tube. Placing a feeding tube is not exactly high-risk, but it's very uncomfortable. When we started to insert the tube, your body's reflexes kicked in and you began gagging and thrashing wildly. We were attempting to hold you down in order to finish placing the tube when you began screaming. I was thrilled to hear your voice and began removing the tubing. That's the last thing I remember."

Dr. Groves looked over to George for answers. George couldn't suppress his smile.

"Sorry, but it was quite humorous. Charlie, in your thrashing, you must have grabbed the metal basin. I heard the water splash on the ground and then you whacked Dr. Groves solidly on the head. I'm sorry. In our whole lives together, Joseph and I have been in plenty of scrapes, but I never imagined his first time being rendered unconscious would come from a lady."

At that, the whole group burst into laughter.

"I have so many questions, Charlotte! You may have insight into a medical condition that has eluded me for years," Dr. Groves said excitedly.

"I'll do my best. But I'm still so confused."

"Confused, and thirsty, and hungry, I'll wager," Dr. Groves added. "Clara can take you upstairs and help you get dressed, and I'll go tell Vivian the good news. She is going to be thrilled to see you again, my dear."

Charlotte looked down and realized she was in nothing but her nightgown.

"Oh, goodness," she cried.

George, with eyes averted, handed her a blanket from the shelf near the sink. Thomas released her and she quickly wrapped the blanket around herself.

"Please don't be embarrassed, Charlie," Dr. Groves encouraged. "No one in this room was focused on your state of dress. Our only concern was your well-being."

"I'll see you soon, love," Thomas whispered and kissed her on the forehead before leaving the room with the other two gentlemen.

"Well, I'll be," Joseph exclaimed as soon as the door closed behind them. He again touched the large bump on his head as all three men burst into relieved laughter. "If I'd known that was the answer, we could have tried it sooner!"

The men moved down the hallway to the kitchen. "Vivian," Joseph Groves yelled exuberantly. "She's awake!"

"Praise the Lord," Big Viv responded, and danced a little jig. Thankfully, the men hadn't cleared the doorway in time to see her celebration.

"She's bound to be hungry, and very, very thirsty," George informed Vivian as they rounded the corner into the kitchen. "You want me to make some lemonade while you whip up something for her to eat?"

"That would be mighty helpful, George!"

"A tall glass of lemonade sounds just about perfect right now," Joseph said. "Please make a double batch!"

Within minutes, Charlotte and Clara entered the kitchen. Clara sat down at the table.

"Don't you ever scare me like that again, young lady," Vivian chided. She left the stove for long enough to pull Charlotte into a big hug.

"I am not planning to do anything of the sort. That was the most…well, the weirdest thing I've ever experienced. I don't even know how to describe it!"

Charlotte took the mug of coffee Vivian offered and sat down at the table next to Thomas.

"Oh, but I hope you will try," Joseph cried, pulling out the chair across the table from her and sitting down. "I want to document every single detail. During my years at the confederate hospital, I treated at least four gentlemen in a state like yours. However, because I didn't know the men before they lost their faculties, I had no idea what their normal state looked like. And, despite the best efforts of everyone at the hospital, none of the four recovered while under our care. Two died, and the other two were sent home when they had convalesced to the point where they could be spoon-fed. I never heard what happened to them after they left. Charlotte, you could provide so much valuable information to the world's medical community!"

"I promise to share everything I can, but there's something I must do first."

Charlotte looked around the room and then smiled at Thomas.

"If Father Joseph is available, I'd like to be married this afternoon. I don't want to wait another moment to be your wife."

Thomas smiled tentatively at her.

"Are you sure you're ready, my dear? You've been through such an ordeal these last few days."

He looked questioningly at Dr. Groves. Before the doctor could give his opinion, Charlotte repeated Thomas' own words from several weeks prior.

"I've never felt more certain about anything in my life, Mr. Linz."

The look on Charlotte's face nearly melted him. Dr. Groves' looked from one to the other, and his genuine smile conveyed great love and relief.

"Based on how you're functioning right now, Charlie, I think I can give you my medical approval. I'm so happy for you both."

"In that case, we have much to do and very little time to do it," Clara said, standing and pushing her chair back under the table.

"Oh my goodness," Big Viv exclaimed. "I need to get to work cooking the wedding meal."

"Miss Vivian," Thomas interjected. "If it wouldn't hurt your feelings, I'd like to forego the planned reception here and just treat everyone to a meal at The Tremont tonight. The situation Thursday and yesterday did not allow you to do any preparation at all. Having it at the hotel will make things easier for everyone and will allow you to focus your time and attention on making the most delicious cake you've ever made."

The older woman considered this for a moment before a big smile covered her face. "I like that idea, Mr. Linz. This will be the best cake you've ever seen!"

Vivian began taking the lunch plates to the sink. "Now, you all need to get out of my workspace. Shoo!"

Her deep, rich laughter brought a smile to each face and they quickly followed her order. In the hallway, Thomas turned to face his friends.

"I'll need to go speak with Father Joseph first, and then I'll make arrangements at the hotel. George, would you mind letting the Albertsons know of our good fortune?"

"Oh, I'd be happy to bear such glad tidings. Is there anything else that needs doing while I'm out?"

"My wedding bouquet is still with Mrs. Johnson," Charlotte said. "I'm sure she's wondering why it wasn't picked up this morning."

"Her home is very close to the hotel," Thomas said. "I'll pick the bouquet up and bring it with me to the church. Once I hear from Father Joseph, I will hurry back here and let you all know the time."

"Mr. Linz, if I accompany you to the church, then I can let the Albertsons and Groves know the outcome. It will save you having to come back here with the information."

"Good thinking, George!"

Thomas turned to Charlotte and Clara. He looked awkward and embarrassed.

"How long do you need to do all the…womanly things that need to be done?"

"You act as though we'll be here casting spells and drinking potions," Clara cried with a burst of laughter. "It's only dressing and doing her hair! I know Mrs. Albertson wanted to come help, and between the two of us, we can have her ready in little more than two hours."

Thomas looked at his pocket watch.

"It's half past eleven right now. That gives us plenty of time if Father can marry us today." Then he winked at Charlotte. "Wish me luck!"

Once George and Thomas left, Clara jumped into action.

"Would you like to start with a bath? Whether or not the wedding takes place tonight, I imagine a hot bath would feel very good right now!"

"Oh, you have no idea! I'm still so confused by all that happened, but I think my time away gave me further certainty about Thomas."

Then, she lowered her voice. "Clara, I've made up my mind. Ever since you and Marnie talked to me about what happens between a husband and wife, I've been thinking about whether I could ever truly and completely be a wife to Thomas in all ways. I saw some things when I was…unreachable."

Charlotte smiled shyly at her friend. "Clara, I think I'm actually looking forward to tonight."

Clara returned the smile and reached for Charlotte's hand.

"I'm so glad, my dear. If you will allow me, I have one small piece of advice."

Charlotte nodded her assent.

"Just try to relax as much as you can. It's perfectly natural to be nervous, but the more relaxed you can remain, the more you will enjoy it. Mr. Linz will lead you and show you what to do. He will not hurt you. And nothing about the marital act will in any way jeopardize your pregnancy."

Clara noticed that Charlotte's face fell with the reminder of the pregnancy, and wished she could take back her words. She quickly continued so that her friend wouldn't spend too much time thinking about the unwanted pregnancy.

"Once you marry Thomas, his body will be yours, and yours his. There is no cause for any embarrassment and I encourage you to ask questions and be adventurous. Have fun, Charlotte. More than anything, relax and have fun."

Charlotte nodded again and Clara released her hand.

"Now, let's begin heating the bath water. I've got some pressed rose oil for after your bath. We'll have you smelling as beautiful as you look."

Chapter Twenty-Eight

Saturday, September 28, 1867

When Thomas and George shared news of Charlotte's recovery with Father Joseph, the priest was filled with joy. "Praise the Lord," he said with such feeling that the two gentlemen knew they were witnessing a profound prayer.

"Miss Gallagher has requested that I ask you if we may be married this afternoon. She said she doesn't want to wait. Since the reading of the banns has been fulfilled and our wedding was already scheduled for today, would it be possible to just move it to this afternoon?"

Father Joseph could see the anticipation on the young man's face. Thomas' love for Charlotte, especially knowing that theirs would be a celibate marriage, was inspiring.

"I would be honored to celebrate the wedding this afternoon. What time did you have in mind?"

"I was assured by Mrs. Groves that Miss Gallagher can be ready in two hours. We will be hosting a dinner reception at The Tremont Hotel after the wedding and hope that you can join us for that, as well."

"Okay, let's say four o'clock for the wedding, then. Praise the Lord," Father Joseph repeated. "I was very worried about your bride. And George, I'm so glad that you and Dr. Groves kept looking for answers and didn't give up!"

"As am I, Father. If you'll both excuse me, I will go share the good news with Miss Gallagher and all the guests."

After George left, Thomas made a request.

"Will you please hear my confession, Father Joseph? I want to enter the marriage sacrament with a clean heart."

"Absolutely, my son. There is no better way to prepare for your marriage than by bringing all your struggles and failings to the Lord and leaving them at His feet. Let's make our way over to the church."

When they stood before the confessional, Father Joseph entered through the center door and Thomas entered one of the side doors. Once settled inside, Thomas knelt. Soon, Father Joseph opened the small screen.

"In the name of the Father, and of the Son, and of the Holy Ghost," both men said together.

"Bless me, Father, for I have sinned. It has been three weeks since my last confession. These are my sins: I continue to feel such hatred towards the men who killed Charlotte's family. I know that feelings aren't sins, but the thoughts I have about killing them are. And, instead of driving such thoughts from my head, I sometimes sit and imagine how good it would feel to act on them."

"I'm glad you recognize the difference between our feelings and what we do with them. In the Gospel of Matthew, Jesus says, 'But I say, anyone who even looks at a woman with lust has already committed adultery with her in his heart.' Thomas, if you are allowing yourself to dwell on thoughts of revenge, you are already committing it in your heart. I know that revenge is not what will bring you happiness, and I pray that God will send you the strength to fight against those desires from now on."

"You know, Father, I had no choice but to kill men during the war. And, every single time, it plagued me. I knew that if I hadn't killed them, they would have killed me. I knew that I had no other option. But it didn't take away the horror of what I'd done. I've confessed this several times, and I know God has forgiven me, but I continue to struggle with remorse for what I've done."

Thomas stopped talking, but Father Joseph remained silent. He knew there was more that Thomas needed to unload. Finally, the young man continued.

"If I'm honest with myself, Father, I know that no relief would come from killing Fred Miller, either. I need to instead focus my energy on loving and supporting Charlie and trying to forgive all those who hurt her."

"I couldn't have spoken it better myself," Father Joseph agreed. "You are wiser than your years, Thomas Linz. Now, are there any other sins you wish to confess?"

"Yes. I have been lazy with my prayers and Bible reading. I have lacked trust in God and instead spent my time worrying. I have used ungentlemanly language at times, and I grew very frustrated with a kindly clerk at the lumberyard a few weeks ago. I am sorry for these sins and for all those I cannot recall."

"You have made a good confession, my son. God knows the burdens you carry. He knows the pain you feel for what Charlotte is going through. If you allow Him, Thomas, He will use this pain for great good in the world. I will be praying for you; for peace and for the strength to forgive. Forgiveness is much like love. Sometimes we feel them, but most often we must choose to simply practice them and wait for the feeling to come. For your penance, please say three Our Fathers and three Hail Marys. Now, please make your act of contrition."

"Oh, my God, I am heartily sorry for having offended Thee, and I detest all my sins because of Thy just punishment, but most of all because they offend Thee, my God, who art all good and deserving of all my love. I firmly resolve, with the help of Thy grace, to sin no more and to avoid the near occasion of sin. Amen."

Behind the screen, Father Joseph raised his hands and spoke the words of absolution.

"God the Father of mercies, through the death and resurrection of His Son, has reconciled the world to Himself and sent the Holy Ghost among us for the forgiveness of sins. Through the ministry of the Church, may God grant you pardon and peace, and I absolve you from your sins in the name of the Father, and of the Son, and of the Holy Ghost. Amen."

Thomas silently recited his penance prayers, then stood up and exited the confessional. Father Joseph was standing outside with outstretched arms.

"God bless you, Thomas. Your faith inspires me."

"Thank you, Father," Thomas beamed. "I'll see you at the church at four o'clock."

"Hopefully a few minutes before that, son! It wouldn't do to keep your lovely bride waiting!"

Thomas left the rectory and went straight to Mrs. Johnson's house. When she answered the door, she gave him a quizzical look.

"Did you miss your wedding?"

"It's a very long, complicated story, but I'm happy to report that I will be marrying Miss Gallagher at four o'clock this afternoon."

Mrs. Johnson smiled in relief.

"Well then, you'll be needing her bouquet!"

George soon arrived at the Albertson house and told Marnie and Nora the good news about Charlotte's recovery. When he informed them that Miss Gallagher and Mr. Linz were to be married that afternoon at four, and all were invited, Marnie quickly called her children to her.

"As soon as I can get dressed and ready, I am going over to assist Mrs. Groves and Miss Gallagher. John David, will you please go to the jail and notify your father? Sarah, I'm leaving you in charge of ensuring that all these rascals make it to St. Mary's by a quarter till four, cleaned and in their Sunday best. Nora, feel free to head home and tell Oscar. I hope to see you both at the church."

"Yes, ma'am," Nora, John David, and Sarah answered at the same time.

George left the house with a big smile, and Marnie heard all her children chattering excitedly as she slipped into her room to get dressed and comb her hair. What a blessing it was that Charlotte had recovered so quickly. Had it really only been one and a half days since her young friend slipped into that frightening unawareness? It felt like two months, at least.

Marnie picked a lovely gown of light blue silk. She had so few dresses now, having lost everything during the fire. But, the dresses she had were new and more fashionable than what she'd lost, and she'd been able to grab the family pearls before fleeing the house, so she was thankful. She thought of the months after the fire. They had been some of the toughest days of her life, but in the end, all that mattered was she had Jason and the children, safe and by her side.

Back at the Tremont, Thomas requested a bath be set up in his room and then asked to speak to the manager, Mr. Frank Taylor. After explaining the situation, he finished with, "We will have approximately sixteen guests for the reception dinner. Would you be able to accommodate that with such limited notice?"

"Of course, Mr. Linz! We will set up a private dining room with our finest dinnerware. I will have my most experienced serving staff available for you." Then his countenance lit with excitement. "Would you also like dancing? I have some musicians I can contact who might be available to play."

"That would be a great surprise for my bride. We've never danced together. Thank you so much for making this happen, Mr. Taylor. I leave all decisions up to you!"

Thomas pulled out his wallet and handed the manager some money.

"Please use this for whatever is needed, and let me know the balance tomorrow."

Then, he smiled at the man and walked up the stairs to his room.

Frank looked down at the money in his hand and his eyes widened. With this amount, he could fill the reception area with flowers, put candles out everywhere, pay his wait staff, and still have money left over. He observed the man quickly ascending the stairs. This Mr. Linz must be very wealthy indeed, but one would never guess it. Every time he stayed, he treated everyone at the Tremont, from fellow guests to the most humble cleaning lady with kindness and respect. Well, Mr. Linz was going to get the best reception Denver City had ever seen!

Upon reaching the second floor, Thomas spied two men leaving his hotel room with large, empty water barrels. A hot bath was going to feel so nice. He'd spent the last two days tending Charlotte and had neither bathed nor shaved. He certainly wanted to be clean before donning the exquisite new suit. Just as he realized that he'd left his suit at the Groves house, there was a knock on the door. He opened it to find Dr. Groves standing in the doorway, smiling and holding up the hanger with his black silk suit.

"It's as if you read my mind," Thomas said with a laugh. "I was about to undress and get into the tub when I realized I didn't have my suit!"

"Yes, when Big Viv noticed it hanging in the front closet, she sent me over here right away. Vivian leaves no doubt as to who's the true head of our household," he said, with a laugh.

"Thank you, Joseph. I really appreciate you bringing this over."

"I'll see you at the church, Thomas. What a joyous turn of events!"

Joseph Groves turned and left the room. Once he was gone, Thomas locked the door and began to undress. There was steam rising from the bathwater and he was looking forward to a relaxing soak. When that was done, he would need to move his things to the bigger room he'd originally reserved all those weeks ago: The Bridal Suite.

As he slipped into the hot bath, Thomas' mind wandered to his marriage night and what it might entail. He knew that Charlotte would expect a great amount of kissing, and braced himself for the self-control he would need in order to prevent things from going further. Even if Charlotte had never insisted on a semi-chaste marriage, he knew that she was not in the right state of mind to have marital relations right now. The unplanned, unwanted pregnancy had really upset her. Thomas didn't want to do anything that might send her back into that unresponsive state. He would never do anything to risk that happening again. It had been absolutely terrifying!

Then he thought about the pregnancy. Charlotte said the baby would be born in mid-April. He was heartbroken that she wanted to place the baby for adoption. Her decision made sense, and he would honor her wishes, but he couldn't help feeling love for this baby. This baby would be so like his beloved Charlotte. He'd had several vivid dreams of the child in the last two days, and already felt her loss keenly. Her, because he felt sure Charlotte was going to have a baby girl. He prayed that he would be allowed to hold her at least once before she was taken away to her new family. He prayed that they would love her as he already did.

Charlotte was bathed, robed, and sitting in Clara's bedroom rubbing rose oil into her skin when Marnie arrived.

"Oh, my dear, dear friend," Marnie cried, crossing the room and wrapping Charlotte in a hug. "We are all so happy to have you back!"

"And I'm so happy to be back. But I'm even more excited to become Mrs. Linz this afternoon!"

Marnie moved to hug Clara. The joy in the room was almost palpable.

"I see you've pulled out the special rose oil, Clara. Isn't this just perfect? Recovery and a wedding all in one day!"

"It will be hard to ever top today, Charlotte! You've set some pretty high standards for yourself," Clara joked.

"God-willing, I hope to lead a boring life from this day forward. There's been way too much excitement in my life lately. I'll happily settle for uneventful after today," Charlotte said good-naturedly.

"Let's get you dressed, dear," Marnie said, and the three friends got to work.

When they were finished, Charlotte looked even lovelier than she had when she first tried the dress three weeks before.

"Mr. Linz is not going to believe his eyes," Clara said in amazement as they all stood looking in the mirror.

"From a little monster boy to the most beautiful woman I've ever seen. What a transformation!" Marnie cried.

The three friends dissolved into laughter.

"Thank you both so much. Not just for helping me get ready, but for everything. I miss my mother and sister every single day, and probably always will. But you two have become family and I'm so thankful for you both."

"Now, don't make us cry before the wedding," Marnie exclaimed, wiping her cheeks.

"Yes, let's head down to the carriage, Little Monster," Clara teased affectionately. "We don't need to start crying this early, and you don't want to be late to your own wedding!"

Together, they made their way down the stairs. Vivian was waiting in the entryway, dressed in a soft yellow dress and matching hat. She held a large cake box in her arms.

"Vivian," Charlotte cried. "You look so beautiful!"

"Oh, what nonsense," Vivian objected, shaking her head as though to dispel Charlotte's words.

She may have objected, but her beaming smile told Charlie she'd enjoyed the compliment. George took the cake box from Vivian and placed it on the driver's seat. He looked handsome in a nice, fitted suit of deep navy color. When all four women were safely ensconced in the carriage, Dr. Groves and George climbed up front. George held the cake as though it were a priceless treasure, and Dr. Groves snapped the reins to get the horses moving. In mere minutes, the carriage stopped in front of the Tremont Hotel.

George dismounted and carefully grabbed the cake box.

"I'll be right back."

When their carriage arrived at the church, Jason Albertson was waiting outside for them. He, George, and Joseph carefully helped the ladies from the carriage. As she stepped out of the blazing sunshine and into the cool, quiet church, Charlotte fought to control her emotions. She could feel her family with her here in this church. She knew they were here in spirit, and yet, she longed to feel their hugs and hear their words of excitement and encouragement. Again, she thought of how much they would have loved Thomas.

Marnie and Clara hurried her into a side chapel so Thomas would not see her before the ceremony. Just as Marnie was fastening the pearl necklace on Charlotte's neck, there was a knock on the door. Clara stepped over to open it, and Marnie saw her daughter, Sarah, holding a large bouquet of white roses.

"Mr. Linz asked me to give this to you, Mother. We're sitting on the left in the front pew. I'll see you soon." Sarah quickly hugged her mother and turned away.

Clara watched as the lovely girl walked away. She tried to keep her longing for motherhood at bay. That was not what today was about.

"Someday," she told herself. "Someday Joseph and I will have children." Out loud, she said, "Sarah has grown into such a beautiful young lady, Marnie. I know you and Jason must be so proud of her."

"She is a wonderful daughter, and a great help to me. I wish we knew more eligible young men her age. I know that she will be dreaming of a marriage of her own soon."

"Yes, love stories like the one we've witnessed in Thomas and Charlotte do tend to ignite the flames of romance in us all," Clara said with a smile.

Marnie turned the beautiful bouquet around in her hands. Then, satisfied with the appearance from every angle, she handed it to Clara. The roses had a pretty white satin ribbon wrapped around their stems.

"It's perfect," Clara said. "Absolutely perfect."

Just then, organ music began to reverberate through the church.

Clara and Marnie looked at Charlotte.

"Are you ready, dear friend," Clara asked.

"Absolutely, yes," Charlotte answered with a grin.

Clara handed her the bouquet and gave her a quick wink.

"Don't be nervous! God-willing, you only get married once in your life, so enjoy every single moment."

As the three women walked through the door into the back of the main church, Joseph met Clara and escorted her to their seats. Sergeant Albertson was waiting for Charlotte. His warm smile melted Marnie's heart. How could all these years of marriage have passed so quickly? Sometimes, it felt like only yesterday she and Jason were standing at the altar.

"You look positively radiant, my dear," Jason said to Marnie, as he offered Charlotte his arm. "As do you, Miss Gallagher."

Marnie made her way to join her family and Jason and Charlotte positioned themselves at the back of the center aisle. Charlotte looked up to the front of the church where Thomas stood waiting for her. When he caught his first glimpse of his bride, his face lit up in awestruck delight. Charlotte's heart filled with joy! Thomas saw past her ugly scar and loved her as she was.

As he watched her walk up the aisle toward him, Thomas felt as though he may burst with love. Would he really be spending the rest of his life with this captivating woman? He could hardly comprehend his blessings.

When they finally reached the front of the church, Jason lifted Charlotte's veil and gently kissed her forehead.

"I am so proud to be here with you, my dear," he whispered. Then, placing her hand in Thomas' he added, "Take care of each other always."

If anyone noticed the big, tough man swipe away a tear on the way to his seat, they never mentioned it. Father Joseph looked at the beaming couple standing in front of him.

"Let us begin in the name of the Father, and the Son, and the Holy Ghost. Be attentive to our prayers, O Lord, and in Your kindness pour out Your grace on these Your servants, Charlotte and Thomas, that, coming together before Your altar, they may be confirmed in love for one another. Through our Lord Jesus Christ, Your Son, who lives and reigns with You in the unity of the Holy Ghost, one God, forever and ever."

"Amen," responded everyone in the church.

"Please be seated," Father Joseph said to the wedding guests. Charlotte and Thomas remained on the decorated kneeler placed in front of the altar. In a solemn, regal fashion, George Groves made his way to the ambo, a small raised pulpit with steps at each end. He looked down at the Bible before him.

"A reading from the Song of Solomon," he began, and looked at the bride and groom. "My beloved speaks and says to me: 'Arise, my love, my fair one, and come away; for now the winter is past, the rain is over and gone. The flowers appear on the earth; the time of singing has come, and the voice of the turtle-dove is heard in our land. The fig tree puts forth its figs, and the vines are in blossom; they give forth fragrance. Arise, my love, my fair one, and come away. O my dove, in the clefts of the rock, in the covert of the cliff, let me see your face, let me hear your voice; for your voice is sweet, and your face is lovely."

Before he could stop himself, George looked up from the Bible and made eye contact with Sarah Albertson. Hoping no one noticed, he quickly looked back down at the holy book.

"My beloved is mine and I am his; he pastures his flock among the lilies. Set me as a seal upon your heart, as a seal upon your arm; for love is strong as death, passion fierce as the grave. Its flashes are flashes of fire, a raging flame. Many waters cannot quench love, neither can floods drown it. If one offered for love all the wealth of one's house, it would be utterly scorned." He paused. "The Word of the Lord."

"Thanks be to God," everyone responded.

George turned and bowed to the altar, then made his way back to his seat, next to Mr. and Mr. Albertson. Dr. Groves made his way up to the ambo.

"A reading from the Letter of Saint Paul to the Romans. Brothers and Sisters: If God is for us, who can be against us? He did not spare His own Son but handed Him over for us all, how will He not also give us everything else along with Him? Who will bring a charge against God's chosen ones? It is God who acquits us. Who will condemn? It is Christ Jesus who died, rather, was raised, who also is at the right hand of God, who indeed intercedes for us. What will separate us from the love of Christ? Will anguish, or distress, or persecution, or famine, or nakedness, or peril, or the sword? No, in all these things, we conquer overwhelmingly through Him who loved us. For I am convinced that neither death, nor life, nor angels, nor principalities, nor present things, nor future things, nor powers, nor height, nor depth, nor any other creature will be able to separate us from the love of God in Christ Jesus our Lord."

Dr. Groves finished the reading and looked up at those seated in the church. "The Word of the Lord."

"Thanks be to God," everyone responded.

He closed the Bible and placed it on a small table to the left of the altar. Once Dr. Groves was again seated next to his wife, Father Joseph walked to the ambo and opened the Book of the Gospel.

"A reading from the Gospel according to John," he said and, with his right thumb, traced the sign of the cross on the page.

"Glory to You, Lord," answered the congregation, signing a cross over their foreheads, lips, and heart.

"Jesus said to his disciples, 'This is my commandment: love one another as I love you. No one has greater love than this, to lay down one's life for one's friends. You are my friends if you do what I command you. I no longer call you slaves, because a slave does not know what his master is doing. I have called you friends, because I have told you everything I have heard from my Father. It was not you who chose Me, but I who chose you and appointed you to go and bear fruit that will remain, so that whatever you ask the Father in My name He may give you.'"

Father Joseph looked out over everyone in attendance. Then he raised the Book of the Gospel and said solemnly, "The Gospel of the Lord."

Everyone responded, "Praise to You, Lord Jesus Christ," and sat down in their seats.

Father Joseph smiled widely as he looked at the bride and groom before him.

"What a joyous event we gather to celebrate today – the holy sacrament of marriage. In our Gospel reading today, Jesus gives us a new commandment. He says, 'Love one another as I love you.' We are called to have God as the center of our lives and to love our neighbors as we love ourselves. The primary relationship in your life is the relationship through which you will become the person God created you to be. If your destiny is to become a saint, the only path is love. Love is the way. For most of us, marriage and family are the first schools of love. These are the first places where we experience love and learn to love in return."

Father Joseph directed his gaze to Thomas and Charlotte and indicated with his arm that the congregation should do the same.

"This man, Thomas, who we love and respect, is who he is because of his parents and his siblings. And Charlotte, this woman that we love and respect, is who she is because of her parents and her family. We have only known them for a short time. But we know they are a man and woman of great faith. Before anything else, they are pursuing Christ. They complement each other so well. For every way that they are alike, they are also very different. This dichotomy is right out of scripture – God sees Adam and says, 'It is not good for the man to be alone. I will make a suitable helper for him.' The man did not need a servant. He did not need a slave. The word helper is actually used in the Psalms in reference to God. David says, 'The Lord is my helper.' When God says 'helper,' He's referring to someone with whom to share the mission. Someone with whom you will unite so closely that you can share your lives, your mission, and your journey to sanctity. Man is called to love and protect and guard his wife. The woman is called to respect and encourage her husband in his trials.

"Jesus is the new Adam. While Adam slept, God removed a rib and created Eve. When Jesus was in the sleep of death up on the cross, the soldier opened his side. Blood and water flowed forth from Jesus' side, and holy tradition has always taught that this was the beginning of the Church. The water represents baptism, which brings us into the Body of Christ. The blood represents the Eucharist, which keeps us in the Body of Christ. And then Paul writes in Ephesians, 'This is a profound mystery—but I am talking about Christ and the church.' The mystery of marriage is so profound that it is the mystery of Jesus and His bride, the Church.

"We see marriages all the time. We see weddings so often that we may lose sight of the great mystery we are witnessing. Do we understand the great mystery of marriage? This couple will stand before this altar, beneath this crucifix, and Thomas will profess his love for Charlotte. Charlotte will proclaim her respect for Thomas. And in the shadow of the Cross, we will see a miracle happen. We will see an image of the great mystery of Christ and His Church. One man and one woman who complement each other, have come together to form one body. They are different, and they come together to become one, just like Christ and His Church. None of us can belong to Jesus without belonging to His Church. And none of us can belong to Jesus' Church without belonging to Jesus. Just like Thomas cannot be a husband without belonging to his wife, and Charlotte cannot be a wife without belonging to her husband. This reality is so profound that it is the reality that moves the world. Thomas and Charlotte, filled with love, and with respect, proclaim 'I will love you in the same way that Jesus loves His

Church. With everything in me, I will lay down my life for you. I'm willing to die to myself to show you the love of God."

"As you come forth, Thomas, and stand in the shadow of the cross and promise to love and cherish Charlotte, we are all praying for you. Charlotte, as you come forth and stand in the shadow of the cross and promise to respect and obey Thomas, we are all praying for you. We pray that this covenant becomes the great sign of God's love for His world. I join everyone in this church in praying that your love will change the world."

With that, Father Joseph lowered his head for a brief moment of meditation. Then, he raised his hand and indicated that Thomas and Charlotte should join him in front of the altar. John David Albertson picked up the Roman Ritual book and stood at Father Joseph's right side. Father Joseph opened the book and found the correct page. John David held it high as Father Joseph read the prescribed words.

"Thomas, wilt thou have this woman to thy wedded wife, to live together after God's ordinance in the holy state of Matrimony? Wilt though love her, comfort her, honor and keep her, in sickness and in health? And, forsaking all others, keep thee only to her, so long as you both shall live?"

"I will," Thomas answered. His green eyes shone with unshed tears.

Father Joseph turned to face Charlotte.

"Charlotte, wilt thou have this man to thy wedded husband, to live together after God's ordinance in the holy state of Matrimony? Wilt thou obey him and serve him, love, honor, and keep him, in sickness and in health? And forsaking all others, keep thee only to him so long as you both shall live?"

"I will," Charlotte answered. Her face was radiant with joy, and Thomas almost couldn't breathe.

"Who giveth this woman to be married unto this man?"

Jason Albertson approached Charlotte, saying, "I do."

He reached for Charlotte's right hand and placed it into Thomas' hand. Father Joseph nodded to Thomas, and he began reciting the vows he had memorized.

"I, Thomas, take thee, Charlotte, to my wedded wife, to have and to hold from this day forward, for better, for worse, for richer, for poorer, in sickness, and in health, to love and to cherish, till death us depart; according to God's holy ordinance and thereto I plight my troth."

"I, Charlotte, take thee, Thomas, to be my wedded husband, to have and to hold, from this day forward, for better, for worse, for richer, for poorer, in sickness, and in health, to love, cherish, and to obey, till death us depart, according to God's holy ordinance, and thereto I give thee my troth."

When she finished speaking, John David approached Father Joseph and handed him the amethyst ring. Father Joseph made the sign of the cross over the ring as he spoke.

"I bless this ring in the name of the Father, and of the Son, and of the Holy Ghost."

Then, he handed the ring to Thomas, saying, "Repeat after me. With this ring, I thee wed."

"With this ring, I thee wed," Thomas said, clearly enough to be heard by all those in attendance.

"With my body, I thee worship—"

"With my body, I thee worship—"

"And with all my worldly goods, I thee endow."

"And with all my worldly goods, I thee endow."

"In the name of the Father, and of the Son, and of the holy Ghost. Amen."

The rest of the Mass continued as prescribed. At the very end, Father Joseph called the bride and groom to stand before the congregation.

"Receive in Your kindness, Lord, the offerings we bring in gladness before You, and in Your fatherly love watch over those You have joined in a sacramental covenant. Through Christ our Lord."

"Amen," was the response.

"You may now kiss your bride."

Charlotte turned to her husband and lifted her face to his. He leaned down and kissed her briefly on the lips.

"I present to you Mr. and Mrs. Thomas Linz."

Everyone clapped their approval, and many guests shed a tear. Even Nora's stoic farmer husband, Oscar, could be seen wiping his eyes. Neither Charlotte nor Thomas had a single blood relative present, but as they turned to face their guests, neither of them felt alone. They were orphans no more. The beaming smiles of their loving friends brought comfort to their grieving hearts, and reminded them that they were forming their own family now.

Chapter Twenty-Nine

Saturday, September 28, 1867

After many hugs and congratulatory handshakes, the wedding party walked the short distance to the Tremont House Hotel. They were met at the door by Mr. Taylor, who was now wearing his finest suit.

"Welcome, Mr. and Mrs. Linz! Please, everyone follow me."

Thomas noticed the man was practically bursting with pride. He could hardly wait to see Charlotte's reaction to his surprise.

Mr. Taylor led them to a set of doors a few paces past the dining room. When he threw the doors open, Charlotte gasped. The room beyond was more lovely than anything Thomas could have imagined. There were flowers everywhere! Each of the four tables had its own arrangement and there were more flowers hanging from the ceiling alongside gauzy, sheer green fabric. Hundreds of candles in the massive chandelier, in sconces on the walls, and in silver candelabras on the tables waited for sundown. A cellist and violinist were providing soft, stirring music from one corner of the room. Charlotte walked to the center of the room and spun slowly around to take it all in.

"Thomas," she said, her voice full of awe. "This is the most beautiful thing I've ever seen! Thank you!"

"While I would love to take credit for this awe-inspiring production, I had nothing to do with it."

Thomas motioned for Mr. Taylor to join him. "Mr. Taylor created this extraordinary transformation with less than four hours' notice. Sir, you have exceeded even my most creative imaginings! Thank you. Thank you so much!"

The look on Charlotte's face as she continued to gaze around the room was all the thanks Frank Taylor needed. He looked around to find that every single guest was in the same rapture. Frank chuckled to himself. Decorating this reception was the most fun he'd had in years, decades even. He wondered if there might be a future in this and decided that he must make a sketch of the room to show future prospective brides and grooms.

Thomas took Charlotte's hand and led her to one of the four tables. Once the bride and groom sat, Clara and Joseph sat with them, and everyone else began taking their seats. Charlotte looked around and was happy to see that everyone was intermingling. Julia and Fulton Albertson sat at one table with Father Joseph and Big Viv. Sarah, Jason, and Marnie Albertson sat at another table with George. Nora and Philip Carlin sat with John David and Damien Albertson at the last table. Charlotte imagined the small tables would lead to easy, comfortable dinner conversations.

Charlotte squeezed Thomas' hand.

"What a wonderful gift this is!"

"What, precisely, is the gift, my dear," Thomas asked.

With her free arm, Charlie indicated the whole room.

"We are sitting in the most beautiful room I've ever seen. We are surrounded by all the love and friendship we need. And we are now husband and wife. How blessed are we?"

Dr. Groves smiled warmly at Charlotte, and taking Clara's hand in his, he spoke from the heart.

"Charlotte, Thomas, I hope your marriage will bring you all the happiness in the world. I hope you will find the joy that Clara and I have found together."

The smile that lit Mrs. Groves' face only added to her beauty.

Once everyone had finished their meals, the efficient wait staff took away plates and floral arrangements. The guests were requested to make their way to the chairs lining the walls so that the tables could be put away for dancing. Marnie and Sarah walked away to talk with the bride and groom and George took this opportunity to turn to Jason.

"Sergeant Albertson, once the tables are moved aside and dancing begins, may I ask Miss Sarah to dance?"

"Why, of course, George. You know you're like another son to me. You may dance with both my girls as much as you like."

"Respectfully, sir, I'd prefer to not be seen as a brother to Sarah—"

George was filled with anxiety, but kept his voice firm and even. He'd wanted to have this conversation with Sergeant Albertson for quite some time. He couldn't afford to mess it up.

"Since I first met your daughter, I have been impressed with her intelligence and ready humor."

George paused to gauge Sergeant Albertson's response. Seeing no horror on the man's face, he continued.

"Over the last three years, I've grown to care for Miss Sarah greatly. I plan to ask you and Mrs. Albertson for permission to write to her while I'm away at medical school. I leave in January, as you know, and Sarah is the person I will miss the most during those months. It's hard to imagine a life without her, sir."

Jason Albertson was taken aback. He admired George greatly for his gentle, strong spirit and his thirst for education. Jason knew that the intelligent black man would make a remarkable doctor someday and would lead a life of dignity and faith. And of course, he'd always noticed the easy camaraderie between George and his eldest daughter. But relationships between whites and blacks were simply unheard of. Not to mention, illegal.

After a few moments, Jason finally spoke.

"George, I'll need to talk with Mrs. Albertson about all this. Please know that she and I have discussed you before, and both believe you a remarkable young man with great prospects for the future. Your integrity and faith make you exactly the sort of man we would choose as a husband for Sarah, and yet…have you thought about how difficult your lives together might be?"

"We have talked of it, sir."

At the startled expression on Sergeant Albertson's face, George quickly corrected himself.

"Not ever in regard to us. I would never presume to discuss such a personal topic without your permission. We've simply debated whether interracial marriage will ever be accepted in the United States as it is slowly becoming accepted in Europe. While not common, by any means, people of color have occasionally married their white counterparts in several European countries. In those places, black people are now able to hold positions in society and even own property. Sarah's belief is that the United States will soon follow suit and allow these rights to people like me."

The music had grown louder and more deliberate; sure signs that dancing would soon begin.

"I hope and pray for that day, George, but I cannot see it happening any time soon, unfortunately. My concern is—"

At this moment he was interrupted when Sarah and Marnie returned to their sides.

"Look how beautiful they are together," Marnie said to Jason and George as she directed their gazes to the dance floor where Thomas and Charlotte were waltzing together.

"A very handsome couple, indeed," Jason agreed. "Mrs. Albertson, I hope that you will allow me the honor of the first dance."

As Marnie placed her hand in his, Jason turned and nodded to George. And that happy young man, his face aglow, immediately bowed to Sarah.

"May I have your first dance, Miss Albertson?"

Anyone who had been watching the exchange as closely as Jason Albertson was, would have noticed the smile and flash of excitement so evident in Sarah's face as she accepted George's outstretched hand.

"You seem distracted, dear. What's on your mind," Marnie asked, as her husband twirled her around the floor in an elegant waltz. For such a strong man, he was incredibly graceful. She loved dancing with him and wished it happened more often.

"I'm thinking that it will be no time at all before we are dancing at the weddings of our own children." He looked down at her upturned face; the face that was most dear to him in all the world. "Marnie, the time has gone so fast! I wish I could go back and live my whole life with you all over again."

"Why, Jason, I've never seen you so reflective."

They maneuvered a difficult spin and then she continued. "The years have, indeed, raced by. But they haven't left us behind. We have many more happy years ahead of us! As for our children's weddings, I often despair of them ever meeting suitable partners. Denver City is growing quickly, but an increasing population doesn't ensure like-minded, God-fearing souls. Sometimes I wish that we still lived in Tuscumbia, where we knew every family around. With all us mothers working together, I imagine our Sarah would already be engaged," she ended with a laugh.

Jason longed for the privacy of their bedroom so that he could tell his wife that their Sarah, while not yet engaged, certainly seemed to be taken with Mr. George Groves. What would Marnie think about that?

As the evening progressed, Jason noticed that no matter who her dance partner was, Sarah's attention frequently returned to George. Now that he was really paying attention, it was evident that his daughter had feelings for the handsome young man. George, for his part, attempted to keep his attention focused on the woman with whom he was dancing. Jason noticed, with admiration, that George was just as attentive to Clara, Vivian, Nora, and Marnie as he was to the new Mrs. Linz, Sarah, and Julia. He treated each of them with an easy dignity and respect. And, although he danced more often with Sarah than with the others, he was quick to make sure no one was left sitting out for too many dances in a row. Jason thought back over the three years that the Groves had been in Denver City. He had never seen or heard of George acting in a way that was less than honorable.

He knew he should wait until they were alone tonight to broach the topic of this budding relationship with Marnie, but he wanted her to be able to observe Sarah and George right away. The next time he danced with his wife, Jason asked her, "Have you noticed the deep friendship between George Groves and our Sarah?"

Marnie smiled and was silent for a long while. He wondered if he'd upset her and was about to change the subject when finally she spoke.

"I've noticed their interactions for quite some time now, Jason. I think we might be dealing with more than just a deep friendship."

"Go on," he encouraged.

"I think our dear Sarah is in love, Jason. And, although I'm not exactly sure how I feel about it, I am certain that George feels the same about her. He's an impressive young man, and exactly the sort of partner that would keep Sarah challenged and engaged. She needs someone intelligent and adventurous. Sarah would quickly grow bored and resentful with a husband less learned than she."

Marnie began to laugh.

"Please share your humor, dear wife," Jason requested as the music swelled on.

"I don't know if you've ever been seated near them during game nights or dinner, but their conversations are so humorous. Oh, Jason, I've never witnessed two young people less adept at flirtation. Their utterances are comprised of scientific theories and historical debates. Why, Sarah would have received numerous punishments had she been a debutante back when you and I were young. We were strictly prohibited from talking about serious topics with eligible gentlemen!"

"Of course you were! Everyone knows we men don't want intelligent women for wives," Jason agreed, sarcastically. "I'm exceedingly glad that you dropped the debutante ridiculousness shortly after we began courting. I love the real Marnie Davis, smart though she may be."

The song ended, and, as they bowed to each other, Jason said, "Let's discuss this more tonight when we are assured privacy. There is much to talk about."

"I look forward to it, dear," Marnie said with a raised brow and wink at her husband.

"Are you flirting with me, wife?"

"I certainly am, Sergeant Albertson!" Then, in her most alluring voice, she whispered softly, for only him to hear, "I hope you're none too tired when we get home."

With that, she turned and made her way over to join the rest of the guests gathering around the table where Vivian's beautiful cake had been placed. Jason Albertson couldn't help but laugh as she walked away. This tiny, demure wife of his certainly had him wrapped around her finger.

At the cake table, Mr. Taylor handed Charlotte a silver cake knife and Thomas a fine China dessert plate.

"Mr. and Mrs. Linz will now cut the cake together to signify their first task as man and wife," he announced.

Once seventeen plates had been prepared and distributed, one even to Mr. Taylor despite his protests, Thomas broke a small piece from his slice of cake and placed it in Charlotte's mouth.

"Mrs. Linz, I am committed to providing for you for the rest of our lives."

Charlotte beamed at Thomas and the guests broke out into applause. Then, she placed a piece of cake into Thomas' mouth.

"Mr. Linz, I am committed to spending the rest of my life caring for your needs."

She shot a glance at Big Viv and then added, "And trying to learn how to bake as well as Vivian Lincoln!"

Big Viv couldn't hide the proud smile that covered her face.

"Well, eat up everyone," Vivian hastily said to hide her emotion. "That girl just loves to make me cry," she muttered to no one in particular.

Thomas looked over and noticed that Mr. Taylor summoned a young waiter and spoke discreetly to him for a moment. The waiter nodded and left the room. Was there another surprise, he wondered. By nine o'clock, it was time for the married couple to retire. As tradition dictated, the guests all cheered loudly and threw handfuls of rice as Thomas swept his beautiful bride up into his arms and left the reception room. Charlotte felt that she had never been more excited and nervous in her life. She longed to feel the sensations Clara and Marnie alluded to. And more than that, she longed to see Thomas' expression when she informed him that she'd changed her mind about the nature of their marriage.

When they reached the top of the winding staircase, Thomas walked past the room he had occupied so often over the last three weeks and, instead, walked all the way to the end of the hallway. The young waiter Thomas noticed earlier was standing outside the door. As they approached, he opened the door for them and walked away. Thomas carried his bride inside the now candlelit room.

"These candles…someone has been busy in here," Charlotte said. She felt that her heart would burst, and wondered if Thomas felt her rapid breathing against his chest. He gently lowered her until her feet reached the ground. The air between them crackled with anticipation, and she found she could hardly stand.

"Alone at last," he said.

Then he covered her mouth with his own and kissed her greedily. She wrapped her arms around his body and held on tight. When he finally pulled away from her, he stood staring for several moments.

"Have I told you yet how beautiful you look today?"

She stood before him as his longing gaze moved over her body.

"You are exquisite. When I saw you at the back of the church this afternoon, your radiance took my breath away."

He placed his right hand on her left cheek and looked deep into her eyes.

"I still cannot believe how God has blessed me, Charlotte. I will spend every day for the rest of my life thanking Him for the gift of you."

He kissed her again until her knees gave out and she felt herself beginning to fall. Chuckling, he pulled away.

"I'm sorry, love. Let me give you time to breathe."

Then, as though realizing something for the first time, he stepped around and stood behind her.

"Umm, do you want me to run down and ask Mrs. Albertson and Mrs. Groves to come help prepare you for bed? This dress looks terribly complicated back here."

Charlotte pivoted to face him.

"It is terribly complicated," she agreed, breathlessly. "But I'd like for you to be the one to prepare me for bed, husband."

Her barely audible words left no doubt as to her meaning.

Thomas stared into her eyes for what seemed like an eternity. Then, he slowly turned her around and began untying the strings that held her tightly bound in the dress. In the silence of the room, Charlotte could hear that he was breathing as hard as she was. Every brush of his fingers on the skin of her back felt like fire. The flickering flames of so many candles only added to the magical moment.

As Thomas fumbled with the ribbons, he could hardly catch his breath. Charlotte was simply splendid. His body was filled with desire, and he feared he would lose all control. He drew in a shaky breath and reminded himself yet again that he must stay strong. No matter how his body burned, he could not allow anything to happen tonight. Charlotte was in such a fragile emotional state, and he couldn't risk losing her again.

When the top half of the dress was opened, Thomas kissed her lightly on each shoulder blade and then on her neck. Charlotte had never imagined anything could feel so arousing.

"Thomas," she moaned.

"How do we remove this dress," he asked, in barely a whisper.

"It must be pulled over my head."

Thomas began gently gathering the yards and yards of skirt material in his hand. Then, he laughed.

"There's so much material, Charlie, and I'm afraid I'm going to ruin something. How am I supposed to do this?"

The laughter brought some measure of relief to Charlotte's racing heart. "I think Marnie and Clara usually lifted from the bodice, not the skirt."

Now that he knew what to do, Thomas quickly freed her from the dress. He walked over to gently lay it over an upholstered chair and turned back to face her. She was surprised by the fact that her barely clothed body did not leave her feeling as self-conscious as she would have imagined. Instead, she felt bold and eager for what the rest of the night held.

"Will you sit down," Thomas asked.

She sat in a beautiful, upholstered chair and he knelt in front of her to remove her slippers. Then he rolled her stockings down her legs and placed them in the slippers. Standing, he took her hand and pulled her into his arms. After another lengthy kiss, he said, "Now, I wonder where we might find one of those frilly nightgowns your friends insisted on."

Charlotte could barely form coherent thought.

"I…nightgowns?"

Thomas chuckled.

"Yes. I'm wondering where your nightgowns might be located."

Charlotte stepped out of her petticoats and stood in stunned silence as he walked over to the far doorway.

"Will you join me, wife," he called softly.

She walked through the doorway to find a bedroom filled with more twinkling candles and a spectacularly ornate canopy bed. Thomas was standing next to the bed looking through the bag Marnie and Clara had packed earlier this afternoon. Someone must have delivered it to the hotel before the wedding.

"Here we are," he said, pulling out a gauzy white creation and smiling at her.

"Do I need it right now," she asked, walking closer to him.

Thomas looked at her and took a deep breath. She was standing so close to him that she could almost certainly feel his chest expanding with every inhale. He backed up a bit.

"Thomas, I've changed my mind. I'm not afraid anymore."

He continued to silently stare at her. Her body burned at his nearness, and she longed for his touch.

"Thomas, I want to do everything that husbands and wives do. I want to fulfill my vows. I want to worship you with my body."

When he still didn't move or speak, she reached up and laid her right hand over his heart. It was beating wildly.

"Thomas, say something, please."

"Charlotte, I've never wanted anything more in my life than to take you to bed tonight."

She smiled at him encouragingly. "That's what I want, too, husband."

He stepped back and took a ragged breath.

"Charlotte, I'm scared. I almost lost you this week, and the act of…what a husband and a wife do…I'm scared it will send you back to wherever you were this week when I couldn't reach you." Thomas was surprised to feel a tear running down his cheek. "I just don't think we should, Charlie. I can't risk losing you, my love."

At the look of shocked rejection in her face, he added, "At least for a while. Maybe in a week or two, if you're still feeling okay, maybe then we can try."

"But Thomas, I want you," she whispered, hating the need in her voice.

"You have me, Charlie. You have me for now and forever. I promise." He kissed her lightly on the forehead. "For now, let me help you with this nightgown."

Charlotte raised her arms and thrust them into the sleeves as Thomas pulled the nightgown over her head. As the material fell to her feet, it was a wall falling between her and Thomas; an insurmountable wall.

Thomas reached past her and pulled back the bedclothes. Charlotte climbed the two stairs up to the bed and sat facing him. Thomas continued to stare at her. He had never encountered such beauty in his entire life.

"This suite has two bedrooms, Charlotte. Would you prefer that I stay in here, or leave you alone?"

Charlotte felt utterly rejected and was trying with all her might to hide her bitter disappointment. She didn't want to ruin such a perfect day.

"What would you prefer?"

"I would prefer to never spend another night without you in my arms, my love."

Without a word, Charlotte reached over and pulled back the covers on the opposite side of the bed. Thomas smiled.

"Excuse me for one moment. I need to make sure there are no lit candles in the other bedroom."

When Thomas returned, Charlotte shamelessly anticipated watching him undress. She wondered if he would sleep shirtless as he had that first night in the cabin. Her face flushed with heat as he began unbuttoning his white dress shirt. He removed it and hung it on a peg in the wardrobe. She marveled at the way his muscular torso was outlined in the soft, flickering candlelight. It was as though he had been chiseled from marble. As he unfastened his belt, she looked down to the bedsheets. Maybe she wasn't as ready as she thought to see all of him. She kept her face lowered as she heard him remove his boots and pull off his pants. Before long, she felt him slide into the bed next to her.

"Did the sight of me upset you, wife," he asked with a teasing laugh.

"It didn't seem proper to watch. I felt like I should give you some privacy."

He reached for her and pulled her close to him. Their chests were touching, and she felt his heartbeat rapid and strong against her breasts.

"Charlie, we are married now. Your body is mine and mine is yours. You never have to look away again." He reached for her hand and placed it over his heart. "I am yours, forever."

Chapter Thirty

Sunday, September 29, 1867

The next morning, Charlotte and Thomas met their friends at nine o'clock Mass. Charlotte felt that Clara was paying special attention to her, and several times she caught her friend staring at her with a questioning look. She knew Clara must be exceedingly curious about whether she had enjoyed her first experience of marital love. Not wanting to discuss her disappointment, she determined to avoid the uncomfortable conversation by sticking close to Thomas' side. If Clara never found her alone, she couldn't ask probing questions.

It wasn't that she would have minded talking about last night. During the days between the candid conversation with her friends and her wedding night, she had thought of little else. This unwanted pregnancy, and the fear and anticipation of the marital act had consumed her mind. It was peculiar that her dread about the pregnancy calmed at the same time as her anticipation and longing to fully unite with Thomas grew. Thinking about the tiny life growing inside her, she absently placed her hand on her stomach. There was still no bulge at all, but her hand was inextricably drawn there, as though she needed to create a connection with her new inhabitant. Something akin to protectiveness passed through her.

"Are you a boy, or a girl," she wondered. A smile crossed her face, and she felt so confused by her happiness. She didn't want this baby, did she?

Before she knew it, Father Joseph had finished reading the Gospel and everyone sat down. Charlie chided herself for daydreaming and resolved that she would pay better attention during the homily.

"In John's Gospel today, Jesus tells a story of a father and two sons. The father asks each of them to go into the vineyard. One says 'Yes,' but doesn't go. The other says 'No,' but ends up going. They both change their minds. Truly, neither of them desired to spend time working in the vineyard. The one who finally does the work does it for one reason alone - because his father asked it of him. That is loving God—doing something because He asks it. It's important to note that in this parable, the father seems to accept the answers of his sons. He accepts the 'No' as well as the 'Yes.' He does not argue with his sons, he accepts their decisions."

"Both of the sons are given this thing that is a requirement for love. The two sons have freedom. Freedom is a pre-requisite for love. The freedom to reject love is a precondition for any meaningful yes. If I can't say no, what does my yes even mean? Love is an ability and part of that ability is the power to say no. Love is a decision. Love always involves sacrifice. Any decision we make necessarily involves sacrifice. The word *decide* comes from the Latin word 'decidere,' which is a combination of two roots: 'de' meaning 'off,' and 'caedere' meaning 'to cut.' To decide means 'to cut off.' Therefore, any decision that we make sacrifices the ability to make other decisions."

"Now, if we look back on our lives, we will see that deciding doesn't usually involve big leaps. It most often involves many small steps. We all occasionally wonder, 'What is God's big will for my life? What mission does God have for me? What is my purpose?'"

Here, Father Joseph artfully paused to allow his parishioners to think about those questions for a moment. Then, he continued.

"The answer to these questions is determined by all the small steps that we take every day of our lives. We start by saying yes to God's invitation to prayer. Then, we might say yes to God's invitation to forgive, or say yes to His invitation to love and serve others. Through one small step after another, one small decision after another, we slowly grow into the fullness of who God created us to be.

"When we make the commitment to love, it is not easy. St. John of the Cross once said, 'Where there is no love, put love, and you will find love.' It sounds so simple, but what are the practical applications of this? We don't consult our feelings when a child needs us. We don't consult our feelings when a horrible accident occurs, and we jump in to assist. We just do what needs to be done. We choose the actions of love, regardless of how we feel. We aren't bothered by whether or not the feelings are there, we just do what needs to be done. What if, in all our relationships, we chose to act, whether or not feelings were there? Think of Christ. As He carried the Cross, as He gasped for breath, He probably wasn't filled with affection for suffering or an overwhelming desire to suffer. He did it because God asked him to. He did it with his whole heart."

Objectively, Charlotte knew that Father Joseph was speaking to everyone in the church this morning, but she had the oddest feeling that this homily was meant for her alone. She hung on every word the priest said, and each of them made its way straight into her heart.

"If we want to imitate Christ, we must ask ourselves daily, 'Where is God calling me to love today?' And then, we must listen for His answer. And we must remember that love isn't a feeling. Love is an ability. Some people can choose love, and some people can't. They haven't developed the ability. Sometimes love is saying the hard things people need to hear. Sometimes love is allowing people to experience the consequences for their actions. Sometimes love is taking on the consequences of someone else's actions and forgiving them; as Christ did for all of us. Sometimes love is rejecting resentment. At the core, there is something even more essential. Sometimes love is the ability, or the power, to love even when I don't want to. At the heart of sacrificial love is the power and the ability to love even when it is not deserved and even when I don't feel affectionate feelings towards someone. The ability to love, regardless of feeling, is true strength."

"We know that love is willing the good of the other. Try to imagine what it would be like if each and every one of us were willing and able to love others regardless of changing circumstances. If I am called to be like Jesus, I must work to develop this ability. If I want to be able to fully love God, I must strive to love others this way. And I must do it with joy. Not because it feels good, but because it is God's holy will for me here in this moment. I can find joy in even the most difficult activity if I remember that I'm in the vineyard and I have the great opportunity to serve with God and for God. Let us all pray for this strength."

As had become their habit, everyone met at the Albertson house after church. During the joyful, boisterous meal, Charlotte repeatedly found Marnie and Clara looking at her. She would have to face them sooner or later. Once everyone had finished eating, she turned to Marnie.

"I had an idea for food storage in the new house, and would love to talk with you and Clara about it. May we withdraw to the sitting room?"

"Of course," Marnie answered. "Sarah and Julia, please begin gathering the dishes. Boys, you may set up the card tables if anyone cares to play. We will be out soon."

When the women left the room, all the men looked at each other.

"Is it just me, or did that seem very odd," Jason asked his friends.

"Very odd," George agreed.

"Oh, you know women. I'm sure they just want to replay every detail of the wedding, and don't need us laughing at their excitement," Joseph surmised.

Only Thomas didn't speak. He suspected Charlotte wanted to talk with her friends about his refusal last night and ask for their advice. Once he got past his initial embarrassment, Thomas felt relieved that Charlotte had such close friends with whom she could discuss her disappointment. He wished he had the same freedom, but men could not discuss such intimate things as women did. What would Marnie and Clara say? Would they agree that it was too great a risk to take? Or would they advise her to try again? Oh, what he wouldn't give to eavesdrop on their conversation! Selfishly, Thomas hoped the women would propose a good solution to the situation. Lying next to Charlotte all night had been blissful torture. The feel of her kisses and the warmth of her body in his arms had been wonderful beyond words. The frustrated longing to consummate their marriage had been unbearable.

As soon as the women entered the sitting room, Marnie closed the door behind them.

"Well," Clara prompted.

Charlotte burst into tears. "He didn't want to…he wouldn't…we didn't consummate the marriage. I practically begged him, but he said he was too scared that I might slip back into my comatose state. I've never felt more rejected or ashamed. I was quite unladylike in my efforts to persuade him."

"Oh, Charlotte. I'm so sorry," Clara said.

"He has a very good point, you know," Marnie admitted. "Marital relations might be a bit risky at this point."

"I don't agree. I want to be with him more than anything, and I don't think it will upset me. Of course, I'd rather attempt it while we're here close to medical care, than wait until we're back at the property. We'd be all alone and far from help if I lost my mind again."

"Sweetheart, you didn't lose your mind. You just went somewhere else for a while," Clara assured her.

"Nevertheless, I'd feel safer knowing that we were near our friends in case anything bad happened. How can I convince Thomas that I'm not afraid?"

"I recommend you simply tell him what you told us; that you're ready and that it's safer to try it here than once you get back home," Marnie answered, as she handed Charlotte a fresh handkerchief. "He's a reasonable man, and I'm sure he desires you every bit as much as you desire him. This will all work itself out, dear."

Charlotte sniffled and shook her head. She felt so much better having discussed this with her friends.

"Now, can we please talk about that beautiful wedding yesterday," Clara asked. "It was the most wonderful wedding I've ever attended!"

Ten minutes later, the women rejoined the rest of the party in the dining room where several tables had been set up for cards. Thomas was relieved to see that Charlotte was smiling. When she looked over at him, he winked. He couldn't wait to be alone with her again.

"May I talk through something with you," Charlotte asked, as she and Thomas lay in bed together that night.

"Always."

Thomas moved his body slightly away from hers so he could look her in the eyes. "What's on your mind?"

He assumed that she was again going to make the case for consummating their marriage right away. He prepared himself to stand strong against her pleas. It was simply too dangerous.

"I can't stop thinking about Mass this morning."

"I'd say that's a good thing," Thomas encouraged, with a smile.

"Yes, you're right. However, the problem lies in how I'm feeling about the readings and about Father Joseph's homily."

Charlotte sat up into a cross-legged position.

"I'm quite convicted that I need to do something…that I'm being called by God to do something, but I really don't know if I'm strong enough to do it."

When she didn't continue, Thomas prompted her. "What are you being called to do?"

He immediately wondered if it had to do with keeping the baby instead of placing it for adoption. A glimmer of hope took root inside him. A child born of his beautiful wife would be a gift, no matter who the father was. Charlotte took a deep breath and looked straight at him.

"Thomas, I feel that I'm supposed to forgive Fred. And, not only that, but I also think I'm supposed to let him know that I forgive him."

Thomas couldn't hide his shock.

"Well, I can certainly see how this presents a problem."

Finding this too serious a conversation for lying down, he pulled himself into a sitting position and ran his hands through his hair. "I mean, recalling the message this morning, I can see how you came to this conclusion. God definitely wants us to forgive and find the freedom forgiveness brings. But what those men did seems unforgiveable!"

"It does. I know it does. Maybe this isn't at all what I'm supposed to do. I'm just so confused."

Charlotte thought of her precious little brother and sister. Of her parents. Of the tiny, helpless baby growing inside her. A tear escaped and made its way down her cheek.

"Charlie, I honestly don't know whether I should beg you not to do it, or shout to the world how proud I am of you."

Charlotte noticed there were tears in Thomas' eyes, too.

"Don't be too proud just yet," she chuckled, grabbing his hands. "I know I'm supposed to do it, but I certainly don't know if I'll be able to do it."

"Would it help to discuss it with Father Joseph tomorrow morning?"

"Immensely! He could certainly clear up my misgivings and point me in the right direction."

Charlotte looked down at their entwined fingers. "It's odd. Whenever I'm around Father Joseph, I feel so much peace. It's as though he loves me, loves all of us, more than we even love ourselves."

"Yes, that absolutely describes him. You wouldn't have any way of knowing this, but two times I visited the church alone after dark, seeking answers and peace. Both times, Father Joseph was in there, silently praying in front of the Blessed Sacrament. He appeared to be in such close communion with God, it was almost like he was in another world."

"That close communion is most likely the source of his unconditional love," Charlotte mused.

Then, she dropped her voice to a whisper and her face took on a mysterious, conspiratorial mask. "Every night, he sneaks into the church and fills his heart from the spring of God's unquenchable love."

She smiled and threw her arms open wide as she continued. "And then he spends the next day pouring it out to everyone he encounters."

Her silliness brought welcomed laughter to both of them. But then, Charlotte looked down at their hands again and grew somber.

"I want to be more like that; more like him."

"Oh, you're going to keep me working hard, Charlie," Thomas said, taking her hands in his. "I already feel that you're so far beyond me when it comes to love and faith. The fact that you're even considering a meeting with that man…well, I don't think I could do it—"

"What are you talking about, my love? You're the one who swooped in and saved a young monster boy from having to burying his family alone. You're the one who loved me even before I was able to be honest with you. You're the one who helped me be brave and survive unimaginable loss."

She was embarrassed to find herself crying again. "Thomas, there is no way that I would have made it to today without you; without your love. You allowed God to use you in the most wonderful ways. When I hear the exhortation that we should be Christ's hands and feet in this world, it makes me think of you."

Thomas couldn't answer her. For the rest of his life, he would treasure her words.

"Charlotte," he began. But there was nothing to say to such beautiful sentiments.

"Yes, husband?"

Thomas leaned over and kissed her. He hoped that his kiss could convey the enormity of the emotions he couldn't put into words. The kiss deepened, and he was shocked when she was the one to end it. That had certainly never happened before.

"I do have one more concern," she said, with a mischievous grin.

"And that is?"

"Well, the way I see it, if we are leaving in the next day or two to return to Kerry Haven, tonight would be the safest time to..."

Charlotte lowered her head and looked up at him shyly. Thomas smiled at her in amusement.

"I know what you're implying. Please enlighten me as to your thoughts about safety."

Her smile faded and she was all seriousness now. "I know that I'm ready, Thomas. Loving you, physically, is all I can think about now. And, if for some reason, I did end up back in that unaware state, Dr. Groves and George know exactly how to rouse me. Wouldn't it be better to take the risk here in Denver City than to wait until we're three hours away?"

Thomas closed his eyes. He'd spent the last twenty-four hours in desirous agony. Every beat of his heart only served to strengthen his longing to consummate the marriage, to truly become one with his wife. Now that he was faced with her very logical argument, all his fear and worry melted away.

"You're most likely right, my love."

At his words, Charlotte looked up at her husband. He sat across from her, staring deep into her eyes. There was so much passion in his beautiful, green eyes that she almost felt afraid. But she couldn't look away.

Finally, after what seemed like hours, Thomas lowered his feet to the floor and stood up. He slowly walked around to her side of the bed. Timidly, she turned to face him. Now that this was going to happen, all her bravado was gone. She shuddered as he slowly untied the laces of her nightgown and bent to kiss her collarbones. Fire raced through her whole body.

"You'll have to show me what to do," she whispered huskily, as he began to slide the nightgown down over her arms.

"Are you assuming I've done this before, wife?"

"Well, yes. I assumed all men…Don't all men engage in this sort of—"

She stopped talking when Thomas lifted her off the bed and into his arms. Her nightgown fell to the floor in a gauzy heap.

"Not men who trust that God is saving them for the right woman."

The next morning, Charlotte lay in bed staring at her sleeping husband. He was still deep in slumber and his vulnerability made him even more handsome. Her face flushed as her mind replayed the blissful activities of last night and this morning.

As though he sensed that he was being watched, Thomas reached over and grabbed his wife.

"Are you spying on me as I sleep," he asked, eyes still closed.

"No. Just admiring you."

"How can you be awake and alert? I am utterly exhausted," he said, as he opened his eyes and looked lovingly at her.

"It's already daylight outside, and besides, there's one more thing I need to discuss."

Thomas smiled and closed his eyes again.

"You're not even going to let me eat first, wife?"

"Oh, I'm sorry. Should I ring for a tray?"

"Well, considering the fact that going down to the dining room for breakfast is the only way I can think to escape this bedroom, a tray would not help me much."

Charlotte hit him with a pillow.

"Are you saying you haven't enjoyed the last few hours?"

That made Thomas laugh heartily.

"Nothing could be further from the truth. I'm just worried that I may not survive your…exuberance."

Charlotte shot him a flirtatious look, and, shaking his head, Thomas sat up and pulled on his sleeping shirt.

"I'm ready. What's on your mind?"

"Thomas, I think I might want…" She shook her head as though to muster her courage. "No, not think. I know that I want to keep the baby."

For the last two hours, while her husband slept, Charlotte had been dreading this conversation. When Thomas jumped off the bed and almost shouted in joy, her eyes grew wide with shock.

"You're not upset?"

"Oh, Charlie. I've been agonizing about this for the last few days. I fully understood what you meant about a constant reminder of the worst moments of your life. I swore to myself that I was not going to try to sway your decision. But," Thomas stopped to calm his voice. "I'm sorry. I didn't realize I already felt so strongly about this."

Charlotte slid off the bed and walked to him. She wrapped her arms around his waist as he wiped away his tears.

"Charlotte, this child will be a part of you. I couldn't bear to know she existed somewhere far away from us. I knew that I would ask you to let me hold her for at least an hour. And then I knew I'd never be able to let her go."

"Her?"

Thomas laughed and wiped his eyes again. "You must be contagious, my dear. I can't recall ever laughing through tears before."

Charlotte squeezed his waist as they laughed together.

"But Thomas, why did you say 'her'?"

"You'll think me silly, but I've had several dreams about a little daughter. She looks exactly like you, Charlie. And I already love her so much."

Charlotte looked up into his beautiful green eyes.

"In my dreams, Thomas, she's named Mariah."

Chapter Thirty-One

Monday, September 30, 1867

After bathing and breakfasting, Thomas and Charlotte set out for the church office. They were surprised to find Father Joseph available. The secretary guided them down the hallway to the priest's office.

"What luck," Charlotte cried when the secretary closed the door behind them. "Knowing how busy you always are, I assumed we'd need to make an appointment."

"Well, God must want us to meet right away because I was scheduled to be in Golden all day today. Last night, I received word that the celebration had to be rescheduled. I can't remember the last time I had a whole day free."

Father Joseph smiled warmly at the young couple.

"Have a seat. What brings you in to see me this morning? Complaints about my wedding homily?"

The newlyweds both laughed and then Thomas spoke.

"No, Father Joseph. It's my wife. She has," he stopped and smiled encouragingly at Charlotte. "She has something monumental to discuss with you."

The new bride smiled at her husband, and Father Joseph felt the sun could not shine brighter than she did at that moment. He felt sure that the light in Charlotte was Christ's light, the Holy Ghost within her. The obvious love between these two was a balm to his sometimes battered, discouraged heart.

"Father Joseph, I feel called to forgive Fred Miller, and the others, I guess," she said, looking down at her hands in her lap. "And I think I'm supposed to go to the jail and forgive him in person."

Charlotte raised her head, looked directly at the priest, and added, "It's not something I want to do at all. But ever since your homily yesterday morning, these thoughts have not left me alone. I know in my heart that I must."

Father Joseph sat silently for a few moments after she finished speaking. He appeared deep in thought.

"Oh, Mrs. Linz, how you do humble me."

"What do you mean, Father," she asked with a confused look on her face.

Father Joseph ran a hand through his silver hair.

"Well, as a priest, I put a great amount of prayer and preparation into every one of my homilies. My constant goal when preaching is to disappear and simply allow God to speak directly to His people through me. But, sometimes, like all priests I'm sure, I can fall into discouragement. I often wonder if what I say is making a difference."

He looked at each of them for a moment before continuing. "I know that the sacraments always confer grace in spite of my unworthiness. But a homily is different. A homily can truly motivate people or be just so much mindless drivel. There were probably three hundred in attendance yesterday morning, and for most of them, the homily was likely nothing special. However, it seems God carefully prepared your heart, and then carefully gave me the words, and then carefully put us in the same place in order to foster a loving encounter for Mr. Miller. It's so beautiful."

Father Joseph looked up at the crucifix on the office wall.

"Just think, Mrs. Linz! If you go through with this, God will get a chance to speak His love directly to someone who might never have heard it in his whole life. How wonderful is that?"

"I never thought of it that way," Charlie answered pensively. "I couldn't understand why, when I am trying so hard to move past the horror, God was calling me to do something so difficult. Now I not only understand, but I find myself joyful about it. Isn't that odd?"

"Not really," Thomas said. "Until just now, I was praying that Father Joseph would tell you that you weren't being called to meet with Miller and that you should just forgive him in your heart. I couldn't bear the thought of you seeing him again. But you are being given the opportunity to show Jesus' love to someone who has likely not experienced love in a very, very long time, if ever. What an incredible privilege!"

"Mrs. Linz, would you mind if I was there, waiting outside, when you spoke to Mr. Miller? I'd like to be available if he decides he wants spiritual guidance after hearing your forgiveness. When faced with something as powerful as your words will be, I wouldn't be surprised if Miller totally falls apart."

"Father, I think I'd rather that you were right there in the room, right next to me," Charlotte said, chuckling nervously. "I'll feel much braver with you by my side. But only if you think that's okay."

"That would be perfect, my dear. When do you think you will meet with him?"

"I haven't made any plans, as I wanted to discuss this with you first," Charlotte answered. "Thomas and I can head over to the jail right now and see if Sergeant Albertson has any objections to us speaking with Mr. Miller. Then, we can come right back and let you know."

"Nonsense," Father Joseph said, standing up from his chair. "Let's head over together. I need the fresh air, and a walk will do me good."

Thomas and Charlotte stood, and the three made their way out of the office and down the street to the jail. When they reached the jail, Thomas held open the door, then followed Charlotte and Father Joseph inside. Sergeant Albertson was surprised to see them, and immediately rose to greet them.

"Sergeant Albertson," Charlotte began. "I'd like to speak with Mr. Miller, please."

Jason shot a concerned look at Thomas.

"Are you sure? I truly don't recommend it, Mrs. Linz."

"I'm very sure, Sergeant Albertson. I really must do this. Father Joseph will be accompanying me, but Thomas can tell you everything."

Thomas nodded at Jason. "It's fine. She's on a mission from God."

Jason moved to unlock the heavy, wooden door that led to the cells.

"Charlie, I am going to leave this door ajar. Please yell if you need me," he said. Then he gave her a big hug. "I still don't think this is a good idea, dear."

"I promise you that I'll yell if I feel threatened in any way. I love that you're so protective of me, Sergeant. You remind me of my amazing father."

"Mrs. Linz, I love you like one of my own daughters, but I must insist that you not make me cry in front of my prisoner." He laughed and released her from the hug. "Here you are," he added, pulling the door open.

He walked back over to where Thomas was standing. Charlotte and Father Joseph walked through the door. Charlotte was relieved to see that Fred Miller was still the only one being held in the jail. Upon hearing them enter, he looked up and a sardonic smile flitted across his face.

"Well, look who's here again! Couldn't get enough of me? And look, you even brought me a priest this time. How kind of you!"

Fred Miller spat on the ground as though to punctuate his disdain.

Charlotte did not speak for several long moments.

"Mr. Miller, you committed unspeakable acts. You killed some of the most outstanding people who have ever lived. You hurt people and you took delight in doing it. I am happy that you have been caught and relieved that you will never hurt another person again. I came today to tell you that I forgive you."

Fred stared at her with an odd look on his face. Charlotte couldn't tell if it was fear, or defiance.

"I want you to know that you are forgiven, Mr. Miller."

"You're the girl from that farm. You had the idiot sister," he said, pleased that he'd finally remembered her. "I thought Dan killed you."

"No, he only left me unconscious. Which is good because it allows me to come and forgive you."

"You can't forgive me. Because I'm not sorry. I had a hell of a time raping you and killing your family, and I'd do it all again if I could."

Father Joseph gasped at the man's response. It certainly hadn't been what he expected. What sort of man spurned forgiveness? Would Mr. Miller's evil response send her back into that comatose state? What had they done? His immediate thought was to pull Charlotte out of the jail and away from the awful man. But before he could take Charlotte's arm and usher her out, he heard her laugh.

"You are a fool if you think I need your permission to forgive. You have no control over me, Mr. Miller. My forgiveness is not contingent on your permission, or your apology. My forgiveness is mine alone to confer on whomever I wish. Like it or not, you are forgiven."

Father Joseph was shocked to his core. He had never seen anything like this. Mr. Miller sat in silence, having no response to her wisdom and her lack of fear.

"That is all, Mr. Miller. If you should have need of Father Joseph at any time between now and your likely death sentence, please send word to him. He has already offered to meet with you. Good day."

Charlotte turned and walked back through the doorway. Fred looked up and stared at Father Joseph. Thinking that he might speak, Father Joseph hesitated.

"Damn that woman," Fred said, and spat again on the ground.

That was all Father Joseph needed to hear. He turned on his heels and returned to the office. Jason walked over and closed the door, locking it behind him.

"How did it go?"

Charlotte looked over to Father Joseph. "What do you think, Father? How did it go?"

Father Joseph raised his eyebrows and, smiling at her, shook his head. "I've certainly never met anyone like you, Mrs. Linz."

"What happened in there," Thomas asked, looking from one to the other. "Really?"

"Mr. Miller simply wasn't ready to accept my forgiveness yet. But I've done all that I was called to do. And now, my dear, you and I can go home."

She smiled at Thomas and reached for his hand.

"Mrs. Linz, thank you for…allowing me to witness this," Father Joseph said. "I still don't know how to process what I just witnessed, but I think it will give me material to think about and pray about for the rest of my life."

"Father Joseph, thank you for everything you've done for Thomas and me. I heard your prayers for me when I was trapped, and I have felt your love in so many powerful ways. You truly are a servant of God."

"As are you, my dear. As are you." The priest shook hands with the men and gave Charlotte a hug. "I hope to see you all soon."

When Father Joseph was gone, Thomas turned to Jason.

"We've already said our goodbyes to the Groves household. We'll head over to your house next to wish everyone goodbye and get our horses. I know we'll be back soon. Take good care of yourself, my friend."

The two men shook hands and Charlotte hugged Sergeant Albertson.

"Thank you," she whispered.

Thomas and Charlotte walked quickly to the Albertson house. Marnie opened the door and welcomed them into the house.

"John David, Damien, will you please go and ready the horses for Mr. and Mrs. Linz?"

"Yes ma'am," the boys answered, and left to the stable.

"I'm sad to see you go. Can I offer you some lemonade or cookies before you leave?"

"No thank you," they answered at the same time.

"I will miss you so much, Marnie, but I'm excited to be heading home."

"You can rest assured we will be back soon," Thomas added. "We have so much to do in preparation for building the new house."

"Well, when construction begins, please let us send the boys out to help. I know they would love it! They have had so much fun out at Kerry Haven with you."

"I'll take you up on that. You and Jason have raised some spectacular sons."

After leaving the Albertson home, they rode back to the hotel to gather their things.

"I'd like to stop by the post office one more time," Thomas said, once their bags were securely fastened to the saddles. "Just in case there have been inquiries to my fliers."

"That sounds fine. I'll wait outside with the horses if that's alright with you."

Soon they were in front of the post office. Thomas jumped down and handed his reins to Charlotte.

"I'll be right back."

Moments later, he walked out with a huge smile on his face. "I have a letter from Emily!"

"Will you read it aloud," Charlotte asked.

Thomas stood next to Meg and opened the letter so that Charlotte could see it as he read aloud.

September 8, 1867

My dearest Big Brother,

I was so excited to get your letter from August 16. Finally, a destination for my letters!!! I've written you ever so many, and I will mail them soon, but I must ensure you will receive this one first.

Thomas, your little sister is married! I've married the most wonderful man, Mr. Gaetano Carvelli, and I am happier than I ever thought I could be!

I know you're shocked and likely hurt that I didn't wait for your permission and blessing. But, dear brother, I had no way of contacting you, and no way of knowing when you might return. As soon as Aunt Shirley got to know him, she came to my room one night and said, "Emily, if you don't marry that young man, then you are the biggest fool I've ever met." I informed her that generally a man must propose marriage before a woman can accept. "Bah humbug," said she. "A rich woman may do whatever she likes!" And she truly meant it, Thomas. Before you are overcome with shame, let me assure you that I did not propose to Gaetano. I practiced the greatest of patience and he eventually asked me to be his wife. I may have shrieked in delight, but, other than that, I was an absolute paragon of propriety!

The wedding was very small, but beautiful. If I couldn't have you there, dear brother, I didn't want a crowd. So, it was just Aunt Shirley, Mr. Chesterfield, who has become very dear to me over the last few years, and my faithful maid, Polly. Gaetano's family are all still in Italy, so neither of us had parents or siblings there.

A part of me feels wretched about leaving Aunt Shirley on her own after everything she's been to me. However, Mr. Chesterfield continues to visit the house every single day, and I feel sure that he will continue to do so for years and years to come. If Aunt Shirley weren't so stubbornly independent, she would have accepted one of his many proposals of marriage. However, she assures me that, at her age, marriage would simply mean having a boss and having to share her loads of money! She actually said that, Thomas, and in front of poor Mr. Chesterfield. I honestly don't know anyone else who could get away with talking as she does. It's simply not polite at all! I was so embarrassed by it, but Mr. Chesterfield just laughed uproariously and said that her sauciness was one of the many reasons why he loved her so much. Aunt Shirley said I shouldn't be pushing her to marry anyway, since she's planning to leave every penny she owns to her only surviving relatives — you and me.

I don't know about you, but I'd rather see her happily married than inherit her fortune someday. You and I already have more money than we'll ever be able to spend in our lifetimes. However, I have great ideas towards accomplishing just that. I'm so, so excited to share Gaetano's and my plans with you. You know I've always had big dreams about making my mark in the world and changing it for good. Well, guess what! I finally know how I want to do it. Gaetano and I met while teaching at Woodward and both have a love for educating the underprivileged. We decided that as soon as we heard from you, we would write to let you know we were planning to join you wherever you ended up, opening a school for those students who can't attend private schools. And now, here I am, writing just such a letter! Thomas, let's make a pact to never live so far apart again. You always have been and will remain my greatest role model, and I want us to share everything our futures bring.

Brother, I simply cannot wait to join you in Colorado. These months apart have been filled with so many adventures for both of us and I imagine it will take days and days to catch up! We will have so many stories to share. And as soon as I get there, I will begin looking for the perfect spouse for you. I only hope that you can find the happiness I have.

Your loving sister,
Mrs. Emily Carvelli

"Oh, Thomas! I can't wait to meet her!"

Thomas folded the letter and returned it to the envelope. He stood silent and dazed for a few moments taking it all in. "My dear, between the baby, and the house, and the Marshalls and the Carvellis, we are in for a very busy year!"

The End

About the Author

A nnie Coffey has spent the last twenty years married to her best friend, David. She is a Licensed Professional Counselor who has worked with clients of every kind, including former child soldiers in Liberia, West Africa, and adolescents in the Texas Juvenile Justice System. Her greatest blessings in life are her husband and four incredibly amusing children. The joyful, loving character of Ruth is based on Annie's daughter by the same name who has Agenesis of the Corpus Callosum. Proceeds from this book series will go to establish "Ruthie's Ranch," a support facility for individuals with special needs and their families. Please visit us on Facebook and Instagram for more information on Ruthie's Ranch and how you can help!

You can contact Annie Coffey via https://anniecoffey.com